Torkil Damhaug studied literature and anthropology in Bergen, and then medicine in Oslo, specialising in psychiatry. Having worked as a psychiatrist for many years, he now writes full time. In 2011 Torkil's third Oslo Crime Files novel, FIRERAISER, won the Riverton Prize for Norwegian crime fiction – an accolade also awarded to Jo Nesbø and Anne Holt – and his books have been published in fifteen languages. He lives with his wife and children near Oslo.

There are four deeply dark thrillers to discover in Torkil Damhaug's Oslo Crime Files series: MEDUSA, DEATH BY WATER, FIRERAISER and CERTAIN SIGNS THAT YOU ARE DEAD.

By Torkil Damhaug

Medusa
Death By Water
Fireraiser
Certain Signs That You Are Dead

TORKIL
DAMHAUG

FIRERAISER

AN OSLO CRIME FILES NOVEL

**Waterford City and County
Libraries**

HEADLINE

Ildmannen © Cappelen Damm AS, 2011, 2012
English translation © 2015 Robert Ferguson

I Wanna Be Loved By You by Herbert Stothart, Bert Kalmar,
Harry Ruby © 1928 WB Music Corp.
Almost Cut My Hair by David Crosby © 1970 Stay Straight Music
Smells Like Teen Spirit by David Grohl, Kurt Donald Cobain © 1991 Primary Wave
Tunes, MJ Twelve Music, BMG Rights Management (UK) Ltd Primary Wave,
The End of Music

The right of Torkil Damhaug to be identified as the Author of
the Work has been asserted by him in accordance with the
Copyright, Designs and Patents Act 1988.

First published as an ebook in Great Britain in 2015 by
HEADLINE PUBLISHING GROUP

First published in paperback in Great Britain in 2016 by
HEADLINE PUBLISHING GROUP

Published by agreement with Cappelen Damm AS,
Akersgata 47/49, Oslo, Norway

1

Cataloguing in Publication Data is available from the British Library

ISBN 978 1 4722 0685 5

Typeset in Granjon by Palimpsest Book Production Limited,
Falkirk, Stirlingshire

Printed and bound in Great Britain by Clays Ltd, St Ives plc

Headline's policy is to use papers that are natural, renewable and recyclable products and
made from wood grown in sustainable forests. The logging and manufacturing processes
are expected to conform to the environmental regulations of the country of origin.

MIX
Paper from
responsible sources
FSC
www.fsc.org FSC® C104740

HEADLINE PUBLISHING GROUP
An Hachette UK Company
Carmelite House
50 Victoria Embankment
London EC4Y 0DZ

www.headline.co.uk
www.hachette.co.uk

To Anders, Joachim, Rebecca and Isabelle

I SIT HERE with a black-and-white photograph in front of
me. It's been lying on my desk for several weeks, but only
now do I pick it up and take a closer look. Two young boys
and a water buffalo. The boys are wearing tunics and wide
trousers, sandals on their feet. There's another figure present
too, behind them, a man in his forties or fifties with a beard
that reaches down to his chest. His tunic is white, with what
looks like an inscription embroidered on the collar. A turban
in a darker colour on his head. He is looking not into the
camera but at the two young boys. The look is severe, and
something that might be grief is also present in his gaze.
One of the boys has the same expression, while the other,
taller and thinner, is hugging the buffalo round the neck
and grinning.

On the day the picture was taken, the family had moved
to a new house. The people who had lived there before
them were Sikhs and had gone east some years previously,
driven from the plains around the rivers Jhelum, Chenab
and Ravi in one of the largest migrations in human history,
an exodus occasioned by the decision of a small group of
men to establish a new state. The abandoned Sikh house
was larger and lighter than the one the family had occupied
before, and was more in keeping with their dignity. The
father was leader of the council of village elders, a man who
was listened to. He was often the village's representative on
ceremonial occasions in other parts of the region, and he

had been blessed with four sons. Zahir, the boy on the left of the picture, was the strongest and had few problems in asserting his rights if a matter were to be settled with a fist fight. The boy on the right, the one with the broad smile, is Khalid. He was one year younger than his brother, but superior to him when it came to riding; he was brighter too, and he was the one who was going to complete his education.

The family owned almost twenty-five acres of land, three water buffaloes, two horses and of course had the four boys, who, when they grew old enough, in due course would be able to help out on the land. Most importantly, they were the owners of one of the wells in the village, making them self-sufficient for water and able to charge others for drawing what they needed. The father was among the first to acquire a radio, and many years later, in the winter dark of a land whose name he had never even heard at that age, this would remain one of Khalid's strongest memories: the village land-owners gathered in their room around the radio, puffing on opium pipes, listening to a test match commentary, or the president's speech, or to music.

His mother was not in the photograph, which perhaps explained why the image of her that Khalid would always carry inside him was so clear. The reddish hair, only partly covered by the shawl, the face with smiling eyes. Maybe she did try to treat all four sons the same, but she could never hide the fact that he was special to her. She called him her prince and said that her life's most important task was to ensure that he would be happy. When he was eighteen, Khalid married a cousin from Kanak Pind, a nearby village. The following spring they were about to become parents, but kismet, or fate, would have it otherwise. The child clung on, and not even the doctor that was called after two days could do much more than coax and squeeze. When they finally got it out, it was too late. And along with him into death the little boy took the one who was supposed to have given birth to him.

The land more than provided for the basic needs of Khalid's family, but the father was a man whose thoughts went beyond the sunset. The surplus could be invested in domestic animals, he could rent more land and increase the yield, though buying land was more or less an impossibility. And when, after his time was up, the sons came to divide the property between them, times would be leaner for each of them, with many more mouths to feed. The solution had to be that one or two of the sons should leave home and find work in another country.

There were several reasons why the choice fell on Khalid. His wife was dead, he was the most intelligent, and had completed his ten years of schooling. He was independent, and no one doubted that he would be able to look after himself anywhere in the world. The argument against was that his mother could not bear the thought of his leaving. But perhaps this was precisely what influenced the father in his decision.

Khalid Chadar arrived in Oslo one December day in 1974. He had heard of the cold, the snow, the darkness. Before leaving home he had read whatever he could about this country that lay about as far north as it was possible to go; he thought he was prepared. But as he walked through the dark streets, colder than he had ever been before, beneath the heavy spikes of ice hanging from the roofs of the houses, he felt for the first time a despair so profound that it would not let go of him. The cold and the darkness he could endure. Worse was that he did not understand the people who lived there; not the language, of course, much more the way the people there treated him, friendly in a distant and shy way.

If he tried to reciprocate this strange way of being friendly, they retreated and disappeared.

He found work at a brewery in the city. Lived in a bedsit with four others from the Punjab. All were of inferior birth to him. The Chadar name could be traced as far back as King Padu of Mahabaratha.

Another man from his own country whom he met at the brewery was a *kammi*, low caste, and was reminded of it in every situation that arose. This *kammi* lived on a farm somewhere north of Oslo. One day in the depths of winter he invited Khalid there. It was lighter now. Still cold, but it was the darkness around midday that had been worst; weeks might go by without Khalid seeing the sun. And what he would later remember best from that day at Stornes farm was the light; suddenly intense and penetrating, reflected by the snow on the fields, coming both from above and below, and so sharp he had to walk with eyes half closed.

The people on the farm were different from those he met in the city. They did not speak to him in that distant, friendly way, which, as he had gradually come to understand, expressed a hidden contempt. He was invited into the living room for coffee and cakes; they asked him about the country he came from, his family, children. When they heard that he was already a widower, he saw that the wife and one of the daughters especially had a sad look in their eyes.

It emerged now that they had had a special reason for inviting him. They had been told he was good with horses, and they needed help in the stables, where they had twenty mares and two stallions. Khalid thought he had misheard when the wife said she would show him round. It was inconceivable that he would be alone with a strange woman in the stables. But the husband had some business in a nearby town, so he handed the task over to his wife without hesitation. And she wasn't ugly, not ugly at all, Khalid had gathered that much, even though he had been forcing himself to look anywhere but directly at her.

It didn't take long to demonstrate that he had a way with the animals. He understood quickly which of them he could approach, and which to keep his distance from. Even in the half-dark in which they were tethered, he noted quickly which one was the leader and he gave this stallion a lot of attention.

The following week he moved out to Stornes farm. He was given a room of his own in the smallest of the outhouses. There was a separate kitchen there which he was to share with the *kammi* from the Punjab, and he was allowed to use the bathroom in the main house where the family lived. His work with the horses still left time for his job at the brewery, so that he now had two incomes, both of them many times greater than what the best-paid people in his village could earn. Every month he sent two thirds of his earnings home, and his father wrote grateful letters of thanks back, making it clear that when the time came for Khalid to get married again, he could choose from among his most distinguished relatives in Gujarat.

There were two daughters on the Stornes farm. The elder was named Gunnhild. She was twenty-two and had what they called a boyfriend, a man a couple of years older than her who boasted about being an army officer. One of the most shocking experiences Khalid Chadar had after arriving in this country was to see this young woman, wearing a short leather jacket and tight-fitting trousers, her hair hanging loose, getting into this boyfriend's car. Early one evening as he was emerging from the stalls, he saw her, leaning back in the front seat, with the boyfriend lying half across her. One of his hands was up inside her jumper.

Khalid spoke to the *kammi* about this. The *kammi* had lived in Norway for several years and said he'd seen much worse things than that in the parks around Oslo in the summer: young women lying in rows on the grass wearing tiny briefs, their breasts bare. Khalid didn't believe him. The *kammi* grinned and said all he had to do was wait and see, once the snow was gone.

The fact that Gunnhild had a boyfriend who undressed her in places where anyone passing by might see them did not mean that she was going to marry him. Maybe, maybe not, she answered vaguely when Khalid asked. Then she laughed: – Tord's a bit slow. Maybe you'll get there before him.

Was she making fun of him?

There was something in her voice, and her look, that made him feel as though she meant it. And in moments of weakness, he let himself play with the thought of returning to his Punjabi village with a wife from this country. She would insist on walking two paces ahead of him along the street, fair haired and grinning, with no shawl on her head. Sometimes at night he had to turn on the light, fetch the photo standing on the chest of drawers, the one of himself and Zahir with the water buffalo, and stare at the figure in the background, trying to get his father's gaze to meet his. Only then did he feel calm again.

But it wasn't only Gunnhild. Her mother, a friendly woman with a ready smile who must have been over fifty, asked him straight out one day if he was hoping to find a new wife in Norway. He had learned to laugh along with them, the mother and daughter, as they sat at the kitchen table and drank wine, even though he never understood what was funny about the way they spoke. It was disrespectful, and there were times when he left their kitchen suppressing a strange white rage within himself.

The younger daughter was sixteen. Her name was Elsa and she was the complete opposite of her sister. Dark haired and with serious deep blue eyes. She didn't say much, didn't laugh much, but when she spoke, he liked to hear her. She thought a lot, in which he saw something of himself, because somewhere inside that prince they always treated him as back home in Punjab, the one who always succeeded, the one so favoured by God, he had always felt the presence of something that could suddenly cause him to fall silent and wander off through the mustard fields alone, into the trees, to the grave of the holy one, and kneel down there and pray.

Sometimes he found himself sitting in the kitchen with Elsa. She spoke good English, better than her big sister, and had decided that she was going to teach him Norwegian. In a different way from Gunnhild she was curious about where he came from, what it looked like there, how the people lived, how they thought. She listened attentively when he spoke, as if it was important for her to know all this. When she asked him about his God, he told her that Allah was not his God but everybody's God, including hers. The *kammi* he shared the outhouse with had warned him against talking about things like this, and Khalid had never felt any particular need to demonstrate his faith to others. He prayed, but not five times a day. He didn't follow the Koran to the letter, and several times that winter he had drunk beer they had taken home with them from the brewery. He had a relaxed attitude to fasting, and the pilgrimage to Mecca was not at the top of his list of priorities. But when this girl with the large dark blue eyes asked him about God, he was able to respond with the most self-evident truths. Without Allah there were no people, no animals, no world. And she nodded slowly, as though she were willing to share that thought with him.

In this upside-down country, where nothing was *haram*, unlawful, and nothing was holy either – people believed in God one day and the next day not – a woman of sixteen

could be told to go to the stables with any man at all. It was
even more shocking than if the wife herself should accompany him. One afternoon it was the sister's boyfriend who
went there with Elsa. Maybe this Tord, as he was called,
was going to fetch something or other, because he was
carrying a crate, and he would have nothing to do with the
horses; he seemed to be afraid of them. From the window
of his room Khalid saw them crossing the farmyard. Five
minutes later they still hadn't come out again. He waited
another minute, two more minutes. Then he pulled on his
jacket and marched over there. They weren't in the stables.
He heard Tord's voice mumble something or other from
the hayloft, then Elsa's voice, then a short scream. Khalid
was in no doubt that it was a cry for help. He grabbed a
spade and pushed the door wide open. In the semi-darkness
he saw Elsa lying in the hay with Tord on top of her. He
took aim and drove the edge of the spade down hard into
his back. Tord howled with pain and whirled round. He
clambered to his feet, walked towards Khalid; they were
about the same height. Khalid raised the spade, ready to
strike again.

Then Elsa was there, standing between them.

– Leave him alone!

It wasn't clear which one of them she meant.

– Fucking Paki bastard, Tord raged.

Khalid took a step towards him. – If you touch her once
more, I'll kill you, he said quietly.

Tord spat on the floor, turned and walked out.

– Tell your father, Khalid exclaimed. – He should know
what kind of a man your sister has for a boyfriend.

Elsa shook her head.

For the next few days, Khalid made sure to accompany Elsa
when she was in the stables, and Tord had sense enough to

stay away. Elsa said he wouldn't try it again, but Khalid wanted to make quite sure. And Elsa obviously liked looking after the horses with him; they both had the same way with animals. She was close to each one of them, talked to them for a long time, soon noticed if there was anything wrong.

One morning as Khalid was feeding the horses, the door opened behind him. He jumped and dropped what he was holding in his hands, and turned, ready to face Tord. But it was Elsa in the semi-darkness, with a harness and a brush.

— Aren't you at school? he exclaimed.

She shrugged her shoulders. — I'm not well today.

— What's the matter with you?

Without replying, she started to groom one of the mares, the one that was pregnant and about to foal any day now.

He finished what he was doing, made ready to leave. He had been alone with her before, but on those occasions one of her parents had always known about it. This time he didn't even think they were at home.

— Come here, Khalid, she said, as though it were the most natural thing in the world for a girl ten years younger than him to stand in a stable and tell him what to do.

He strolled over to the pregnant mare, stroked her neck.

— Feel here.

Elsa took his hand and placed it under the horse's belly.

— Can you feel that?

There was movement in there.

— How many do you think there are?

He let his hand glide back and forth, keeping an eye on the mare's head.

— Two, he said. — I think there are two.

— I agree, she said, standing right next to him. — As many children as this mare gives birth to this spring, that's how many I'll have.

He had to smile. She could say things like that. She

dreamed something or other and was convinced it was a sign that something was about to happen. She had premonitions and visions, she had confided in him; she could see things that were invisible to other people. Where he came from, it wasn't unusual for people to possess powers like that. In the village, there was a holy man they could take their troubles to, and he could read their kismet, their fate. Khalid had no reason to doubt that this young woman, if it be God's will, had powers like those of the old man.

When he lifted his hand, it brushed against a lock of hair that had fallen across her face. He put the lock back in place, and what happened after that was kismet. That was the thought he clung on to as he stood there in the dark stables. Ordained by fate, just as this journey to the land in the north had been, and that he should have come to this farm and been welcomed with a warmth he had not experienced anywhere else on his journey here.

He said that to her. That it was fate she was standing there so close beside him that he could feel her breath against his neck. And when she nodded, fate grabbed hold of him and did what it wanted.

They went riding together many times that spring. They walked the horses along the beds of streams where the water had risen up and flowed over the banks, galloped them along paths where the patches of grass and moss grew larger by the day. They stopped by a tarn up in the woods. She had a blanket that they could spread on the hard ground. And while he lay there looking on, she stood up in the bright sunlight and undressed.

– We can move to the country you come from, she suggested one day as she lay beside him.

– That would be wonderful, he smiled, without mentioning

a single one of the obstacles that made such a thing impossible.

– I would *love* to live on your farm and ride the horses. I could help out in the fields. Or maybe be a schoolteacher in the village school.

– You would be very good at that, he nodded. – But you would have to be a Muslim, have you thought about that?

– It can't be that difficult to be a Muslim.

– No, not difficult. But you would have to take a new name.

– Could I choose it myself?

He thought about that. – It would have to be a Muslim name, completely Pakistani.

– I would call myself Yasmin, she said. – I love that smell. Would that be allowed?

He didn't know anyone called that. – I don't know.

The spring in this country was even more perplexing than the winter. Now it seemed as though the sun shone all the time, so that he awoke restless, tossing and turning in the grey light that forced its way through the curtains. The *kammi* told him it would get stronger and stronger, until it lit up the whole of the night.

On one such night towards the end of May, he was woken by Elsa standing beside his bed. It seemed to him that she was a djinn, a spirit come to tell him something. He was afraid but didn't show it. Only when she touched him did he feel calm.

– Did I frighten you?

He shook his head firmly, didn't want her to come to his room, but it was too late now to stop her.

– I have to talk to you, she whispered, sitting down on the edge of the bed.

This was different from going riding together, different from caresses in the hayloft behind the stables, or hands that slipped beneath clothes, hidden from sight behind the bodies of the horses. This was his bedroom; she had no business being there, and no one must know what they did together: not Tord, who had made him an object of hatred and spat each time he saw him, not Gunnhild, not her parents, not the *kammi* he shared the outhouse with. Above all not him, because if he found out, the rumours would spread through the Punjabi community in no time, and would not stop until they reached Khalid's own village.

– You can't be here, he said in a low voice.

She remained sitting. – I'll go, she murmured finally. – But I have to tell you something first.

That morning he stayed in bed, couldn't manage to get up. As if a huge hand had laid itself across his chest and was pressing him down. The husband came in, asked if he needed a doctor. He said no thanks, and could hardly raise his head from the pillow. He felt completely wiped out, he explained, an expression he had picked up after arriving in this new country.

In the grey light that seeped into everything, he lay and thought over what Elsa had said. She had decided that they would live together for the rest of their lives. She was certain that her parents would accept it. They would be angry, tell her off, threaten all sorts of things, but in the end it would blow over and they would calm down. If not, she was prepared to go back with him to the country he came from. He had told her stories about it and, she said, she had thought a lot about these. Several of them were about the way the love between a man and a woman reflected God's love for human beings, and how it conquered all, even death. She was sixteen, and in this country it meant she was still regarded as almost a child. And still thought like a child. She had even decided the Muslim name she would choose. *Yasmin* was originally from Persia, she had discovered, so that would probably do.

He lay the whole day, sweating and afraid, turning this way and that. In the course of the afternoon, he became genuinely ill.

If this were his story, then a great deal more would be told about Khalid Chadar: how they came down on him, threatened him with prison, with being thrown out of the country, threatened to destroy his life. But the family on the farm at Stornes couldn't do anything to him; he hadn't broken any of the laws of this country. And it emerged that they were as keen as he was to make sure that nothing be said about what had happened. But he *had* broken some of the laws that governed his own life, and for this he turned to his God and let Him be the judge. He prayed more often now, observed the stipulated hours for praying, and promised that one day he would make a trip to the holiest of all places. And his prayers must have been heard, because after a few months he realised that no one would ever know anything about it, excepting those few who had very good reason for wanting to keep it to themselves.

This story is going to be about events that led to the deaths of many people. I knew several of them personally. I shall let it start with Khalid, with the black-and-white photo of his brother and himself with his arm around a water buffalo, beneath their father's gaze. I found this picture after it had become clear to me how the things I am about to describe happened. When I was still trying to understand why.

PART I

April 2003

AN EMBER CAN glow and expire. It can glow and flare up. The time when it can still go either way is the best. You have set things up and withdrawn. Consigned everything to circumstances beyond your control: the combustibility of the material, moisture content, availability of oxygen.

This particular glow, which is not yet fire, is located at the tip of a half-cigarette. It smoulders for a minute, maybe longer. It is possible to work out the likelihood of its not dying out but spreading to the other end of the unfiltered cigarette. There it may well light one of the three matches attached to it by a rubber band. This is the second of the critical points: the question of whether the ember has enough energy to transfer to the paper the matches are made of. If it has, the ember will become a tiny flame, and the flame will creep like a blind worm in the direction of the head of the match. The journey will take less than twenty seconds, and if it reaches this point, a small, spluttering explosion will follow. The flame is now at the threshold dividing what is possible from what is inevitable. If it crosses the threshold – and the likelihood is now high – the fire will catch and begin to eat its way through the cotton strip soaked in lighter fuel intended for use when barbecuing meat and fish outdoors in the summer.

It is not summer; it is the first night of April. The horses have known for some time now that something is about to happen. They stand, hooves scraping on the stone floor;

some toss their heads, some lower their necks as a warning to the others. *We must stay together now* is perhaps what it means; no one must leave the herd.

Certain people react in the same way when sensing danger. Squeeze up against other bodies, trying to protect themselves by huddling together as close as possible. Others will break out and make a run for it, and a few will turn to face the threat. This interests him. The way animals behave when in danger, and the way danger makes people behave like animals. Horses don't think, he has concluded, and this unthinking life fills him with a wonder that is not far off anger. This animal, which so many people find beautiful, and which has been credited with qualities it cannot possibly possess, is in reality extremely primitive, with its remarkably simple brain. He seems to remember reading somewhere that, of all animals, the horse is the one most susceptible to panic. This explains the cruelty it can arouse in some – well, in everybody. No other animal can lead a person to take cruelty to such lengths, he thinks as he climbs on to a rock between the pine trunks.

Through a gap between the trees he can look down at the farm. Four minutes have passed since he left the stable, pulled shut the door with its broken catch and slipped round the corner, heading in the opposite direction from the farmhouse. He visited this farm a couple of times a few months ago. Not to learn to ride. And not because he felt drawn to the unthinkingness of these animals or the large, muscular bodies, the stallions' enormous penises pressing out from the sheaths beneath their bellies, the motion of their buttocks as they trotted down the track and across the field. Not because he was interested in those who swarmed about the place, the girls thirteen and fourteen years old, young women, older women, even if their relationship to the horses had to have a bitter darkness in it. The little girls who could spend hours in the stables, stroking and grooming, mucking out, or just being close to the animal bodies. As though seeking protection. Incomprehensible, the way these unthinking and panic-driven creatures could arouse such feelings.

It was not until his third visit that he realised this fascination angered him. On one occasion he lost control and struck one of the horses across its soft muzzle, not particularly hard, but enough to make it rear up and its eyes turn white. He thought he was alone in there, but one of the girls had just entered without his noticing it, and when he turned, he saw in her eyes that she would tell on him. He took a step towards her; she held on tight to the mane of the horse she had come to groom, and he pulled himself together and left the stable.

He had not been back again until last week. They had an open day, and he wandered about there in a group of people, mostly parents with little children in tow. The kiddies were lifted and held up in front of the horses' faces. It made him feel ill, as though he were about to puke at any moment, but he forced himself to stay, to listen to those babbling mothers, watch the childish fingers pawing at the damp muzzles. It was then that the thought that had been smouldering inside him took shape and became a decision.

He looks at his watch. Six minutes. The critical moment has passed. The horses sensed something was wrong as soon as he began feeling his way about inside the stables; they started to move, a harbinger of the panic that might break out. The waiting feels good. Everything uncertain. It can still be prevented. If nothing happens, the horses will calm down again, and the sleep of the humans continue undisturbed.

Seven minutes. He still doesn't know for sure. Or does he? Can't he hear the restlessness behind the walls of the stables, more than a hundred metres away? The tramping of more and more hooves, even a whinny? He can't keep still himself. The waiting time, the uncertainty. The fact that it could go one way or the other; one way and everything will be different and mean that he will never again be part of the herd. Not of any herd.

Another whinny. And then he knows. The ignition device has worked. This is no longer about a likelihood. That which is critical cannot be measured; forces that surge towards each other, invisible, inaudible. That's how Elsa would put it. Will and reluctance that are not noticed because they are everywhere, in everything. What he has done is to ask a question, compel an answer. He has facilitated things, bundled hay up against a wall, sprayed lighter fuel on that too. He notices that he is stamping with one foot, and the grin this realisation evokes catches fire, as it were, and becomes laughter. He needs to piss, jumps down from the rock, opens his flies and empties his bladder on to the frozen moss. Steam rises from the ground below him, and when he clambers back up on to the rock, he sees a thin braid of smoke seeping from the roof and up into the dark, clear night sky. He pulls out his mobile phone and begins filming. They might still wake up in the house. Tumble out to see what is happening. Some people, such as Elsa, believe that humans who work with horses become alert to the faintest of signals. She says that being around these animals can bring out hidden powers. He doesn't know if he believes stuff like that, but he takes due note of everything she says.

Eight minutes. The racket from the stables is now considerably more distressed. Sloppy of the owners not to wake up. Maybe they are on sleeping pills. So much for supernatural sensitivity. And there is a smell now, of scorched tar, that filters across the field and reaches him there at the edge of the wood. He has to jump down from the rock again, walk around a bit between the trees, slapping himself with his arms, even though he isn't cold. It makes him laugh, laugh at himself, laugh at what is happening. Because by the time he is back up on the rock again, he can see a glow through one of the openings halfway up the stable wall.

Nine minutes have passed since he set things in motion, and now that it is decided, nothing can turn it back, not even if he called the owners and told them to get up. Thick black smoke begins billowing out from the wall openings, and the whinnying from more than thirty horses rises into the darkness, cutting and slicing through the cold air. He can imagine them in there, gathering close to one another, pressing those huge smooth bodies together. There are foals in there too – he noticed them during his visit – and now they force their way in under their mothers' bellies, their whinnying much thinner; it seems to him he can distinguish the sounds. Suddenly he is furious with the owners for lying there in their beds. Fucking hell, he shouts, wake up, you fucking morons, and as he does so, a light goes on in one of the rooms. Immediately afterwards: the sound of a door opening, and a woman's voice screaming.

2

FOR ONCE KARSTEN had overslept. Less than fifteen minutes, but enough to disrupt his regular morning routine. One thing was that he had to wait for Synne to be finished in the upstairs bathroom. He wouldn't have time to read the newspaper, that was the other, maybe just the sport. He could make up lost time by driving to school, but if he asked to borrow the Volvo, he would have to put up with a lecture about CO_2 emissions. The truth was more that his father was so worried about his XC90 getting scratched that he hardly dared use it. He couldn't ask his mother; she'd already left in the Golf. That was what had woken him up, the bang of the door downstairs as she left.

He hobbled out into the corridor, like an old man, he thought, and exaggerated his hobble, let his body go lopsided and halting. When he knocked on the bathroom door and demanded that Synne, who started a half-hour later than him, should let him in, there was even something old-mannish about his voice, and this game made it easier not to get too worried. From the other side of the door his little sister said something sarcastic. He gave up and padded down to the kitchen and shook out a bowl of muesli.

The next time he knocked he was careful to sound annoyed, and maybe he was too; at least that was how Synne understood it. She opened the door and emerged with a yellow bath towel around her body and a pink one as a turban. Karsten was informed that it was only out of the kindness of her heart that she was willing to get dressed in her ice-cold bedroom, and that now he owed her a favour. He agreed and said he would do something for her, maybe drive her to the stables, for example.

Eleven minutes later, as he hurried into the kitchen, she was standing by the radio, staring at it as the news-reader went on about something or other. The slice of bread and salami lay untouched on her plate. Twice before he had discovered her in a state in which she was far away and didn't react, but the last time was more than a year ago now. He touched her shoulder, breathed a sigh of relief as she moved her gaze.

The voice on the radio was talking about a fire.

– Something happen?

– Stornes, she stammered.

The news went over to something about the National Audit Office. He lowered the volume. – The farm? Has there been a fire there?

She didn't answer.

– Anybody dead?

– The horses, she whispered. – Nearly thirty of them burned to death.

He saw the tears welling up in her eyes. Before her first attack, Synne had been riding at Stornes farm for several years. Afterwards the doctors had decided that it was too risky for her to carry on. Because who knows what might happen if she suddenly had an episode while she was on horseback and galloping at full speed? Her furious protests were ignored, though she continued to go to the stables to look after these animals she was no longer allowed to ride. Now none of the tests showed she had epilepsy after all, and they had promised she could try riding again.

Her whole body shook with crying, and he patted her

shoulder. She was five years younger than him. After the attacks began, there were a lot of activities she could no longer take part in, and even more she voluntarily gave up. He didn't like her being alone so much. He wasn't particularly sociable himself, but that was something different.

– That's bad news, he said comfortingly, with a glance up at the clock. – But surely they managed to save some of them?

– Only seven, she wailed.

– Well that's some, after all.

She began to sob. – The horses don't want to leave each other.

– Don't *want* to?

– When there's a fire or something, they all herd together, to look after each other. She closed her eyes and shook her head. – There are horses that do manage to get out but then run back into the fire to be with the rest of the herd.

Just then their father came in. – Don't try any April Fools on me, he said. – I know perfectly well what day it is. His eyebrows rose a few millimetres when he noticed that Synne was crying.

– There was a fire at Stornes farm last night, Karsten explained. – Apparently a lot of horses were burnt to death.

– Really, Father remarked as he took his coffee mug from the cupboard. It was light blue, with *World's Best Dad* written on it in faded red lettering. – But no people?

– Is that all you can think to say? Synne sniffed.

Father poured himself coffee, cast a quick glance at her. – I don't think it's *completely* irrelevant that no people died.

Synne made a noise somewhere between a growl and a wail and ran out; they heard her footsteps up the stairs and the slam of the bedroom door.

– Quite a performance, Father said, and slotted two slices of bread into the toaster. He picked up the newspaper and his mug of coffee and slumped down into his seat next to the window.

Karsten felt certain it was about more than the horses. Several times in recent weeks his little sister had had outbursts of rage and refused to go to school. When these moods came over her, she made herself completely inaccessible, shut herself off both physically and mentally. It worried him. Had done for a long time.

– I overslept, he said tentatively. – Can I take the car?

His father glanced at him over the top of his spectacles. – And you find that is defensible in a world such as ours?

– No, Karsten hurriedly assured him – It is indefensible, but I don't want to miss the first lesson. Anyway, I need to drive a bit to get more practice, that's another thing. And in the third place, a car needs to be driven once in a while.

Less than a year ago, suddenly and without warning, Father had upped and bought that Volvo with its 2.5-litre engine, the only investment he had ever made that might be said to be an extravagance. His excuse was that they needed a four-wheel drive to navigate the track all the way to their cabin in the winter.

Now he shrugged his shoulders in a way that indicated that the arguments volunteered so far had made an impression on him. Having received assurances that Karsten would not park anywhere near cars belonging to reckless boy-men, or clumsy girls who opened doors into neighbouring vehicles, he agreed and approved the unnecessary and environmentally destructive trip.

3

As DAN-LEVI JAKOBSEN passed Exporama and began to drive up towards Gjelleråsen, his phone vibrated. He saw that the message was from Sara. He turned off at Mortens café, switched off the engine, called her. Her voice was weak; he could tell she was lying down.

– Still nauseous? he asked cautiously. – Can't you manage to take Rakel?

– No, she groaned.

The last time she was pregnant, Sara had also been sick a lot during the early months, but not like this. She lay moaning in bed the whole morning, and it was almost asking too much of him to leave her in that state.

– I'll tell them I'm not well, he said, even though he knew it would cause trouble.

– No, she whispered. – Don't do that. But call in when you get the chance and take Rakel over to Mum's. If you have time.

She was brave. When he heard her voice, he counted himself luckier than anyone else he knew. What was more, he was aware of it, and that doubled his reasons to be happy. He had a daughter, too. Trebled them. They were going to have another child. Quadrupled them. He put his hands together. *Lord, I thank you for everything. Most of all that you let me feel this gratitude, your voice inside me.*

Again he considered whether he should ring the paper and explain the situation. He knew what Stranger would say. Dan-Levi had already had more day shifts than the others in the duty group, and the news editor used every opportunity to remind him of the fact.

He put the phone down and started the engine. The CD at once picked up again as the windscreen wipers pushed a layer of slush aside. *Almost cut my hair. It happened just the other day.*

The track up to Stornes farm was closed to traffic. He parked by the old sanatorium and walked the last kilometre of the way. Two fire engines passed as he was walking. Police tape also closed off the entrance to the farm itself. Dan-Levi spoke to the policeman standing there, but didn't get much out of him. He made his way towards the edge of the wood and took a few pictures of the ruins, saw at once that they were usable. Climbing up on to a large rock, he got an even better angle. The blackened end wall still standing, the jets of water dousing the ruins from three sides. Again he noticed how this calculating of the best angle and lighting for his pictures caused him to forget that what he was looking at was a tragedy. It still bothered him, although less now than when he had first started working on the paper.

As he returned to the cordoned-off area, another police car swung into the space behind him. Two men stepped out, one of them in uniform. It was Roar Horvath, Dan-Levi's best friend since their days at secondary school.

– I see the tabloids are here, he said by way of a greeting.

– Always first, Dan-Levi nodded. He had a crude joke in mind but decided it would be inappropriate at the scene of a tragedy like this.

The plain-clothes officer raised the tape and ducked under. Roar Horvath stayed where he was. – Been eating fish all week?

It was just over a week since they'd spent a Sunday together at Roar's cabin in Nes. They'd been ice fishing on the half-rotten ice and brought back a trout meal for Sara and Roar's new girlfriend. There had been tension between the ladies from the start. The girlfriend's name was Monica; she was an estate agent and the type of person who always had to control whatever situation she was in. Moreover, she had absolutely no idea how anyone in the twenty-first century could speak in tongues, and it was evidently important for her to repeat this to the point of boredom. Sara got tired of it and turned off, but Dan-Levi let her carry on. His pal changed partners about once a year, and he couldn't see this one lasting any longer than the others. For a short while at secondary school Roar and Sara had been a couple, and she still complained about how he couldn't find anyone to settle down with. Dan-Levi didn't voice any opinion on that. His friendship with Roar was a sort of exclusion zone in which both observed an unwritten injunction never to discuss matters of faith, salvation and personal morality.

– What can you tell me about what happened here? Dan-Levi said, pointing at the ruins. – Any hot tips?

Only after he'd said it did the macabre pun strike him.

– The fire technicians haven't been in there yet, Roar told him with a grin as he wiped something from his reddish moustache. He'd started it in his last year at the police academy. Recently he'd begun waxing the tips, but this morning he'd obviously not had time to twist them up into points, and the thick clumps hung limply under his chin, making him look like a walrus.

– What about the cause of the fire, Eggman?

Roar glanced over at Dan-Levi. – Eggman?

– *I am the Walrus.*

He still didn't get the point, even though old pop and rock hits were an interest they'd always shared. Dan-Levi had to explain that he was referring to the sad and drooping moustache.

His friend rolled his eyes. – It isn't part of my job to talk to tiresome journalists, he growled.

– Do I have to go up to the police station to hear exactly the same thing as you're refusing to tell me?

– We need to go through the whole list. Technical faults, carelessness and so on.

– And so on?

– You know something, Dan-Levi, it doesn't suit you, being an investigative journalist. How on earth did you end up with that gig?

It was something Dan-Levi wondered about himself. He was going to apply for a post in the culture section as soon as a vacancy opened up there.

– So there's nothing to indicate that the fire might have been started deliberately? he persisted.

Roar pulled a tin of dipping tobacco from his pocket, unscrewed it. – What makes you suppose that I would share my innermost thoughts with your readers?

– Take it easy, Horvath, said Dan-Levi. His glasses were steaming up. He removed them, cleaned them with a corner of his shirt. – When I've made up my mind to keep something to myself, not even a bottle of Toilet Ninja is going to open me up.

Roar grinned and stuck a fingertip with its liquorice-like load behind his upper lip. – I might just test that out sooner than you think. I was thinking of popping in tonight and taking a look at that kitchen.

Dan-Levi hesitated. They'd been living in the house for a little more than a year, taken it over after his in-laws. The kitchen and living room were both in need of a total makeover. And Roar was a born handyman, Dan-Levi's polar opposite in that department.

– We're probably going to have to postpone the whole renovation thing.

– I thought so, Roar grinned. – Sara still feeling sick?

She'd started to feel unwell that Sunday at the cabin. Dan-Levi hadn't said anything about why. It was too early; there were still a lot of things that could go wrong. But the main reason was that they wanted to keep it to themselves. That precious time when they were the only two in the whole world who knew what was going to happen.

– She's still feeling a little bit under the weather, he conceded.

– So you don't rule out the possibility that the fire was started deliberately?

– We've got a few statements from witnesses we need to take a closer look at. Pregnant?

Roar fixed him with a detective's gaze and Dan-Levi couldn't bring himself to respond. As far back as he could remember, he had been indoctrinated with that single sentence that formed the basis of all rules: to tell a lie was the worst sin of all, because it incorporated all other sins. Not just at home, but also in his sermons from countless pulpits, Pastor Jakobsen always returned to the curse of the lie. And the older Dan-Levi grew, the more he realised how right his father had been.

– Don't you two feel any responsibility at all in the face of overpopulation? Roar scolded him. – You're a Pentecostal, aren't you? I thought it was just Catholics who weren't allowed to use rubbers.

Dan-Levi tried to laugh it off. He could joke about most things with Roar, but this was one area he didn't want his friend trampling around in. It belonged to him and Sara alone.

– It's still not definite.

– What's that supposed to mean? Roar seemed surprisingly interested. – Either Sara's pregnant or she isn't.

Dan-Levi gave in. – Just don't say anything about it.

Roar wedged the snuff into place with his tongue. A brown drop dripped on to his moustache.

– Don't worry, he winked. – Sure as Toilet Ninja, me.

4

He tossed the newspaper and a bunch of ads down on to the table. Twenty-four hours since he'd last slept. Still didn't feel tired. He switched on the computer, opened the online edition of *VG*. The article about the fire had been revised. Not twenty-six animals taken by the flames, but twenty-nine. He went to *Dagbladet*'s site. They too were now giving a figure of twenty-nine. It was about a herd of horses. But still, he wanted to know the exact number. Twenty-nine meant that six horses had escaped. Maybe they hadn't managed to catch them all; maybe some had run off into the woods and were now charging about in the wet snow up there.

VG's page included a video of the fire, obviously made with a primitive camera, but close up and much better quality than the one he had recorded himself on his mobile phone from the edge of the wood over a hundred metres away. He played the video again. The stables were consumed, with only the framework remaining, outlined against the blinding yellow-white of the flames. Grey smoke wafted about in the night, mingling with black smoke from an outhouse that had also caught fire. In the jagged light a few naked birch branches trembled. The fire crews on the scene spoke calmly, as though discussing the best way to deal with some ordinary everyday problem. So the recording must have been made after the noise from the horses had stopped. On his own recording the shrieks of panic were so clear that it was painful to listen to them, and that pain conjured up a feeling of being confronted by something he controlled, but which was nevertheless bigger than him. And when neither horses nor people were screaming, and the fire crews had moved further away, he suddenly heard the fire itself. The crackling was like the sound of greedy little animals eating and eating, and behind, like a faint wind, a powerful voice whispering as it drew breath. That was something he'd heard before. He played the recording over and over again. The smoke raced about in the night, and something moved inside that greedy light. But it was not the sight that fascinated him. It was that whispering inhalation, the fire's own, almost inaudible voice.

He wandered out into the bathroom, cracked open the three capsules he had made ready. Injected two millilitres of Trenbolone in one arm and a mixture of Testo and Primo in the other. He was in the building phase, but had learnt not to try to go too fast; made up his mind not to lose control again. In the bedroom he undressed, did push-ups and sit-ups, over a hundred of each, could have carried on for the rest of the day without tiring. Afterwards he lay there looking up at the ceiling. Suddenly he knew: the next place that would burn. He could see it in his mind's eye, even though he hadn't been there for many years. If he concentrated, he could hear the sounds from in there. The voices of the grown-ups. And the smells: the linoleum, the oil paints, now and then chocolate and freshly baked bread.

He got up, opened the wardrobe, pushed his hand in under the boxer shorts and the socks and pulled out a bra. Yesterday evening before going up to the stables he'd let himself in to Elsa's place. The smell of the perfume she'd put on before going out still lingered in the bathroom. The bra was hanging on a hook along with two dark red towels. He'd stuffed it into his jacket pocket. Now he stood there with it in his hand, naked in front of the wardrobe mirror. Finally he realised how exhausted he was and lay down on the bed on top of the blanket, feeling the faint breeze from the window, how it dried the sweat that ran down his back. He pushed the bra between his thighs.

A bird sang directly outside; another one answered in the distance. The bedlinen was clean, the clothes he'd been wearing during the night were now in a rubbish bin, and in the morning he had showered and washed every inch of his body. Yet he could still detect a faint smell of tar when he raised the back of his hand to his nostrils. The smell brought with it the sight of the burning stable. But now he felt differently when he thought about the horses. It no longer enraged him. He closed his eyes and conjured up the crackling sound of the flames once again. And somewhere behind it, the faint whisper of a mighty voice.

5

THE LILLESTRØM GRADUATES had the reputation of being the biggest bunch of wimps in all Romerike when it came to the annual pre-graduation celebrations, and Priest had decided to do something about that. Some pretty mean stuff was being planned around the kitchen table. Something about baptising the Lørenskog soon-to-be school-leavers with fire extinguishers. They were the ones who'd put it about that the Lillestrøm lot were more interested in swotting than partying. Priest claimed to have a natural talent when it came to dreaming up armed operations and volunteered to lead the attack on the next officially designated party bar. Not out of any need for status; he had plenty enough cred after the night he'd spent in the cell for being drunk and disorderly following the first party of the season.

Now he wanted to hear what Lam, as a Buddhist, thought of the plans. Lam had drunk a few beers and sat laughing at every idea Priest came up with. But when asked directly, he suddenly grew very serious. They should drop this business with the fire extinguishers. Not only would they wreck the interior of the bar and get reported to the police and have to pay for the damage, but if anyone got powder in their eyes it would hurt. Priest rose to his feet and hailed Lam as the voice of common sense in a mad world. They drank a toast to him: *chia,* as the Vietnamese say.

Karsten was standing at the door munching on a slice of pizza. He raised his glass too but didn't drink. He made no secret of the fact that he never touched alcohol. All the same, Priest had just filled it with vodka, maintaining that the occasion was the equivalent of a Holy Communion. He claimed that the father had given him authority to do so; if not the Heavenly Father, then at least his own father, who was the parish priest.

To get away, Karsten opened the door to the living room. At once there was music. Tonje was sitting on the sofa, and he recalled that she had been sitting in exactly the same place the last time he had been to a party at her house. On that occasion he had slumped down beside her and she had suddenly rested her head on his shoulder. There ought to be a dictionary that explained what something like that meant. If a girl gave you a hug, it meant she liked you. If she put her head on your shoulder, that also meant she liked you, and it *could* mean she wanted to get it on with you. But not necessarily. Not if you only had one testicle, for example. If you were found wanting when it came to passing on your genes and were an evolutionary cul-de-sac. Karsten had tried to find out what he could about this business of sperm count. In the average ejaculation, between two and three hundred million sperm streamed towards the waiting egg. Did that mean there were only half as many if you just had one testicle? Wouldn't the other one work even harder to compensate? So far he hadn't found an answer.

Tonje glanced up at him, shouted something through the music. It might have been *Are you okay?* and he nodded. Tonje wanted everyone to be okay. The seat next to her on the sofa was vacant this time too. And as Karsten registered this, the question cropped up again, the one he'd been asked up to twenty times a day for a period at secondary school. *Who's the poorest man in the world?* Don't know, he always used to say, prompting exactly the same answer every time: *Karsten's Willy, because he only has one stone in his sack.*

The party had reached its chaotic phase. He withdrew from the living room again, wandered out into the corridor. It was nearly twelve thirty, the time at which he'd planned to get out of there.

Lam noticed him and came over. – Let's walk back together.

He was one of the few in his class who Karsten felt was on the same wavelength. They often solved maths and physics problems together. Had quite similar ways of thinking about things, even though Lam was a Buddhist and Karsten an agnostic, the only position he felt himself able to defend rationally. But Lam was much too smart to go on about being right, and Karsten didn't think religious questions were worth spending time on.

As he pulled on his jacket, Inga appeared behind him. She wrapped one arm around him and immediately the smoke from her cigarette began to irritate his eyes.

– And where do you think *you're* going?

He half turned towards her. Her white blouse was unbuttoned and the lacy edge of her bra clearly visible.

– Got to get up early, he offered, but immediately regretted that he hadn't thought of another answer.

– Aw, are we going home to beddy-byes? Is Mumsy going to pull up the bedclothes and go poochie-poo?

She reached up and kissed him on the cheek, stroked his hair and repeated that *poochie-poo*. He had no way of knowing if she was taking the piss or actually meant something by it. He worked out that it had to be something on the list of things to do, one of the challenges that would earn her the right to tie another knot in her graduation cap tassel. One he hadn't heard about: *Make it with a nerd*. She'd done the same thing at the coffee bar a few weeks ago. She'd just been voted 'School Leaving Babe of the Year' by the other students, and him 'Dullest School Leaver in Northern Europe'.

Lam went out into the hallway and stood waiting, a smile playing around his lips as Karsten tried to free himself. Last time Inga had made quite a fuss when he'd made it clear he didn't want her hanging on to him like that, shouting out that he was a snob, that just because he was a bit smarter at maths than the rest, he thought it made him better than them. That kind of thing.

Then Priest arrived. – Need any help, mate? From the corner of his mouth he added: – Can fix you up with a box of Viagra. Premium quality. All the way from Latvia.

Inga pushed him away. – Karsten is a stud. Think he needs stuff like that?

– Who doesn't need stuff like that when they're with you?

– I'll bet he can keep it up longer than you.

– I don't doubt it, Priest said with a wink. – I shoot off quicker than a hare.

Inga blew smoke into his face, turned back to Karsten and put an arm around his neck, pulled his head down and kissed him. He felt her other hand caress his buttocks.

– Stay a bit longer, she murmured, and the exaggerated horniness in her voice made him even more certain that this was all about getting another knot in her cap tassel. The fact that she stank of vodka and cigarettes and that her lipstick was smeared on one corner of her mouth didn't help matters.

He was rescued by a ringing on the doorbell. Three long rings. Karsten pulled himself free and was about to open up. Priest stopped him.

– Don't let anyone in unless Tonje says it's okay. Too many psychos out there.

He turned and shouted for the hostess. Again the doorbell rang, a long, harsh note that didn't stop.

Tonje appeared in the hallway. – Find out who it is, she said to Priest.

He opened the door. A guy wearing a black jacket with the collar turned up was standing on the top step.

– Lam, he said.

He was a Pakistani, Karsten saw. A Pakistani or something like that.

Priest turned and asked: – Wasn't Lam standing here just a moment ago? He interrupted himself. – What do you want with Lam?

– Talk to him.

Four other figures now appeared at the foot of the steps. Priest's gaze moved from the Pakistani and over his shoulder to Tonje. – Don't let them in, she whispered fiercely.

– Who are you? Priest said.

The person shook his head. – You don't want to know, right?

Priest began to close the door, and with lightning speed the guy blocked it with his foot and pushed it wide open. The next moment, all four of them were inside the house. The first one pushed Priest up against the mirror in the hallway.

– I don't like your girlie face.

He hit him on the nose with his bunched fist. There was a sound like dry twigs snapping. Priest collapsed with a strangled cry. Inga and Tonje had disappeared into the living room, pushing the door shut and screaming. It occurred to Karsten that he ought to stand in front of that door, guard it with his body. He gestured with his arm. The guy who had just knocked Priest down turned towards him.

– Don't move, he hissed, his voice black, his eyes even blacker.

Karsten shook his head. He intended to convey that no one had the right to tell him what he should or shouldn't do, but dimly realised that his meaning had been misunderstood.

One of the others who had just arrived pulled the fire extinguisher down off the wall and broke the glass in the living-room door with it. For a moment the girls' panicky screaming stopped, only to start up again after a few seconds. The door was kicked open, shards of broken glass flying everywhere along with a cloud of foam from the extinguisher. The one who had punched Priest shouted: – We're looking for Lam. You're the ones who're making trouble.

Karsten was still standing there, frozen, but his brain carried on working, as usual looking for things that could be sorted together. Lam lived in Lia, the Lia gang's turf. The Vietnamese had been at war with a Pakistani gang for a long time. But Lam wasn't a member; he was a smart guy, he was aiming to study architecture, he wanted to build houses.

– Lam isn't one of the Lia gang, he shouted to the four intruders, who were already in the living room. As the music was cut off, he heard a groan from Priest, who lay writhing on the floor below the mirror, the sound instantly drowned by the shattering of more glass, screaming girls, footsteps running on stairs, something heavy that might have been a TV set crashing on to the floor. Karsten felt a prickling that spread along his arms and made them numb and incapable of movement. It was as if the rampaging was taking place somewhere else, far away from the house where he was standing bent against the wall.

He glanced down at Priest. – You in pain?

Priest stared at him. Blood was pumping from his broken nose, but he was breathing and able to move his head. Suddenly Karsten realised what he had to do. He tore himself out of his frozen trance, stepped over his classmate, out on to the steps, pulled out his mobile and called the emergency services. Almost a minute passed before there was an answer.

His voice sounded distant as he explained, gave the address, how many attackers there were.

In the same instant, two of the interlopers came running out. They were dragging Lam between them. He was in his stockinged feet and bleeding from the mouth. In the pool of porch light Karsten noticed the look in his eyes. It was rigid, his pupils the size of dinner plates, as though locked in the maximum dilation.

He followed them down the steps.

– Hey.

One of the intruders turned.

– Hey wha'? he said in broken Norwegian.

– Don't, was all Karsten managed before somebody pushed him over. He lay there in the slush, his head by the hedge.

– Just stay where you are and we'll let you live, got it?

The guy planted a foot on his chest. He had a roundish face with a beard like a pencil line along the edge of his jaw. His broad eyebrows joined together above the bridge of his nose, and in one ear he wore a ring with a dark stone.

– Got it?

He's not going to make me answer, thought Karsten. – Can you read? he muttered instead.

– What are you on about?

– Have you learnt to read? Karsten repeated, more clearly this time, but still the guy didn't understand what he was saying.

He's a nothing, he thought to himself. He'll end up doing time in Ullersmo, or on disability benefit. Something like that.

Over by the car, Lam was shouting. Karsten heard the punches, hard and dry against bone, muted on softer areas. The screams turned to groans and then stopped. Only the sounds of punching hung in the air. He could feel the snow beneath him melting, penetrating his pullover and shirt, running down inside the waistband of his trousers. He lay alone beneath the dark sky. A twig from the hedge prodded into his cheek. The person watching him was no longer there, but Karsten didn't get up. Could hear the punching going on and on. Until it was drowned beneath the sound of an engine starting, revving up a few times and then disappearing. Even then he didn't get up.

6

He stood naked in front of the mirror. Flexed the muscles of his arms, and in his chest felt the pain that had settled there after his workout earlier that evening. He had just been online and read several articles about arsonists. Setting fire to something was a cry for help, it said somewhere. In another article he read that people who did it were relieving tension they couldn't get rid of by normal means. And even though they might join in the work of extinguishing the fire, it gave them a sexual thrill to watch the flames spread and get out of control. People who experienced this were sick and needed treatment.

Nothing of what he read applied to him. He was in primary school the first time he deliberately started a fire. The man named Tord who called himself his father was burning a pile of dead leaves on a piece of ground close to the house. Busy with his rake, putting it out, starting it up again in other parts. Striding about the field in his black tracksuit, master of the flames, hunched over watchfully, into action the instant the flames threatened to go against his will.

He'd found his own rake and wandered around after his father. Allowed small tongues of flame to spread and swallow up clumps of dead straw, and struck down on them when he felt they'd gone far enough. Tord glanced across at him a couple of times, said nothing, but no one could doubt that they were a team.

At one end of the field a wide footpath ran diagonally across. The flames could get that far, but no further; they went out by themselves once they reached it. The tongues of flame licked their way across the grey-black gravel and died away as though poisoned. He tore up a handful of dry straw, pushed it into the fire; it began to smoke and hiss because there were green and juicy blades of grass in there too, and spittle oozed out of it. Tord stood there with his back to him, bent over; didn't notice him as he took a couple of steps out on to the path and tossed the hissing torch over to the other side, mostly to see how long it took to go out. He timed it. After half a minute, it started to smoke and whisper. There was still time for him to run across and beat the defenceless sparks to death, but then Tord would have realised what he'd done. Instead he went up to the house and hid behind the garage. Lay there until he heard shouting from down in the field, pulled his trousers up again and ran down the driveway. Tord was standing on the other side of the footpath, swishing and swiping at the flames that burned in a circle round him. This was just a few metres away from the neighbour's hedge, and behind that brushwood and raspberry bushes, and beyond them the neighbour's yellow house.

He ran down. The neighbour had arrived, and a couple of older boys. Shoulder to shoulder they advanced in the direction of the hedge, hitting and beating at the flames, which fought back now. The fire was wearing a huge grin, and it hissed around him, the voice whispering as it drew breath, and it made the men furious. He could see it in Tord's face. He was afraid now, there was something stronger than him, he fought with his mouth half open, his eyes staring. The fire didn't give up until it was less than a metre from the hedge. It didn't give up, because it could flare up again at any time, anywhere, and no one, not even the man who called himself his father, could ever feel completely safe. But now it did surrender, with another grin, stopped whispering and gave the men a temporary victory.

He ran his finger across the patchy scars on his underarm. That this memory should surface again on this of all evenings was a sign. It was going to happen again. He got dressed, went into the kitchen, emptied the dregs of his coffee. It was tepid, bitter; he poured another, forced it down.

Back in his room, he got out the packet of cigarettes, the rubber bands and the strips of cotton. At a hotel where he'd spent the night once he'd found a whole package of paper matches and taken them. Now at last he had a use for them. He busied himself with his ignition device, improved it, placing two fuses next to each other, dousing them with lock oil, took the device into the bathroom and tested it in the bathtub. If Elsa had been home, maybe he would have told her about the fire that time. Told how he had been sent up to his room afterwards with instructions to think about what he'd done. But when Tord came up, it wasn't the fire he stood there raging about. He could still remember every single word that was said. The words mingled with the smell of paint thinner, because the floor of the hallway had just been painted. Afterwards he was to stay in his room and carry on thinking about what he'd done.

And that was what he did. Crept into the wardrobe, and in behind the loose plank in the wall where he had a room no one else knew about. He sat in there thinking over what Tord had said. The woman who called herself his mother came up looking for him. It was late by then, and shortly afterwards, he heard her outside the house calling for him. But he remained sitting in the room inside the wardrobe, not just thinking, but bringing the thoughts to life, flicking the lighter he'd taken from Tord's drawer, staring at the flame until he knew what was going to happen. He scratched it on to the wooden beam, burnt scorch marks around it, like a frame, and it was decided once and for all. The sentence over the house they lived in.

Later on, he went further in finding out what flames could do. They destroyed things, and people were things too. Usually he used his place for these studies, the room behind the wardrobe that no one else knew about. There he would flip open the lid of the lighter and ignite it. Even in that tiny flame he could hear the voice whispering if he listened long enough. Not that he could hear the words, but he could feel what it was the flame wanted. He moved it closer to the skin of his underarm, felt how it jabbed at him, pulled it away, brought it closer again, allowed it to scorch away the light hairs. If it was close enough, it penetrated the skin. He held it there so long it began to smell. In this way he was able to study what the flame wanted to do to the body, how it wanted to transform it into something that was nothing but pain, damage it so badly it could not be repaired.

He had never mentioned any of this to Elsa. She had asked him a lot of things about those days, but he could never bring himself to talk about this. And this evening she wasn't home, she was out having dinner with her prince. He was the one who filled her thoughts now. As if she'd just been waiting for years.

He got into the car, peeled back a section of felt beneath the dashboard, pushed the bag holding the four ignition devices inside. As he started the car and began to reverse, still thinking about Elsa and her prince, he stamped on the accelerator and hit something, the wheels spun, and he jumped out and went round to the rear of the car. Three fence posts destroyed. He swore loudly, calmed down, decided to ring Elsa and explain what had happened. Then she might tell him to stay home that evening and not finish

what he'd started. He changed his mind. She believed
in what was good. But she was the one who had spoken
about the purifying power of fire.

A few minutes later, he turned on to Erleveien. Years since
he'd last been there. He'd been sent away when he was
fifteen.

The house had turned a brownish colour, but next door's
was still yellow. On the field where the fire had been, a
small block of houses had been built, red with white door
frames. He parked by the side of the road, sat there a while
looking out into the dusk. A few children were playing in
the little strip of garden where the field had once been.
There were no signs of life in the house he used to live in.
He climbed out of the car, strolled over to the letter box. It
said *Jakobsen* on the lid. When he opened the small gate,
the hinges creaked. In the days when he was living there,
they were always well oiled. Tord looked after everything,
couldn't stand slovenliness. He was a major and used to
things being done. Now the house needed repainting, and
the wheelbarrow outside the garden shed looked as if it had
been there all winter, full of stones and with a layer of ice
at the bottom.

The front door was visible from the road, but not from
any of the nearby houses. The porch light wasn't on; he had
to bend down to read the name plate in the dusk. *Sara,
Dan-Levi and Rakel Jakobsen live here*.

Just then he heard a car approaching further along the
road. He darted down the steps and round the corner, pressed
himself up against the wall of the garden shed. The car
glided past the gate and turned in towards the garage. He
could have run for it, jumped over the fence and off between
the trees in the garden next door. He waited until the car
had pulled up and the garage door been closed. Until he

heard footsteps on the icy gravel path, up the steps, the front door being opened and then shut. Only then did he glide out of the shadow, walk calmly down the flagstone path and out through the creaking gate.

He stopped a little further down the road and saw lights going on inside the house. First the kitchen, then the living room. A few moments later upstairs. But his old room remained in darkness.

On the way home, he called in at Studio Q. Hadn't planned another workout that day, but had to get rid of that itch before it spread through his whole body. It was already crawling around in his arms and legs.

He did a simple programme of bench presses, biceps curls and thighs. A woman in dark red workout tights was using the treadmill. He'd seen her there before and nodded back when she gave him a brief smile. She had a hooked nose that was too big for her small, narrow face. He let his gaze take in the rest of her body. From the neck down she was great. He looked again, no more than vaguely interested, but probably what she was expecting.

In the toilet he took out the bag with the capsules and syringes, gave himself two mils each of Testo and Trenbo, still determined not to rush things. He glanced at his face in the mirror; three or four pimples had appeared just below his hairline. Elsa had some herbs that would fix that. It would give him an excuse to drop in that evening.

Back in the studio, he noticed a man in police uniform at the reception desk. He gave a start, struck by the thought that the guy was there because of him. Calmly, without so much as a sideways glance, he headed for the weights room. Turning to close the door, he saw the woman with the hooked nose on her way over to the reception desk, then stretching up and giving the policeman a quick kiss.

He pulled back from the glass door. From a corner of the weights room he could still see them reflected in a mirror on the opposite wall. The man in uniform had a reddish handlebar moustache vainly twisted into points at the ends. He had to grin, relieved and curious. It's a warning, he thought. He would have to build up slower; the mixture of Testo and Trenbo was making him paranoid. Just showed how easy it was to lose control.

7

THEY WERE STILL talking about what had happened at Tonje's party in the last lesson on Monday. They had a supply teacher, the type who made it his business to overhear everything. He picked up what they were saying.

– So you were attacked by a gang.

Karsten stared at his desktop. When he'd left the party, the floor in the hallway and living room had been covered with bits of shattered glass and foam from the fire extinguisher; the TV had been smashed, CDs and ornaments lying all over the place. Some were sobbing, some puking, others talking about revenge.

– How many of them were there? the supply teacher wanted to know.

– Four or five, said Tonje.

One of the boys added: – There was another gang of them waiting outside.

– Then it was some kind of strategically planned attack, the teacher concluded. – And you say they were Pakistanis? Do you know that for sure? Why not Kurds, or Iraqis, or Afghans?

The teacher appeared to be in his mid twenties and was probably a student at the university. He was wearing a suit jacket that looked quite expensive, dark trousers with a crease in them and a shirt with a wide collar, and when he had introduced himself it emerged that, among other things, he had served as a soldier in Afghanistan.

– I don't give a shit where they were from, Priest said from his desk in the middle of the room; he had a plaster that went right across his swollen nose. – It was totally a gang thing. They came to get Lam. There's total war between the Lørenskog Pakis and the Lia gang, Lam's brother's gang.

There was a Pakistani girl in the class. The way Priest was speaking caused Karsten to glance across at her. Her name was Jasmeen. For the whole of that school year she had been sitting a knight's jump behind him; several times they'd worked on class projects together. When she met his gaze, he turned away.

– Isn't gang war like that a type of cultural conflict? the teacher persisted.

A number of voices were raised in protest. Priest said: – It's got nothing to do with culture. They're criminal arseholes, it's just fucking wicked.

The supply teacher was tall and broad shouldered, with longish hair swept back and a neatly trimmed chin beard.

– How many were at the party?

Only now did Karsten notice there was something about the way he spoke, some kind of almost imperceptible accent.

– About thirty, Tonje replied.

– And how many lads?

She looked around. – Maybe about half.

The teacher ran a finger over his stubble. – So that means there were at least twice as many lads in the house as there were interlopers, maybe three times as many. I'm sure some of the girls could have helped out too if there was any talk of self-defence. But that didn't happen?

A vague disquiet spread through the room. – What d'you mean? one of the boys muttered.

Inga interrupted: – Maybe he means that someone might have lifted a finger if our lives were being threatened. Apart from Karsten, no one did shit.

Karsten stared straight ahead. A hot flush invaded his skin at the hairline and crept downwards. He was about to protest, but she carried on: – Karsten isn't exactly Rambo, but at least he tried to fight back, even if they did slash him in the face with a knife.

The burning sensation gathered in the centre of his cheeks, in the cut made by the hedge outside Tonje's house.

– And what's more, he doesn't get hammered every time you need to have your wits about you, Inga went on. – Half of the boys lay there puking up and the rest were completely paralysed. It's pathetic.

Karsten glanced up at the teacher, hoping he'd start the lesson soon.

– Quite a few of us tried to stop them, Priest protested. – It's not that bloody easy to organise a defence when you get taken by surprise.

The teacher pointed at him. – You've got a point there, Finn Olav.

Priest touched his broken nose, clearly surprised that the teacher had learnt his name.

– As I say, I was a soldier for several years, the teacher went on. – I've been in situations where the element of surprise is crucial. Suppose you'd been given a warning that an attack was imminent, that you had a few minutes, what would you have done?

Various suggestions were aired, gradually more and more drastic. The idea of wasting vodka on making Molotov cocktails gave rise to protests, and after that, to Karsten's relief, the discussion turned into a joke session. The teacher grinned and let them carry on for a while before interrupting.

– We're going to be talking about the period after the Cold War. In other words, more or less what we've just been doing.

He fell silent. The talking stopped in the classroom. There

was something about this teacher that encouraged them to sit quietly and wait to hear what he was going to say.

– During the Cold War, the world was in theory divided because of political ideologies, the liberal West against the communist East. The struggle in the world today is between civilisations with different cultures and religions, first and foremost Islam and the Western world. Maybe we'll end by seeing a connection between what you're going to learn in your history lessons and what you actually experience in your own lives.

He let this prospect hang in the air for a few moments before resuming.

– I asked you if what happened at the party had anything to do with culture. Of course it does. Everything is about culture.

He began talking about civilisations, tracing the connections between the ancient river cultures of Mesopotamia to present-day Iraq, led by the most hated man in the West, that same West which had armed this tyrant to the teeth before invading his country to get rid of him. He spoke without raising his voice, but there was an intensity to the narrative, a battle between opposing forces, a drama in which they were themselves participants and in which they might find themselves playing a crucial role. Their history exam was only a few months away, and their regular history teacher had given them the topics they would be going through a long time ago, and now here was this supply teacher getting into something that wasn't even on the list. No one complained. That the girls sat there staring at him as if he came from another world wasn't all that surprising, thought Karsten, but the boys were behaving in an unusual way too. This was the second time he'd taken the class. He used their names when he spoke to them, and when he was asked how many he had learnt, he pointed to each of them in turn and said what their names were. He didn't get it wrong once. They stared at him in astonishment, as if he'd just performed a conjuring trick. Even Karsten, who people said had a photographic memory, was impressed.

– Let's have a show of hands, the teacher suddenly announced. – How many Christians in the class?

Three students raised their hands. A murmuring started up and spread around the room. Priest spoke up.

– What right do you have to ask that? Isn't that a personal matter?

The teacher nodded. – Good question, he said with a little smile. – Naturally it's a question of whether you mean a legal right or an ethical right or some other kind of right. Of course it's entirely up to you whether you answer or not.

Another couple of hands were raised.

Five altogether, the teacher concluded. – What about the other faiths? Buddhism, Sikhism, Hinduism, Islam?

Karsten wasn't the only one who looked over at Jasmeen. Hesitantly she raised her hand.

– Jasmeen Chadar, the teacher said.

It sounded funny, the way he used both her first and second names. It occurred to Karsten that maybe that was the way people showed respect for girls in the countries where the teacher had been as a soldier.

– I'm a Muslim, said Jasmeen, and something passed through the class, as though they were surprised to hear her say out loud something everybody knew. In the previous school year they'd gone through all the great religions, and one guy in a parallel class, another Pakistani, had given a talk. Not a word about religious wars or 9/11. Nothing about arranged marriages or infants with mutilated genitals. And no one had confronted him about it. In the name of inclusiveness he got away with it. That their regular history teacher didn't bring it up either wasn't surprising;

he was an absolute fanatic about everything to do with multi-cultural and rainbow societies and wouldn't dream of saying something that might offend a minority. Karsten himself wasn't the type to discuss such matters in a classroom. He was interested in other things and contented himself with the observation that part of the world was still living in the Middle Ages.

The supply teacher sat on the edge of the desk.

– So then, five Christians and one Muslim. From which I conclude that the rest of you are atheists.

Tonje was sitting closest to the teacher's desk. The whole time she'd been staring at their supply teacher in a way that Karsten sometimes fantasised girls would stare at him. Several of the girls in class took turns at being visitors to these fantasies, and just lately some of them had started visiting at the same time. But never Tonje. Even in his fantasies she was unattainable, and the thought of her sitting there and being interested in the teacher in that way caused little jolts in his stomach that replicated themselves down through the rest of his body. Sometimes Karsten consoled himself with the thought that since after all he had the poorest man in the world between his legs, he might as well make him even poorer. If he had his remaining testicle removed, he would be freed from this type of disturbance. He could devote himself completely to the world of research, live a useful life, exploit all the talents he possessed so effortlessly.

Suddenly he raised his hand.

– Atheists have beliefs too, he declared. – They believe God doesn't exist.

The teacher turned towards him. – Do we have an agnostic here? Someone who declines to express a view on something we can know nothing about. Tell us more.

Karsten tried to think clearly. Had the situation been

different, he would have remained silent. But now it was him Tonje was looking at. He took a grip on himself.

– I believe in genes.

There should have been more after this, but now the eyes of the whole class were glued to him, and that burning feeling that had started up at his hairline had extended to cover every inch of his body. Of course he knew what he believed. His mother was a tepid Christian who had made sure both he and Synne were baptised, but she never talked about any God. His father, on the other hand, who was a nuclear researcher and an atheist, was forever holding forth about the origin of things, those molecules in the primordial soup that took the great leap from the inorganic to the replicating and could propagate themselves. Karsten was slightly interested. Maths and physics were more his field; there was too much chaos in biology.

– Genes have a lifespan of thousands, maybe millions of years, he said, and thought of something his father often said. – Even the greatest civilisations collapse after a few centuries.

He realised he wasn't quite sticking to the question, but the teacher was watching him with something like curiosity in his eyes.

– Genes reproduce themselves at the expense of their competitors. They keep the world going and create evolution, and to do that, they use us individuals.

– At last, someone with an opinion, the teacher exclaimed. – Go on.

Karsten was stuck. He mumbled something about all religions arising because people needed something to comfort themselves with. Finally the teacher released him and addressed the class again.

– There are plenty of examples and plenty of new arenas in which Islam and the Western world are in conflict with each other. Are there any particular aspects of Islam that might account for this?

– Are you saying it's Islam's fault that there's war in the world? said Jasmeen. Her voice was loud and clear. They had been in the same class for nearly two years, but outside those projects worked on together, Karsten had hardly spoken to her. She didn't talk much in the class, and in the early days he hardly noticed her presence at all. At break time she hung around with the other immigrant girls. She lived in Lørenskog, he gathered; her father had a couple of shops, including a sweet shop in Strømmen.

The teacher was looking at her, and when Karsten again turned, it was as though he was seeing her through the teacher's eyes. The boys who made lists thought she was hot, between eight and nine on a one-to-ten. Her tits were supposed to be as good as Inga's, though those who said so couldn't possibly have seen them. Inga's, on the other hand, could be accurately described, and from primary school onwards they'd been the gold standard. Karsten had never taken part in these contests. Sure, it was all based on verifiable criteria like size and shape, but there were fundamental flaws. Tonje was small and thin, with hardly any breasts at all. But she'd recently been selected to participate at a gathering for the junior national handball team, and she was leader of the students' graduation party committee. Not one of the boys who made these lists would have said no to her, no matter what she asked for.

– I'm about to ask the opposite question, the teacher said calmly. – Is there anything in Christianity, or some other aspect of Western culture, that leads to conflict? What do the rest of you think?

Karsten waited before getting up once the lesson was over. He was hoping Tonje would hang about so he could walk out with her and at last confess to his pathetic behaviour when the intruders arrived. But there was evidently something she wanted to talk to the teacher about, and she disappeared through the door with him. Priest sidled behind them, crestfallen. Karsten stayed where he was; there was no one else he wanted to talk to. But Jasmeen was still sitting at her desk.

– I don't think he was having a go at Islam, Karsten said, not really sure why he felt the need to defend the teacher.

– You get used to stuff like that, she answered as she shoved a pile of notes into her bag. She'd changed her appearance after the Christmas holidays, Karsten had noticed vaguely. Something to do with her hair. She'd had it cut and it was hanging loose; before that she'd always had a metre-long plait hanging down her back.

– That stuff about genes, you only said that to impress the teacher.

– Why should I want to impress him? Karsten protested.

– Why does everyone else?

He shrugged. – So you don't think I believe that genes decide everything?

She shook her head firmly. – If that's the case, you've got nothing to live for.

He was on the point of asking her what *she* had to live for, but resisted. Recently he'd watched a TV programme on the biology of faith, and he was convinced that this was the truth of it: religious experiences corresponded to hyperactivity in certain areas of the brain. This produced intense sensations of meaning and universal connection among people who had developed particular neural patterns in precisely those areas.

She took a step closer.

– Is that where they cut you?

He touched his cheek. Suddenly had a desire to tell her

what had really happened. Someone had to know that actually he was the most cowardly of them all at the party. It might as well be her.

– You're brave, she said, and then it was too late to explain.

He looked out of the window. – I was just there. It was as close to the truth as he could come without directly confessing. – Lam's going to be away for weeks.

If he hadn't done anything to stop Lam being hurt, he had at least accompanied a neighbour who drove him to the hospital in the middle of the night. Priest was allowed to go home after an examination, but Lam was admitted. Not because several teeth had been kicked out and his jaw probably broken, but because he had pains in his stomach and the doctors couldn't find the cause.

– What did they look like, the ones who attacked you?

Karsten had been asked that several times, and he still couldn't provide a good answer. Could remember only the one standing over him, a stocky guy with a round face, a thin strip of a beard and a flashy earring.

– What about the car they were driving? Jasmeen wanted to know.

– Black, I think. It was dark, I couldn't see so well. I'm not blaming Pakistanis, he said to change the subject. – It's wrong to start talking about clashes of culture just because of a few gangs.

She looked at him. – It's okay that people talk about it, she said, smiling so the dimples in her cheeks showed. – It makes us think. Isn't that why we're here?

It was natural for them to leave the classroom together, go down the steps.

– How is Shahzad? Karsten asked, though few things interested him less. Her brother had been two years ahead of them. He stole mobile phones and other electronic stuff from the shopping centre. Used to brag about it: only the best makes were worth the trouble. There were rumours he had connections with the Young Guns, and even though he wasn't a very big guy, no one would want gang members turning up at their door no matter how much iron they'd been pumping. Shahzad had dropped out of secondary school in his third year. Probably made so much money that education was a waste of time.

Jasmeen wrinkled her nose by way of an answer; maybe she was even less interested in talking about her brother than Karsten was.

Down in the assembly hall, he had an excuse ready to say so long and head off for the library, but Jasmeen suddenly wanted to know what kind of music he liked. He wasn't interested in music and had never heard any Pakistani music, if that was what she was thinking. The Pakistanis had their own music, had their own everything. That was just the way it was. She was one of them. He wasn't one of them.

On the way out, he held the main door open for her. As she passed, he smelled her sharp smell, a mixture of spices and soap, and he wondered whether it came from her clothes or the skin beneath them.

There was rain in the air; it fell in a slippery film on the asphalt. The church clock struck three. She trotted out into the school yard in her black bootees. He was wearing climbing boots with thick soles. Somewhere above them a plane passed low through the clouds; from the sound, he guessed it wasn't heading in towards Gardermoen but was on its way up. His bike was leant up against a snow bank with three or four others. He nodded over to indicate he was heading that way. She stopped and looked up at him. Her eyes closed and then opened again. She said: – I like you. Can you tell?

He regretted having delayed and not disappearing from

the classroom once the lesson was over. He felt the burning creeping down from his hairline again, knew he had to say something, but if he opened his mouth he was afraid he might swear, and that would made it even harder to stand there.

– Like you too.

It was he who said it, but the voice sounded different. As though it came from far away. And the roar from the plane meant he had to say it far too loud. Still no sign of a smile on her face, just that strangely intense stare, and in a crushing moment it struck him that he had misheard her, that she'd said something else, something about a class project, or maybe something about trigonometry, because to his short-term memory it sounded like that when he thought about it: *I like trigonometry*. Then she touched his hand, and relieved that he seemed to have understood her correctly after all, he gave her hand a quick squeeze. He glanced up towards the front of the school. Through the bare horse chestnut branches he saw a figure in the classroom window, someone standing looking down at them. It might have been the supply teacher.

8

He parked by the high school, walked along the footpath, came to what was left of the woods he had once wandered about in. Through the trees he could see the house down in Erleveien. There was light in almost every window now, including his old room. He had found out who they were. The man of the house, the person who had left the wheelbarrow out all winter by the tool shed, was a journalist working on the local paper. He didn't find much on the wife, only something about a congregation in Bethany, the Baptist church. The thought that this meant they were Pentecostals excited him, and he began humming quietly to himself: *Nearer, my God, to Thee, nearer to Thee*.

Almost a week since the stables burned down. If he thought about the horses now, it was still without a trace of anger. As if the fire had consumed all the rage, purified his thoughts once and for all. Maybe it would be like this every time something burned. He'd been very low that winter. Couldn't face getting up in the mornings, stayed in bed until late in the day, the curtains drawn. Again it was Elsa who had come to him and helped him. She took him to the room where she worked with the cards. She read his life and knew what he needed. She was the one who told him he was born under the sign of fire. Fire purifies, she said, and now he seemed to be on the verge of finding out what that meant.

He returned to the car, drove further up the hill. It took

him two minutes to locate the kindergarten. A new wing had been added, the playground apparatus had been changed, but apart from that everything was just like it used to be. He drove past slowly, found somewhere to park a couple of hundred metres further up, sauntered back down, hands in the pockets of his jacket, as though he were out for an evening stroll, as though he were savouring the cool April evening, as close to spring as you could get before it actually arrived.

He let himself through the gate, carried on by the wall with the dark windows. *Welcome to the carnival*, it said in big cut-out lettering on one of them. Coloured paper streamers hanging from the frames, some masks. The door was locked.

He headed over towards the copse. A conical Sami tent, a *lavvo*, had been put up between the trees. They'd made a fire inside it; the smell of burnt logs and ash still hung in the air. The earth around it had been trampled flat, as though an Indian tribe lived there. Once he'd run around between these trees himself. He couldn't remember playing. Growing up was about something else. Keeping watch, keeping a distance. Waiting until your turn came.

In a shed he found two large rubbish bins, one of them with something stinking inside, nappies maybe, and scraps of food. The other was half full of magazines, packaging, boxes folded flat. He tipped it over and pulled it towards the wall of the kindergarten. In his pocket were the ignition devices he had developed and improved. The half-cigarette with the tip torn off, fastened with a rubber band to three cardboard matches. Woven in between the match heads a twisted thread made of thin cotton. He took out the bottle of lighter fluid, carefully dipped the thread into it, making sure nothing got on to the cigarette. He poured nearly half a bottle into the paper rubbish. Then he rolled the fuse inside some wrapping paper, carried a pile of newspapers over to the doorway at the rear of the building and laid another ignition device there.

He reset the timer on his wristwatch and lit the fuse. Ran back over to the rubbish bin and set fire to the cigarette. It would take just over a minute and a half for it to catch fire, he'd worked it out, more than enough time for him to reach the car. *If* it caught fire. He thought of Elsa. She was the one who had said there was no such thing as chance, that this was just the name we gave to the invisible powers that guided us.

He drove past the fire station and pulled up at the far end of the parking lot on the other side of the road, pulled on the buttons for both windows but only the driver's-side window slid down. He leant across and thumped the other one; the window lift mechanism still didn't work. He swore. He'd bought the Chevy less than six months earlier. A guy he used to work with had brought it back from the States. It would be a drag trying to locate a window lift motor for a ten-year-old model, going through the lists of dealers in second-hand parts for American cars, making sure it was the right part that was sent.

He climbed out and slammed the door shut, squatted down in the dark corner by the wall, glanced at his watch, tried to quell his irritation. Ten minutes had passed. Nothing was definite yet. He closed his eyes. Imagined the tiny flame as it sucked its way down towards the end of the cotton thread. Imagined the papers and cardboard boxes soaked in lighter fluid flaring up. The rubbish bin suddenly turning into a huge greedy bonfire attacking the wall. He imagined the fire burning an opening in the building. The oxygen supply was good there; the flames lived on that oxygen the same way a vampire lived on blood, sucked and sucked and grew strong and heedless.

The time was ten past nine. At this hour there was no one at the kindergarten. Twelve hours earlier, the place had been full of children. He could see them in his mind's eye. Little hands holding scissors and paper, tottering round in teddy bear slippers and tights or swishing down the slide in the playroom. Red noses and runny eyes, shrieks and laughter. He tried to imagine what these small faces would look like if they were there now, trapped inside the building as the flame tore away a wall and advanced upon them in a whirling column. Softly gliding over to the sides of the room and starting to dance around them. He could see the children's faces as they realised that every exit was blocked. He could be there then, with them. Comforting, holding them, a couple of them in his lap, a little girl with a pigtail and huge brown eyes behind her glasses. Then he would get up, walk slowly through the burning doorway, close and lock the door behind him. Lock the screams inside that raging whisper and disappear into the darkness between the spruce trees behind the *lavvo*.

He was roused from his fantasy by a car that came tearing up to the fire station. Fifteen minutes from zero on his stopwatch. A man leapt out, rushed over to the entrance, disappeared inside. Lights appeared in a couple of the windows. He saw shadows inside, hurrying about. A minute later the garage door rolled up and an enormous fire engine growled into life. Cruised slowly down to the road, headed off. Only now did the siren start.

9

KARSTEN RAN. IT wasn't one of his evenings for working out. Usually he ran three evenings a week, same route every time, but now he had broken with his routine, dropped his chess session too, set off without a word to anyone, and no one at home asked him where he was going either.

He ran along Fetveien, past the end of the runway, then took Storgata, into the school, past the spot where he had stood with Jasmeen a few hours earlier. There was a thick layer of slush on the pavements and his trainers were already soaking wet. Bits of what had been said came and went in his head. *I like you. Can you tell?* It was the most unexpected thing that had ever happened to him. As he ran along, he turned it into a story: *Together they walked across the schoolyard. A plane flew low overhead. He was on his way towards his bicycle, she to the bus stop. They walked side by side. And then she said it.* Like you too, *he answered, and didn't even know if it was true.*

He passed the outdoor swimming pool, closed for the winter, carried on along towards the river. Increased his speed a touch, needed to feel tired. Was the likelihood of these fleeting memories being just part of a dream any greater than the likelihood of them actually having happened? He stopped, rested his hands on his knees, a faint nausea. Suddenly he pulled out his mobile, navigated to the address book, found her name. Her number couldn't have got there by itself. And he wasn't dreaming now. He could hear the roar of traffic from Fetveien. The siren from a fire engine. He sent her a text. It all happened so fast he didn't have time to ask himself what he was doing. He carried on running through the slush, heading up towards Nittebergtangen. Felt a vibration in his pocket, halted, pulled out the phone again. *Thinking about you too. Haven't thought about anything else since I saw you.*

He set off running again, as hard as he could, over the footbridge, stopped again. Leaned over the railings in the middle of the river, another of those thoughts he had no idea what to do with: throw yourself in, feel your body crashing through what's left of the melting ice, sink down through the muddy water.

On his way back, he heard more sirens. Up on the hillside he saw blue lights, and for a moment it occurred to him that maybe it was his house they were heading for. Before this thought had time to establish itself, he saw a first response vehicle disappearing up past Erleveien. He jogged along after it. The road on the right was closed off. There was a farm there, and the kindergarten he'd gone to himself. People had made their way into the field and were standing in a crowd up on the slope. A shower of sparks was hurled up against the dark sky. He ran over in that direction. Saw someone he knew.

– The nursery school? he said, and got an affirmative nod. He noticed Dan-Levi walking round with a camera.

– Who would do such a thing? he shouted.

– What do you mean?

– Who would set fire to a nursery school?

Dan-Levi turned towards him. – Who said it was started deliberately?

– Well it would have to be, wouldn't it?

He wasn't certain of it, wasn't certain of anything as he

stared at the flames that came licking out through the roof, the loops of water glinting in the darkness, the blue lights spinning and spinning.

– Sorry I never made chess class tonight, he said, remembering that he'd arranged to play Dan-Levi that evening.

Dan-Levi shook his head, seemed suddenly very sombre. – Doesn't look as though I'm there either.

He disappeared through the crowd of spectators, but reappeared a few moments later and began packing up his photographic gear. – Another thing, Karsten. I'm doing a piece about the problem of gangs in Lillestrøm. You were at that party that was attacked.

Karsten bit his lip. – Don't really want to talk about it much.

Dan-Levi removed his green woollen hat. He was a Pentecostal, and his hair was at least as long as Jesus had in old pictures. He wore it gathered in a kind of tail.

– Think it helps to keep things to yourself? he asked.

– The police'll sort it out, said Karsten.

Dan-Levi thought about it. – Well let's hope so. But they weren't there when you needed them.

Karsten regained his self-possession. – I'm sure you'll find others who can tell you more about what happened. I was out of it.

– Quite literally, I gather.

Karsten attempted a grin. – Literally.

Dan-Levi's small round glasses were misting over. He removed them and wiped the lenses with a cloth. – I've talked to quite a few of the others. Including the girl whose party it was.

– Tonje? What did she say?

– That you were the only one who did anything to try to stop the gatecrashers. She said you ran out after them when they dragged your pal off, and they slashed you with a knife when you tried to help him.

Karsten rubbed his skin where the twig had scratched him. – Please don't mention me when you write about it.

Dan-Levi looked at him for a long time. – You afraid they'll come after you?

The thought had never occurred to Karsten. – Christ, no. Just don't want to be in the papers. I didn't do anything special. Got to get home, he interrupted himself, turning and running off.

In the bathroom, he stepped into the shower, tugged off his boxer shorts, turned on the hot water and peed into the drain. Everything could be interpreted in the light of passing on the genes. Animals that fought and defeated their rivals had a good chance, but at the cost of diminished strength. The ones that lay down and played dead probably had just as good a chance of succeeding. For an instant he felt he was done with what had happened in the schoolyard with Jasmeen; it wasn't something he needed to think about any more. It lasted just a few seconds, and then it was on him again.

He dried himself, picked up his mobile, read the messages again, first the one he had sent, then her answer. Then he deleted them. Regretted it instantly. He tried to imagine a flowchart. The alternatives were to call her, or not to call her. Each choice pointed to a new box in which new choices led in different directions, more and more boxes.

The sound of classical music came from the living room, so that must mean his father was home. He took a quick look into the kitchen. Synne was sitting at the table reading a book. A half-eaten slice of bread with salami and a ton of butter lay on her plate. For a while he had tried to get her to eat something else, vary things more, but he'd had to give up. She refused to go anywhere near fruit and vegetables; she wouldn't even touch jam.

– There's a fire up at Vollen, he told her. – The nursery school.

– You think I'm deaf?

He didn't think that, just wanted to see how she would react. For the past week she had hardly talked about anything but the horses that were burnt to death.

She carried on reading. At any moment she could disappear into a book and stay there. And then it was impossible to reach her until she decided to return to this world. Sometimes he envied her this ability.

– Someone just called for you, she said without looking up from her book.

– Well who?

– No idea.

– Boy or girl?

– A grown-up. I think he said he was your teacher.

– You think?

He suspected she had a tendency to lie. Just like now, she would suddenly say that someone or other had rung and asked for him but couldn't tell him who it was. The first time he believed her, but not the fourth or fifth time. And there were other things too, always little fibs it was hard to catch her out on. He wondered sometimes whether this was why she didn't have any friends. As far as he could tell, she was always at home when she wasn't at school or the stables. Very occasionally a girl from her class would come round, a girl who was adopted and was also an outsider. Sometimes even he had to make an effort to understand what was going on when he was in the middle of a group of people. He had an idea his father's genes were to blame. But in Synne's case it had to be more than genes. He couldn't understand it all, but it upset him that she was like that.

As evening fell, he sat at his desk without switching on

the light. Looked down towards the runway and the wide river running beyond it, a pale light reflected in its waters. The house had fallen silent. The clock in the living room struck ten thirty. He tried to call Jasmeen, planned to say something about the maths test they were going to have, because right now the only thing he was capable of talking about was trigonometry.

She didn't answer, so he sent a text. A reply came back immediately: *Can't talk now. Call you later.*

He lay awake in his bed. A plane approaching. Sounded as if it was flying right over the roof. As the sound of it faded, his mobile on the floor began to ring. He turned over, grabbed it.

– Sorry it's so late, she said. – Were you sleeping?
– Yes.

She gave a low chuckle. – We had visitors. I couldn't get out of it.

No asking why he had called. Only that lowered voice, as though they were intimates. As though that touching earlier in the day had been a binding agreement. He tried to imagine her lying in bed, wrapped up in a duvet; he was on the point of asking her what she was wearing.

– Have you gone to bed? he asked instead.

She confirmed that she had.

– Do you have a room of your own?

– Yes, she whispered. – Because I'm a girl, I get to have my own room.

That was why she had called. *Because I'm a girl.* Still not a word about trigonometry.

Suddenly she yelled something or other, and he understood she wasn't addressing him. A few seconds passed; he couldn't take the phone away from his ear.

– Is your name Karsten? he heard suddenly. It was a man's voice, or a boy about his own age.

– Sorry, got the wrong number.

– No you didn't. What do you want?

All he wanted to do was hang up.

– Nothing really. He pulled himself together. – It's about our trigonometry homework.

– This is the last time you call this number, said the voice at the other end. Karsten had long ago realised whose voice it was.

10

He pushed the barbells up towards the ceiling, held for a moment, lowered them slowly. After the fifteenth time, his arms began to burn. He should manage another ten. The burning turned into a pain that penetrated every fibre of his muscles. He didn't know how he managed the last lift; his arms wouldn't obey him, but still the bar went up. He managed to park it in the cradle, got to his feet, picked up the towel that had been spread beneath him on the bench, stood by the apparatus and shook the blood back into his dead arms. A gang of Pakis had come in while he was working out. He'd seen them before; they'd started hanging out there. Like a pack of jackals, he thought, talking noisily in that language of theirs, with a few words in broken Norwegian chucked in. They invaded the room, took control of it. The way they did wherever they went. They did what they liked and no one tried to stop them. He felt a sudden fury, an urge to tell them to speak Norwegian or shut up, provoke them into attacking him so he could smash a few faces.

He rubbed his knuckles over his scalp. The Pakis exchanged looks, passed some remark or other, maybe about the weights he'd been lifting. None of them could have managed even half as much, and that thought made him turn his back and get out of there. He left the weights still on the barbell, so they would have to start by taking them off before they could begin their bench presses.

Out in the main hall he did a quick survey. It was still quite early in the evening. A couple of kids on the biceps curl machine. A guy in an Adidas suit who'd tried to sell him some roid of dubious origin. At the table over by the soft drinks machine the woman in the dark red workout pants. She was sitting reading a newspaper. The thought that she was going with a policeman still excited him.

He pulled a Bonaqua from the machine, sat down on the other side of the table. She didn't look up. There were several newspapers lying about. He'd trawled the net that morning. None of the big papers had bothered with the fire. He'd gone down to the postbox and fetched *Romerikes Blad* for Elsa. They had the story in there, and in one of the pictures he could just make out himself, with his back turned. Now he turned to the same page in the newspaper on the table: *Nursery school burned down*. It felt even better reading the story with other people around. The biggest picture took up nearly half a page. He sat there looking at the fire breathing sparks up into the evening sky.

– Nasty business, he said to no one in particular, not expecting any response, but the woman in the dark red tights looked at him with the same half-smile as last time.

– That fire?

He nodded.

– Good job it was at night, she said. – Imagine if the children had still been there.

He waited for her to say more. Had absolutely no objection to sitting there and talking about what had happened, be someone on the outside looking at it from a distance together with this woman. But she contented herself with a shake of the head.

– Don't even want to think about it, he lied. Because he had thought about exactly that. Not just as he waited outside the fire station for the engines to emerge, or as he wandered around the scene of the fire filming, gliding in and out of the crowd of curious onlookers whose safe daily routines had been broken, who had been drawn to the catastrophe. Afterwards too he'd thought about the children. He'd sat up most of the night at his computer, transferring images and videos, going through the sequence of events. Was trying to stick to the facts of what had actually happened, but what could have happened kept breaking through and wouldn't leave him alone. The thought of being in there with them, saying farewell to them and then locking them in, standing outside and watching them through the window. They flocked together in mindless panic, just like the horses had done, squeezing themselves into the furthest corner as the flames licked closer and their faces opened. They didn't scream with their mouths as their clothes caught fire; they screamed with their whole bodies. But in the morning, when he'd returned to the scene of the fire, he felt filled with a peace he had not experienced in a long time. The thought of the children no longer moved him; the fire had purified it, removing every trace of what was exciting and alarming.

– They think someone started it, she said.

He glanced over at her, that hooked nose in the narrow face, the breasts beneath the clinging outfit.

– I can't see any mention of that here.

She leant across the table, the smell of perfume mingling with sweat, and it occurred to him that this combination was better than each one of them individually would have been.

– I know someone in the police who's working on the case, she revealed. – And the person covering it for the newspaper.

One of the first things he had noticed was the name of the journalist who had written the story about the fire. It was none other than the guy who lived in the house in

Erleveien. Unless he had a namesake, someone else called Dan-Levi Jakobsen who worked on the same newspaper. Now he had to make an effort not to laugh out loud.

– And the police think it was started deliberately? he said, as evenly as he could. – Who on earth would do something like that?

– There's a lot of weirdos out there, she said with a nod in the direction of the window and the mid-morning light.

He dried his neck with the towel, had to be careful not to show too much interest in the fire. – Do you work with children? he asked, changing the subject.

Her eyebrows shot up, two lines drawn with a thin pencil. – Not bad. That's what we call male intuition. She laughed and added: – I wouldn't last more than an hour in a nursery. I'm an estate agent.

He brought his lips together in a smile. Behind everything assigned to chance all sorts of forces were in operation. Somehow or other they had caused her to sit there and wait for him to join her.

– My name is Monica. She looked up and met his gaze. – With a c, she added.

He nodded, as though this c instead of a k was important for him too. Just then his phone rang. He took it out, looked at the display.

– I have to take this, he explained as he stood up.

His body was steaming when he got outside. The vapour was light grey and mingled with the cold sunlight before evaporating.

– Got a date? Elsa asked. He listened to the inside of her voice for some sign of whether she was happy or angry. She wanted something, otherwise she wouldn't have rung.

– I'm working out, he explained. – Studio Q, he added, because he liked the thought of her knowing where he was.

– Good, she said. – Can you pop into the shopping centre and get a couple of things for me?

It was the least he could do. He peered in through the window as he repeated what it was she wanted him to buy. Red wine in a box, rocket salad, feta cheese. The woman – Monica with a *c* – got up from her chair. If she left now, he thought, he would leave her alone. But if she stayed until he came back, he would follow her home. She cast a glance in his direction, looked as if she was thinking something over. Then she sat down again in the chair where he'd been sitting, continued flipping through the newspaper. The sweat from those dark red tights would blend with his on the back of the chair.

– And another thing, said Elsa, and he noticed the tiny little shadow that crept into her voice. – Have you seen what's happened to the fence?

He swore silently, had forgotten to mention it to her. Now it was as if she'd caught him red handed.

– Sorry, he began, and heard the breath escaping from between her compressed lips, a sign that she was on the verge of being annoyed. He promised he would fix it without delay, and the darkness in her voice went away.

Monica lived in a flat near the square. A top-floor terraced flat, modern interior. She obviously wanted him to see all the rooms, as though he was at a viewing. But suddenly he realised she wanted him to choose the spot: the kitchen with the black tiles, the living room in which daylight reflected back off the parquet floor, or the dim sleeping room that faced in towards the courtyard.

He decided on the bedroom. It was the greyness of the light that attracted him. He pulled her down on to the edge of the bed, put his hand up under the short skirt, tugged her knickers down. She was ready and didn't need any foreplay, or else everything that had happened since she sat down to wait for him in her sweaty tights by the drinks machine had been foreplay enough. With his other hand he opened his flies, pulled down his trousers and boxer shorts, lay across her, excited about how she would react as he entered her, because that was the closest he could get to excitement in all of this. She lay there with her eyes open, bit her lip, no exaggerated noise, no deep moaning. He liked that.

She was narrow, he noticed, he had to wriggle a bit to get in. First she lay quite still, face stiffened to a mask, teeth pressing so hard against her lip that a tiny drop of blood appeared below it. He put more force into it, almost like adding an extra weight to the barbells, pressed down hard, and at last a whimper escaped her mouth. He screwed in deeper, saw from her face that that was exactly the way she liked it. She tried to squeeze her legs together, as though to stop him getting in any deeper, but he grabbed her thighs, pulled them apart and carried on. She opened her eyes and looked at him. He put his lips against her shoulder to get away from that look, let his mouth glide across the skin that smelled of soap and luckily no nauseating scent of deodorant, bit her nipple. She came twice, with a few minutes between each time. Then he let himself come too, not because he had to, but because she expected it. And as it poured into her, she whispered something or other in his ear, and that whispering reminded him that he must remember to call in at the building supplies store after he'd been to the shopping centre.

Usually he didn't stay, but this time he made an exception. She made coffee and put some pieces of chocolate on a blue plate.

– Party, she said with an apologetic smile. The smile was

different now; it had lost that practised stiffness he had noticed at Studio Q.

– We deserve it, he agreed, – after all that exercise.

She laughed shortly. Maybe she blushed, or was it redness that lingered after the events in the bedroom?

– You're not the type that talks about himself, she said as she sat down next to him on the sofa. She was still naked, but he didn't want to sit on what was obviously a very expensive piece of leather furniture without his boxers on.

– I was in the army, he said, to avert further personal questions. – How come you know that journalist?

She gave him a quizzical look. – You mean the one who wrote about the fire?

– You said you knew him.

She wrinkled her brow, as though she couldn't understand why they should want to talk about that.

– Met him on a trip to the cabin a couple of weeks ago. Him and his wife. They're Pentecostals.

He acted surprised. – Cool.

– Weird people. What are you supposed to talk about with people like that?

– Talk in tongues, maybe.

She laughed again, a quick, bright laugh, picked up another piece of chocolate, broke it in half and pushed it in between her thin lips, quickly, as though she was doing something illegal. Her hand landed on his thigh; a finger slid up under his boxers.

– In a hurry, Mister Soldier?

He glanced at the clock and drank the rest of his coffee. There were several things he had to do. The thought of going home to Elsa without the things he'd promised to bring annoyed him. Without replying, he snatched the other half of the chocolate from her, put it in his mouth and pushed her down on the sofa; he took her with her face pressed up against the cold leather, feeling no desire, not even hers, even though more and more sounds came, some of them resembling words he had no interest in hearing.

The bathroom cupboard was full of make-up and lotions. But at the back of the top shelf he found the medications. Valium and sleeping tablets and something he couldn't identify. There were a few capsules loose in a bag. He recognised them. Not that he was surprised. He knew of other women who used roids. Not to build up muscle tissue but to get rid of fat. And to have more energy, or quite simply because they liked feeling horny all the time.

He was about to flush the toilet when he heard a door closing. To be on the safe side he locked himself in. Directly afterwards he heard her voice from the living room, saying something about showering. He heard the rumble of a male voice in response. He pressed his ear against the door, picked up snatches: it sounded as though the man had forgotten something. He imagined it was the police guy with the ridiculous moustache. He heard the sound of boots clacking across the parquet, in the direction of the bedroom, returning a few moments later, approaching. He waited for the doorknob to turn. He decided that if it did, he would unlock the door and be standing there stark naked.

– I give up, he heard from outside; the voice sounded exasperated rather than threatening, and no one touched the doorknob. Again the sound of footsteps, retreating this time, then Monica saying something or other and then the front door opening and closing.

He let himself out. She was standing in the middle of the room wearing nothing but a top and a G-string, panting like a deer that had just got away from the hunters and their hounds.

– I thought I was going to die, she groaned.

— Was it the cops? he joked.

— You could well say that.

— And you were scared he was going to handcuff you?

She squatted down, pushed her hands in below the sofa, pulled out a bundle.

— Is that any way to treat my clothes? he grinned.

She gave a quick smile. — He very nearly went into the bathroom. I said I'd just been.

He glanced over at the bathroom door. Not difficult to tell from the outside whether it was locked or not. A policeman should notice something like that.

— He hasn't got time to go to the toilet. Not with all these fires, I mean.

She glanced at him. — Have there been more?

He hesitated. — One up at Stornes farm, last week.

She took the rest of her clothes off.

— I need a bath.

— Isn't that what the police think? he wanted to know. — That there's a connection.

— Yes.

He looked for a way to keep going, ask without seeming all that interested in the answer.

— Because both are arson attacks, right?

She glided past him into the bathroom, put the plug in and turned on the taps.

— Don't you ever think about anything else? she said and turned towards him.

For a few seconds he stared at her. Something stirred in him, began to whirl, brought his muscles into a state of readiness. He calmed himself and forced a smile. — Obviously your boyfriend tells you just about everything.

— A lot more than he should, if I can put it like that. Sounded as if she was boasting about it.

– That's why I picked you up, he said as he grabbed her by the arm. – To talk about a few fucking fires.

– Wait, she groaned and pulled down the toilet seat, slipped down on to it. – My bladder is pleading for mercy.

He stood in front of her, feeling her breath against his stomach. As it streamed out of her, she took hold of the elastic in his boxers and pulled him in towards her.

11

DAN-LEVI ARRIVED FOR work two and a half hours late.
Rakel had been awake half the night. She didn't have a
fever, and there didn't seem to be anything else wrong with
her. But she was thirsty all the time and Dan-Levi had to
get up and bring her water at least three times.

On the way up the steps to reception, he met Stranger
trotting down.

– You need to follow up that nursery school fire.

– Didn't you say last night that Gunders should do it?
The thought of what had happened just a few hundred
metres from his own home was disturbing enough.

Stranger raised both his hands in the air. – The rest of
us have had a meeting since last time you and I spoke. He
shook his head. – It's sheer hell up there at Maura.

Dan-Levi had heard about the car crash on the local radio
station. The mental picture he had formed of events corresponded pretty accurately to the reference to hell, and Gunders
had probably been on to it the moment he caught a whiff
of impacted bonnets and diesel mixed with blood.

– And another thing.

Dan-Levi turned. Stranger came back up the steps, stopped
just below him.

– That piece you did about gangs, he said, coughing in
a way that sounded more like a snarl.

Dan-Levi had been satisfied with the article. He had
interviewed two researchers who were working on a project

about gang-related violence in the community. Kids could form a mob just by punching in a few numbers on a mobile phone. It was all about vengeance and honour. Politicians and police alike were taken unawares and powerless to prevent it, and the thought of his own child growing up in the middle of all this made him despair.

– Anything wrong with what I wrote? he asked the editor.

Stranger lowered his voice. – We can't print something like that. You're getting very close to the edge there. Quite okay that you dislike Islam personally, but for Chrissakes, Dan-Levi, we're not exactly a mouthpiece for the Progress Party, are we?

– All I did was report the research findings.

– All you did? All you did? Stranger was getting angry. – Take a look on your desk. I've deleted the sort of formulations we can do without, thank you. *Gang violence may be related to certain ideas in Islam*. Pull yourself together.

He turned and resumed his dancing little run down the steps, even though there was no way he could be busy.

The entrance to the nursery school was still cordoned off. Dan-Levi left his car in the industrial park on the other side of the road. Crossing the muddy plot of grass where ripped-up shreds of a home-made football goal fluttered in the wind, he became aware of a sweet and synthetic smell such as might come from burning plastic. He stopped in the middle of the field, took out his camera, photographed what was left of the building: the collapsed roof and the front wall like a worn-down gumshield against the green copse behind. It struck him that it could have been Rakel's nursery school, if she hadn't had grandparents who were willing to help. Suddenly these images connected: his daughter lying asleep in her bed, and a house on fire. He had always been afraid of fire. He could go back to check the hotplates on the oven and the light switches several times before finally retiring for the night. Sara said he was neurotic.

He dismissed the thought, applied himself instead to wondering how to take the story further. The fire service, the police, talk to the nursery head, maybe a few of the teachers. It was doable, and once he'd dealt with his pictures he'd have no problem in popping back home for a while. Sit down on the edge of the sofa, stroke Sara's pale forehead. Place his hand across her tender stomach.

Back in the car, he sat looking out at the scene for a few moments. He had worked till past midnight on his article on the Romerike gangs. It was unquestionably the best thing he had ever written. Stranger had cut most of it. Dan-Levi could admit that here and there his scepticism in regard to a religion that would not accept his own showed through. A religion whose standard-bearers went to war to establish a worldwide caliphate in which the Koran and a few other texts decided what was punishable under the law. In which lawbreakers were punished by whipping, stoning, the amputation of hands. And in which all who refused to convert would have their heads chopped off. But he had been careful to keep his feelings in check.

He could junk the article, but compromises make the world go round. He decided he would tone it down a bit. What he couldn't write in the newspaper he could take up at the meeting at Bethany that evening. There was no culture of political correctness in the youth group. The dangers of real life could be discussed there, while elsewhere kids were lulled to sleep with a lot of waffle about being tolerant and how everything was equal.

The phone rang and he saw that it was Roar Horvath.

– Hello, Eggman, he said by way of greeting.

He heard his pal groan at the other end. – I haven't got time to babble on about moustaches. It's bad karma. He made no attempt to explain what he meant. – I hear you were up taking pictures while that fire was actually burning.

Dan-Levi was able to confirm this. – I'm there now, he added. – Needed a few more.

– It's your pictures from yesterday I'm interested in. Can you send them to me?

Dan-Levi had nothing against helping the police, but he didn't like handing over material just like that. At work they'd had discussions about the problems associated with the blurring of roles. In the old days there were some who thought the paper was too close to the police, and Stranger had made it his business to do something about it.

– I just need to look at them first. Does this mean you're searching for an arsonist?

– Too early to say.

– But you've found something.

– Listen here, Dan-Levi. You know perfectly well that fires are just about the most difficult cases we have to deal with.

Dan-Levi persisted. – You're not getting any pictures unless you tell me what it is you're looking for.

Roar gave his throat a thorough clearing. – How does a fire start spontaneously in a rubbish bin standing outside on an April evening?

– Is that all? Dan-Levi urged him on.

After several more exasperated groans, Roar gave in. – We've found something. Looks like the remains of a primitive ignition device. And now you already know more than you should do.

– Might there be a connection to the fire at the Stornes place? Nod your head twice if I'm close.

Now Roar chuckled at the other end. – No comment. How about a beer tonight?

It was a while since they had last been out together.

– Got a youth group meeting. Maybe later this week?

– I'm off to Trysil on Thursday, Roar informed him. – Need to get away for a couple of days. You could come along.

– Bit short notice.

– That's family life for you, you can never get away.

Roar never missed an opportunity to complain about the trip to America they'd had planned for a couple of years that had been cancelled the first time Dan-Levi became a father. They both felt drawn to the USA: motorcycles across the prairie, crossing the Rocky Mountains, down through California, end up at the Pacific.

Dan-Levi distracted his pal before he could start getting into it. – I seem to recall you were taking your lady up to the mountains?

Roar grunted. – Something cropped up.

– Not over, is it? Dan-Levi wondered.

– No, no.

– But?

– There are no *buts*.

Dan-Levi let it drop even though he could hear that something wasn't quite right. A certain tone always crept into Roar's voice whenever there was any trouble on that front. Dan-Levi had never understood his friend's relationships with women. Even less how Sara and Roar once, albeit for a short time, could have been a couple.

One of the few things they never talked about.

12

ACCORDING TO THE passage in the exam paper, Archimedes wanted his tombstone to be a sphere enclosed within a cylinder and touching its edges. How high should the cylinder be for the relationship between the volume of the two bodies to be equal to the relationship between the surfaces?

Karsten set out the formulae and solved the problem using half a page, but knew that there was a simpler way. Though who actually believed that Archimedes sat down somewhere in Greece and poked with a twig in the sand to work out the height of his own tombstone?

Yet it wasn't primarily this that was bothering him. What he called his mathematical brain, which was usually allowed to work undisturbed, was being invaded by all the other parts of his brain. He'd been trying to contact Jasmeen all day, but she'd been with people every break time, Pakistani girls from other classes. He needed to say something or other to her about what had happened last night. Again he turned towards her desk; she sat there concentrating, calculator in one hand, pencil in the other, and didn't look up. He made a last attempt to concentrate on the height of Archimedes' tomb, gave up the idea of finding the simplest solution, strolled up to the teacher's desk and handed his paper in. Still not so much as a glance from her. He could have gone home, but sat down again, took out a history book and began leafing through it without reading.

Tonje packed up her things and headed for the door. At some point last night he had decided not to delay any longer in telling her what had really happened when they abducted Lam. He couldn't bear the thought of Tonje believing that he had tried to help his friend, that he had fought with the Pakistani gang and had his face cut with a knife.

He hurried after her. Had nothing against Jasmeen noticing, but even now she didn't look up from the paper she was writing on.

Tonje stopped and turned at the end of the corridor when he called her name.

– How are things at home? he asked, and was about to go on, say something that meant he couldn't back out.

She walked out on to the balcony above the assembly hall. – It's good of you to care, Karsten, she sighed with a glance at her watch. – Dad has reported it to the police. They were in shock the whole weekend.

I am such a jerk, he was going to say. A jerk and a coward. Instead he asked: – Did you manage it?

She looked at him in surprise. – The test? Think so.

– What did you get for the last question?

– Surely *you* don't need to ask *me* that? Again she checked her watch. – The square root of something or other. What did you get?

– Two r.

– Thought I'd got it wrong, she said with a wan smile.

– I haven't seen the answer, he said, trying to comfort her.

She sighed. – If my answer's not the same as yours, then I've got it wrong.

He liked her saying that. – What method did you use?

– Are there that many different ways?

He nodded. – A lot of complex ones, and one very simple.

Suddenly she stood on tiptoes and gave him a hug.

– Have to run, I'm meeting Thomas.

– Thought that was over, he blurted out; someone had said so in the canteen.

She shrugged her shoulders and disappeared down the stairs.

After a visit to the toilets, he went back into the classroom. Couldn't have been gone more than three minutes, but Jasmeen was no longer there. It occurred to him that she'd grabbed the chance to slip away. There were two sides to it, he reasoned. All in all, the advantages weighed most, the sum of things he wouldn't have to go through. He chucked his books into his rucksack, glanced out of the window. Then he saw her at the main entrance, in front of the white plaster horse in the winter garden. She was talking to someone. Really it was a matter of complete indifference whom she was standing there with. It was the supply teacher, the history teacher. He was a good head taller than her, wearing a black combat jacket, his longish hair swept back. It looked as though Jasmeen was doing most of the talking; she kept moving her hand and looked very worked up about something. Yet another reason to steer clear of her, Karsten decided. In a couple of months' time they would be leaving school, and after that, there was little chance they would ever meet again.

When he came down a few minutes later, there was no one in front of the winter garden, and he was relieved. He needed a run, needed to feel exhausted, decided to do his usual circuit, even though it was a breach of his weekly routine.

As he was unlocking his bicycle, he noticed that the rear tyre was flat. He checked the valve; the lock nut was still screwed tight. The front tyre was flat too. He started to wheel the bike through the slush, tried to figure out what the odds might be against something like that happening by chance.

A black Golf with its engine running was standing outside the school gates. Two guys leaning on the bonnet. They were Pakistanis. Karsten recognised one of them. By a bit of pure bad luck he'd spoken to him on the phone yesterday evening. And in the same instant he realised what had happened to his bicycle, and why they were standing there.

As he walked by without looking at the two boys, the taller of them said: – Stopped saying hello to people?

Karsten glanced at him without stopping. Shahzad Chadar was wearing a suit with a white shirt beneath it, open at the neck. He nodded to the other man, who strode forward and stood in front of the bike.

– Busy guy.

Shahzad's pal was short, his round face framed by a pencil-thin beard and eyebrows that met in the middle. He wore an earring with a dark stone.

– It's you, muttered Karsten, because at that moment he knew where he had seen him before. He could feel the little cut on his cheek begin to itch. He had never been able to stand the thought of physical pain. He used several tactics to avoid such thoughts, because they were much worse than the pain itself. Thoughts could make a slight burning in the throat or an inflamed pimple unendurable. Not to mention toothache. From his early childhood, he had refused to go to the dentist. He always brushed his teeth thoroughly, three times a day, but still he got cavities. In the end they had to give him a general anaesthetic before he could be treated. Something like that was starting to whirr about in his head now: if only somebody could anaesthetise him until this was over.

Shahzad Chadar came swaggering towards him. He was

still not much taller than Karsten, but he had grown a lot sturdier since the last time they met.

– Almost thought you were going to make a run for it. Done something wrong?

Karsten made a face that might have passed for a smile, because it was still possible that all Shahzad Chadar intended to do was muck him about a bit. The chances were more than ten per cent, less than twenty, but the whole calculation was founded on a pretty shaky base.

– I heard you've started taking an interest in the ladies. Shahzad winked. – Always had you down as a homo. You're that type.

He jerked his hips. The other one gave a thin snort of laughter.

– Don't have the balls, do you. Or at least not enough of them.

Karsten pulled the handlebars to move on. The other guy blocked the way.

– You're a snob, Shahzad said, his voice darker now. – The kind who can't even bring himself to talk to people he once went to school with. Won't even say hello. Calls up and then slams the phone down.

– What do you want? Karsten said, hearing at once how wrong the question was, because that was precisely what he did not want to know.

Shahzad leaned his head in towards his pal. – The guy's asking what we want.

– It doesn't matter, Karsten mumbled.

Shahzad turned slowly towards him. – You're asking what I *want* right now? He pushed his face up close. – You are bothering my sister.

– Bothering?

– She's got enough on her mind without having someone like you pawing at her, Shahzad growled. – I'll tell you what I *want*. And I will *show* you what I want. Motherfucker.

– Everything all right, Karsten?

He turned. The supply teacher was standing there eating a piece of fruit; it looked like a nectarine. Karsten suddenly remembered that his name was Adrian. The way things were looking, it was probably as well to be on first-name terms.

– Don't quite know.

The teacher threw away the stone, stood alongside him. He looked straight at Shahzad Chadar.

– If you've got anything else to say to Karsten, get on with it.

Shahzad didn't look at him. – I've said all I want to say. He added: – As of this particular moment.

In his relief at hearing these words, Karsten almost burst out laughing. He managed to swallow it down; all that came from his mouth was a low burble. Shahzad took a step towards him – maybe he was rethinking that *as of this particular moment* – and his pal cleared his throat thoroughly, bent forward and spat on to the saddle.

The teacher put a hand on Karsten's shoulder.

– This monkey is trying to tell you something.

Karsten glanced at the greenish lump glistening there. Beneath the viscous surface, it was speckled with tiny brown particles.

– That's okay, he said, not looking at any of those standing around.

– That's okay, the supply teacher echoed.

Abruptly he grabbed the man by the wrist, twisted him round and pressed his underarm across his throat. – That's okay, he repeated, and forced the man's upper body down so that his face landed on the saddle. He rubbed it back and forth several times before yanking his head up by the hair.

– Satisfied? he asked.

Karsten stared at the guy, who now had most of the spittle smeared across his cheek and the corner of his mouth.

– Is the saddle clean enough? the teacher continued.

– That's fine, Karsten managed to say.

The throat hold was released; the man stood there wheezing, supporting himself with his hands against his knees. Shahzad Chadar stared at the teacher, his eyes narrowed. Ten seconds passed, maybe more. Abruptly Shahzad turned and jumped back in behind the wheel of the Golf. His pal slumped in beside him. The engine roared a couple of times, and then the car leapt away and disappeared in the direction of Storgata.

– Dunno if that was all that smart, Karsten groaned. – They'll come after you now. *Me too*, he might have added.

The teacher laughed. – We'll find out soon enough, he said, dusting off the arm of his jacket. He seemed quite unaffected by what had just happened. – Did they do that as well? He nodded down in the direction of the tyres. – If you'd told me, they would have had to come up with a repair kit before they disappeared.

Karsten had forgotten about the state of his tyres. – The laws of probability would suggest it was them, yes.

– A genuine realist, the teacher observed. – And that, I suppose, was the brother of your classmate Jasmeen?

Karsten gave a start. – What do you know about that?

The teacher shrugged. – I can't help noticing certain things when I'm teaching.

Karsten pulled out a handkerchief and blew his nose.

– Your name is Adrian, isn't it?

– You know what my name is.

Karsten couldn't deny it.

– And exactly what things did you notice?

The teacher smiled broadly. – You would have to be

unusually dull witted not to notice that there's something
going on between you two. It's amazing how much you can
find out just by keeping your eyes open.

– You were with her just now, down in the schoolyard.
Now the teacher grew serious. – I've got no interest in
messing things up for you. You can do that all by yourself.

– The fact of the matter is, nothing at all has happened,
Karsten protested. – Just spoken with her a few times. Stuff
like that.

The teacher looked to be considering something. – I'm
living just down the road here at the moment, he said. – We
could go to my place and have a cup of coffee.

Karsten didn't know what to say. It felt as though he was
in the teacher's debt and couldn't refuse. As they started
walking, he tried to explain the business about Jasmeen.
The teacher, Adrian, seemed to be interested, for some reason
or other, and listened without interrupting. Not until they
were turning into Bjørnsons gate did he say: – And so you
rang her? Well, you're no chicken.

– What have I got to be afraid of? Karsten exclaimed.
– This is a free country.

Adrian pushed his lower lip out and wagged his head
slowly from side to side. – That is a matter of opinion.

He didn't expand on that.

Down in Strandgata he turned in through the gate of a
red-painted semi. It looked just like the other houses, fairly
well maintained, with a thicket of bare rose bushes growing
up against the wall. But several of the fence posts next to
the gate had been broken off, Karsten noted. Their own
fence at home had been damaged in a similar way after his
father reversed into it. That was six months ago and it still
hadn't been repaired, something his mother remarked on
more or less every day.

They kicked their shoes off in the hallway. There was a

sweet smell from the corridor inside. Not food and not perfume, but something else. Karsten didn't know what it was.

– Home alone?

– Nope. Adrian gave a brief nod in the direction of the stairs up to the first floor.

– Lived here long?

– Only now and then.

Karsten was taken down into a large living room in the basement. It was furnished with a bed and chairs, two shelves and a writing desk. The single door to what had to be a wardrobe was covered by a large mirror. Adrian took a kettle from the table in one corner. When he left the room with it, Karsten looked at the CDs on the shelves. Metallica and Death Metal. But a lot of classical stuff too.

– You dig Beethoven? he asked when Adrian came back with the filled kettle.

– You have a problem with that?

– Oh no, that's cool.

Adrian poured steaming water into the cups. – What do you plan to do?

Karsten slumped a little in his seat. – What do you mean?

– You know perfectly well what I mean. You've got something going with a Pakistani girl. Her family has found out about it. Are you going to chicken out or go ahead with it?

As though they were talking about a game of chess. Offer a draw in a difficult situation, give up, or make a daring move that might change the game.

– You think she's nice looking?

– Yes, Karsten admitted.

– I agree. She is undoubtedly the best-looking girl in your class. And she fancies you.

Karsten felt the prickling around his hairline. – Yeah, right.

– That's not what your problem is. Adrian smiled. – This has the makings of a classic. Young Pakistani girl takes a fancy to young Norwegian. The family are not the most extreme Muslims in the world. Even so, because you've been alone with her, not to say possibly even touched her . . . because you did do that?

Karsten gave a non-committal nod.

– Her father has made an arrangement for one of the girl's elderly relatives to marry her, Adrian said.

– Do you know that?

– That's the way it usually happens. There's money on the table. Status. Honour. There are alliances to be made.

Adrian kept his eyes on him. They were deep set, and so dark that he could almost have been a Pakistani himself, it occurred to Karsten. He was still not sure why the supply teacher had invited him home.

– Where did you used to live? he asked.

– Here and there.

– And you were a soldier?

– Bosnia, Kosovo, Afghanistan.

– Are you going to Iraq as well?

– I wouldn't rule it out. Adrian leaned back in his chair. – And you've lived your whole life here in Toytown. He looked at Karsten for a few moments. – Do you remember what you said in class a few days ago? When I asked what you believed in?

Karsten tried to remember. – You mean all that about genes?

– Exactly. What you were saying is that the only purpose in life is to pass on our genes.

– I don't think the world is quite that primitive.

Adrian laughed. – So you were just bluffing? And I was so certain you meant it.

He handed Karsten the mug of coffee. – For a long time

Toytown was a place where there were no conflicts and no evil, he said. – But sooner or later the world had to come here too. And suddenly you find yourself right in the firing line. That's why I'm asking you what you intend to do.

Karsten looked at him, confused. Do I have to do anything? he was about to say. Then he heard footsteps from the floor above, someone opening and closing a door. He wanted to ask who it was, but didn't do that either.

Adrian rested his feet on the glass table. – You've got talents that a lot of people are going to want. You've got possibilities. And you're not afraid to stand out from the crowd.

Karsten didn't recognise himself in this description, but enjoyed hearing it. Adrian was his teacher, but he wasn't talking down to him. More like a pal.

– I want us to keep in touch, Karsten. I'd like to know what you decide to do.

Karsten put down the coffee cup.

– What would you have done? he asked.

Adrian rubbed a finger over his stubbly beard. – I would never allow the Pakistanis to dictate my choice. And I never take orders from people I don't respect.

Karsten nodded; it was well put.

– Will you see her?

He had no answer to that. There were arguments for and arguments against. Adrian continued.

– Don't allow yourself to be ruled by fear. You'll never get anywhere if you do.

It sounded cool, the way Karsten wished he could have thought.

– Makes no difference if I want to meet her if she doesn't want to meet me, he objected. – After we spoke to each other last night, she's been avoiding me. I don't think anything'll come of it now.

— She's got enough to think about, said Adrian.
— What do you mean by that?
Adrian shrugged. — She'll get in touch with you.
He said it as though he was the one making the decision.

13

HE HAD ASKED Elsa if they could do something together. They did that now and then, went out for a meal, went to the cinema. He would even have gone with her to a concert or an exhibition if that was what she had planned. But now she said she couldn't and didn't give any reason. He couldn't bring himself to ask why, headed off into his room, undressed, pulled the curtains, flopped down on the bed. In his hand he was holding the Zippo lighter. Lit it, extinguished it, lit it again. The point of the thin flame stabbed at his skin. He sat in the dark looking straight ahead as he moved it up and down the inside of his underarm, between the old scars.

Then he heard her voice outside. She laughed. He jumped up, peered out through a gap. Had known it all along, that she was off out with the prince. They were making their way across the yard; he was telling Elsa something or other that made her laugh even more. She leaned towards him and gave him a hug, linked her arm with his as he closed the gate behind them.

He could have followed them. Found out where they were going. Stood outside the restaurant, watched as they ordered, as the table was laid for them, as they were served. Then he could have gone in and tipped the table over.

He did a hundred and twenty sit-ups. Took two extra capsules of Testo even though he'd already taken his weekly dose. Went into the shower, turned the temperature up as high as he could bear and stood there without moving, imagined the skin coming loose and falling off. Soaking wet he walked back to the bedroom, opened the window wide to the cold wind. Elsa had said again this business about how he should get out more, meet people. – Of course she's right, he murmured. – Ought to get out more.

He couldn't find any clean boxer shorts. He pulled on his workout trousers and hoody without drying himself, grabbed the car keys from the hook by the chest of drawers and went out. On the steps he stopped, stood there for a few seconds and breathed, captured by a thought that had been wandering about inside him. He went back into the flat, up to his room, took the ignition devices from the writing-desk drawer, four that he'd prepared earlier. From the cupboard below the sink he took two bottles of lighter fluid.

As he turned down into Storgata, he had an idea. When he'd left Monica's apartment that morning, she had made it clear that she would like to see him again. And within two hours she had sent him a text. He hadn't replied. Once was just once. Twice meant the beginning of something. He had no plans for that. Half a year earlier, he'd broken his rule, given a woman his phone number and let himself be persuaded to make a second date. It had caused him endless problems.

He parked in Solheimsgata. A couple of minutes later he was standing outside the street entrance and studying the row of doorbells. Realised he didn't know her second name. He glanced up; there was light in the living-room window that had to be hers. Maybe he saw something moving there. Maybe the policeman was paying a visit. There were two toothbrushes in her bathroom, each in a separate mug, and a razor with remnants of red stubble. His name was Horvath and he had been interviewed about the nursery school fire. According to Elsa, everything was connected. Now and then we catch a glimpse of the pattern behind what we call chance, like a veil suddenly being pulled from our eyes.

At the roundabout by Kjellerholen, the road surface was covered with a thin layer of black ice. He let the car skid sideways before straightening up and heading on in the direction of Olavsgård. Still a strip of light in the western sky as he swung down on to the motorway heading north, moved over into the outside lane and put his foot down. Over two hundred horses galloping along under the bonnet of the Chevy. He could have closed his eyes and let them take over, take him wherever they wanted. But that was not how it was going to end. He wasn't going to die in a car. He had asked Elsa about it. To begin with she refused to answer, because such things belonged in a room she didn't want to enter. That was what she said, but he had persisted, mostly to see how far into death she was prepared to look. Whether she would break off and say: *You mustn't leave, stay with me, forever.* Instead she told him that the way he was going to die had something to do with fire.

That was a few weeks ago. Just before her prince showed up. She had studied his cards for a while before putting them down and mixing them in with the others. Fire purifies, she said. It destroys, it prepares the way for the new. It was after that he had decided that the stable with the horses had to burn. To see if thoughts could disappear too. And as he sped past the fields at Kløfta, an image of the burning stable rose up again. Along with it all sorts of other images, streaming out from dark corners, tiny mice and rats and lizards shooting out and heading for the fire as it took hold.

He hit the wheel so hard that the car swerved over into

the inside lane, and he had to pick up a CD and turn the music on full, *I feel stupid and contagious*, he'd played that track over and over again on his Walkman eleven or twelve years earlier, and as he bellowed out that line along with Cobain, he knew that he wouldn't be going any further along this road that continued ever northwards. He moved across into the turn-off for Gardermoen. Not that he had any business at the airport. It wasn't the idea of travel that impelled him, because he didn't want to go any place where she wasn't. Not until he had driven past the airport and was heading west did he realise where he was going.

The first kilometre of road after the motorway was narrow and twisting. He could remember how nauseous he had been the first time he was driven up here. He'd been sitting in the back. Neither of his parents, as they called themselves, were there. He was told it was best for him to go without them.

Not until he passed the local shop did the road straighten out. Now it was a Rema store, but apart from that it didn't look any different from back then. He'd been there and stolen beer along with two of the other lads. *They* got caught, but they didn't grass. He was never caught for anything. Not for the stealing, nor the windows that were broken, nor for the fire. He was too smart for them.

A few hundred metres before the driveway there was a forestry track, just as he remembered. The time was ten minutes past eleven. He followed the bumpy track a way, parked by a cattle grid. He'd put the bag with the ignition devices behind the felt flap in the driver's-side door post, and the rest of what he would need was in the boot. It was all still open, anything could happen. For another half-hour he sat in the car. Elsa and her prince. Those two words put together and pulled apart again. *Prince* and *her*. He steamed the side window with his breath, saw the outline of the trees disappear in the grey and then reappear before he blew it away again.

Even in the dark he could see that the main building had been painted a lighter colour. He studied it from the parking lot. Furutunet remand home was still run by the Child Welfare Service. He'd hacked their server not long ago, found out who was working there and how many kids were being held. Twelve years ago there had been ten of them; now there was just half that number, but still with fourteen staff. Two were the same as back then. One of them he'd liked. She was twenty-something, name of Siv. There was something about her, the way she spoke to him. She thought he should never have been sent to Furutunet. At least that was what she said, even though she wasn't allowed to say things like that. Elsa also said he had no business being there. But it took a long while before she could get him out, almost a year after she returned from England. He had never asked her why she waited so long.

He walked across the yard, stationed himself at one corner, just beyond the circle of light from the outdoor lamp above the main entrance. Only then did he know that he had to get into the building, move around inside it. It was a matter of finding the right place. The zero point. Where absolutely anything at all might happen.

The cellar door faced the slope down towards the stream. He had broken in that way before. On that occasion they had smashed the window with an axe, and if the adults hadn't been so dopey they would have heard the racket a mile away. He and his pal didn't care a damn if anyone heard them. Not that they had any business down in the cellar. It was a question of getting in there because it was locked. Now he used a crowbar. A few creaks and a snap of metal and the lock gave.

The classrooms were still located at the far end of the basement corridor. On one of the doors was an embroidered cloth sign with the word *Schoolroom*. Unmistakably the zero point. Probably full of easily combustible material. And perfectly situated. Smoke alarms had been fitted to the ceiling at each end of the corridor. Even if he disconnected them, the ones in the floors above would work and everyone who was in the house would have time to get out. It wasn't the people he was after; this was about the building itself. He alone decided what would happen to it. It was his building now.

He remembered that there were changing rooms further down. Opened the door to the first one. The girls' changing room. Still a smell of perfume in there. He'd sneaked down several times, when he knew that Siv was there.

Past the boys' changing room were the stairs. He stopped and listened. Heard a faint, dark voice, a lighter one that responded, then music. The night-duty guy watching TV, he realised. The living room was at the end of the corridor above, directly over the basement door he had just come through. At the top of the stairs he stood and sifted among the smells in the brightly lit hallway, examining each one individually. Something had been baked in the kitchen: bread, pizza maybe. The smell of spices mingling with green soap, dust, people who sweated and breathed and farted and went to the toilet. The sound from the TV was still low, but clear; the door to the sitting room was ajar. Light flickered in the dark room. The film was American, he could tell by the accents. The night watch was probably dozing on the sofa; they always did that.

The stairs up to the first floor were halfway along the corridor. He walked quietly. At one point the linoleum was sticky. His sole stuck to it, released itself with a pop. He stopped, waited; nothing happened.

Upstairs had been redecorated. Brighter colours, new cornices, new doors too. There were names on some of them. *Marita*, written on a cardboard sign below a pressed flower. *Sveinung* on another, printed along with some characters from *Star Wars*. Someone named Bizhan had contented himself with his name scribbled on a yellow Post-it note. It was the next door he was interested in. Fourth room on the left. There was no sign outside it. Maybe the room was empty. Maybe the person who lived there would have nothing to do with the place. The way he had been himself.

He eased the door open slightly, listened into the darkness. Silence at first, then a faint whistling sound, breath so light that it just about escaped from sleep. He slipped inside, pulled the door to behind him, stood there with eyes closed. This room had haunted him for years after he was let out. It could still appear in his dreams, or at any other time. Smelled different now. The strong whiff of deodorant made him think of 'Teen Spirit', a scent with noise inside it. *I feel stupid and contagious*. In the days when he was kept at the home, there was rot somewhere or other, the smell of damp in every room.

He took a step into the room and knocked against a chair. Clothes slung over the back of it. He felt them. Jeans, pullover, socks. He held a pair of knickers in his hand. They were tiny, and he stood there inhaling the smooth material, drawing that strong and bitter girl-smell down inside himself.

A sound made him start. He heard her more clearly now. The rhythm of her breathing had changed after he came in, was faster, as though she had tipped over into a different type of sleep. Maybe she was dreaming that a strange man had just entered her room. That he crawled in under the blanket and lay down next to her. But he hadn't come here for something like that. There was a way of getting rid of memories. Everything he had thought into the walls during the year in which he was held there. Purification by fire. Therapy, it struck him, I have worked out my own fucking therapy.

He kept the laughter inside, moved soundlessly across the floor. The bed was in the same position it had always been, with the headboard in the corner by the window. The outline of a head, short dark hair, could just be made out against the white of the pillow. Suddenly he felt that the girl was lying there staring at him.

– Bizhan, she whispered.

A few seconds went by before he remembered that was the name on the Post-it note on the room next door. He bent down slowly over her. Her eyes were open, and now he could not stop the movement towards them, had to keep going until he saw them properly in the dark. So close that he could see the mouth open, because now she knew that it wasn't Bizhan who was leaning over her bed.

He was quicker than her, pressed his fist against her lips, forcing them together, felt the scream come, forced it back down the narrow throat, held it there. Should say something to this girl, something to calm her, but she mustn't hear his voice. At that moment a pain from his index finger shot up through his arm. He hissed, pressed harder, already knew that there would be a mess, drops of his blood that ran down her cheek and dripped on to the pillow.

– You should not have done that, he growled. Then she bit again, even harder, and he put all his weight on to his hand. It was like holding the jaws of a small animal shut, a vole or a ferret. With his other hand he pulled the pillow out from under her and put it over the biting mouth. She turned, her hands shot up and began to claw him. He covered the whole face with the pillow, sat on it, the movements became wilder, he had to turn round and hold her body down.

Somewhere in his thoughts he was counting off the seconds, because he knew he could not sit there like that for very long. But the little animal twisted and thrashed, began kicking out too now, and he could hear the scream that would rise out of that little mouth if he got up. He counted slowly. Allowed himself to think of nothing else but the numbers. After forty-five she was still jerking from side to side, but the kicking had stopped. He carried on counting. At sixty he would let her up. There was an interval there, he decided, a gap between the phase in which she bit and screamed and the point at which she would never scream again.

– It's you I'm counting for, Elsa, he whispered, – even though you went off with your prince. You are the one who will let me stop in time, you want me to choose the good.

He reached sixty-five. She was still now. He stood up and took the pillow away. The eyes still stared up into the darkness, but in a different way, and he put a hand against her mouth. No sign of breathing. He pulled the duvet off her, pressed his ear to her chest. Leant forward and covered the little mouth with his own, blew into it, twice, three times, stopped, waited for the chest to begin to move by itself. Carried on blowing, pushing the ribcage, pressed down so hard that the bottom of the bed snapped, did it again ten or twenty times, breathed again down into the mouth, tasted blood, his own.

Suddenly he heard something from out in the corridor, the pop of a sole sticking to the linoleum. He jumped up, stood in the corner by the cupboard. He could hear that the approaching footsteps were a man's. They stopped outside, a door was opened.

No light. Motionless and bent over, he stood there and heard the night watch talking in a low voice to someone in the next room. In the darkness by the window he could just make out the bed, the duvet on the floor, an arm dangling over the side.

He ran the four or five hundred metres to the copse where his car was parked, opened the back and grabbed the carrier bag with the bottles of lighter fluid. From behind the felt flap in the doorpost he pulled out the bag with the ignition devices, knew that he couldn't risk using them but still shoved them into his pocket, felt that there was already something in there. His fingers closed around the silky piece of cloth he had taken from the room. In a flash it occurred to him that the girl to whom it belonged had become a part of the building, a part of what had to disappear.

Back in the basement, he stood gasping for breath. As though he were still breathing for the tiny little girl in the room as well. Other thoughts would come, he knew that, and with them would come the sight of that dangling arm, the smell of deodorant, the stabbing pain of his bitten finger. But for now he concentrated on what had to be done, step by step. The part of him that had been asleep all winter had now woken up again. He was trained to lead a group of men in battle. Tactics that had to be changed while approaching an enemy position. He forced the crowbar into the crack of the schoolroom door and pulled. The sounds of the building had changed; something was rushing through them. It dawned on him that it was his own breath he was hearing. He held it. Then there was only the throbbing of his pulse that echoed around the basement corridor, filling it.

The room he now entered was just as it had been, with a blackboard, the teacher's desk and a few work tables. In a cupboard he found rolls of cotton cloth, cut it up and made heaps of it. He made three fireplaces around the room, drenched in lighter fluid. Still not satisfied, because the play of chance must not be allowed to decide here, he had to insure himself by creating several more such points. The door between the two schoolrooms was unlocked. The second room was mainly used for timeouts if someone was causing too much trouble. He pushed the door open; it knocked into something or other. As he arrested the movement, he realised he was too late. Something collapsed and toppled over, chairs stacked together probably, and a zinc bucket or something like that, which hit the washbasin with a resounding crash.

For a few seconds he stood motionless, trying to suck the sounds into himself, prevent them from leaving the room. Then he ran out into the corridor. He heard a door upstairs. Already the sound of footsteps, the same ones he had heard approaching the girl's bedroom, that little pop of the sole as it came unstuck from the linoleum. He slipped into the girls' changing room, stood still in the darkness beside the row of cupboards. Now the steps were down in the basement.

– Bizhan?

The voice was light for a man's. He was seized by a painful need to do something to it. As the footsteps passed on their way towards the schoolroom, he banged the crowbar against the changing room cupboard. The footsteps stopped.

– Bizhan?

He scraped the side of the cupboard a few times. The screeching sound of metal against metal slowed his pulse rate; abruptly he felt calm and clear headed.

– Are you in there?

Light from the corridor spread out like a fan. He stood in the darkness just beyond it and stared at the outline of the night watch in the open doorway. Someone small and thin, suited to the voice. He saw the hand on the wall, fumbling for the switch. As the neon tubes in the ceiling blinked into life, he stepped forward; his eyes met those of the night watch in the mirror. Then he struck out. The crowbar hit the man on the side of his back. He struck out again as the night watch tried to turn, his hands held up, hit him higher, on the back of the head. The guy was thrown against the wall. He grabbed hold of the wispy neck hair and beat the head against the mirror so hard that it broke and the shards showered down into the sink. Kept on beating until the man collapsed, toppling the rubbish bin, and lay slumped at his feet like an empty sack.

He raced back to the schoolroom, emptied the rest of the lighter fluid across the floor, squirted it as high up the walls as he could reach. Then he set fire to the strips of cloth and tossed them about. The flames leapt up, as though the room had been waiting years for this to happen. In a window between the tongues of fire he caught an image of himself, his face glowing white and unrecognisable.

As he backed out into the basement corridor he noticed that the door to the girls' changing room was wide open. The figure on the floor in there still lay motionless in a twisted pose. It occurred to him that he ought to drag the man out.

For two or three seconds he held on to that thought. Then he shut the door and ran out into the cold night.

14

JASMEEN WAS SITTING at a computer next to the counter. Glanced up as Karsten came down the steps. He walked past her, over to one of the bookcases. He had never been to the library in Lørenskog before. While he waited for something to happen, he took down a book on fish, flipping through it as slowly as he could. Two minutes, maybe three, and she was behind him, moving closer, her hand touching his back. At the end of the bookcase she stopped and bent over to one side, as though she were reading the titles on the spines of the books.

He took a step towards her.

– Don't talk to me, she whispered, and moved her eyes in the direction of the floor above.

He stood there half turned away. Noticed that she wrote something in one of the books, saw her put it back and disappear out the other way.

The book was protruding from the shelf; it was about fish too. At the bottom of the title page, written in a thin, even hand, he read: *Go out the top exit, cross the road, past the entrance to the garden centre, wait for me at the end of the block.*

The flakes that came floating down made him think of white insects. They landed in his hair and dissolved. In the pitch dark a car swung up and away from the garden centre. Karsten didn't know anyone here, but even so he withdrew into the driveway to someone's garage. Fifteen minutes passed. The melting snowflakes trickled down from his hair and over his forehead. She had asked him to meet her. He was there to talk to her, nothing else. There could never be anything between them. But Adrian was right: fear mustn't be allowed to dictate our choices. At least not all of them. Why Adrian was even interested in what he did was something Karsten still hadn't understood.

Twenty-five minutes. He stepped back on to the road again. – What does she want with me? he muttered in exasperation. Then he saw her heading towards him along the footpath.

– Sorry you had to wait, she exclaimed. – Bilal just kept going on and on.

She stroked his cheek, twice. He forgot how annoyed he'd been, took her hand.

– Someone might see us, she protested quietly. – Everyone round here knows me.

That couldn't be true, but she turned, walked ahead further down the road, across a snowdrift and into some trees next to a factory. He caught up with her.

– Who's Bilal? he wanted to know.

– My brother, who else? she said, sounding angry. – Drives me crazy having him follow me about everywhere.

She explained that her nosy little brother was being told to spy on her for the family. Then she stood there looking at him, saying nothing, as though waiting for him to do something or other. In an attempt to kiss her, he pressed her body up against a pine trunk and a shower of droplets fell on them.

– Sorry, he muttered, and now she began to laugh.

Twice before he had kissed a girl. Once was on a sofa at a class party in junior school and he thought it had gone pretty well. But then the girl got up, allegedly to go to the toilet, and never came back again. The second time was also on a sofa and he had decided never, ever to think about it again. But beneath that dripping pine on an industrial estate in Lørenskog one evening in April, it was exactly this memory that returned, and the image of Tonje backing away, staring at him open mouthed as though she had just found an insect in her food.

Now he pressed his mouth determinedly against Jasmeen's. To his surprise he felt it open, felt his tongue suddenly dart between her lips and encounter another, small and slippery. Something about the taste of her made him think of fresh chlorine water, but sweet rather than bitter, and in his mind's eye he saw the diagram of a tongue in his biology book with the different taste buds drawn in. When he opened his eyes, he was looking directly into hers. Suddenly she gave him a careful bite on the lip. He bit back, much too hard, he realised, because she pulled away.

– Sorry, he said again, and again she gave that little laugh.

– I've been thinking about you all night, she whispered as she pulled him in to her, and he concluded that she would hardly have said those exact words if he'd already been voted off.

– Thought about you too.

It sounded okay, but he knew that soon he would have to say something that wasn't just an echo of what she had said. Something occurred to him, something about the genes of the fish, but he realised it would be the wrong thing to start talking about. – Can't we just say screw them? he heard himself suggest. But that was wrong too. He didn't even know what he meant by it.

She laid her forehead against his. – You don't understand anything. You who know everything about trigonometry and differential calculus. And now I have to get back.

He nodded. At least that was what it felt like.

– And you mustn't call me any more.

He looked down into her eyes. In the pale light they seemed to loom towards him, like jellyfish or some other aquatic creature drifting up to the surface on the currents of the deep.

– We need to think of something, she said, and he nodded again, as though this was the type of problem that had to have a solution. – Wait here until you can't see me any more.

He held her from behind and wouldn't let her go. Then she unbuttoned her coat, the top buttons, put his hands inside and pressed them against her breasts. For a few moments he felt as though he was in free fall, and he was about to shout out or laugh. He clenched his teeth as hard as he could.

– Jasmeen!

It wasn't him shouting. The voice came from somewhere on the street, a child's voice. She tensed and pulled away.

– Hide, she whispered, pushed him towards the tree and walked away over the snowdrift.

He did as she told him, stood there half shadowed and tried to fade away, become one with the hard bark of the pine tree.

The microwave started to ping. Karsten padded into the kitchen. Took out the lasagne and called out to Synne. His sister looked tired as she came down the stairs.

– Were you asleep?

She didn't answer.

– You can't start going to bed and sleeping in the middle of the day, he warned her.

– None of your business.

It would have been okay if things were that easy. He had enough to worry about already. He'd met a girl he shouldn't have met. He would rather not see her again. And most of all he wished the doorbell would ring right now, that she would be standing outside when he opened the door.

– Are you still thinking about that fire? he said to switch to something else.

Synne put her fork into her mouth. – What do you expect?

She had sauce on her chin. He pulled a wipe from the roll, laid it in front of her plate. It was over a week since the stables had burnt down, but he realised that it wouldn't be a good idea to point that out.

As he stood up she said: – There was another fire last night.

He turned to her. – At the stables?

– Of course not, she groaned. – That's already burnt down.

– I gathered that.

– I don't think you understand much, do you? Do you actually pay any attention at all to things that are happening in the *world*?

For emphasis she made an exaggerated gesture in the direction of the kitchen window.

He avoided giving her an answer that might hurt her. Anyway, she was right: most of the time he was lost in his own thoughts.

– Update me on what's going on out there, he contented himself with saying.

She looked as if she was wondering whether he was worthy of it. – There was a fire at a remand home in Nannestad.

– I gathered that. One dead, and one serious.

She gave him an exasperated look. – That's the third time there's been a fire near here in just over a week.

– Nannestad isn't exactly near here.

– Well it's not far away.

He thought about what she had just said. – Does it say anywhere that they think there's a connection?

She shook her head. – But it must be obvious.

Not everyone is as smart as you, he should have said, but didn't. His sister *was* smart, in a completely different way to him. She devoured all kinds of books, fantasy and crime and horror.

He sat back down. – Have you been to the scene and found some clues?

– Haha.

– Tell me what you think.

She brushed a lock of thick hair off her forehead; it was full of knots and didn't look as though it had been washed for some time. When she wedged it behind her ear, it stuck out a bit and made her look like a cartoon elf.

– First the stables burn down, then six days later the nursery up at Vollen, and then, only two days later, this home in Nannestad.

– You mean like it's more and more frequent?

– It looks like it. And then there's similarities between all the places.

– In what way is a stables like a remand home?

She rolled her eyes. – Don't you get it? Places where something is kept and looked after. Same with the nursery.

Karsten couldn't hide his smile. – You mean that every place where someone or something is looked after could be set on fire by a madman?

– Is that so strange?

– You read too many weird books, he told her. – You should get out more. Out in the *world* out there. It's not enough to sit in here and understand all kinds of weird stuff.

He put his plate into the dishwasher. She looked up, obviously annoyed.

– Says you. The biggest nerd in Lillestrøm.

– In northern Europe, he corrected her. He had told her about the dubious award he'd been given at the coffee bar.

– The police will give it high priority now that someone's dead, he went on after thinking it over.

Synne threw down her fork. – Now that someone's dead? Twenty-nine horses died in those stables. But that doesn't really count, because they're not people.

– Of course it counts, he said to placate her.

– A horse's life is worth just as much as a human life, at least. But people like you don't understand.

She jumped up and left the room, slamming the door behind her. Footsteps like drumsticks on the staircase, another door slamming. He thought perhaps he should go up to her but changed his mind. It bothered him that she had hardly any friends, that she spent so much of her time alone with her books and her computer games in her room. She'd had a couple of appointments with a psychiatrist at the clinic in Lillestrøm. Last time she'd come home exasperated and angry because the psychiatrist had gone on about how things were at home, as though *that* had anything to do with her attacks.

His phone rang, startling him. Jasmeen had said she would ring. He'd been thinking it would be best if she didn't. He looked at the display. For a few seconds he considered not taking the call, then he shut himself in the living room, as far from Synne's ears as he could get without leaving the house.

– Wanted to hear your voice, Jasmeen said, and it made him think how embarrassing it was to listen to a recording of his own voice, how strange it sounded, so much thinner and lighter than he expected.

– Did your brother see you? he asked.

– He sees all, hears all.

– Did he talk?

She hesitated. – They're not home yet.

– Hope it won't get you into trouble.

– Don't think about that.

There was a pause. He should have said they ought not to meet again.

– When can we meet again? he asked.

– I don't know.

Suddenly the problem from the maths test mixed itself in among his thoughts. Archimedes' tombstone; he still hadn't managed to find the simplest solution.

– What are you doing? she asked.

– Nothing special. Solving a few problems. Talking to my sister.

Jasmeen wanted to hear more about Synne and he told her how obsessed she was by the fires. It was easier to talk about his sister's world of horses and weird books. He mentioned her attacks too, even though Synne had forbidden him to say a single word about them to anyone in the entire world. He didn't tell her how strange Synne was, or that she had no friends and could lie about anything at all. That he was getting more and more concerned about her.

– You really love your sister, said Jasmeen.

– In a way. What are you doing?

– I pray. Think and pray.

He needed to hear something like that. Be reminded that she belonged to another world, one in which every smell and sound was different, where people got down on their knees to pray many times every day.

– I think about a story my father used to tell me when I was a child, she went on. – It's from the place where his family comes from. Every Pakistani knows it. Do you want to hear it?

He wasn't sure that he did.

– It's about a very beautiful and brave woman from Punjab named Heer. She falls in love with a boy named Ranjha.

Karsten slid down in the sofa, tried as best he could to follow the story. Ranjha and Heer loved each other more than anything in the world. But a jealous uncle reported them, and Heer had to marry someone else and was taken to a village far, far away. Ranjha wandered lonely and unhappy around the streets of his village. But then he met a holy man who taught him to renounce everything.

– Do you understand?

Karsten didn't. He looked at his watch, it was quarter past eight; soon his parents would be home.

– Ranjha finds the place where Heer is living an unhappy life with her new husband. She gets her parents' permission to divorce and marry Ranjha, but just before the wedding the jealous uncle poisons her food.

Jasmeen paused, then said quickly: – Someone's coming, I have to hang up. Call you later.

Karsten lay with his face buried in his maths book. He didn't want to wake up, but sleep had begun to withdraw into the pages of the book, and the images dissolved. A last one hung on for a while. He's walking through a zoo. There are no animals there any more. Someone calls his name. This can't be a dream, he reasons, because my legs are cold. A car with its engine running stands at the entrance. He opens the door. Jasmeen is in the front seat. She's naked. Adrian is behind the wheel. *We're waiting for you, Karsten.*

It was his father's return home that woke him. Karsten could hear that it was him. His mother always slammed the door shut, Synne usually left it open, whereas his father opened and closed it with a click, not too hard and not too gentle. But something was different this time. His footsteps continued straight down the hallway without him pausing to remove his shoes.

– Karsten, I'm waiting.

His father hardly ever shouted to him. Sometimes he would enter the room, stand there a while looking at what Karsten was working on. *Not a cloud in sight*, he might announce by way of affirming what he already knew, that there was nothing to worry about. He rarely raised his voice. Karsten could remember the two or three times when he'd seen him angry. The last time must have been about five or six years ago, when two boys from their neighbourhood had captured Synne and taken her clothes off, then doused her with a garden hose.

Now he was standing by the hall table with the telephone receiver in his hand.

– Hello? Karsten said.

His father straightened up and put down the phone. Looked more afraid than angry.

Karsten tentatively started down the stairs. – What is it?

– Come.

His father disappeared out into the yard, waited by the open garage door. The light inside was switched on. Karsten crossed over to the car. Two broad white scratches from the rear bumper to the front, running together towards the middle and then parting from each other in an uneven pattern that no function in a co-ordinate system could have described. His father indicated for him to go around to the other side of the car. A similar pattern, even more irregular.

– Was the garage door open?

– Closed, but not locked. His father's voice was shaky. In the cold wind, a few hairs in his thin fringe lifted.

Karsten walked around the car again, mostly to avoid the sight of his father, who was standing there, arms dangling forlornly at his sides.

– Bloody hooligans, he said loudly as he emerged.

– Do you have any idea at all who might have done something like this? his father muttered.

Karsten did. He shook his head.

He ran as fast as he could down towards the roundabout, followed the pavement and crossed the boggy ground on the other side of the runway. His body took over, the hunger for air, the acid accumulating in his muscles. But something happened to his thoughts too: they split apart, didn't snag so easily, moved along more smoothly.

Not until he turned into Strandgata did Karsten realise where he was headed for. If he'd known it before, he would have run in another direction, but now he came to a halt at the gate. At the sight of the three broken fence posts an image of his father outside the garage flashed up, his hands hanging still at his sides, the wind in his thinning hair. For some reason or other it was this image that decided him. He stepped across the yard and rang the bell on the nearer of the two doorways in the red semi. Was about to run on when the door slid open. The woman standing there was wearing what looked like a dark red dressing gown.

– Is Adrian here? Karsten gasped; it sounded like a groan.

– Not just at the moment.

He greeted the information with a little nod. The woman was pretty, he noticed as he turned and was about to leave.

– Maybe you'd like to come in and wait for him? He'll be back shortly.

Karsten thought he probably wouldn't. But then saw in his mind's eye that scratched car and couldn't say anything.

– Are you Karsten?

He gave a start. – How do you know that?

She opened the door for him. – Adrian was telling me about you.

And then he was in the hallway. She had dark blue eyes and dark hair. She kept her eyes on him the whole time. It felt like being out on a wide-open heath, with nowhere to shelter. He bent forward and fiddled with his shoelaces.

– My name's Elsa.

She held out a hand. He straightened up, gave it a quick shake.

– Karsten, he managed to say, – but you already know that.

She smiled, and it made her look even prettier. – I'll put the kettle on. Tea or coffee?

– Yes please.

He bent forward, fiddled with his shoelaces again. His father was going to the police station to report the vandalism. Not impossible that he would ask him to accompany him. If Karsten could spin this out long enough, he might at least be able to avoid that.

– So tea *and* coffee then?

He could hear that she was still smiling. – Coffee, he said, even though he would have preferred tea with four spoonfuls of sugar.

She showed him into the front room. He tried to protest that he'd been out jogging, that his clothes were dirty and wet, but she told him to sit down on the sofa anyway. It was a reddish colour, not unlike the colour of her dressing gown. – Just excuse me while I go and get dressed.

He muttered some response or other.

– I work nights, she explained, and then disappeared up the stairs.

He sank down into the soft plush. Her name was Elsa. At this very moment she was walking into a room above him to get dressed. Maybe she'd left the door ajar.

When she came back down, she was wearing jeans and a knitted bottle-green sweater. She put cups and a cafetière on the table, poured coffee, slipped down into the chair directly opposite him.

He reached out for the blue cup. – How long have you and Adrian—

He interrupted himself with an abrupt gesture that splashed coffee on to the tabletop.

– Excuse me, I'm sorry.

She assured him it was okay, fetched a tissue and draped it over the little puddle. The white paper turned brown, and Karsten could see how the fibres inside it swelled up.

She sat down again, sipped from a large glass mug containing some greenish brew that didn't look like either tea or coffee.

– You're a maths genius, I gather.

She didn't sound as if she was being ironic.

– Always been interested in that kind of thing, he said. – Pretty much of a nerd, actually.

– Adrian says you're good in all subjects.

For some reason or other Adrian had been talking to this woman about him. Elsa, he thought. She said her name was Elsa.

– Are you going to study maths?

He shrugged his shoulders. – I've applied to several places. People at home want me to study medicine. It sounded stupid. As though it was his parents who were going to decide his career choice. – But I don't fancy it.

– Why not? Elsa wanted to know, looking intently at him.

– Dunno. It struck him that she wanted a proper answer. – Not really all that good with people.

She wagged her head slightly. It was like something he'd seen Adrian do. – Well that's what you'll learn when you study.

They had discussed this at home. It was his mother who

kept going on about medicine. His father was more relaxed, reckoned he still had plenty of time. Can you see Karsten sitting at the bedside of a woman who's about to give birth? he asked, with a little chuckle to indicate that he found the thought amusing. Why not? his mother had persisted. And anyway, he could be a researcher. His father had to admit that wasn't such a bad idea. He was a nuclear physicist himself and had done his doctoral thesis on dark matter. The thought of his father recalled to Karsten the sight of the vandalised car in the garage, and it was a sight he associated with Shahzad Chadar.

He took a swig of coffee that was much too big and much too hot.

– Probably be research, he managed to get out once he'd finished coughing. – That's the kind of thing I'm best suited to.

Elsa looked at him as though trying to determine whether or not this was correct.

– What do *you* do? he dared to enquire. – You said you were on night duty.

She put down the cup containing the mystery brew. – Work at a nursing home. It's just a part-time job. Apart from that, I help people who need advice and guidance.

– I thought as much, Karsten blurted out.

– Is that what I look like?

He felt the prickling at the roots of his hair. – You seem like, so open.

– That's a nice thing to say.

– Are you a psychologist? he ventured.

She smiled with her whole face, but mostly with her eyes.

– I use various methods. Mostly the Tarot.

He must have looked pretty funny, because she burst out laughing, and there was nothing else to laugh at but him.

– Do you know what that is? she asked.

He shook his head.

– The Tarot is an ancient way of finding out what's happened in the past in people's lives, and what's going to happen. People who are uncertain about things can be helped to see more clearly and make sensible decisions. We use a special pack of cards.

– You're a fortune-teller? he exclaimed.

– You could put it like that.

She leaned back in the chair and the pullover tightened across her breasts.

– There are certain areas of life in which common sense alone can't help us.

Karsten drank the rest of the coffee. Superstition and magic were things that primitive people did, out of ignorance. And yet he sat there nodding his head at what she said.

– I can see you're sceptical, and that's quite natural.

He even nodded at this. – I am sceptical.

He lifted the mug, which was now empty, and pretended to drink. Put it down again, looked at his watch, thought he'd better say something more.

– If I told you something about my life, could you predict what's going to happen next?

She looked at him for a long time. – I could give you some idea, at least.

– With a pack of cards?

– Not just any old cards. Tarot cards have distinctive properties. They inspire thoughts, fantasies and premonitions.

With relief Karsten heard the front door opening. A few seconds later Adrian was standing there.

– Blimey.

Karsten got up from the sofa. – I was out jogging, he explained, – and I just thought . . . There was something I wanted to ask you.

– Sure.

Adrian disappeared into the kitchen, returned with a cup, sank down into the chair next to Elsa's. Karsten noticed a vague resemblance between them, and it was only now that he realised Elsa wasn't Adrian's partner. She must be ten or twenty years older, he thought, the same age as his own mother, over forty, maybe more. Adrian was twenty-four; the girls in class had managed to get that out of him.

– And Elsa's been looking after you, he smiled.

– I wasn't going to . . .

Adrian waved it aside, got him to sit back down again.

– And quite right too.

– I'm going upstairs, said Elsa. – Then you two can talk in private.

Karsten glanced at her. In among the brown, almost black hair he noticed a few thin wisps of grey.

– More trouble? Adrian asked once she'd disappeared.

– Someone's scratched up my dad's car.

He explained. Adrian's eyes narrowed. Afterwards he said: – Well from all this I deduce that you have had another meeting with a certain girl from a different ethnic background, to put it formally.

– In a way, yes.

– And have you *in a way* been making out with her?

Karsten nodded.

– Or *in a way* gone further than just snogging?

– Nothing happened really. Almost nothing, he corrected himself silently.

Adrian smiled broadly and it made him look even more like Elsa. – Let's have the details.

Karsten hesitated. He started to describe the encounter outside the library. Left out most of it.

– And you're wondering if this has something to do with the car being trashed?

– It hasn't been trashed. Just the paint scratched.

– And at home they've no idea why?

– They work a lot, Mum especially. And my sister might have some kind of illness. They've got enough to think about.

Adrian poured himself coffee, offered Karsten a refill. He couldn't bring himself to say no, even though he could feel his hands shaking. Coffee always wound him up, and he was pretty worked up to begin with anyway. He needed to go the other way, get things to slow down.

– What kind of illness does your sister have?

Karsten squirmed in his chair. – She has these attacks now and then. She falls out of bed. Once she passed out at school and hit her head. It's possibly a rare form of epilepsy.

Adrian leaned back and looked up at the ceiling. – What you've just told me is very interesting.

– Is it?

– You learn something about the world you otherwise wouldn't've known anything about.

Karsten didn't know what to say to this. – I don't know how they can do something like that, he complained.

Adrian ran his fingers down his close-cropped beard. – The girl is their property. You offend them, they take revenge and their honour is satisfied. That's what it's all about in the world outside this little Toytown: honour and vengeance.

– I've got to report them.

Adrian laughed. – The police will arrive with lights flashing and start looking for fingerprints and traces of DNA. By the end of the evening, the entire Chadar family will be under arrest.

Karsten couldn't sit still any more; he had to get up. He was bursting with caffeine. He needed to run more.

Adrian stood up as well. – I understand you're pissed off. I would be too.

Karsten wasn't sure if pissed off was the right expression

for how he felt. – I shouldn't've come, he apologised. – It's really nothing to do with you.

Adrian put his hand on his shoulder. – You did absolutely the right thing in coming here. It sounded as if he meant it. – It's too bloody bad them trying to drag your family into this. But I can assure you, the kind of thing that happened to your car will never happen again.

Karsten looked over at him. He couldn't understand what Adrian meant, or how he could be bothered to get involved at all. But he felt a sense of relief.

He heard footsteps on the staircase. Before he could ask Adrian what he was thinking, Elsa came back into the room.

– You could ask Karsten if he wants to stay for dinner, she suggested.

– Could do, Adrian replied without sounding too enthusiastic about it.

Elsa brushed a lock of dark hair off her forehead. She had rather slanting eyes that weren't like Adrian's at all. But the mouth was the same.

Suddenly Adrian said: – Karsten and I have been discussing the conditions of love.

– Have you?

– The question is, should culture and religion be allowed to stand in the way of a young couple?

Elsa turned to Karsten. – Have you met someone from an immigrant family?

Karsten felt himself shrinking.

– Relax, said Adrian. – Elsa will never tell anyone. He smiled at her. – Karsten and Jasmeen Chadar are in the process of becoming sweethearts.

Something in his voice suggested that he was amused. Karsten glanced across at Elsa. She stood in the middle of the floor, looking at him with an expression close to surprise. Then abruptly she turned and went into the kitchen.

15

AFTER THREE ATTEMPTS, he gave up trying to start the Chevy. Not so much as a cough from under the bonnet. He'd trawled the net and still not found the right type of window winder. And now the battery was flat too. He let himself into the house. Listened. All still. Elsa had been on night shift and was probably sleeping now. In the cabinet he found the spare key to the Peugeot. No hesitation from the tiny French engine once he'd turned the ignition; it was still warm and purred like a lazy cat between his knees, weak and feminine.

At the building materials store he chose the planks of the size he needed and cut them to length. They just about fitted into the little boot. As he started up the engine again, thoughts of the night watch came to him. He wasn't dead; smoke divers had pulled him out of the changing room. He was in intensive care at Ahus. Still critical; that was how his condition was described in *VG*'s digital edition.

He got the three fence posts up, knocked in the last nail. Let his fingers glide over the impregnated wood before getting into the Peugeot and reversing it into the garage. Was the night watch conscious, even if in bad shape? Had he been able to tell the police anything? Did he remember the face he caught a glimpse of in the mirror before the lights went out? He'd been thinking about that for the last twenty-four hours, how to get inside the hospital and find the right room and make sure the guy would never say anything.

The girl would never talk again. He was almost surprised to find that all he felt was relief. There was a picture of her up on *VG*'s website. She was a Somali. Didn't matter how often they said she was a Norwegian with a Somali background, or bilingual, or a girl with parallel cultural connections; she was a Somali, and not even her name had any effect on him. She was called Abiya. Fourteen years old.

After leaving the basement, he'd driven on in the direction of Hadeland, turned back after an hour. On the journey back, a roadblock had been set up. As he parked further off, he looked at his watch and registered that she'd been dead for almost three hours. As though time meant anything to her. A crowd of people had gathered, moths, drawn by the light. He slipped in amongst them, pulled out his mobile and starting filming. Two lips of fire stretched up into the deep purple sky, turned into a mouth that sucked at it and left floating dark specks in its wake. When he played the recording back, he could see how, behind the exterior wall that was still standing, the flames worked their way through wall panels, cut through piping and cables, chewed their way in towards the heart of the building, where the material now and then gave off hoarse, groaning shouts. He'd read that the temperature inside a burning building could reach over a thousand degrees; metal, concrete, all structural material, no matter what it was made of, had to admit defeat. The fire could develop unfathomable warmth; it could reshape anything.

When he transferred his pictures to the computer and screened the film, the sounds were so greatly amplified that behind the hollow coughing of the building, he could make out that same whisper as before: the sound of the fire itself. He lets it lead him on from the schoolroom and up the staircase. Walking with the fire, searching each room for something to devour, and in the fourth room on the left they come across a lifeless arm hanging down towards the floor, and find the body in the bed. The fire enfolds it, melting the skin, melting the hair, the nails, the eyes, softening the skeleton until it can be bent.

This trip into the heart of the burning building kept him awake for the rest of the night. He played the video segment over and over again as he pictured her, how she had moved around inside that building before the fire came, talked, laughed, eaten, showered, used the toilet. He went through the whole story, got out her panties, which he had stored in a box at the back of the cupboard, sat with them in his hand, the smell now even sharper and stronger. Abiya was the girlfriend of Bizhan in the next room, he imagined; they used to visit each other at night, he used to undress her, and the thought got him excited in a way he hadn't known since he lay in that bed and heard Siv's footsteps outside, or followed her down into the basement and stood outside the girls' changing room with his ear pressed against the door. The same door he had tricked the night watch into opening.

He was still seated behind the wheel of the Peugeot. And he still had the hammer in his hand. He tossed it aside on to the seat, turned off the engine. For a few more minutes he remained sitting in the dark garage, staring out through the windscreen. The fence posts couldn't be painted for months, maybe not even until the autumn. He could offer to do the whole fence. Was suddenly consumed with the desire to do more for Elsa. He got out of the car, stepped into the light. For a few seconds there was no room for any other thought than this, of doing something for Elsa. He took hold of the newly repaired fence, closed his eyes, breathed in the clear air. The wind was different now, raw and sharp, and yet warmer. He had never liked the spring, but this one would be different, he decided. He forgave Elsa for having neglected him these last few weeks, because she was so preoccupied with someone else. He would win her back, once and for all.

The day grew lighter as he jogged towards the centre of town. The heat of the sun made the gables drip, and the light from the steaming asphalt was so strong he had to half close his eyes against it. He stopped by the corner shop. The fire was front-page news in the national dailies too. The general view was that it was probably an arson attack. The police were looking for the perpetrator. He had to laugh. Good luck with that. The only thing was that night watch, if he should ever regain consciousness. If he remembered. If he was able to identify him. He'd managed to find out what his name was. The brief glimpse the guy had got of him, it couldn't possibly be enough to cause any trouble. Yet there was still that little jab of doubt. One way or another, he had to get rid of it.

He spent a lot of time warming up. Increased the resistance and kept the bike going at over thirty kilometres an hour. Watched his pulse monitor closely, kept it at around eighty per cent of max for ten minutes. His phone vibrated. Without stopping, he took it out. Sæter had said not to put his name on his contacts list but he recognised the number anyway, jumped off the bike and went over to a corner of the hall.

– It's me.

Sæter didn't even like people to use names in conversation. Ridiculous, bearing in mind that not a single soul in the whole bloody country cared what he was up to.

– You sound out of breath.

He explained why.

– It's about the meeting this evening. We need to move it.

He forced himself to breathe normally. It wasn't the first time Sæter had decided at the last minute that they had to move a meeting. He was convinced that the security services expended a lot of resources in keeping track of him. He went in for diversionary manoeuvres and cover operations in the obvious belief that this made him important.

– I'm sending you a message from a second phone, Sæter said in a low voice. – Pass it on. Yellow alert.

He smirked, making sure it couldn't be heard at the other end.

– Everyone needs to take this check, no exception.

– Check?

– You'll get a message, said Sæter, and disconnected.

He positioned himself in front of the mirror to work his biceps. Lifted the dumb-bell. He'd increased fifteen kilos since he started bodybuilding again. Each time he flexed, the muscle came bulging out of the arm of his vest, like the belly of a giant fish. He increased another five kilos. The sweat marked out a deep, wide gorge from his neckband down across the chest of his vest. As he was about to lift again, he saw her in the doorway, Monica with a *c*, tripping along on high heels towards reception, probably headed for the changing room first: change, go to the toilet and all those type of things women did before starting a workout. He could use the time to get out of there, pull on his outdoor clothes and disappear without her seeing him. He followed her in the mirror on the opposite wall. Her body was firm, not over-muscular. Knowing she was going with someone else made him hot. The thought that it was a policeman who was looking for him brought on a feeling that was almost like wanting to have her again.

Horvath, that was his name. He noticed the names of everyone who had dealings with these fires. Had a separate file on his computer with a list of them. Fire brigade people, police officers, journalists, relatives of the victims. It was already a card index. This policeman was under control.

And as he stood there watching Monica disappear into the changing room, he knew what it was he wanted her for. If that night duty guy regained consciousness and started remembering things, he would be one jump ahead of them.

He did another two rounds on the bench press. Then he got up and opened the door to the main hall. She was sitting with her back to him on one of the machines, working on her abdomen and chest. He slung the towel around his neck, strolled over to her.

– Not bad, he nodded.

The weights she was lifting tumbled down and hit the metal block with a nasty crack. She sat there staring at him and said nothing. Not until her pupils had started to narrow again did he let one hand brush past her thigh.

This one's gonna be for the night watch, he said to himself.

He chose the sofa in the living room because of the strong smell of leather. From the kitchen the sounds of the percolating coffee had just started, but he had no intention of sitting there and waiting to be served. He pressed her down on to the cold leather; she was still wearing the training pants, but no panties. The previous time her comb of hair had been dark and trimmed; now it had been shaved off entirely. He let her keep her top on, spread her out below him and forced his way inside. Same biting of the lip as last time, he noticed. He waited for it to start to bleed, and suddenly he saw in his mind's eye the mouth of the girl at Furutunet, smeared with his own blood. Abiya, he thought, and maybe he said it out loud, because Monica opened her eyes and he had to put a fist over them to close them again. Then she began babbling beneath him, and he grabbed hold of her hands and held them in an iron grip above her head. She twisted from side to side and he let her do what she wanted until she was finished.

Afterwards he got up and stood by the window, which was slightly open. He listened to the voices down in the square, music from a café, a road-sweeping machine approaching from the other end.

– What was it you called me?

He turned with wrinkled brow.

– Did I call you something?

She nodded decisively. Around her neck was a ring of tiny bruises. – You called me a name.

He laughed, shook his head and glanced at his watch.

– Have you got a partner? she persisted. – Sabina or something like that?

– You're the one with the partner, he countered.

She thought about it. – Not necessarily.

A ridiculous answer. – How far have they got with their investigations? he asked.

– Of what?

– Isn't your bloke still working on these fires? You must have noticed that there's been another one.

She waved an arm. – What do you think? That's all Roar ever talks about.

– Not surprising really. When a young girl gets burned to death like that.

He was still standing by the window, looking out, the sun just making its way through the cloud cover high above the roof on the other side of the square.

– They don't think she died in the fire.

He acted startled, exaggerated his surprise. – What do you mean?

She got up, picked her exercise pants up from the floor. – Roar would be furious if he knew I was talking about it.

She went out to the bathroom, left the door half open. When she came back, she was wearing a G-string.

– What killed her if it wasn't the fire?

She sat on the glass-topped table. – You still on about that girl?

He stepped across the floor, stood naked above her.

– I guess they did a post-mortem on her, she said as she lifted a hand and stroked his underarm. – Where did you get these scars?

– When I was a kid. An accident.

– Don't look like that.

He withdrew his arm. – What did the post-mortem show?

She gave an exasperated sigh. – They believe she was dead before the fire started.

– Which means?

– I've said enough now.

– That she was murdered?

– That's what they think. I don't know any more than that.

– And that the fire was started to cover the traces?

– Can't we talk about something else?

She leaned back, her thighs parting and taking on a different shape against the brownish glass. A gap opening beneath the silky material of the G-string.

– Thought maybe the fire might be connected with the nursery school, he said vaguely, and it was not the sight of the naked lips beneath the material that made him decide it was time for another round.

– They think there is a connection, she said. – Even if the girl was murdered.

He knew how to get her to say more. Abruptly he bent and lifted her up.

– What are you up to now? she whimpered.

– You'll find out.

It was colder in the bedroom; the window was wide open. He dropped her on to the bed, closed the window, closed the curtains.

– Don't go making me nervous now, she said, as if that was the last thing in the world she wanted.

There was a dressing gown draped across the back of a chair; he pulled out the belt.

– I'm freezing, she complained in a thin, little-girl voice, pulling the duvet half round her.

– It'll pass, he told her, taking hold of her hand and squeezing it round the shaft of his penis, holding it there until he went hard. Then he dragged her up to the head of the bed, pulled her hands together and tied them to the wrought iron.

– Not so tight, she pleaded, but he didn't loosen the knot.

– Just so you don't run off, he told her as he opened the wardrobe in search of what else he could use. He found a belt and, on the floor near the wall, a blue and white striped tie.

– Hope he doesn't turn up looking for his fashion accessories, he grinned.

She shook her head. – He's at work all day.

He fastened the tie around her ankle, drew it tight. – You've always got the latest news. Does he call you up at lunchtime to tell you what's he up to?

She nodded. – He tells me everything.

– And now you're going to pass it all on to me.

She shook her head. – I promised not to say anything.

He fastened the tie around her ankle to the edge of the bed. – We'll see how long you hold out for.

He pulled the other leg to one side, leaving her wide open. – Sooner or later you'll talk, when it gets dangerous enough.

She looked up into his eyes. – How dangerous are you?

– You have no idea.

He lowered himself over her. – There was someone else there who nearly got killed.

She gave a slight nod. He stopped his movement.

– The night watch at that place. It says in the paper that he's being treated at Ahus. Have they spoken to him yet?

Now she shook her head, acting serious and sad. – He's unconscious.

He put his hands around her throat. – How bad is he?

– I'm not saying anything.

He waited a while before releasing his hold on her throat and let her breathe.

– Smoke inhalation, she groaned.

– And now your boyfriend's hanging around up there waiting for him to wake? he said as he pulled out of her.

She jerked at the belt, pressed her groin up against his. – They're waiting. But I hate waiting.

16

Jasmeen wasn't at school. At first it was a relief not to have to sit three metres away from her and act as though nothing had happened. But as the morning progressed, the relief grew heavier and heavier, and by the time the mid-morning break came, it was so weighty that Karsten chose to stay seated in the classroom. He picked up a book and looked at the physics problems. If she was ill, she could have sent him a message. He was pleased she hadn't. If nothing at all happened, the problem would disappear of its own accord.

– Hallo, Karsten, earth calling, do you receive?

Tonje was standing in front of his desk waving both hands. He recalled that she had cropped up in one of the half-dreams he had had earlier that morning, as he lay dozing and waiting for the alarm clock to go off. Wearing nothing more than a tiny pair of panties, she had disappeared into a room with Adrian.

– Are you so fascinated by your physics book that no one can get through to you?

He blinked a few times, the flush burning along his forehead and down through his cheeks. – I was just sitting here thinking.

She leaned a hand on his desk. Round the wrist was a broad gold bracelet that looked as though it was woven out of a number of fine strands. Karsten knew it was a Christmas present Thomas had given her. She hadn't been wearing it for the past few weeks. There were rumours flying about that Thomas had been invited to train with the elite team at Easter, but Karsten refused to believe that *that* was the reason she had started wearing it again.

– A few of us are having a get-together at Martin's Pub this Friday evening. You want to come? I mean, it's not really an official arrangement, she added. – Just celebrating that it's the Easter holidays.

He scratched his neck. It was the first time Tonje had ever offered him this kind of invitation. Maybe it was meant as a joke. Maybe it was another challenge, to win a knot for her cap: ask a nerd to go out with you and see how long you can stay awake?

– Aren't you going away for Easter?

She shook her head. – Got a lot of catching-up to do. Especially in maths and physics. And we've got lots of practice matches lined up.

– Did you say Martin's?

– Just to have somewhere to meet. Afterwards we'll go back to someone's place, watch a film or something, don't know what yet.

He could've stood up and lifted her little body into the air and danced round with it.

– Think about it, eh? she said, heading for the door.

– Who else is coming? he managed to compose himself enough to ask. – Apart from you?

She turned, tossing the thin braid behind her back. – Priest and a few others. Maybe Inga.

Thomas? he nearly asked, but managed to keep his lip buttoned.

The headmaster was standing out on the landing. – A word, please, he said as Karsten walked past.

He turned and walked ahead, up the stairs to his office, closing the door behind them.

– Sit down. He pointed a finger. Karsten did as he was told, and the headmaster sat at his desk, behind documents of all sorts arranged in piles that were surprisingly symmetrical.

– How well do you know Jasmeen Chadar?

Karsten looked over at him. – Jasmeen in my class?

The headmaster studied him. The lenses of his spectacles magnified not only his eyes but also the surrounding areas. Small bluish veins were visible just beneath the skin. They looked like tiny worms about to crawl on to his eyeball to feed.

– The fact is, her father telephoned me last night. And I want this to remain just between you and me, Karsten.

The headmaster removed his spectacles and scratched the back of his head with one of the arms. – They're talking about taking her away from school. For the time being they're going to keep her at home until after Easter. Do you understand why I'm telling you this?

– Sort of.

– Now I'm asking you straight out, Karsten. Have you been with her?

– Been with whom?

The counter question gave him a breathing space, but it was one he didn't really want. What mattered was to get this over with and get out of there. There was one day left until the Easter holidays. And then ten days off school. Go running, study, play chess. Maybe go to the cabin after all. Far away from here. And by the time he came back, it would be all over. He didn't know how, but it must be over by then, and no one would talk about it again. And then he would need never think about it any more.

– Jasmeen's father says she has been harassed. That someone has assaulted her. And he mentioned your name.

The headmaster's words whirled around the room,

smashed into the wall, crashed into one another, dissolved into meaningless sound. Karsten realised that he was staring at a point on the headmaster's forehead, just above one eyebrow, where there was a brown patch that resembled a coin.

– Assaulted her? He fidgeted with one of the straps on his rucksack. – Assaulted her? he said again, struggling to understand the meaning of the words.

The headmaster rose and walked round the desk. He bent slightly over him. – I have great difficulty in imagining that you have done any such thing, he assured him. – But her father maintains that you have been pursuing her for some time now. And that is why I want to hear your answer to the question I have just asked you. Have you been with her in such a way as to . . .

He straightened up, stood in front of the window, put his arms behind his back and stared out across the schoolyard.

– If something has taken place that was entirely consensual, such as citizens in our society are at complete liberty to do, then that is an end to the matter. So to speak. But where conflicting moral visions come up against one another, things tend to get a little more complicated.

He turned again and peered down at Karsten before embarking on a lengthy explanation of what he meant. It was just as well, because Karsten was still in no state to give any answer at all.

– I've talked to her a few times, he managed to say once the headmaster was finished.

– Out of school?

– Met her at the public library.

At this the headmaster seemed to breathe more easily. It was as though the words *public library* were better than any other words that could have been said at such a time, as though they explained everything and put the matter in its proper perspective. – I thought it was probably something like that. I'm sure we'll manage to sort this out. If we invite her and her family to sit down and talk things through.

Karsten kept his mouth shut. He didn't trust what might come out if he opened it. He could have told the headmaster that the world wasn't the kind of place where you all sat round a table and talked to Muslims whose honour had been compromised. He could have told him they weren't living in Toytown any more.

– And if, as seems unlikely, things are still unresolved, the headmaster reasoned, – then of course there is always the mediation board.

As Karsten descended the staircase from the headmaster's office, Adrian was standing outside the staffroom talking to one of the other teachers.

– I'd like a word with you, Karsten said as calmly as he could.

Adrian nodded. – Two minutes. Wait outside for me.

When he came out, he looked pleased. – So you had an audience with the head himself. Let's walk together and you can tell me what you were talking about. They headed towards Storgata. Karsten struggled to explain the content of the conversation.

– The mediation board, Adrian exclaimed with a big grin. – There, you see.

– I'm sure it's not Jasmeen who's making all this fuss, Karsten stammered, and tried not to pursue the thought any further.

– Not Jasmeen, but the rest of the Chadar family, Adrian announced in a surprisingly firm voice. – They've changed tactics. We'll try to find out what's going on.

It was a relief to hear him use the word 'we'.

– Any fool knows that you don't get anywhere by involving the police.

– My mum and dad mustn't know anything about this, Karsten burst out.

That was the thought that had tightened around his chest up in the headmaster's office and was still squeezing and squeezing. He couldn't bear to think about how they would react, especially his dad, who was repelled by anything embarrassing; he slipped out of the room the moment people on TV started snogging, even if it was a film that even Synne was old enough to watch.

– You think that's the most important thing?

A warm wind blew along the street, but Karsten was still feeling cold. – Dunno. Maybe.

– Actually that's very interesting, Karsten. You meet a Pakistani girl, and before you can get your flies zipped up, her whole family is involved. Whereas whatever happens, *you* want to deal with it alone. Your family's not to know anything about it. That's something to think about, it really is.

Karsten couldn't bear the idea of thinking about anything at all. – What are we going to do? he muttered.

Adrian stopped and looked round. – Good question. He seemed satisfied, and the sense of calm he exuded was contagious. – Actually, as things stand at the moment, it's the only question you need to ask.

– One thing's for sure, I have to stay well away from her.

Adrian drew two fingers across his chin, smoothing down his short beard. – I'm not so sure about that. He looked to be thinking something through. – We've got to keep one step ahead. I have a suggestion to make to you, Karsten.

– Okay.

– I know several people who've been giving a lot of thought to what's happening.

Karsten looked at him quizzically.

– We meet up now and then to discuss what's going on around us. Things we have to have an opinion on, whether we like it or not. I can get you in. Next meeting is this evening.

– Get me in? Karsten looked at him. – Is it secret?

Adrian shrugged. – For the time being it's best that as few people as possible know about it. There's no need to go round shooting your mouth off about it.

– Don't think I can make it tonight.

– You mean you don't like the sound of it? Without even knowing any of the details?

– Maybe.

– I'll call in on my way there, Adrian decided. – In the meantime, you can think about it.

Karsten speeded up, running down Fetveien. The slush splashed up his legs; his trainers were soaking wet. The fine rain plastered his hair flat across his forehead. He forced himself into a last sprint, heading up towards Erleveien. Then an easy jog home, stopping in the driveway until he'd got his breath back before pulling out his phone. Squatted down behind the corner of the garage and called directory enquiries, got what had to be her home number.

– Who is this?

A child's voice answered, sounded like a boy.

– I'm calling from Lillestrøm Secondary School, he said. – I'd like to talk to Jasmeen Chadar, is this the right number?

He heard the boy shout something or other in a different language. People talking together somewhere in the room. Then suddenly her voice.

– Jasmeen.

– It's me. I have to talk to you.

A brief pause, then she said politely: – It's difficult, but

I'll see what I can do. I'll call you back in about fifteen minutes.

He couldn't stay still, walked down the street again. Had just passed Dan-Levi's house when his phone rang. He grabbed it from his pocket.

– You mustn't ring me at home, Karsten.

– You don't answer my messages, he protested.

– I don't have my mobile phone. They've taken it.

– Where are you calling from? he asked, immediately suspicious.

– Just somebody that's helping me. Don't ask any more, I only have a few minutes.

– You're going to report me for harassment and assault, he informed her. – I've got a right to talk to you about that.

– Assault?

He told her what the headmaster had said.

– Is that true?

– Think I'd lie about something like that?

She was silent at the other end.

– Are you still there? he asked, relieved that she obviously knew nothing about the accusation.

– I hate them.

He was startled at the anger in her voice. It sounded as if she had started crying, and that made him even more relieved.

– How can they do something like that without you knowing anything about it? he asked nevertheless.

– You don't know them! You've no idea what they want me to do.

He didn't want to know either.

– My dad shouts at me and calls me a bad person and even worse things than that. Somebody's scratched his car and I even get the blame for that.

Karsten stiffened. – Scratched it?

She was now clearly crying.

– If we don't meet any more, he began, – everything will just blow over of its own accord.

– You don't know them, she repeated, and suddenly her voice was gone.

Karsten had to set off on another run. Past the Statoil station, past Åråsen Stadium. Could've kept on running along Fetveien; it stretched for kilometres on end towards the river Glomma. Carry on across the bridge at Fetsund and on through the forest into Sweden. He could keep on running until he collapsed and was unable to think any more.

When he returned home an hour later, a blue Peugeot was parked right outside the drive. As Karsten passed, the window slid down.

– You don't look ready, said Adrian.

Karsten stopped in his tracks. – Ready?

– Have you forgotten the meeting we talked about?

– Someone's scratched their car too, he burst out.

Adrian looked at him completely straight faced. – Whose car?

– Jasmeen's.

– She has a car?

– Shit, Karsten panted. – Her dad's. You know what I'm talking about.

He looked around. No one within hearing distance, but a window in the house next door was wide open.

– Did you go over there and . . .?

– Calm down, Karsten. Adrian got out of the car. He was wearing the same leather combat jacket, but his dark hair looked as if it had just been cut, a lock of it hanging over his forehead. – Calm down, he repeated, not raising his voice. – Someone has obviously had a word with them. It wasn't me, but that doesn't matter. He rested a hand on

Karsten's shoulder. – It's the kind of language they understand. You won't have any more trouble from the Chadar
family. Trust me. Are you alone in the house?

Karsten looked over. – Think so. Maybe my sister's home.

– Then I'll wait inside while you have a shower.

Karsten realised that Adrian was still trying to get him
to go along to the meeting.

– Forgot about it, he apologised. – Maybe you should just
go without me.

– No worries. How long do you need?

Karsten hesitated. – Who else is going?

– Some people with an opinion on what's happening in
this country.

– So not some kind of political party or anything like
that?

– We've got enough of those already.

Karsten abandoned any thought of getting out of going
to the meeting. He let them into the hallway, heard Synne
playing music up in her room. When he emerged from the
shower fifteen minutes later, his sister was sitting in the living
room with the guest.

– Synne's taking good care of me, said Adrian with a
broad smile. There were biscuits on the table, and a bowl
of fruit. – And I believe she's an absolute whizz with the
coffee machine.

Synne headed off into the kitchen and returned with a
steaming cup, which she placed in front of Adrian. He took
a sip. – That's just as good as you said it would be. Actually
even better.

She blushed and perched on the edge of her chair. Adrian
gave Karsten a wink. – Have you any idea how bright your
sister is? She knows everything there is to know about the
French Revolution.

– She reads all the time, Karsten conceded.

– Adrian knows a lot more than I do, Synne said coquettishly.

– I went to university, Adrian protested. – When I was thirteen, I didn't know the half of what you know.

Synne was bursting in her chair. – Shall we play some music?

– Doubt if Adrian came here to listen to Michael Jackson, Karsten groaned.

Adrian dismissed him with a wave. – Michael Jackson is cool. You got any videos?

Synne had videos. She ran upstairs and came back down with three or four. Adrian looked them over and asked her to put 'Thriller' on. Karsten didn't mind at all if Adrian had changed his mind and preferred to spend the evening with them. But once Michael Jackson had danced his way through the cemetery of the living dead and kissed his girl good night and left it open to doubt whether he himself was actually a monster, he stood up and drained his coffee cup.

Synne followed them out into the hallway and shook the hand that Adrian offered her. Karsten had four, maybe five problems he couldn't find a solution to, but when he saw how brightly her eyes shone, he suddenly felt a huge sense of relief. It lasted until they were seated inside the car. Then he had to let off some kind of steam.

– I feel as though I'm swimming around in thick soup.

Adrian grinned. – You can forget all about that business of the harassment and assault. That's history now.

– What do you mean? Have you talked to them?

Now Adrian laughed. – That's one way of putting it.

– If someone's vandalised their car, they'll get their own back. You said yourself the only thing they care about is revenge.

Adrian turned up in the direction of Skedsmokorset. – That won't happen.

Without stopping the car, he unfastened his safety belt and wriggled out of his leather jacket, tossed it into the back seat. A wall of chest muscles pushed out through his T-shirt. – For the time being, just accept what I say. Trust me.

His phone rang; he took the call. – We're on our way, he said. – Be there within forty.

With the brief telephone conversation over, he turned on the CD player, pressed a few buttons, settled for some piano music. – You have to understand the way the Chadar clan thinks. Of course we don't want to underestimate them, but to walk around in holy terror of them is even worse. How did you find out about their car?

– I called Jasmeen.

Adrian glanced at him. – So she's got her mobile phone back?

Karsten explained what he had done.

– Not bad, Adrian smiled.

– Had to tell her that that's it now, no more.

Adrian drummed with his fingers on the steering wheel. – So you've decided to let the powers of darkness triumph?

Karsten tried to get things in some kind of order. – Why are you taking such an interest in all this?

Adrian didn't reply. He indicated and made a turn. Shortly afterwards, he left the main road and drove up through some woodland. – Try to see your life in a slightly larger perspective, he said at last. – For four centuries our civilisation has dominated the world. We've had our age of greatness and now we're in decline.

Karsten blinked a few times. He wasn't ready to see the scratches on his father's car and the accusations of sexual harassment in the context of the rise and fall of civilisations.

– You, who are so preoccupied with evolution, you've got a much larger perspective on existence than I have, Adrian continued. – As you said yourself in one of the lessons, in the really big scheme of things the history of civilisations is just a passing moment.

He turned down the piano music.

– Of course, you have to decide yourself whether to meet Jasmeen Chadar again or not, but there's no doubt in my mind what I would do in your place. She's not having an easy time of it right now.

– How do you know that?

– I'm trying to help her, said Adrian. – And you can do the same thing.

– But I can't even get hold of her, Karsten said. – They've taken her phone away, and she's not allowed to go to school. How am I supposed to help her?

They drove over a hilltop and Adrian pulled into the side of the road. – Give me your phone.

Karsten did as he said. Adrian punched in a number and handed it back. – I'm just going out to see a man about a dog. You call her.

He switched off the ignition. The music was cut; silence came flooding in from every direction.

Karsten peered at the number on the display. Before he could ask any more questions, Adrian had slammed the door shut behind him. He stood with his back turned right in front of the car. A powerful arc steamed out from him. Karsten could feel that he needed to go too, but knew that he wouldn't manage a drop unless he was completely alone.

Abruptly he punched the call button, hoped there would be no answer.

– Rashida, said a female voice at the other end.

Karsten cleared the phlegm from his throat. – Jasmeen? he managed to say.

A few seconds, and then she was there.

– We've only got a few seconds, she said quickly.

– I understand, he said, though he understood nothing.

– Will you be at home tomorrow? she asked.

– I think so.

– Your parents, will they be around?

He hesitated. – They're going to the cabin with my sister.

Adrian was still standing there with his back turned. Karsten tried to stop staring at him, peered instead out of the side window, followed the fading evening light down through a gap in the trees. It looked as though there was a lake down there.

– I'll come to your place tomorrow.

– My place?

– In the evening. When my dad and Shahzad are at the mosque.

Adrian was obviously finishing up with a final shake. Karsten couldn't say a word.

– You must be there when I come, Jasmeen went on. – I'll show them you haven't done me any wrong. Again he heard the anger in her voice. – This is none of their business.

– No, you mustn't, he finally managed to blurt out, but she'd already ended the call.

– She says she's coming round to my place, he groaned as Adrian slid back into the driver's seat.

Adrian turned. Looked at him without saying anything. Now something's going to happen, thought Karsten. But Adrian started the engine and the piano music came on again. A theme repeated over and over. They drove on down the hill, the lake coming into view between the trees, like a dark eye, and then disappearing again.

Twelve minutes later, they pulled up in front of a large house that looked as if it had stood there for centuries. There was a smaller house next to it, and behind that a barn. Two cars were parked in front, a Mazda, and an Audi with patches of rust on its doors. Dogs were barking hysterically somewhere. A tall and massively built figure approached across the lawn. Adrian wound down the window.

– Sæter doesn't want hundreds of cars parked right outside the house, the guy said. He had a dark coxcomb of long hair running across the centre of his scalp, with the sides of his head shaven. It made Karsten think of some great Indian chieftain he had read about once. – Spread them out across this area here.

Adrian reversed out again. – Noah is in charge of security at these meetings, he explained.

– Is his name really Noah?

– Any reason why it shouldn't be?

Karsten couldn't resist. – Named after the person who saved mankind from drowning? He looks more like an Iroquois.

– You don't mess with a guy like Noah, Adrian told him. – If he gets angry with you, he never forgets it. And nor do you.

They continued another two hundred metres or so up the woodland track, parked at the edge of a field, walked back to the farm. The dogs were kept in a pen next to the barn, four or five enormous mongrels biting at the wire and still barking as furiously as when they had arrived in the car.

Adrian pulled on a bell rope hanging to the left of the door to the main house, and the sound of a horn was heard from inside, like reveille at an army camp. The door was opened. The giant Noah with his Iroquois hairstyle stood there; he looked to be about the same age as Adrian.

– Trouble?

Adrian shook his head. – Karsten here had something he had to do first.

Noah turned to him. – So you're the maths genius. The

small eyes carried an expression of irritation. – Let me have your jacket.

Karsten looked at Adrian.

– Do as he says.

Reluctantly he took off his jacket. The enormous man laid it flat on a table and then patted it with both hands, as though searching for something, before hanging it on a peg.

– Standard procedure, said Adrian as he handed over his own combat jacket. This received the same treatment.

– Don't touch that gun, he joked, nudging Noah's shoulder.

– The old fella's getting more and more cautious about stuff like that, the giant growled as he led them along a corridor. At the end of it, he opened a door that led into a large sitting room. There were twenty or thirty people inside. They sat facing a wall in which an open fire burned. An elderly man, tall and bony and wearing a knitted jacket, was standing next to it. His hair was grey but the eyebrows looked black. He interrupted what was evidently a lecture to nod briefly to the new arrivals. All those present turned. What am I doing here? Karsten thought as he slipped into one of the vacant cane chairs at the back of the room. Adrian remained standing at the door beside Noah.

The man in the knitted jacket carried on speaking. Karsten gathered that he was talking about the Second World War. He looked around. The furniture in the room was made of wood, with a floral pattern on the coverings. A diploma hung on one wall, some kind of military honour. Most of those sitting there looked to be about his own age. A few pale skinheads in camouflage pants, their faces studded with various piercings, the others more normal in appearance. There was a good-looking woman in a denim jacket; she had to be over thirty and resembled an actress whose name he couldn't immediately recall.

– On the other hand, continued the man in the knitted jacket, – the murder of hundreds of thousands of innocents in Dresden has been turned into an act of heroism. And that brings us to the subject of the Five Great Lies.

He bent and picked up a log. The broad brows made it look as though he had a black moustache over each eye.

– The first is that we are living in a democracy, he continued once he had worked the log into place among the glowing ashes in the fireplace. – Democracy means, as we know, the rule of the people, but today's Norway is ruled by money and by the political manipulators.

He held up two long fingers.

– The second is that Christianity made Norway into a more civilised society.

He took a drink from a glass, put it down again and remained silent. It appeared as though he was trying to raise the level of anticipation among his listeners, but judging by the weary faces in front of him, the intended effect failed. The log gave off a sharp crackle as it caught fire. Apart from that, there was silence in the room. Karsten made an effort to concentrate on what the man was saying. His voice was reedy and hoarse, but certain words, like *lie* and *Christianity*, were thrown out into the room.

When he had finished his talk, some people started clapping, and the others joined in. The man in the knitted jacket sat down in a deep armchair by the fire, pulled a pipe from his trouser pocket. Just then a door on the right opened and a woman came in, drawn and bow backed, with hair the colour of straw. She was carrying a tray with three large thermos flasks, which she placed on a table. A chubby girl of eleven or twelve came in after her carrying another tray with piles of cups.

The man in the knitted jacket released a cloud of smoke from his pipe that hid his outline for a moment.

– After the break, we'll talk about what's going to happen this weekend, he said. – Those who are participating, please remain. The rest of you are welcome at our next meeting. You will be informed of the details.

Some left the room. Karsten went over to Adrian, who was standing talking to Noah.

– We're staying, Adrian announced before Karsten could say anything. He turned his back, effectively preventing any protests.

Thick banks of smoke drifted about the room, most of it coming from the leader's pipe. He was standing by the window talking to the woman in the denim jacket. Beyond him Karsten could just make out the edge of the forest and the grey clouds impaled on the tops of the spruce trees. As though noticing Karsten's scrutiny, the elderly man turned. Then he crossed the room and held out a large, wrinkled hand.

– I'm Sæter, he said. – And you, I presume, must be Karsten. Without waiting for confirmation, he went on: – Excellent. We need people who are bright. Very much so.

He turned and said a few quiet words to the people standing by the door. Adrian nodded briefly. Then he and Noah accompanied Sæter as he left the room. Suddenly a short guy was standing there. He seemed as broad as he was tall, with bleached hair and skin a solarium brown.

– Come with me, he said.

Karsten followed him out into the kitchen. The woman with the bent back and the chubby girl were told to leave the room.

– Sit down.

Karsten did as he was told.

– No need to look as though you're about to be hanged.

– Have I been reprieved? Karsten said, and the short man laughed.

– I'm just going to ask you a few questions, that's all. Everyone who comes to these meetings has to go through the same thing. I'm Kai, by the way.

He pulled a piece of paper from his pocket. It looked like a form. He asked for full name, date of birth, address. Karsten asked what they needed all this for.

– Sæter sets certain conditions for anyone who wants to join.

Karsten raised both hands in protest. – I've no intention of joining anything!

The man called Kai looked very surprised.

– In that case, why are you here?

– Dunno. Just tagged along.

Kai looked at him for a few moments, then showed his unnaturally white teeth in a big grin.

– Okay, Karsten. It's up to you. But I need a couple of answers anyway. Nothing secret, only stuff that's already available from public records.

Karsten was soothed by his friendly tone. He gave concise answers to the questions that followed. No, he was not a member of any political party. Yes, he lived with both his parents. His father worked at the Institute for Energy Research, mother a lawyer, with a seat on the council as a Conservative. No, he was neither Christian, Jew, Muslim or *other*. What am I doing here? he asked himself again. What the hell am I doing here? It helped him to repeat the question over and over again, because that way he could keep all the other thoughts out of his head.

17

He parked by the vehicle licensing centre. Stuck his hand down behind the lining of the car door, pulled out the bag with the fuses, put three of them in his pocket. As he was opening the boot to take out the two bottles of lighter fuel, he changed his mind and left them. Not more than a few hundred metres' walk up to the house on Erleveien. It would take a couple of minutes. A bit too near, he calculated. The car would have to be moved before he could set things in operation.

He took a walk around the property. The frozen wheelbarrow was still standing there outside the tool shed. He had to smile. That told you all you needed to know about the man of the house who found it no easy matter to shove a wheelbarrow under cover for the winter. Let the snow cover it and then melt and it would reappear covered in rust.

The lock on the front door was an ordinary Yale. No safety catch. No warning signs about alarms and security firms. He made another round of the property. At the back of the house he glided up the icy veranda steps, peered in through a gap in the curtains. A golden-brown cone of light slipped from the hallway on to the living-room floor. He had a sudden impulse, tried the latch. To his surprise, the veranda door slid open.

He stood just inside, taking in the smells. Food leftovers, a hint of fish, dust, wet clothing. Clearly this Pentecostal

journalist and his wife had a different attitude towards clean-
liness to the people who had called themselves his parents.
In those days it was always clean in here, always he sharp,
tangy smell of soap with a touch of lemon in it. For a few
days the stench of paint thinner filled the rooms before the
smell of lemon took over again.

He crossed the living-room floor, out into the hallway,
trying to filter out the things associated with the new
occupants, trying to get to the house's real smell. There was
a pram there, and the smell of wet clothes grew stronger,
of sweaty shoes, and something rotten. A bulging plastic
bag full of rubbish stood by the front door. Even taking the
rubbish out before he went to bed was too much trouble
for this guy.

Two bunches of keys hung on hooks next to the fuse box.
Only two of the keys were Yale. They were identical, and
he twisted one off and shoved it into his pocket before
continuing on into the kitchen. There too the smell of rubbish
and naturally of the fish supper. He turned on his flashlight
and glanced around. Piles of dirty dishes stood in the sink.
He noticed how the sight made him shake his head. But
the plugs for the coffee machine and the toaster had been
pulled out. The kettle too. The sort of stuff the fire brigade
recommended, to avoid tragedies at night, when people lay
sleeping. At once he saw the site and the burnt-out remains
of a house. Burnt-out ruins, he thought, and separated the
words: burnt, out.

He tested each step of the staircase up to the first floor.
Checked to see if the same steps still made a noise. Two of
the doors upstairs were ajar. He guessed that the journalist
and his wife slept in the largest room, because that was
where Tord and Gunnhild used to sleep. He stood at the
top of the staircase. Closing his eyes, it was as though he
could hear them again, talking in the room below. He knows

that he's not supposed to hear what they're saying – *We've got to tell him* – but he goes on standing there, listening, the voices washing towards his ears like breaking waves. *He's still so little. Can't we wait?*

It's the evening when Tord has painted the floor in the hallway, and now there's that smell of thinner again, almost as real as it was back then – *We've got to tell him* – and he knows without thinking about it that something is going to happen in this house. Something that once and for all will put an end to the smell of thinner and stop the voices below from ever bothering him again.

He pushed one of the doors open a little wider. Heard the sounds of the two people sleeping in there, the journalist and his wife. And just at that moment it came back to him that he'd gone into Tord and Gunnhild's bedroom after they'd gone to bed that night. With lighter fluid and matches. Stood beside their bed and looked at them. Didn't do anything, because it was enough to know what he could've done.

The room that used to be his was on the right. That was where he was headed. He turned the handle; it moved smoothly. As though the room has been waiting for me, it struck him as he slipped inside. It had a musty smell, stale sweat. He carried on over to the window, opened it slightly. Tord always used to march straight in here and throw it wide open, airing the place, changing the temperature, regulating. Regardless of the time of year, he was in charge of the air that was to be breathed.

By the light of the street lamps that seeped into the room, he looked around. The room still had its pinewood walls, flat planking punctured by knots. At night he used to lie there and trace the patterns made by the dark markings, as if something was written there in a language he must learn to understand.

The wardrobe was full of clothes: jackets and coats, a

suit. He pushed them to one side and shone his torch on the inside short wall. A board was leant up there, at an angle. He crept in, shoving aside the shoes and boots, coaxed it off, shone his torch inside. It smelt like it always had, wood, cardboard, and glass wool that had powdered down from the gaps between the roof beams. This room was still secret, he decided. Neither the Pentecostal nor his wife nor anyone else who had lived there had found it. He shone the torch on to the beam where he used to carve things. The words were still there, ringed around by the burn marks. He had to struggle not to laugh out loud. Had to replace the board, back out of the hole, sit down on the sofa by the long wall, lean his head back and breathe in the night air streaming in through the window. Not a sound in the house, not a sound outside. He sat there and felt himself laughing soundlessly out into the dark, went on sitting there with his eyes closed until the bubbling feeling in his chest eased down.

There was a computer on the desk up against the other wall. It hadn't been turned off, just left in hibernation. He got up and opened it. The desktop was covered with folders. Some of them looked like they contained journalism; one of them was named 'Furutunet'. He realised that the journalist had sat here at this desk and written about the fires, written about him. He found something he'd read in the local paper only that morning. Another document was new, created earlier that evening at about ten o'clock. A detective inspector had made a statement. They'd allocated considerable resources. They were working on certain leads. He sneered. Clicked on a link that was copied there; it opened an article on *VG*'s online edition: *Killer fire claims second victim.*

The article had been posted late in the afternoon but he hadn't had time to check the online editions since the meeting at Sæter's.

The 48-year-old employee rescued from the fire at Furutunet remand home in Nannestad last Wednesday night died of his injuries earlier this evening.

He read the words over and over again. They had nothing, they understood nothing. He could see them, they couldn't see him. Neither the detective inspector nor Sergeant Horvath with the corny moustache and the girlfriend getting laid by another man, and not the journalist sleeping in Tord's old bed. Abruptly he jumped to his feet, crossed to the wall, pressed his ear against it. At first he heard nothing, then a grunt, then silence again.

Once he'd calmed down, he sat in front of the computer again. In the bottom corner of the screen was a document entitled 'Miscellaneous thoughts'. It contained a sort of journal, with dated entries. He checked its details: the document had last been changed at 22.50; that was less than three hours ago.

Rakel asked: Is Uncle Scrooge God? Sara appalled: What are we teaching our children? I had to laugh, she took it so seriously. It was the same last time she was pregnant, she took everything so seriously. I try to get her to laugh more.

God, how much I have to be grateful to you for. Most of all that I feel gratitude. Every day, every evening.

Suddenly a noise behind him, out in the corridor, a door opening. The door to the other bedroom, the smallest one, that was never used when he lived here. It's going to happen again. The thought flashed through him. I'm going to hurt somebody. He turned around. There was a child standing in the doorway. An infant. Hardly more than a year or two old. He held his clenched fist behind his back, forced it to stay there, forced it to keep still. *Don't scream now*, he prayed, *please don't scream.*

– Dwink, said the child.

By the light from the screen he could just make out the

long blond hair, recalled the name *Rakel* on a sign on the door.

– I'll get you some water, he whispered. – Wait here.

He tiptoed down the stairs, could've sneaked out, be gone. He listened. No adults awake. He could allow himself to do anything he liked in this house; they would never catch him. He found a glass on the draining board, turned on the tap, rinsed the glass and filled it half full. Took it out into the hallway again, saw the child still standing there, up at the head of the staircase. Slowly made his way up, listening, ready to turn, get out of there, but there was not a sound to suggest that he was about to be disturbed in the middle of his good deed.

– There we are, Rakel, he whispered as he handed the glass to the child. He stayed where he was, listening to the sound as the little girl drank. It wasn't the thought of this family that caused him to change his mind, not the thought of the pregnant wife and still less of the journalist who used his room as an office and sat there writing about his gratitude to God. None of this that caused the weight to slide back so that the people who had moved into this house would wake in the morning without knowing what had been about to happen. If there was an explanation for the postponement, then it was probably to be found somewhere in the frail sound coming from that little girl's throat as she swallowed the water.

– Now go back to bed, he whispered. – Go to sleep.

He turned and went back down the stairs again, out into the hallway, filled with an agitation he had no idea how to quell. With a laugh too quiet to be heard by anyone else, he picked up the bag of rubbish, let himself out and threw it into the correct container outside the gate.

He had to take a walk through the deserted streets of the town. Couldn't get rid of that laughter. The night watch was dead. Had never regained consciousness. Or had he, and had he told them what he'd seen before he passed away? Hardly possible. But he wanted to know, even though he didn't need to. It had become a game now. He'd seen their cards, knew what they were up to; he was keeping tabs on them and they hadn't a clue.

In the middle of the square he stopped. The moon had settled on the rooftop of the house where she lived, a sharp, curving edge that carved thin slices off the surrounding clouds. He sent a text. *Any chance of a visit?* Didn't expect an answer, but within a minute the display glowed, and another minute after that, he was standing in her hallway. She didn't seem to be wearing make-up; she had on a vest but her lower half was naked. She smelt of sleep. He liked that.

– I would've brought you some flowers, he sniggered.
– But the shop was shut.

She glanced at him in the mirror above the chest of drawers. – Are you on something?

He laughed. – How about fresh air and love?

She opened the kitchen door. – You want some coffee?

He studied the way the muscles of her buttocks tensed when she stood on tiptoes to get the cups down from the cupboard.

– Give me a couple of minutes. I'm not properly awake yet, she said, and drifted into the bathroom.

There was a key cabinet beside the mirror. He found a bunch of car keys, and another one that looked like a spare set of house keys. He opened the front door and checked the lock, then stuck them in his jacket pocket. The thought that he could let himself in any time he felt like it turned him on even more.

When she came out again, she was wearing a pair of tracksuit bottoms.

– That's bad luck, she said. – I just got my period.

Age-old excuse for not having sex. He stood up, grabbed his jacket, mostly to see how she would react.

– Can't you stay anyway?

He shrugged his shoulders. – What about your policeman?

– He's not *my* policeman. Anyhow, he's away.

– Thought he was out catching pyromaniacs. Can't just go away like that.

– He's been working round the clock for the last two weeks. They gave him this weekend off.

He sat down at the kitchen table. – I see the bloke from Furutunet died.

– Yeah, that's right.

He waited for more, but she yawned and was obviously thinking about something completely different.

– Maybe it was him started the fire up there, he suggested.

– And then knocked himself out and dragged himself into the basement?

She shook her head, looked sort of exasperated.

– Did they get anything out of him before he died?

– How should I know?

– I thought your sergeant told you everything.

She gave a quick smile. – Anyone would think he was the one you came here to see.

He laughed. She had no idea how right she was. He could've told her that he knew more about them than they would ever know about him. Horvath, her policeman's name, was a Hungarian name. He lived on Rælingsveien, and his income before tax was about three hundred thousand. A couple of days ago he'd been standing outside her bathroom door, but then turned away with his tail between his legs.

– So you think I'm more interested in what the police get up to than I am in you?

– Are you interested in me?

He pulled her down into his lap. It felt strange – couples

did stuff like that – but she relaxed and leant up against him.

He stroked her throat with a finger.

– Did they get to question him? he repeated.

– What do I get for telling you?

He grinned into her ear. – Whatever you want.

– Whatever I want? She rubbed her cheek against his. – I can tell you're not very smart.

– Well I'm not. But now you have to tell me.

– He died without regaining consciousness. They didn't get anything out of him.

18

Dan-Levi grabbed for the mobile on the bedside table, tried to turn off the alarm before it could wake Sara. She needed all the sleep she could get. He put his glasses on and glanced over at her; she was lying there with her eyes closed, but as he crept towards the door with his underwear and slippers in one hand she murmured:

– Will you take care of Rakel? Can't face getting up.

He walked back to the bed, pressed his lips against her forehead.

– Of course. You just sleep on.

She grunted her thanks, and he sneaked a hand under the duvet and stroked her stomach. This time it was going to be a boy, she thought. It was up to God what it would be. Dan-Levi had always wanted a daughter, and he'd got one. It wasn't good to think like that; it wasn't up to him to prefer one to the other.

He switched on the landing light, and at the same time saw Rakel. She was half sitting and half lying on the top step. Dan-Levi grabbed her up and held her tight. Her body was cold and lifeless, and it seemed to him that her lips were blue. He gave a great shout and ran into the bedroom with her. Sara sat up with a start.

– She was lying out on the landing, he managed to say as he laid Rakel in the bed.

At that moment their daughter opened her eyes and looked at them in surprise.

– Thank God, shouted Dan-Levi. – Thank God on high.

Sara switched on the light. – Have you gone out of your mind?

He stroked Rakel's hair. She smiled sleepily and cuddled up beside her mother.

– I found her on the stairs. She must have got out of bed and sat down there.

Sara felt the girl's chest with her hand. – She's cold.

Dan-Levi leant over her. – What were you doing out on the landing?

Rakel looked up at him with big wide-open eyes. Once before she'd managed to climb over the bars of her cot; they'd spoken about securing it in some way or other, but Dan-Levi hadn't got round to it yet.

– Dwink, she said.

Now he jumped to his feet, as though this request finally told him that his daughter was all right.

– You can have milk, as much as you want.

He hurried out of the room. At the top of the staircase, where he'd found her, stood a glass with a little water left in it. He took it into the bedroom.

– Did you get up and give Rakel a drink of water?

Sara had slid back down into the bed; she peered out through the tiny gap between her eyelids.

– Been lying here the whole night, far as I know.

Again Dan-Levi bent over his daughter. – Did you get up and get yourself something to drink?

Rakel had started to speak early; she often woke up in the night and was always thirsty. But that she should have made her way down to the kitchen and helped herself to a glass of water was pretty well unthinkable.

– The man, she replied with a coy smile.

– The man? What man?

– The man bring water.

– Leave her alone, Sara interrupted. – She's tired, I'm tired and I'm feeling sick.

– Water Man, Rakel insisted.

Dan-Levi went downstairs, fetched a glass of milk. When he came up again, he exclaimed: – I don't understand this at all. There was no chair by the sink. Can she have put it back again?

– Water Man, Rakel repeated as she slurped milk from the glass.

Sara managed a smile. – Can't you hear what she's saying? The drinks man with the water was here. You're just going to have to make do with that, Dan.

She fitted the duvet around Rakel and turned her back on Dan-Levi. He sat on the side of the bed and said his morning prayers. Ended by giving thanks for having such a lovely daughter. And such a lovely wife. He valued them more than anything else he could think of.

It was mild out. It was the Friday before Palm Sunday, and the last of the snow hung like a dripping tongue over the eaves. Dan-Levi had planned to knock it down where it was thickest, but now it was disappearing by itself. He locked the door behind him, only now able to laugh at the way his daughter had wanted a *dwink* in the night and the *Water Man* had come to her rescue.

As he was about to go down the steps, he remembered that he'd put the rubbish ready to go out in the hall. He'd been so tired the previous evening he'd fallen asleep on the sofa, too worn out to make the eight metres down to the front gate. He stuck his head inside, couldn't find the bag, was about to call to Sara, but the thought of the two of them sleeping up there in the bed, Rakel curled up next to her living tummy, made him change his mind.

Out on the steps once more he saw Karsten Clausen come

ambling towards him across the frozen flagstones. His bicycle was leant up against the open gate.

– Bit early in the year for a spin, isn't it, he joked.

Karsten shrugged his shoulders. – Imagine what the world would be like if everyone drove a car.

Despite the jocular tone, Dan-Levi felt a twinge of conscience. He used his car too much. He only needed it for work occasionally.

– You off to your cabin in the mountains for Easter? he wanted to know.

– Mum and Dad are leaving this afternoon, Karsten replied. – Think I'll stay at home. Haven't made up my mind yet.

– Chess club on Tuesday for those who can make it, Dan-Levi informed him. – I'll give you a game, if you dare.

Karsten had been a member of the chess club since he was nine. In the early days their games had been pretty much even, but it was years now since Dan-Levi had had even the faintest glimmer of a chance against him.

– I probably won't be able to make it. Got quite a bit on my mind at the moment.

Dan-Levi had the feeling Karsten wanted to say more, and stood there, looking round and waiting. Next to the nearest flagstone was half a cigarette. He picked it up. Three matches of the kind you got at hotels were fastened to it with a rubber band. None of their recent visitors were smokers, so the cigarette must have been lying there a while. But on the other hand, it wasn't frozen to the ground.

– Is it you who's been making matchstick men?

He held the little figure up.

– Is that some kind of toy? Karsten peered at it.

– You should know. No one else could have dropped it here.

Karsten shook his head. He looked troubled.

– Don't give me that, Dan-Levi persisted. – This is your footprint, isn't it?

Joking, he bent down and examined the footprint next to where he had found the cigarette.

– The pattern of the sole here looks like a map. Let me see the bottom of your boot.

– Ha ha, said Karsten.

Dan-Levi held the cigarette up next to his ear. – Don't deny it was you who made me, Karsten, he said in a hoarse voice.

Karsten grinned fleetingly but still didn't look too happy.

– You know what happens if you won't quit sucking away on things like me? Dan-Levi croaked, thinking that this was actually a good idea for a puppet show: use cigarettes and butts for the different parts. Something to try out on the kids at the Bethany centre. But he didn't want that kind of thing lying about in his own front garden. Rakel was not only always thirsty, she also had an astonishingly strong urge to put everything she came across into her mouth. He tossed the matchstick figure into the bin.

– Was there something you wanted to talk to me about, something else beside chess?

Karsten cast a quick glance at him, and Dan-Levi felt pretty sure he was right in his surmise. But before he could say anything else, Karsten mounted his bicycle, waved goodbye and headed off down Erleveien.

19

HE JUMPED UP. A thick grey light seeped through the curtain. He swore quietly and pulled on his trousers. Shouldn't have slept, not in this room, not beside her. He turned towards the bed. Monica wasn't there. The bedroom door was ajar; he saw her sitting in the living room, half turned away from him. She was holding a mobile phone in her hand. Her own was lying on the living-room table. He was about to open the door wide. Just then he heard a faint sound. It came from the mobile she was fiddling with. The sound of a siren. With an effort he was able to pick up other sounds, because he knew every detail of that particular video. It was his own commentary he was hearing now, and the distant booming of the burning stable.

He took charge of his anger. Turned it into something that could be melted down and reused, no matter what it was he was going to have to do. Without moving a muscle, he watched her as she sat there and played the video clips from his phone. Her wet hair just about reached her shoulders. There was a plate on the table in front of her, a glass of juice half full, a steaming cup. She found the clips from Furutunet and the nursery school before returning to Stornes farm. She played it over again before getting up and putting the phone back in his jacket pocket. She carried on fumbling there; he knew what she'd find. Her hand re-emerged holding the spare keys he had taken. She stood there a moment, studying them, and he heard her muttering something or other to herself. But not until she had replaced the keys in the pocket, picked up her own phone and started to dial did he emerge from the bedroom. She jolted as though hit by an electric shock. For a second she stared at him, two seconds, her pupils dilating, then her glance slid away. The hand holding the mobile sank to her side.

– Hi, she said, her voice unnaturally loud. – I didn't want to wake you.

He took a few steps towards her. No decision had yet been taken. He stopped no more than half a metre away from her. There was a smell of coffee and toast. She glanced up at him, and he searched for something in her eyes, some kind of solution, something they could both laugh about, but he couldn't find anything but fear in her gaze. She was wearing a white blouse and narrow skirt. Ready to go to work. She stood there as though frozen. She wouldn't be going to work. Abruptly he felt sorry for her.

– I need to make a call, she said, so quietly it was almost inaudible.

He took the phone from her. It said *Roar* on the display, but the call had not been placed. It was just the touch of a fingertip away, a slight pressure on the OK button. And then he knew how it would happen.

– Go into the bathroom.

– I've just showered, she murmured.

– You have showered, he said. – You smell good.

– Got to go to work, she whispered. – Got a meeting, starts in a few minutes.

He shook his head.

– They'll wonder where I am, she said. – I'm never late.

– They'll wonder where you are, he said, and took her by the arm, not hard, mostly to feel the tension in it, weigh the resistance.

A tremor passed through her chest, as though a scream

had just been born in there, and he shot out a hand and clamped it over her open mouth. The scream collided with his palm and was thrown back inside her, coming out through the pores of her skin and through her eyes. She began to struggle, but it took no more than a twist of the arm and her body was locked.

– Come on, he said, and walked her into the bathroom.

Still steam in there. It had coated the mirror and windows. Mingling with the smells of herbal soap and creams. On the edge of the washbasin an open box of tampons. So she hadn't been bluffing about that, he registered.

– You're a good girl, he said, and relaxed his grip.

She struggled for breath. – I have to go, she tried again.

– Fill the bathtub.

– No.

Her voice had taken on contours now, as if it focused in the steam. He took hold of her arm again, still not hard, but hard enough to make her bend forward and put the plug in.

– Turn on the tap.

She did as she was told.

What are you going to do?

He smiled, but everything was different now and he saw that it frightened her.

– Nothing that will hurt, he assured her. – You told me what I came to hear. You don't need to speak any more.

She reached out a hand, placed it against his flies. He took it away.

– I'm not like that, he said, avoiding the use of her name. Mustn't start to mess up now. Don't think too much.

– Get undressed.

She looked down. – I'm bleeding.

– You can keep your panties on.

When she stood there, half turned away, he saw that she was trembling.

– You're cold. Get in.

She didn't respond.

– Get in, he said again, and heard how his voice was suddenly sharp, though he felt no anger, nor even annoyance.

He didn't want her to be afraid. He opened the bathroom cupboard, pulled out a packet of Valium and a tray of Imovane, filled a glass with water and handed it to her with a tablet of each, but she turned her head away.

He looked at his watch. Twenty past eight.

– Take them. Not a lot else is going to happen.

She took the tablets, dropped them in the bathwater.

A grimace flickered across his face. – That's a shame, he sighed, and took another two tablets from each packet. – Now we're going to have to double it up.

She shut her mouth tight. He took her by the hair, bent her head back, forced the tablets in between her lips and followed them with the water. She coughed and gasped; bits of tablet and spittle ran down across her chin.

He waited until she was breathing normally again. – It's a pity you're making this so difficult, he said calmly, and handed her another four tablets.

Reluctantly she took them and swallowed them down. Afterwards she squatted at one end of the bathtub, holding around her knees with her hands. The water still reached no higher than to her ankles. He stood by the washbasin and waited as it crept up over her legs.

– If you go now . . . she began to say.

He sat on the edge of the bathtub. – If I go now?

She stared straight ahead. – I'll never say anything.

– Say anything?

– About the fires, she whispered.

He laid his hand on her shoulder, stroked it. The skin was ice cold.

– That's good. Don't say anything about it.

She looked up at him. – Will you go? An almost imperceptible slurring had crept into her voice. – Can I finish this alone?

He continued to caress her neck.

– I don't want you to be alone.

She lowered her head. – I can help you.

He liked her for saying that, regardless of what she meant; it was a nice thing to say. Just then her mobile rang. It was still lying on the living-room table.

– Can I take that? Please?

She looked up at him again, and for a few seconds he met her pleading gaze.

– You don't need anyone else now, he said.

The water had risen halfway up her legs.

– Wait here.

He stood up, taking the pills with him. There was a mortar on the kitchen worktop. As he emptied them into it, he heard splashing sounds from the bathroom and then steps in the hallway. Within two seconds he was there. She stood fumbling with the lock on the front door. Momentarily he thought of letting her open it and get out on to the staircase.

He grabbed her from behind. She screamed and kicked at the door. He wrapped both arms around her, one hand under her chin, pressing it upwards so the teeth clashed, lifted the dripping body, carried her back to the bathroom and placed her carefully back in the tub.

– Finish your bath first, he said quietly into her ear. Back in the kitchen, he stood so that he was able to keep an eye on the bathroom door as he pounded the tablets to a dust in the mortar. She might scream again. It would take a couple of seconds to get to her. She might have got up, broken a glass, found a pair of scissors. He dismissed the thought with a shake of the head. That trembling girl in the bathtub wasn't capable of anything like that any more.

He was very thorough about it. By the time he was finished, there were fifteen Imovane and twenty Valium in the powdered mix. He found orange juice in the fridge, emptied the powder into the drink, stirred and stirred until most of it had dissolved.

In the bathroom, the tub was full, water splashing down on to the floor. She sat in the same position, staring straight ahead. He turned off the tap, handed her the glass.

– Here.

She didn't move.

– Then I'll just have to help you again, he said quietly and lifted up her chin with a finger, squeezed his hand around her mouth, opened up a gap between her lips into which he could pour.

– Don't be afraid, Monica. I'll look after you.

20

THE WINDOW WAS slightly open. There was a chaffinch sitting on the roof guttering; it sounded happy. The feathers on its head rose up into a crest as it sang in the afternoon sunlight, its own little Mohican. Karsten knew perfectly well that the song wasn't an expression of joy but that the bird made these sounds as a way of marking out its territory. It didn't want any other males there competing for the females and the food. He closed the window, tried once again to concentrate on the drawing he'd made, a round disc penetrated by a cylinder. It might just as well have been a manhole cover. The business of Archimedes' gravestone was one of his maths teacher's bad ideas. He leant forward across his desk, studied the drawing, went through the formulae again, knew that a simple solution lay just around the corner, but his thoughts kept wanting to go off in another direction.

It was Friday. He'd had a text from Jasmeen. *6 o'clock*. That was all. Nothing else. It came this morning as he stood in the bathroom brushing his teeth. He'd tried to call back: no answer. He was about to change his mind, go with his parents to the mountain cabin anyway, but just then Adrian had rung. The conversation didn't last long, a couple of minutes maybe. Adrian did most of the talking.

A few minutes later, on his way down Erleveien, Karsten had seen Dan-Levi come out on to the steps. He parked his bicycle, suddenly determined to tell him everything. About

Jasmeen, about Adrian, about the meeting with that Sæter. But as he was about to begin, Dan-Levi started fooling around with a cigarette he'd found on the ground. After that it was too late.

When his father looked in on him, Karsten was busy with his physics assignment. The change in the speed of an atom of oxygen when emitting a photon. That kind of thing. How much mass the sun loses per second, given the total effect of its radiation. Simple problems. His father peered over his shoulder. The little cough was a sign that he had seen at once that Karsten's solutions were correct.

– No clouds in sight, he reported. – But if you do tear the house down, make sure it's back up again before Maundy Thursday, five p.m. at the latest.

He chuckled, probably to show he was only joking. Karsten followed him downstairs and out on to the steps. Synne had wound down the back window of the car.

– Remember what you promised to do?

Karsten rubbed his chin and pretended to be thinking. – What was it again? Am I supposed to be feeding your pets?

– I'll kill you, she warned him. Just recently her language had got a lot rougher; he wasn't sure that he liked it.

– I'm supposed to record a programme for you. *Sesame Street*, wasn't it?

Her eyes narrowed, but he could tell that she was struggling not to laugh.

– I'll kill you, she said again. – I'll drip poison in your ear while you're sleeping.

A strange way to kill someone. Something she must have got from a TV series or one of the hundreds of books she read. She had almost finished *The Lord of the Rings*; he'd never even started it.

– Stop teasing, his father ordered. – She'll only take it out on us.

Karsten nodded his head several times. The same way Adrian did, it occurred to him. – Okay. Michael Jackson.

– The whole programme!

He stood on the steps and watched them drive away before going into the living room and flopping down on to the sofa. The silence came in waves, almost like something that hurt. Suddenly he leapt up, wandered around from room to room. It was five thirty. He fetched his maths book, drew the gravestone and the cylinder once more on one of the blank pages at the back. Instead of writing out the formulae, he carried on playing about with the drawing. He didn't write Archimedes' name on the gravestone but instead put his own initials and date of birth, followed by a hyphen. Played with the idea of adding a date after the hyphen. Fifty years on, maybe, or just one. He thought of Adrian's mother, who sat with a deck of cards and told people's futures. Why not ask Elsa Wilkins about that date, as an experiment?

Another idea struck him. He fetched a dice from his yatzy box. Made out a table giving values to the different numbers of dots that came up and started to roll it. The day of his death came out to be this year, even this month. He shook his head at all this nonsense but still realised that he was reluctant to roll the dice twice more to find out what day.

At that moment there was a ring at the doorbell. Two short rings. Despite the text, he had never believed she would show up. Had hoped she would change her mind. It would be a relief, it would be a disappointment. He didn't know which was worse.

It had started to rain, and before he had opened the door properly Jasmeen was inside. He'd turned off the light by the front door. She stood there in the half-dark, a black scarf around her head.

– You came, he managed to say at last.

– Did you think I wouldn't?

– No, course not. Well, I wasn't sure.

She unbuttoned her coat. Underneath she was wearing an outfit in some kind of silky material. It was light brown, with a reddish sheen. A large floral motif was sewn on the outside, across the hips. She was from another world.

– You think I look weird.

– Not at all.

– Had to say I was going to visit my cousin. So that meant I had to wear this.

She was still holding her coat in her hand. He took it off her and hung it up.

– I trust Rashida better than anybody else I know.

He let her pass; they went into the living room. – Will you be going back to school soon?

She turned towards him. – I don't know.

– Can't you just go?

She shook her head. – You don't understand, Karsten. She took a quick look around the room before adding: – They want to take me with them to Pakistan. They've arranged for me to be married there. In the summer.

She walked over to him, took his hand. – He's thirty-five and he has bad teeth and can hardly read. I'll never do it. Understand?

– You've spoken to Adrian about this, Karsten asserted. She nodded. – He's helping me

– How?

Now she hesitated slightly. – He's telephoned my dad, she said after a while. – Dad acted funny afterwards. He was both angry and upset. Adrian told me he knew my family from before. I had no idea.

– Have they said anything more about making this complaint?

– They've given up that idea.

– Because Adrian rang?

She turned away. – My father's changed his mind about it anyway, and Shahzad's always been opposed to it. Karsten, can we talk about something else?

– Shahzad would prefer to beat me up, isn't that what you mean?

She looked at him for a long time. – He won't do that. Not now.

They were still standing in the middle of the floor. She leant forward, pressed her cheek against his. She smelt different. Maybe the rain had washed away the sweet sharpness that usually surrounded her.

– I think about you, Karsten. All night, all day. That's why I'm here.

Now she'd said it. If she were to leave without anything more happening, he would remember this. He put an arm around her, pulled her down on to the sofa, pressed his lips against her neck. Suddenly she stood up again.

– I need to use the bathroom.

He was still sitting there when she came back. She stood in the middle of the room. A kind of dark red cape hung down behind her dress, all the way to the floor. She followed his gaze, lifted it and rolled it up. – I look stupid.

He leant back and looked up at the ceiling, and suddenly she was there beside him, stroking his hair. He put his arms around her, his fingers gliding over the silky material. She pulled herself free and sat down beside him on the sofa.

– Be careful, Karsten. She took his hand away from one of her breasts, where it had found its way without any effort on his part. – We have to be careful, she repeated quietly. – If it's going to be us.

He didn't know what to do with the rejected hand. He sneaked it casually down into his groin, where everything was squashed painfully together. She put her hand on top of his.

– Do you have a bed? she asked in a low voice. – A big bed.

– Yes, he almost shouted, and was on his feet and out into the hall.

She followed him up the stairs. He pushed open the door of his parents' bedroom. Or actually, his father slept in his office down in the basement.

– It's cold in here, he said, and turned the radiator on full.

– Have you got a candle?

He ran down to the kitchen, sped back up again with a three-armed candlestick holder, prepared for the fact that she might have changed her mind. But she was still standing there by the foot of the bed. He fumbled with the matches, finally managed to light the wicks.

– I want us to undress and lie naked on the bed together, she said.

He nodded, too breathless to say anything.

– But you mustn't touch me, do you promise me that?

He must have nodded again, because she turned away and unbuttoned her dress. The candlelight cast nervous shadows across her naked back, like strange creatures that wriggled and bucked and tried to swallow each other. Still with her back turned she let the dress fall down over her hips, unfastened her bra, pulled down her knickers. Then she turned to face him, stood there with her arms by her sides, one leg slightly in front of the other.

– Now it's your turn.

He started to fiddle with his buttons, gave up and pulled the shirt off over his head. Somehow or other his belt buckle was already undone and the zip on his flies had opened itself. He stepped out of his trousers, into the cold room, lay stretched out on the bed, less than a metre away from her, the first girl who'd ever undressed for him, the first ever to see him like this, with his stunted balls dangling on the bedclothes.

She reached out and picked up a belt from the heap of clothing, laid it along the centre of the bed.

– You mustn't cross this belt, she said, her voice low.

He grunted something or other, the sound from his throat transformed into small shivers that traversed his body to end up between his legs, a reminder of the intolerable agonies he'd suffered the night he woke up because one of his testicles had twisted round its own axis and cut off the supply of blood that kept it alive. That same night it was surgically removed.

– I want you to come close to me, she whispered. – But don't touch me.

He felt her breath against his shoulder. The body lying on the other side of the belt occasioned tiny movements in the springs of the mattress. She lay like that for a long time. Then her breath moved down across his chest.

– You mustn't touch me, he heard her whisper again.

– No, he moaned, and then it occurred to him that she was going to examine him, see if what she had heard was true, that he was practically a cripple, walking around with the poorest man in the world dangling between his leg, just the one rock in his sack, an evolutionary cul-de-sac. But her breath approached ever closer. As he readied himself for it to disappear again, it closed itself around him. He saw an image of Archimedes' gravestone, the cylinder that penetrated it. Suddenly the simple solution to the problem came to him; it was so obvious he had to shout it out loud.

*　*　*

He stood in the middle of the kitchen floor, saw the reflection of his naked body in the window. A thought struck him; he slipped out into the hallway and picked up the mobile from the chest of drawers, took a picture of himself in the light from the living-room door.

– What are you doing? Jasmeen sat on the sofa, dressed now, with a blanket wrapped around her.

He turned around, took a few steps in her direction, lifted the mobile and clicked.

– You mustn't, she cried out and raised her hands. – You've got to delete it, understand?

He promised to do that, went out to the kitchen again and put the kettle on, heard a text arrive. *We're at Martin's. You coming?*

Tonje hadn't forgotten. The old fear rose again, that the whole thing was a kind of student rag week stunt: you invite a nerd along and laugh yourselves sick when he takes it seriously and actually turns up. Inga was capable of that, or one of the other girls, but not Tonje. She wasn't like that.

When he returned to the living room with the kettle, Jasmeen was still sitting on the sofa. He sat down beside her.

– Tea for you.

– You're nice, she murmured.

At that moment he was certain she meant it. He poured the boiling water over the tea bag in her cup. Saw how the grey, felt-like material became more and more translucent, how the fibres of the tea leaves absorbed the liquid in the steaming cup.

– I must go soon, she said. – But I'll never regret this. No matter what happens. She glanced at the clock. – I don't regret it, she repeated, and placed the dripping tea bag on the saucer. – What are you thinking?

He had never liked to share his thoughts with anyone, at least not when anyone asked him to.

– I've found the other solution, he told her anyway.

– What other solution?

He leant back on the sofa. – The maths problem. The cylinder and the gravestone. I could see there was a simpler way of solving it. Just now, up there, I found it.

She gaped. – Were you lying there thinking about maths problems?

He realised he should have been thinking about something else. – That too, he admitted.

She shook her head.

– But it's so ludicrously simple, he said, and explained that the relationship between the cylinder's surface and its volume had to be the same as that between the sphere's surface and volume, so that it was just a matter of establishing a simple formula that could be resolved in a single calculation. What was incredible was that it had taken him three days to come up with such an obvious answer.

– Do you think you'll ever be able to believe in God, Karsten?

He sat up, took a swig of coffee. What he believed in was a game where the pieces were measurable entities of various sorts. That organic life arose in a particle soup. It was an act of chance. Within that soup, molecules formed which were able to make copies of themselves. He got bogged down in an explanation he couldn't find a way out of.

– You fool yourself into believing a much too simple story, she interrupted. – None of what you say could have happened if there wasn't a God behind it all.

– Maybe you're right, he said. – And maybe you're wrong. We can't know anything about it.

She turned the warm cup around in her hands. – Could you be a Muslim?

He'd just taken a sip; had to cough and just about managed to swallow it down. Even though she couldn't possibly be asking in all seriousness, he had no wish to laugh at her. Not after what had happened.

– Could just as easily be a Muslim as a Christian at any rate, he said diplomatically. – You thinking of having me baptised?

She put the cup down, and he wrapped both his arms around her. Clearly nothing he did counted as touching her body, because there wasn't a single place his fingers weren't allowed to wander, as long as they stayed outside her clothes.

– You don't get baptised a Muslim, she said softly. – You join a fellowship. She pressed herself in close to him. – I could never share my life with a non-believer.

He didn't answer. The caffeine was already racing around inside his brain, and what had happened upstairs in his mother's bed might happen again. He was holding a five of diamonds, or a three of clubs, but for some inconceivable reason it was still possible to win after all.

21

KARSTEN GAVE BREAKFAST a miss, drank a half-litre of orange juice, pulled on his tracksuit and trainers. It was still raining out; that suited him fine. No wind, just thin, cold threads dropping in straight lines from the sky.

Dan-Levi was busy in his garden, trying to free a wheelbarrow that seemed to be stuck to the ground. Again Karsten felt the urge to tell his chess-playing pal what had happened. He didn't know what had happened. Only that the world had turned upside down and been shaken up so much that everything had come loose and landed somewhere else. He'd spent most of last night going over things. One was what she had said as she was leaving. It was just after ten. She'd stopped at the bottom of the stairs, climbed back up again, stood on tiptoes and kissed him. And then she'd said those three words. Astonished, he had repeated them. Actually, it had sounded more like a question. But then afterwards, once she'd disappeared out the gate, the words had continued to whirl round in his head. Words didn't necessarily mean all that much; what mattered was that they'd been naked together. In other words, they had a relationship. But one they couldn't have. She was from another world. He must avoid her. He must see her again.

As he was passing the end of the landing strip, his mobile began vibrating. He stopped, pulled it out of his pocket. But the message was from Tonje. *Pity you didn't come yesterday.* The strange thing was not that she had sent it, he reasoned.

The strange thing was that he wasn't surprised. He answered: *Are you home?*

It took ten minutes for him to run there. As he was crossing Storgata, a black BMW passed. A man was out walking his dog; it was black too. And the clouds towering up in the west over the river Nitelva were, of course, also black, or at least almost black. He carried on enumerating black objects, and by the time he rang on Tonje's doorbell, he had reached seventeen.

Her mother opened the door.

– Hello, Karsten, she exclaimed, as though it was the most natural thing in the world to find him standing there. – Do come inside.

– She was slender and blond. Tonje looked like her, but her colouring was darker. Evolution tossed features around like that. Combining and recombining over and over again.

He stayed outside. – There was just something I wanted to ask Tonje.

She appeared in the hallway. The mother withdrew with a little smile that might have meant anything.

– Was just down the road when I got your message, he assured her. – Thought I might as well pop in.

– You didn't come yesterday.

– Something cropped up.

She seemed to accept the explanation. He climbed up a step, bent forward and gave her a quick kiss that landed on the side of her mouth.

She looked at him in surprise. – What's going on?

– Is something going on?

– You seem different.

She stepped back inside, over the threshold.

– We can always meet some other time, she said, and straight away it reminded him of the first line of a song they were made to learn in primary school.

– What about tonight? he suggested, and almost began singing.

– Maybe.

– Have any plans?

– Don't think so.

He breathed as calmly as he could. – Are you going out with Thomas?

She shrugged her shoulders. – That was ages ago.

A few days? he should have asked but couldn't. He suddenly felt dizzy, took a step backwards and nearly tripped over the top step.

– Call you later, he said quickly.

She crossed the threshold again, ran her finger between her lips and pressed it against the tip of his nose.

– Don't forget, she urged him. – Wow, you seem really out of it.

He hopped down the steps and jogged over to the gate, turned right, speeded up and ran as fast as he could. He would run far. Further than his usual route. Run himself to exhaustion and slow his thoughts down that way. At the narrow railway underpass he saw a BMW, black and newly polished, and it occurred to him that he had seen it somewhere else not long ago. Through the tinted windows he could make out four or five passengers. He continued under the main road, towards the marina, turned up in the direction of the industrial estate. A greyish-brown shaggy dog snapped at him as he passed; it wasn't on a leash, but the owner gave it a telling-off and brought it back to heel. An F-16 took off from the airport, filling the town with a monstrous roar.

At that moment a large black car came speeding by, turned in towards the factory and screeched to a halt a few metres in front of him. It was the BMW again, and the thought that this manoeuvre might have something to do with him just had time to occur to him before two of the doors were slung open wide. He spun round, saw a guy in a dark jacket walking towards him across the yard. Pakistanis, it flashed through him, they're going to get me. He whipped round the corner of the building; the fenced-in parking lot was deserted, it was Saturday, Easter holidays. He wrenched at the gate, it was locked. By the time he turned round, they had encircled him. The guy in the black jacket on the left, another one, big guy, wearing a suit. A third, just in his shirtsleeves, came straight for him, took aim, lifted something: a bat, Karsten just had time to register. The blow struck him in the side, he staggered back towards the fencing, fell.

Got to get away, he moaned. Somewhere far off a dog barked. Two of the men stood over him. One of them said something in a foreign accent. Karsten heard the words, but had trouble making sense of them. Something about him having a debt, that he owed them something or other. Then the other one bent over him and waved a knife in his face. The blade was broad, highly polished, slightly curved.

– Listen real good now while you still can.

They're going to do it shot through him.

The guy bent even closer. There was a smell of raw meat from his mouth, as though he'd just eaten an animal alive, or dead.

– We're not going to kill you straight away. We've got another way of doing it to guys who rape. Know what we cut off?

He fumbled inside the waistband of Karsten's trousers, ripped off the button. Karsten screamed and bent double, a warm wetness squirting down the inside of his trouser leg. He could hear the guy laughing and saying something to the others in a foreign language.

– I haven't raped anyone, Karsten yelled. – She came to me. The explanation clearly made no impression.

– We know all about you.

Several hands grabbed him, turned him over.

– The same thing could happen to your sister. The same thing you did. Have you thought about that?

He was held down while his trousers were pulled off. Laughter. Knife blade against his stomach, cutting into him. Karsten's bowels emptied in a flood; he registered the stink instantly. One of the guys pulled his hands away. – What the fuck, are you shitting on me?

Another sound into the mix now: the barking of a dog, which came slinking round the corner. The same one he'd jogged past earlier. The men backed off a few metres, speaking to each other low and sharp in their foreign language.

Karsten was on his feet and clambering up the fence. One of the men chased after him. The dog leapt at him, barking wildly. The man let go and tried to kick it away. Karsten reached the top of the fence, rolled over and dropped down on to the other side. The guy in the suit, the biggest of them, climbed after him. Karsten got to his feet, pulling his trousers up as he ran over the open ground. Passing a warehouse, he cast a glance behind him. The guy in the suit was still following. Another one was climbing over the fence. He saw no sign of the dog. He leapt up on to a ramp, pulled at a sliding door. It didn't move. He jumped down again, sped round the corner. There was a container there, he jumped up on to it, pulled open the lid. There were a few cardboard boxes at the bottom. He wriggled in under the lid and it closed behind him with a crash that sent thunderbolts through his ears. What have you done? he babbled to himself, and knew that nothing would ever be right again. What have you done? he said again as he crept under a flattened cardboard box and moulded himself into an unmoving form.

Voices outside, one dark and one light; he couldn't hear what they were saying. They went away, came back again. The side door was opened. The waiting was unendurable. He counted the seconds, pulling each one up from an unfathomable depth, dragging them over the side, rolling them away. He'd got as far as ten and was on the point of giving up and handing himself over when the door slammed shut again and the light voice shouted something.

He pulled out his mobile. It was ten past twelve. He'd been lying there for half an hour. He waited ten more minutes, fifteen. Then he sat up, peered up at the door. Waited a few more minutes before creeping out and jumping down to the ground. He heard a sound from the warehouse and ran for all he was worth, not turning round. He clambered over the fence at the end of the yard, ran through a bog, sank to his knees, hauled himself up again. He found a track on the far side that led to the footpath running along the riverbank. He looked up, looked down, up again. Then he collapsed, blacked out for a moment, and heard the voice of the guy with the knife. *The same thing could happen to your sister. The same thing you did.* Nothing must happen to Synne, he groaned as he staggered along the footpath, heading towards the bridge.

Adrian answered the call immediately. Karsten didn't know what to say. He was leaning against one of the arches of the bridge, surrounded by empty beer cans and plastic bags of rubbish. He mustn't stay there. If they came at him from one direction, he could outrun them, he knew he could. But if they worked out where he was, split up and approached from both sides, he had nowhere to run, nowhere else to go but into that muddy, swift-flowing river with its spinning chips of thin ice.

– Trouble? Adrian asked.

– They followed me in the car, Karsten managed to say. – Tried to kill me.

– Are you hurt?

He pulled up his jacket and vest. Blood seeped from a thin cut that ran across his stomach.

– They cut me. I'm bleeding slightly.

– The Pakis?

– Yes.

– Where are you now?

Karsten told him. – Must get to the police, he stammered.

– Think about it, Adrian interrupted. – There are two places they're going to be looking for you. One is by the police station. The other is at your house.

– They're threatening to get Synne, Karsten sobbed.

– Shit, Adrian growled. – That is never going to happen, do you hear? Leave it to me.

The anger in his voice was something to hold on to. Mustn't let go, Karsten thought.

– Can *you* call the police? he gasped.

There was a pause before Adrian answered. – Let's just wait. Got to keep a cool head here.

– What shall I do? He said the four words over and over again.

– The Pakis won't go all the way out to your cabin, Adrian said. – Synne's safe for the time being. And we'll help you.

– Where are you?

– Not far from where we had the meeting. We're in the woods. I'll come and pick you up in two hours.

– Hours? Karsten sobbed, unable to stop.

– Go round to my place, said Adrian. – Make sure no one sees you. I'll tell Elsa to let you in.

As he dragged himself up from the footpath, into Strandgata and along in the direction of the open-air swimming pool, he was frozen to the bone. He cast an exhausted glance in both directions before opening the gates of the red-painted semi.

Elsa opened the door even before he'd rung.

– What do you look like!

Karsten turned away, unable to meet her eyes. He'd messed himself and waded across a bog. Couldn't even feel any shame. Not yet.

– Adrian says you were attacked. Her voice was warm and friendly and calm. – I was thinking about you just today, she added.

Impossible not to believe she meant it.

– Adrian's got some clothes here.

Without waiting for him to respond, she disappeared into the cellar and came back up again with a pair of underpants, a T-shirt and a pair of old tracksuit bottoms.

– These'll have to do for the time being. What you need now is a shower.

She opened a door just outside the kitchen, dug out some towels, which she put over the edge of the bathtub. Karsten went in, pulled off his stinking clothes and rolled them into a ball. Then he turned the water on full and huddled beneath the warm shower.

Elsa came into the room with a bottle, poured him a glass. He'd never liked red wine, but now he took whatever he was given.

She sat in the chair opposite and looked straight at him. She was wearing a red pullover. She was pretty. Suddenly she exclaimed, – Oh, but you're bleeding! Let me have a look.

He stood up, pulled up the T-shirt, which was stained a colour similar to that of the red wine. Blood oozed from the cut below his navel. It seemed deeper now than last time he'd looked. Elsa fetched some antiseptic and bandaging, dried it carefully. The blood had run down below the waist-band of the trousers. – You won't need any stitches, she noted. – But who would do a thing like this?

– Some people. They're after me.

– Well that's pretty obvious. Of course you don't have to tell me what happened if you don't want to.

He did want to. He wanted to talk to her about everything that was troubling him. And suddenly he was telling her about Jasmeen, about the meeting at the library, about the accusation of abuse, about her wanting to come to his house. And that she came. He searched for the right words.

– I'm a total idiot, he muttered. – No girl has ever been interested in me, not until now. And I screw the whole thing up.

Elsa patted him on the arm. – Regretting isn't going to do you much good, Karsten.

He glanced over at her, her face, the dark red pullover. He felt distant, uneasy; he didn't know what was going on. And in the middle of it all, this urge to say out loud how pretty she was.

– What happens to me doesn't really matter. It wasn't exactly true, but it helped to say it. – The worst thing is, they're threatening Synne.

– Synne's your little sister?

He nodded. – If anything happens to her . . . He couldn't think the thought through to the end. Tears welled up inside him and ran down his cheeks. He raised his head, wanted her to see them.

– You're a good boy, Karsten.

– You don't know me, he protested.

– Oh, better than you think.

He opened his mouth, couldn't bring himself to say anything.

– You've been showing up in my cards recently. Several times.

Even that sounded right now. He wanted to show up in her cards. He wanted to credit her with possessing all those powers he would normally laugh at. With knowing things about him without anybody having told her, with knowing what was going to happen. He could have asked her to read to him, fairy tales even, as long as things made sense.

– What happens when I show up in your cards?

She took a sip of her drink, stood up. – I'll show you.

The room upstairs was bigger than he had imagined it. A table with a dark red cloth stood in the middle of the floor. The curtains, also red, were drawn, and the light came from a lamp in one corner. Smoke threaded its way up from two bowls on the table; that must be the source of the sweet smell that filled the house.

She indicated for him to sit in a chair at the table, lit a candle, sat down opposite him. For a while she just looked at him. It felt natural for her to do so, not embarrassing the way it might have been in different circumstances.

– Close your eyes, she ordered.

He did as he was told.

– First I want you to relax. You've had a frightening experience. Someone's threatened to kill you. And they've threatened your sister, whom you love more than anyone else on earth.

He nodded. What she said was right, though he'd never thought of it before.

– Breathe in deeply, Karsten. Feel how the calm spreads through you. No matter what happens in your thoughts, none of it will happen to you in this room. You're quite safe here, no one can harm you.

I am safe with you, he thought, but then the sight of the

three men was there again, and the voice saying what they did to men who raped.

He had to open his eyes. She sat there with a deck of cards in her hand.

– This is you, Karsten.

The card she placed on the table had a picture of a knight riding over the crest of a hill. He was holding a sword in his hand.

– The Jack of Swords. That is how I see you. And that is how Adrian sees you too, an intelligent young man. You are curious. And you are decent. A mind awakening. But you have this in you too.

Beside the Jack she laid the picture of a figure, male or female, in a red cloak and with a light in his hand. Beneath it the words *The Magician*.

– You are strong willed and creative. You already know that. But there's something else here, something you're keeping out.

She pointed to a sign above the Magician's head, a reclining figure eight, the mathematical symbol of infinity.

– The Magician is the intermediary between the physical and the spiritual worlds. And you have this in you too.

Only now did he begin to find it embarrassing to sit there. He wanted to get up.

– Wait, she said, as if she knew what he was feeling. – There is more. Much more, and I want you to listen to at least some of it. It will help you. And it will help Synne.

She continued to lay the cards, expounding the significance of them. It was as though the smells in the room became sweeter and stronger. He tried to concentrate, focusing on a couple of the images: a tower on fire with people leaping from the top; a man sitting sleepless in a bed, nine glinting swords hanging above him; a kind of clown dangling upside down from a tree. Elsa's hands were pale, her fingers very thin. On three of them she wore rings with large stones in them.

– You think too much, she said to him, and he couldn't deny it.

– Doesn't everyone?

She gave a brief laugh. One of her eye teeth was crooked and crossed slightly over its neighbour. Adrian had said she was a trained nurse. Did Adrian believe in these cards?

– Just the fact that you are willing to listen is enough, Karsten, she said. – I know you don't take this completely seriously.

That was true. What she actually said wasn't important. He sat there and listened to the sound of her voice.

– You will encounter trials. She pointed to the burning tower. – I think you wish for a profound change in your life.

– I want everything to be just the way it used to be, he tried to protest.

She held him with her gaze. – This is something much deeper. You will have to pay a price for this. It could be dangerous.

He peered at the tower. A crudely drawn bolt of lightning struck the top of it.

Suddenly a look of sadness came into her eyes. – I'm glad we've had this conversation, she said. – And I want you to know that you have people around you when you need them.

Adrian started the car, swung out into the road.

– And you hadn't seen any of them before?

Karsten shook his head. He could still hear the voice of the guy with the knife. The smell of him, the stench of raw meat mingled with perfume. He started to shake. It started in his stomach, spread to his arms; his legs went numb.

– There were one or two others, he stammered. – They stayed in the car.

– Doesn't matter. We know who they are.

– Synne, Karsten moaned. – Don't care what happens to me, not really. But if they find her . . .

– They won't, Adrian assured him.

– Not Mum and Dad either. I don't want them to know anything about this.

– Leave it to me.

– That's what you said last time.

Adrian opened a bottle of fizzy water. When Karsten declined, he took a few swigs himself.

– We miscalculated. It won't happen again. Old Man Chadar has clearly left Junior in charge. You're still sure you want to go home?

– Where else could I go?

Without slowing down, Adrian picked up his phone and punched in a number. – Are you operational? Someone at the other end answered before he continued: – They're threatening to go after his little sister.

To Karsten he said: – What's your address?

Karsten told him the name of the road; Adrian passed it on. – Brown villa, he added, – white stone basement. You've got Vemund and Sweaty with you. We'll wait until we get the all-clear from you.

He pulled in at the Statoil petrol station on Fetveien. Karsten huddled up in the passenger seat.

– You're not the only one who's experienced something like this.

– That's not much comfort, Karsten complained.

Adrian made a smacking sound with his lips. – So you think it helps if someone pats your cheek and says how sorry they are for you?

Karsten didn't respond.

– Aren't you angry? Adrian persisted.

– I think I am.

– Feel for it, look for it.

He tried. – I think so, he said again.

Adrian drank the rest of the water. – Comforting isn't what you need. You need to learn to hit back. Open the glove compartment.

Karsten pulled it open. He fumbled inside, found a charger for a phone, a service booklet and a hammer. Adrian glanced at the hammer, took it from him and slid it into the door pocket.

– Keep looking.

At the back of the compartment he found something that felt like a gun. He withdrew his hand.

– You don't drive round with a revolver in your car?

– Revolver? Adrian grinned. – Of course not. That there's a pistol. Take it out.

Karsten did as he was told.

– Is it real?

Adrian laughed. – What would I want with a toy gun?

– Dunno. Scare someone maybe. It's not loaded, is it?

– Twelve bullets in the chamber. Don't wave it about like that. Have you used a weapon before?

Karsten stared at the pistol. Something's going to happen, he heard himself think. He said it over again, the exact same words. Something's going to happen.

– What you've got in your hand there is a Luger, Adrian informed him. – It has a story all its own.

The pistol wasn't heavy. Carefully Karsten squeezed his fingers around the nut-brown stock, jumped as a siren-like wail suddenly sounded from Adrian's phone.

– Black BMW?

Again his whole body began to tremble.

– They're waiting for you outside your house, Adrian told him once he had ended the call.

Karsten tensed the muscles of his arms in an attempt to control them, but it only made the shaking worse. – What do we do? he said through clenched teeth.

– Good question. Let's look at the options. One, go to the police. Put all your cards on the table.

– Put my cards on the table? Karsten protested. – I haven't done anything.

– Depends which legal code you're talking about. You've been groping one of their girls. They don't care if it was consensual or not. You've taken something that wasn't yours to take.

– You were the one who said she could come round to my house.

Adrian shrugged. – Your life, your choice. Did you fuck?

– Not exactly, Karsten said weakly.

– You sure?

– Think I don't even know?

Adrian burst out laughing. – Tell me what happened, he said, leaning back in his seat.

Hesitantly Karsten began to tell his story.

– I don't think your future Paki in-laws are going to care that much about what you *didn't* do, Adrian said, interrupting.

Karsten ignored the joke, gave him a few details, but still Adrian wanted to know more. Whereabouts in the house they undressed, what Jasmeen said, every little detail of what she did.

When there was no more left to tell, he sat up straight.

– Let's try to look at this objectively. That's what the police will do. You were attacked. What about the registration number of the car?

– It was a black BMW, Karsten mumbled.

– I know that. That won't get you far.

– There was that guy with a dog.

Adrian bobbed his head from side to side a couple of times. – He might have seen you running off. Maybe saw the car. But how likely is he to have made a note of the number?

Karsten lifted up the gun, stared dully at it.

– That is the safety catch, said Adrian, pointing. – Leave it on, please. You interested in a couple of days hanging out with people who are willing to defend themselves?

Karsten was suddenly alert. – Why do you ask?

– You can come along with me to the next meet.

– With that old nutcase?

Adrian gestured with his hand. – Your choice.

Karsten rubbed his forehead. In his mind's eye he saw again the dark figure bending over him with a knife in its hand.

– I can get you clearance, said Adrian. – But you will have to make up your mind. If you say yes, then there's no way back.

– And the people you're calling, are they going to be at that meet too?

– You can trust them. That's what this is about now, Karsten. Being around people you can trust.

– I can't go anywhere like this. Karsten indicated the clothes he'd borrowed. He'd stuffed his own into a rubbish bin.

– What do you need? Adrian wanted to know.

He needed peace. He needed to get away, be on his own, maybe go out to the cabin. The idea that the Pakistanis might follow him out there loosed another avalanche of thoughts.

– We'll make sure you have what you need for the next couple of days.

Karsten must have nodded, because Adrian punched in a number on his phone and gave their location. A few minutes

later, a silver-grey Toyota pulled up behind them. There
were three people inside. Someone jumped out and strode
over to them. Karsten recognised him: the sturdy, muscular
little guy with the bleached hair, the one who'd asked him
all those questions in the kitchen at Sæter's. Seemed to
remember his name was Kai.

Adrian wound down his window.

– You need to get inside the house and pick up a few
things for Karsten. He's coming back with us.

– Hi, Karsten, the short guy nodded. – Got yourself a
girl, I hear. He grinned. – What do you want us to fetch
for you?

Karsten resigned himself to it. Described where his room
was, where in the chest of drawers to find clean boxers,
jogging pants, socks. And his maths book, still lying on the
kitchen table.

– Maths book?

– Do as he says, Kai, Adrian interrupted.

The dogs began howling and carrying on as they turned
into the farm. Sæter appeared and shouted at them, not that
it had any noticeable effect.

– The action go as planned? he asked as they climbed
out of the car.

– Yessir, said Adrian.

Sæter shook his hand, as though congratulating him, and
then it was Karsten's turn. The squeeze, the gaze drilling
into him.

– We heard about the incident involving the Pashtuns.

He was wearing brown corduroy trousers and a moss-
green pullover and military boots. The thin grey-brown hair
was combed back flat over his head.

– That's what I call the Pakistanis, he explained. – The
Pashtuns are the group that most clearly show what we are

up against. Tribal culture, honour, ruthlessness towards their enemies.

He must have been out walking, Karsten thought. The bushy black eyebrows were soaking wet, and an enormous drip dangled from the tip of his nose.

– There's a lot we can learn from them, make no mistake about it. A lot of the things they believe in we once believed in too. But I gather you were attacked?

Karsten glanced over at Adrian.

– We talked about it after you called. It's important that people know why you are here.

– We'll discuss it later this evening, said Sæter. – Perhaps you'll share your experiences with us.

Karsten felt his stomach writhe, like a worm jabbed by pins.

– Perhaps, he managed to say.

– Jolly good. Sæter cleared the drip from the tip of his nose as it was just about to fall. – I'm sure you'll have heard this before, but I want to remind you that we see no reason to use surnames here. It's safest for all. First names will suffice. Karsten, or whatever you decide you want to call yourself.

He let them into the hall, turned again to Karsten. – Do you have a phone? If so, it is to be turned off and locked away until you leave.

Reluctantly Karsten pulled his phone out of his jacket pocket.

– That's the way it is here, said Adrian with a wink.

The hunchbacked woman was standing at a kitchen counter and looked up as they passed. According to Adrian her name was Sonja and she was Sæter's sister. Seated at a table was the chubby girl Karsten had seen last time. She was holding a Game Boy in her hands, but she looked older than he remembered her; could be about Synne's age. He nodded, and she glared at him without reacting.

Adrian led him up to one of the rooms in the loft, where there were two bunk beds. Clothing and rucksacks on one of them.

– I'm guessing you think it's best to have the top one, he said with a grin. – So I'll take the bottom one and keep an eye on the door. Maybe you should take a nap. Don't be surprised if you get woken up tonight.

He went out. From the window Karsten saw him cross the yard with Sæter and a couple of the dogs, Adrian straight backed, Sæter bent and waddling like an enormous bird. They disappeared into one of the outhouses, emerged with skis and ski poles, which they carried over towards the edge of the forest.

A few minutes later, two cars turned into the yard and parked next to Adrian's. It was dark by now, but once everyone had climbed out, Karsten was able to count nine people. A little later he heard the tramping of boots on the staircase and the door to the room was pushed open. The pair who came in looked to be about his own age, perhaps slightly older. Both were wearing combat trousers and army boots. One was scrawny, thin as a shrimp, a fringe plastered across his forehead. The other was taller and overweight, his curly hair cropped short and with acne scars on both cheeks. He pulled off his sweater; the shirt underneath had huge patches of sweat below the arms and on the back.

The Shrimp tossed a plastic bag on to Karsten's bed. Inside were a few clothes and the maths book. He said: – Gonna sit around here doing maths, are you? Shit, I think we should call you Einstein.

– Okay by me, said Karsten, and fished the book out. – And I'll call you two Heisenberg and Schrödinger.

– *Funn-ee,* the fat one said, pretending to understand the joke.

– You the one who shagged that Paki slag? the Shrimp went on. – How *intelligent* was that, then?

I'll stay here until tomorrow, Karsten thought. Not one day longer.

Sonja had made thick pea soup, and omelette with bacon and potato. The chubby girl helped her serve it. Karsten was starving, but too tense to eat much. He looked around the room, counted fifteen people. Several he recognised from the meeting two days previously. At the top of the table was Noah, with his Mohican hairdo and broad, flat nose. Next to him, the good-looking woman. Her name was Gail; she had an English accent and called herself head of the female section. Not exactly a demanding responsibility, since she was the only woman there. Sonja and the girl spent most of the time in the kitchen.

Opposite Karsten were his two room-mates. The Shrimp made a few efforts to be funny, but when Kai joined them at the table he fell silent. Kai was no taller than the Shrimp, but twice as broad.

After the plates had been cleared away, Sæter rigged up a flipover.

– Welcome to the second day of our seminar, he announced. – Our country is about to embark on what is known as the 'quiet week'. Well it won't be quiet here, I can promise you that.

A couple of people chuckled. Gail pulled a face that was perhaps intended to be a smile. Adrian said she had a masters degree from an English university and was sharp as a razor. Philosophy or something like that; Karsten hadn't been listening properly.

– As soon as I'm finished, we're going to hear someone's

personal story, Sæter went on, looking over at Karsten. Then he went on to talk about what was going to happen the next morning, something he referred to as *manoeuvres*. He spoke of chains of command, and about dividing the group into teams. Karsten gave up trying to follow it. In the brief interval before it was his turn, he sat stiff as a winter-frozen insect in his chair. Adrian came across and patted him on the shoulder.

– You okay about this?

– Dunno. Not exactly how I imagined things.

Adrian sat beside him. – Got a suggestion. Instead of you standing up there with nothing prepared, let's do it as an interview. I ask you a few questions, and you answer to the best of your ability.

Karsten nodded weakly. – Sounds better.

Once everyone had returned to their seats, Sæter spoke again. He introduced Adrian, even though most of those in the room must have already known who he was. – Adrian Wilkins is a front-line soldier, someone who has fought in the battle for the future of our civilisation.

Adrian stood up and didn't appear at all embarrassed by the introduction. He confirmed that he had been a soldier in Kosovo, Bosnia and Afghanistan, and revealed that he was planning to join the British forces in Iraq. Suddenly there was an air of intense interest in the room. He went on to say a few words about Muslims and their view of the world. We would be making a big mistake if we generalised and underestimated them. Muslim culture has retained many of the values now lost to us. The courage to defend what one believes in. The value of honour. Taking care of those closest to us, our families, all of those with whom one has close ties.

– But take a look at the statistics. How many Norwegian women are going with Muslim men and giving birth to their children?

He looked out across the gathering.

– Quite a few, someone answered.

– Far too many, Noah shouted.

– And how many Muslim women with Norwegian men?

– None.

– Well, said Adrian, – at any rate it's very rare. And why is that?

– They're not allowed to.

– Exactly. It actually says in the Koran that it is a punishable offence. Now we might suppose that Norwegian men are simply too feeble to be of any interest to a woman from, for example, Pakistan.

A mixture of laughter and grunting from the room.

– But that of course is not the whole story. If we tried this as an experiment, we would soon find our hypothesis confirmed. Pakistani men in Norway guard their women in the same way as they do back home. They don't hesitate to make threats and use violence. We'll hear an example of this very soon.

He gestured in Karsten's direction.

– The Pakis and Somalis and the others who come here are allowed to carry on as before. They can have their own closed and internal economies, establish a Muslim society within society. The only thing they have to fear is if some of their women start mating with Norwegian men. So they do their best to make sure it hardly ever happens. It's perfectly natural; this is the way things have always been. The struggle for territory, and for the women to bear our children. If only a fraction of the most pessimistic prophesies of the environmentalists turn out to be correct, natural catastrophes and the disappearance of the most basic necessities of life in other parts of the world is going to lead to a migration of peoples on a scale the world has never seen before. Compared to it, the flight from the Huns and the Mongols in the Middle Ages will be nothing more than a trickle. Within a few years these migrating people will be in the majority in Europe, and in Norway too. Do we intend to do nothing to prepare ourselves for this situation?

He let the question hang in the air for a few moments.

– Some people are worth more than others, he said suddenly. – The first thing is to dare to think this. Then dare to say it. Then take the decisive step. Action is the only thing that shows who you are. What distinguishes those who lead from the rest of the herd? They act, while others hesitate.

Karsten looked around the room. Gail with the pretty face was sitting behind and to the side of him. She was wearing a denim skirt and a skimpy black pullover, and the look she was giving Adrian left no doubt that she was ready to follow him into battle. Probably up into the bedroom, too. Karsten suddenly thought of what it would be like to have them in the bunk bed below his. Just then Adrian approached him, patted him on the shoulder, left his hand there. Karsten staggered to his feet and stood beside the chair, his mouth so dry that his tongue was glued to his palate.

– I spoke earlier about my pal Karsten.

Just that word, pal, and the hand holding round his shoulder was enough to make Karsten lift his head and look at the people sitting there. The Shrimp gave a big fake yawn, but Gail was smiling at him, her head slightly to one side. Sæter, sitting beside her, nodded slowly.

– As I was saying, Adrian went on, – Karsten has landed himself in trouble. His mistake, if that's what we want to call it, is that the girl he's dating is a Muslim. And suddenly he finds her whole family is involved.

He described the attack by the Pakistanis in the black BMW. How Karsten had called and asked for help from the only people he could trust. The rescue was made to sound like a commando raid carried out behind enemy lines. They'd got him to safety by the skin of his teeth, and unharmed apart from a small knife wound to the stomach.

Once Adrian was finished, everyone applauded, and he stepped to one side and led the applause for Karsten, who had yet to say a word. Karsten stood there, his face burning, like some kind of hero, a rescued Private Ryan, and he found it impossible not to dip his neck. Not deeply, in fact scarcely noticeable, but that was what he did, several times. He bowed.

22

He jumped down to the floor, woke up and stood there, staring round the room in confusion. The sound of the sleeping bodies in the bunk beds, the draught from the open window, the light outside. It was night, but the moon was visible between the curtains.

The phone!

Deep in his sleep he had heard her voice. It came up towards him, pressing itself through layer after layer. That was what had forced him up and out of bed.

He had done everything right before leaving her apartment, as though following a set of instructions. Wipe the mortar, wipe the bath tap, straighten the sheet on the bed to make it look as though only one person had been lying there. Afterwards he had destroyed the card file, burned every newspaper cutting about the fires, burned the panties he had secreted at the back of the cupboard. All the data on his computer and his phone had been saved on to a USB stick, which now lay hidden behind a beam in the loft, together with a bag of capsules he had grabbed from her bathroom, and the keys to the apartment.

He had remembered everything, but not her telephone. When he left, it was still lying there on the table, with the message he had sent her just before she let him in. *Any chance of a visit?*

He pulled on his clothes and boots, slipped out into the corridor. It was ten minutes past midnight. Almost two days since he had left her apartment. Somebody had to have been in there.

He let himself out. One of Sæter's dogs began barking out in the enclosure. He felt like running over there, grabbing the beast by its fur and killing it with a single punch. Need to calm down, he thought as he jogged towards the car. Get down there, think of something on the way.

It was the night before Palm Sunday. A chilly night, spring still not quite arrived, not quite made up its mind. A few gangs hanging round the streets in Lillestrøm. He drove slowly down Storgata, turned left, parked. Three or four teenagers skateboarding on the stage in the square. A police patrol car at the other end. He moved into the doorway of the bank, looked up and located her living-room window. A weak light shining there. It was morning when he'd left; if the lamp had been on, he wouldn't have noticed.

He looked over at the police car, thought he could make out two figures inside. The time was now one forty. He walked around the block, stopped outside the street entrance, let himself in with the key he had picked up from home. Her postbox was so full, circulars were sticking out through the opening. That was when he made up his mind. Had made up his mind long before, because he had no choice.

The stairs were bathed in bright light. Loud music and the roar of someone laughing from an apartment on the first floor. He didn't look out through the large windows. Hurried on up as though he lived there. Didn't stop until he reached the top floor. He pressed his ear against the door to her apartment, heard nothing from the other side.

He ran through the risks one more time. She'd been away from work on Friday without giving any reason. He had discovered she had a sister, but that sister didn't live here.

And then there was the policeman, whom she was about to break up with. Didn't she say he was away somewhere?

He let himself in. Stood still inside the doorway, sniffing the air. The smell of something putrid that had not been there before. It made him feel safe; it wouldn't have smelled like that if they'd found her. He peered into the front room. The phone still lay there on the table, and he had to stop himself from crying out. He darted over and stuffed it into his jacket pocket. That familiar feeling of inviolability took hold of him. He couldn't be cornered; the margins were always on his side, even when he made a mistake. It was fate, and it made him think of Elsa and the cards she had read. Things would be different after Easter, she had predicted, and he had always trusted what she said.

On the way out, he stopped outside the bathroom. The light was still on in there. He thought about it for a moment. Then he opened the door. The rotting smell hit him. It was mingled with a touch of perfume. The dark, heavy one she put on before going to work. The shower curtain he had drawn across remained untouched. He pulled it back. The water was a reddish brown and smelled like a bog. A hand, chalk-white and wrinkled, above the surface of the water. He bent forward, compelled to touch it. It was cold and slippery, and when he stroked it, the skin came away beneath his fingers. He raised the arm, felt it; large patches of skin had come loose from the muscles below and glided effortlessly away as he rubbed up and down on it.

Just then he noticed the head, had to let go the hand and stand up straight. It was bent backwards, dark brown, and looked to have swollen to twice its size. Around the mouth and nose a yellowy-white scum like cauliflower had formed. He couldn't resist touching it, and put his hand down into the water. The doorbell rang. For a fraction of a second his brain related the sound of the ringing to his touching the face below the water. He jumped back, slipped on the wet floor, fell and hit his head against the rim of the toilet bowl. He lay there for five seconds, maybe ten, before there was another ring. He got up, went into the living room. He started to open the catch on the veranda door but changed his mind, hurried into the bedroom. As a key slipped into the lock and was turned, he lay down and wriggled underneath the bed.

– Monica?

It was a man's voice. He imagined the policeman. Horvath, that was his name. He was powerfully built, but if he took him from behind, he could easily knock him out. Lying there, he tried to imagine it. Horvath leaning over the bathtub, his fist pounding into the back of his neck.

– Monica?

Now the voice came from the living room. He drew his breath, held it, counted the seconds. Reached five before a cone of light swelled into the bedroom. Steps across the floor, stopping next to the bed. The tips of two boots less than twenty centimetres from his face. The shoes retreated a step; the duvet hanging down on to the floor was lifted up. Now I'll see his face, he thought. But the boots turned and moved away again, back to the living room.

He took two long, deep breaths, held it in again. A sound from the bathroom. Not as loud as a scream, nor as low as a groan. More like the wordless grunt of some huge animal. And then the footsteps again, a low moaning probably from out in the hallway, and then silence.

Go away now, he urged from his hiding place, but from out in the hallway he heard the voice again, and in his mind's eye he could see the policeman's face, and that silly red moustache.

– Something's happened here, he heard the voice say. – Dead person.

That's the way he talks about his woman, he thought.

– Five minutes. I'll wait. I'm a police officer.

As though he hadn't known it. And now the place was going to be crawling with all sorts of God knows what because of this *dead person*.

– The street door's locked. I'll go down and unlock it.

The address was repeated. Then the front door latch clicked. He slithered out.

The light in the stairwell seemed very much stronger now, and the windows on to the street grew bigger with every floor he went down. He passed the first-floor flat where someone was having a party. Looked out. In the yard below, ten metres from the street entrance, stood the policeman. He was holding his phone and moving with short steps in a tight circle, as though chained to an invisible bolt. There was no loft in the building, but he had noticed steps down to a cellar. The door at the foot of them was probably locked, but there was no other place for him to hide. He went down another step, heard the street door being unlocked. Heavy footsteps, voices. He spun round, began running back up, thought of the veranda, the possibility of getting up on to the roof. Ran down again, stopped outside the door where the party was going on. As they came tramping up, he leaned against the wall, put his finger on the doorbell and pretended to be waiting for someone to open up. They passed behind him, the first two carrying something between them. Without turning his head, he sensed they were wearing red and yellow overalls. After them what had to be the policeman. Further up the staircase the footsteps stopped.

Now he rang the bell properly, so the sound of it could be heard out in the corridor. He bowed his neck, cursed silently, waited for the policeman to speak, could hear his voice already: *Who are you? What are you doing here?*

The footsteps continued on up.

As he slipped out through the street entrance, he heard the door opening at the flat where the party was. The volume of the music rose, before he closed the street door behind him and as calmly as he could headed for the corner of Solheimsgata.

23

KARSTEN IS RUNNING along a beach but seems to be hardly moving. Someone has made a bonfire, he can see it in the distance; that's where he's headed. Adrian is beside him. He can't turn his head to look at him, but he knows that he's naked, and it makes him angry. Then Adrian puts an arm around him.

He woke suddenly when the blankets were pulled off him. The ceiling light in the room was on and the Shrimp, the scrawny one called Vemund, was standing there bare chested in his combat trousers.

– Better get up. We're going on manoeuvres.

The chubby guy was there too, busy getting dressed.

Karsten glanced over at the window. No trace of light outside. – But it's the middle of the night, he protested.

– No it ain't, it's nearly half four.

– Leave me alone, Karsten mumbled, pulling the blankets over himself and turning towards the wall.

Vemund pulled them off him again.

– We've got orders to get everyone out of bed. Big fucking girl, that's what you are. Lying there tickling yourself between your legs. He picked up the maths book that was lying at the foot of the bed. – Fucking hell, laugh yourself to death. What a sicko.

The chubby guy sniggered as he buttoned up his shirt. It was stained with patches of sweat. – He's actually *reading* a maths book.

For the first time Karsten noticed that he spoke with a lisp. He was about to offer the guy elocution lessons but controlled himself.

– Give me that book, he said instead to Vemund.

The Shrimp tossed it into a corner of the room. Karsten clambered down from the upper bunk. Adrian's bed was empty. He wrapped the woollen blanket around himself. Vemund pulled it off him. Karsten stood there in just his boxer shorts, his skin covered in goose bumps.

– No way have you ever shagged a Paki girl. You're a girl yourself.

Karsten tried to retrieve the blanket. Vemund dropped it on the floor then stood on it, waiting, his fists bunched. The chubby lad stayed in the background.

– Get those boxer shorts off, Vemund ordered.

Karsten stared at his face, the pointed little nose and the red-rimmed eyes.

– We're going to examine you. Sweaty here knows a kid who was in your class. He said you had your balls removed in an operation. No one here believes you could even shag a sheep. He took a step closer. – Get 'em off.

The fat lad came at Karsten from behind, grabbed the waistband of his boxers. Karsten twisted free.

– Either you take 'em off yourself or we'll cut 'em off you. Fuck knows what else we might cut off while we're about it. If there's anything down there that *can* be cut off, that is.

They both started laughing as they pushed Karsten up against the windowsill. The fat lad grabbed his hands, twisted them behind his back, bent him forward and held his head in a lock. His shirt was soaking wet and smelt of stale urine. Vemund stood in front of him and farted straight into Karsten's face. The fat lad cheered. Right then the door opened. Kai stood there.

– Don't you get it, we're leaving.

The hold on his neck was released and Karsten pulled his head free. Vemund started to dance around him. – We're going a few rounds. Need to warm up before we go out into the cold.

He threw a few jabs in the vicinity of Karsten's head. Kai watched them impassively.

– Two against one, he declared. – If there's going to be a fight here, then it'll be two against two. You get to choose whether it's you or me who fights with Einstein.

Vemund grinned.

– I mean it, Kai continued as he pulled off his vest. His hairless brown chest looked like a wall and his arms like oak trees. He danced towards Vemund, landed a punch on his shoulder. The Shrimp staggered backwards into the wardrobe. – So it's Einstein and me against you and Sweaty, Kai decided, and landed another punch on Vemund.

– Give over, Vemund whimpered.

– Give over, Kai mimicked, hitting him again, quite hard. – You blow over like someone out of Belsen.

He turned towards Karsten. – You take care of him. Give the guy a couple of black eyes.

He demonstrated with a bit of shadow boxing how to do it. If Vemund had been on the receiving end of those punches, his neck would have snapped.

– I'll tackle Sweaty, so you can get straight to Vemund.

He turned to the fat lad. Sweaty put his hands above his head and Kai grinned, not that his face looked any less menacing.

– Come on, Karsten, he urged. – Now it's man against man. Or maybe girl against girl.

Karsten turned and picked up the blanket and his maths book.

– Don't want to? Kai smirked. – Or don't dare to?

– The guy is a moron, Karsten said. – And Fatso can't even speak properly.

Kai dropped the guard that was keeping Sweaty neutralised. – Probably not the smartest thing to say, he declared, pulling his shirt off the top bunk and drying his short bleached hair with it.

In the doorway he turned and pointed his finger at Vemund.

– If you're tough enough to take on Einstein alone, okay. But if you involve Sweaty then it's my fight too. I want you sitting in the car in five minutes' time.

Karsten got dressed and slipped away in search of a place where he could pee in peace. In the grey dawn a couple of snowflakes came drifting down. There was a small garden at the rear of the house. The mongrels in the pen had already caught scent of him and were leaping up and down against the wire. He made a wide arc around them and approached the barn from the back. Through an opening he peeked into a dark space. At the end of the wall a few planks were loose. He poked his head inside. There was a smell of manure and old paint. He made out a few buckets on the floor. Suddenly an animal's head emerged from the darkness. He shrieked and tumbled backwards. Not until he was back on his feet again did he connect the agitated grunting sounds with the face he had seen. He leaned heavily against the barn wall. The snow had stopped, and a thin sliver of moon slipped in and out through the sharp tips of the spruce. You're not scared of some poor bloody pig, he thought, but it sounded more like a question, because even that was something he didn't feel completely sure about.

It was Palm Sunday. They assembled on the lawn, were ordered into four of the cars and drove around, first along the main road and then up side roads. Karsten sat squashed in the back of the Toyota that belonged to the guy they called Sweaty. In the enclosed space of the car the smell of him was even worse. Several times he turned sharply and skidded, causing the toy spider hanging from the rear-view mirror to leap about and wiggle its legs.

Karsten had always suffered from carsickness. – How about leaving the rally cross stuff for another time, he groaned. – Think I'm gonna puke.

Noah, the giant with the Iroquois hair and the flat nose, turned in the front passenger seat.

– You've got two choices, he growled. – You can get out here and find your own way back. Or you can shut your mouth.

Karsten looked at the forest whizzing past on both sides of the slushy road and chose the second alternative.

It was still only five thirty when they turned into an area of low buildings and construction machinery, an enormous lunar landscape that terminated in a wall of rock. Enormous chunks of stone that had been blown free lay strewn about. Vemund obviously worked there, and he showed them a factory unit that was no longer in use. This was what they would be warring for. Adrian split them into two groups and issued them with overalls and helmets. The paintball guns were simple to use. Aim and fire.

Vemund went ahead up a crooked staircase on the outside of the building. The corridor inside smelt of a mixture of damp and chemicals. He opened a door that led into a huge hall. Daylight was just about visible through the broken windows high up on the walls.

Kai was their team leader. He rigged up two revolving spotlights on the floor and turned them on.

– The uniforms look pretty similar in the dark, he said. – In a situation like that, there's a real danger of friendly fire. So we need to make some arrangements.

Karsten's post was next to a pile of pallets. He rubbed his hands together to keep his fingers from going stiff. The lights from the two spots met just below the roof, then turned and continued on their separate rounds. He squeezed the shaft on the thin muzzle, checking that the gas bottle was firmly in place. Noticed how he thought more slowly when he was cold. That was fine; fewer thoughts to worry about. Suddenly he remembered more detail of what he'd been dreaming when they woke him. Adrian had walked up to him on a beach. Jasmeen had been there too. There was something involving her and Adrian, and he tried to think what it was.

He hadn't heard the door, so he presumed that the figure on its way down the ladder was one of his own. But abruptly there was a sound from a gun over there. He heard something hit the wall behind him, squatted down. At the same instant a door on his right burst open. Running footsteps up in the gallery. The sound of guns. He peered over the topmost pallet. Caught sight of a figure just exiting the cone of light; it might have been Vemund, but he couldn't stop himself from firing. Heard someone howl, recognised the sound of the Shrimp's voice.

– Fuck you, you clumsy twat!

Three hours later, they were on their way back to the cars. Vemund stopped them at a ledge. He obviously wanted to play at being the guide, and got everyone to walk to the edge and look down. A deep rift opened up below them. Rocks from the quarry were wedged down it, the largest of them probably weighing several hundred kilos.

– This is the crushing chute. What comes out the other end measures less than a hundred and twenty millimetres.

Just a couple of months ago, he told them, one of his workmates had almost fallen into the chute.

– I expect you're wondering what would have happened to that soft body of his once they started crushing the granite blocks down there. He looked over at Karsten. The chest of his overalls was drenched in red paint. – After you've been turned into chippings, you're on the conveyor belt that leads to the pulveriser. He pointed over at a pile of grey sand. – Worst-case scenario, you end up as asphalt.

Karsten moved back from the edge of the platform. Sweaty was behind him and pushed him forward again. – Suppose it was you who fell down there, he lisped. – That way at least you'd be some use.

– C_3H_7COOH, Karsten muttered to himself, the formula for butyric acid. He'd worked out what it was the guy smelled of.

Not until they had eaten the leftovers from yesterday's meal did Adrian appear, along with Noah. They stationed themselves by the kitchen door, bowls in hand, slurping away. Karsten hurried over.

– Gotta talk to you, he said to Adrian in a low voice, urging him a few steps away from the surly giant.

– Trouble?

– This stuff isn't for me.

Adrian went on eating.

– Those guys we're sharing the room with . . .

– You don't like them?

– How long do I have to stay here?

– You're free to go whenever you like, said Adrian, putting down his bowl.

– What should I do when I get home?

Adrian took him out into the corridor. – I understand why you're worried, Karsten.

He said it in a friendly voice, and Karsten felt like leaning his head against his shoulder.

– I've discussed it with a few of the others. We'll work something out. So you can feel safe. And your family. Until the Pakis stop making threats.

– You mean it?

– We'll be here for a couple more days. And you've got tonight off. A heathen like yourself doesn't have to participate in the sacrifice.

– Sacrifice? Karsten exclaimed. – Now you're kidding me.

Adrian patted his shoulder. – You can relax up in your room. Enjoy yourself with your maths book while we're out celebrating in the woods.

The chubby girl emerged from the living room with glasses and the empty soup bowls in her hands.

– Hi, Vera, Adrian said, and smiled.

– Hi, said the girl, her face blushing furiously behind the freckles.

– Sonja is her grandmother, he explained once she'd disappeared into the kitchen. – Her mother isn't capable of looking after her. He gestured with a hand towards his upper arm, like someone giving himself an injection. Maybe to make it clear to Karsten that there were other people besides himself who had problems.

24

DAN-LEVI LOOKED INTO the sitting room at the Fagerborg Hotel. There was a cheerful log fire burning, but no one around. It was still not four o'clock, a Tuesday in the middle of the Easter holidays. He delayed going in, went downstairs to use the toilet. Roar had called him earlier that afternoon; it was obvious he needed to talk. Dan-Levi felt pretty sure he knew what about.

By the time he came back up the stairs, his friend was seated at a table close to the fire. His glass of beer was already half empty.

– I don't suppose you drink beer at Easter? he said as Dan-Levi approached. – Or is it only Whitsun that's holy for you lot?

The humour was a little strained, and Dan-Levi let it pass without comment. His friend's fingers toyed with his glass; he seemed out of sorts.

– How was Trysil? Weren't you supposed to spend the whole week there?

Roar shook his head slowly. – Monica, he said, staring into the fire.

– Trouble?

– In a manner of speaking. She's dead.

It took Dan-Levi a few seconds to take the news on board. When the waitress reappeared, Roar pointed to his almost empty glass and held up two fingers.

– I found her, he said in a surprisingly professional way. – Her sister called and asked if she was with me in Trysil.

– Wasn't that the plan?

Roar thought about it. – She changed her mind. We were probably just about to break up. He glanced at Dan-Levi. – Never did understand that woman.

Me neither, Dan-Levi almost said.

– I tried to call. She didn't answer, neither Friday nor Saturday. Couldn't get hold of the caretaker either. Her sister kept calling me up, and her mother. Come night I gave in and promised to find out what I could.

The beers arrived.

– I hadn't given her back the spare key, so I was able to let myself in.

In two swigs he drained half his glass.

– She was lying in the bathtub. Drowned.

– Is *that* possible?

Roar wiped the foam off his moustache. – It is when you're stuffed full of Valium and sleeping pills.

– I'd no idea she had that kind of problem.

– She did not have *that kind of problem*. She was not the type to fucking kill herself.

– No, Dan-Levi agreed, though he wasn't so sure. And even less sure that suicide had anything to do with the type of person you were. One of the youngsters in his group had committed suicide two years ago, the most cheerful and outgoing of the lot. No one could make any sense of it.

– She must have been lying there since Friday morning, maybe Thursday evening.

– Can't have been a pretty sight.

– I've seen a fair bit in my time.

– But not someone you knew that well.

Roar glanced at him. – Actually she was the one who wanted to call it off.

Dan-Levi realised that what might have been hard for his friend to admit was now a sort of comfort to him.

– Didn't get the impression you two had a lot to talk about.

– Talk? No, that wasn't the reason. She didn't have much interest in sex, to tell the truth.

It wasn't the first time Roar had given this as the reason for the break-up of a relationship.

– I'm feeling pretty bad about a lot of things. He emptied what was left of his beer, turned to the bar, pointed to his glass again. – Not just that it was me who found her. There are a number of other things that don't add up.

– Such as what?

– Her mobile phone wasn't there. Nor the spare set of keys.

– Well you had those.

– She had another set. And another thing: why would the chick get into the bath with her panties on?

Dan-Levi scratched his throat. He understood that his friend needed to create a distance from what had happened, but he didn't like hearing him refer to the dead woman as *the chick*. They hadn't even broken up yet.

– So you're not completely convinced it was suicide?

Roar didn't reply. The third beer glass appeared on the table. Dan-Levi picked up his phone and informed Sara he would be home later than he'd said, because it was obvious his pal needed him.

They moved on from the fireside, which had actually become a rather gloomy place, and visited a few of the bars in town. In the square, Roar stopped and pointed up at a window. He didn't need to explain to Dan-Levi that it was there that she had lived.

They ended up in a window seat at Klimt's. Roar was

well away by this time, not that it was noticeable to people who didn't know him, but he had a particular way of waving his hand as he spoke, his voice was a couple of notches louder than it needed to be, and his flirting with the girl behind the bar was now an openly physical business. Dan-Levi had switched to fizzy water some time earlier.

– You working tomorrow? he asked with a nod in the direction of his friend's sixth or seventh beer of the evening.

Roar twisted one end of his handlebar moustache around his finger.

– I have to go through everything we've got on these bloody fires, he burst out.

Dan-Levi looked round; there was no one sitting near them.

– Have you found more evidence of a connection?

Roar grinned sarcastically. – If we wanted it all to be in the papers, I wouldn't hesitate to let you know. He took another couple of large swigs. – But okay, there *is* some connection.

Dan-Levi removed his glasses and wiped them, mostly to disguise his curiosity.

– Give me a little bit of what you've got, he said calmly. – I've always shared with you.

Roar squeezed more foam out of his moustache. It was a sorry sight by this time.

– Do you swear it will go no further? By God in Heaven and His only begotten Son?

He looked at Dan-Levi, probably wondering if his blasphemy had managed to provoke his friend.

– We think the arsonist is using some kind of ignition mechanism.

– You already mentioned that. Time to be a little more specific.

– We found one that was almost intact at the nursery school. Fires were started in several different locations.

Roar took out a ballpoint pen and began to sketch on one of the serviettes on the table.

– A cigarette and matches held together by an elastic band, fastened to a kind of fuse. It gives the arsonist the chance to light it and get some distance away before the fire really takes hold.

Dan-Levi picked up the serviette and sat staring at the primitive drawing. He knew at once where he had seen something like this before.

– This is just too crazy.

– What's too crazy?

He lowered his voice. – I found something exactly like what you've drawn here.

Roar dropped the glass he was about to raise. It hit the tabletop with a loud bang. – You're kidding me, right?

Dan-Levi turned the serviette around and drew. – One cigarette and three matches, fastened together with an elastic band.

– Ordinary matchsticks?

Dan-Levi thought about it. – No, they were flat, the kind of matches that come in a little book, at hotels and restaurants.

Roar leaned across the table. – Where did you find this?

– On the steps outside the house.

– Your house? Jesus fuck, Dan-Levi, pardon my language. You do realise that this conversation has just turned into a witness interview?

By the time Dan-Levi got home at around eleven, Sara had gone to bed. He grabbed a yoghurt from the fridge, picked up the newspaper and sat at the kitchen table, flipping distractedly through it as he ate. Before they parted, Roar had insisted that they go round his place with an expert fire investigator. By that time of the evening his thinking wasn't exactly clear. The rubbish had been emptied ages ago, but they ought to take a look around the garden, in his opinion. As though there would be anything to find there. Someone had dropped the ignition device, if that was what it was, on his front steps, Dan-Levi insisted. He said nothing about who it might have been. Not a word about Karsten Clausen being right next to him when he found it.

He refused to bring Karsten into it. There had to be some other explanation. He would talk to the lad himself. He knew of cases where people had been unjustly accused of something criminal. He had seen the suffering and the problems experienced by innocent people after a cross-examination, the suspicious looks of neighbours and friends. He knew of at least one case in which a life had been ruined. A false accusation of child abuse arising from a tragic family conflict in which a cynical mother had used every possible means to deny her former husband custody of their children. This was different, but Karsten Clausen was a sensitive boy. A loner who struggled with friends and girls. Two other things had struck him as he sat at Klimt's with Roar. Karsten had seemed in a strange mood that morning when he had come to his door, as though there was something or other he wanted to tell him. And on the evening of the fire at the nursery school he had also behaved strangely, not that Dan-Levi could recall the exact details of what was said.

His stream of thought was interrupted by a sound from the staircase. Sara was standing there. She was wearing a tracksuit.

— Not gone to bed?

— Fell asleep on the bathroom floor.

She came over to the table, gave him a weary smile. He held her, pulled her down on to his lap. He loved to take in the smell of her. It made him calm at the same time as it excited him. Especially what she exuded when she had just been sleeping.

– You smell so good, he murmured in her ear.

– And you smell of beer and cigarettes.

– A victim of passive smoking, he said in his defence.

– And the beer, you old boozer?

– Again, passive.

She laughed sleepily into his hair. – And Roar, he's OK?

Dan-Levi hesitated. He had to tell her about Monica, but she was tired and needed to sleep.

– So-so, he said vaguely, and looked into her face, the grey eyes that were at once happy and sad. – I'm the luckiest man in the world, he said, and kissed her.

– Carry me up to bed, she ordered.

He lifted her up. He'd never been the big strong he-man type, but she was as easy to carry as a little girl.

– Carrying you like this has made me hot, he told her as he kicked open the bedroom door.

– I'm much too tired to resist, she murmured.

He unbuttoned his shirt. Just then Rakel called out.

– Stay awake, he warned Sara as he headed off to the child's room.

His daughter was sitting up in bed. – Thirsty.

– Okay, I'll get some water for you.

– No, she protested. – Water Man get it.

Dan-Levi leaned over the bed railings and gave her a hug. They had had so much fun from this story about the Water Man that the little girl had become obsessed by it. A true story that would be repeated in years to come, maybe even feature in the wedding speech Dan-Levi was planning, when the time came to give her away.

– The Water Man couldn't come tonight, so he's asked me to fetch your drink for you.

– Water Man, Rakel insisted.

By the time Dan-Levi returned to the bedroom, Sara had fallen asleep. He swallowed his disappointment, tucked the duvet carefully around her warm body, bent over and said a prayer for her. Downstairs he put on shoes and a jacket, walked up the street and turned into the little cul-de-sac. A black car stood there with its engine running, a BMW he could not remember having seen in the neighbourhood before. Someone was sitting inside it. He could just make out the glow of a cigarette through the dark windows.

He couldn't see lights on anywhere in the Clausen house, but Karsten had said that he wasn't going to the cabin with the rest of the family for the holiday, and Dan-Levi decided to wake him up if he was home. Just then he saw someone by the door.

– Can I help you? he called out.

The man standing there whirled round and walked towards him. Dan-Levi noticed that he didn't look Norwegian; probably a Pakistani or from somewhere in the Middle East. He repeated his question. The young man shook his head and crossed to the car, which backed out into Erleveien, accelerated away through the residential area and was gone.

25

KARSTEN JUMPS OVER a fence, comes to a snow-coated ledge, stops at the outer edge. Immense stones are fed into the deep chute below him to be crushed. Someone down there shouts his name. He runs off, opens a door, stumbles on to a staircase. Somewhere in the building a baby is crying, but as he makes his way up the stairs, the crying changes until it sounds as if it's coming from an older child. Just then he realises he's back home, on his way up to the first floor. He has to find Synne before it's too late.

He sat up in bed, drenched in sweat. Slowly he remembered where he was. In the other top bunk Vemund turned over. It felt as though he was looking at him in the dark, but Karsten could tell from his breathing that he was asleep. He leant down over Adrian's bed. It was empty.

He lay back down, his body stiff after all the exercising. Once again he'd had to squash into the back of Sweaty's Toyota and sit in the nauseating stench of butyric acid that came from his body, try to stop looking at that ridiculous spider dangling below the rear-view mirror and the way it was supposed to jiggle whenever they drove over a bump or turned a corner.

Someone was crying. Karsten jumped down from the bed, stood in the middle of the floor, listening. He heard it again. He slipped out into the corridor, over to the stairs. He heard the sound of a low voice coming from the chubby girl's room. Just then the door opened. He recognised the silhouette of the person standing there.

– What are you doing here?

Adrian sounded more angry than surprised.

– Someone's crying, whispered Karsten. – I had to see what the matter was.

– Everything's fine, said Adrian. He led him back to the bedroom, closed the door behind them. – No need to wake the whole house, he said quietly.

Karsten leaned against the bunk beds. – What's the matter with Vera?

Adrian turned towards him. In the dark, Karsten could just about see his eyes.

– Something happened. I had to take care of it. It's all right now.

– Take care of what?

– Can you keep it just between the two of us?

Karsten nodded.

– Vera's mother wants to see her, but Sæter won't allow it. Vera's been crying every night, waking me up too. I had a word with her. She's in a terrible state.

– That's good then, said Karsten, relieved, as he climbed back up into his bed. – That you comforted her.

He slept soundly. Didn't notice the light falling in through the thin curtains. Didn't notice the blanket being tugged off him, and then his boxer shorts. Awoke suddenly as something wet and ice-cold hit him in the face.

He jumped down from the bed, naked from the waist down. Vemund was hopping around the floor, bent double with laughter, Sweaty choking and beating his head against the wall. They'd pinched not only his underpants but his trousers and pullover.

– The little boy's sleeping so soundly, Vemund howled. – Doesn't even notice that his pants have come off.

– Oh that boy's had the operation all right.

– Give me my clothes, Karsten raged.

– That's the price you pay for sleeping in in the morning. Vemund pointed to the open window. – You'll have to go down and get them yourself.

– Price to pay, Sweaty echoed, lisping.

Vemund took out his phone, bent down in front of Karsten and started taking pictures. – Is that what you were hoping to impress the Paki slag with?

Something snapped in Karsten. He took two steps forward and sank his fist into the Shrimp's face. He withdrew momentarily, astounded by what he had done, surprised by the dull thud, the pain in his knuckles, the feeling of something breaking. Vemund's fist struck his lip, and then it was as though a fuse had blown, and everything went dark. He grabbed hold of the wispy hair, pulled, twisted the thin body down on to the floor, sat on top of him, pinioning his arms beneath his knees, then threw another punch at his mouth. He could feel Sweaty's hands around his neck but kept punching and punching away at the bloodied rat-like face beneath him. Distantly he heard the door being opened.

– Let them fight, Kai ordered.

– He's killing him, Sweaty protested, but Kai pulled him away.

Karsten felt the darkness lift. He raised his fist again, and the skinny body beneath him twisted and bucked, but with Kai's entry, the rage had subsided. He looked down at the bleeding mouth and the frightened eyes, dropped his fist, got to his feet, grabbed somebody else's blanket and wrapped it around his body. When he crossed to the window and looked out, he saw all his clothes spread out in the dirt.

– Shit, he muttered, and felt the jab of anger again.

– How are you going to sort this out? Kai stood next to him. – Who's going to fetch your clothes?

Vemund had got up and was sitting on the edge of the bed, whimpering and spitting blood.

– Him, Karsten said, pointing.

– You've got to say it to the lad.

– You go down and fetch my clothes.

– Wasn't me that threw them out, Vemund wailed.

Karsten thought it over. – I don't give a shit who it was, he announced, astonished at how his voice still sounded angry. – You fetch them.

Vemund glanced over at Sweaty, but his pal was busy packing his rucksack, no help to be had there.

– I'll kill you, he howled at Karsten. Then he got up and headed for the door.

26

HE LET HIMSELF in using the TrioVing key he had taken
last time he was there. There was a light on in the corridor;
otherwise all was in darkness. He listened. The even hum
of the refrigerator; apart from that, nothing. He climbed
the steps slowly, avoiding the ones that made a noise, the
fourth, the eighth, the tenth. Headed on towards the room
that had once been his. That still was his. As long as that
room existed, it was his.

The curtains were open. He stood there awhile, looking
out. On the other side of the copse lay the ruin of the nursery,
on this side the sleeping houses. The kind of place where
nothing could happen. Not until it did happen and everything got torn up and turned upside down. And then it
would take years for things to fall back into place again. If
they ever did. Even when everyone now lying asleep behind
these dark windows was gone, the stories would still live
on: *the house that stood there a hundred years ago burnt down
to the ground. No one knows why.* Forces that people had no
control over struck at the heart of their lives. It might all
begin with a spark from the friction between a small, round
sulphurous surface and a strip of card saturated with tiny
splinters of glass.

He was carrying four ignition devices. The last time he
was there he had lost one somewhere or other along the
way. He took the two bottles of lighter fluid out of his
pocket, placed them on the table. Once again the computer

was on standby. He woke it up, opened a few documents the journalist had recently written. Articles presumably intended for the local newspaper. Something about a drunk driver, something else about vandalism in a cemetery. He found the document he'd read last time he was there, the one containing an ongoing series of dated notes.

15 April: Sara is in the bath. Rakel been sleeping all evening. I have everything.

16 April: Karsten still not home. Need to talk to him before he gets called to attend an interview. He mustn't become a victim of groundless suspicion. The Judas dilemma.

He looked out of the window again. Karsten Clausen lived up at the top of the road: was it him the journalist was talking about?

He opened the cupboard, shone his torch inside. There was a suitcase on the floor that hadn't been there last time. He lifted it out and crept in underneath a pair of overalls, some coats and shirts, removed the board and squeezed his upper body in between the two sides. It all came back to him, what it felt like to sit in that room that nobody else but him knew about. Hearing the tramping up the stairs, the door slung open, the furious voice calling his name. Knowing that no one could find him.

He shone the beam on the rear wall, found where the little letters had been scratched in, running in and out of each other in a restless pattern. *Fire Man come tak them hom with you.* The scorch marks that framed the prayer were still there, along with a stain that he recalled was blood. This was the dark side of the room; all the blackness that possessed him was gathered here. On the other beam was her name. He'd scratched it in day after day. Counting them now, he reached a figure of thirty-five. Took out his knife and carved it once more. Because it was Elsa he was thinking about in here. She was the one he could always bring to life in this dark recess.

When she spoke to him, her voice was stronger than the one he heard in the flames. Hers was the voice that held him back, that made everything that didn't want the house to be burned down triumph over everything that did. When he carved her name into the beam, the tiny recess turned into a great white room, a temple in which she appeared if only he pressed his fingers hard enough against his eyes.

Now the balance between the forces had changed, the weight was tipping in the other direction. She herself had used this image when she read the cards for him, when she spoke about death and the fire that purified. *Everything in this world lies in a balance, and the slightest thing we do can change the way the scales tip.* Maybe it was Monica who had provided the crucial weight. Her body in the bathtub half eaten by the water, the skin peeling away from the bones beneath his fingers.

He took out one of the ignition devices, straightened the cigarette, which had been bent slightly. This was where it should begin. Among the clothes hanging against the bone-dry woodwork. He felt the itch, felt it spreading through his body, from his bones and up into his spine. And beneath it the tiredness that threatened to suck everything inside itself. If he listened into the silence, he could hear faint voices. They came from the bedroom; the door was ajar.

We have to tell him, Gunnhild. Sooner or later, for Chrissakes, we have to tell the boy.

A little pause; his lips moved as he mouthed her reply.

He's still so little. Can't we wait?

He goes out into the corridor, stands outside the bedroom door.

Why should we have to raise her Paki kid? She's rolling in money.

You know why, Tord. And I'm not prepared to go on talking about it every single evening.

Then silence. Back in his own room, he takes the lighter out of the desk drawer. That was the evening when he scratched the prayer to the Fire Man on to the beam. Decorated it with a border of scorch marks. But just as he is about to set light, Elsa is there, talking to him, holding him back.

He woke to a sound. A child's shout. Not loud, but where he was lying, there was only the thin rear wall separating him from the room on the other side. He wriggled out of the cupboard, slipped into the room.

The girl was standing up in her cot.

– Are you thirsty, Rakel? I'll get you some water.

She didn't answer, but even in the dark, he could tell from her large, bright eyes that this was what she wanted.

Down in the kitchen, he took the trouble to get her a clean glass from the cupboard. Waited a few seconds after filling it, but still the only sound was the humming of the fridge. He made his way back up the stairs.

– Drink this, and then you must sleep.

This time too he stood listening as the little throat swallowed and swallowed. It took time, and he noticed that what had interested him last time was now beginning to irritate him.

The girl held the glass out to him. – More thirsty.

He thought about it for a moment, then took it. The bathroom was at the other end of the corridor. There was a smell of rotting in there. No surprise, because this journalist was the type who put things off, let his house fall to pieces around him, had probably never held a hammer in his hand since woodwork lessons at school. He filled the glass. As he was turning off the tap, he heard a door open, and the next moment the landing light was switched on. He didn't move a muscle; every fibre of his body was tensed.

– Are you still not sleeping, little rabbit?

The voice came from the door to the child's room. A woman's voice.

– Shall I get you some water?

– No! The Water Man.

As her footsteps approached, he slipped into the shower, drew the curtain halfway across. It was almost transparent. The door and the light switch were less than two metres away; he could already feel the movement in his body, the jump across as the light came on.

She didn't switch it on. He saw her in the light from the landing. She was wearing a white nightdress; he could make out the outline of her body in the doorway, and the shape of the long fair hair. She was small and as thin as a bird. The kind of neck that snapped when you bent it slightly.

She lifted the toilet lid, pulled up her nightdress and sat down, no more than thirty centimetres away from him. He could smell the sleep on her, hear her breathing. Then the trickling down into the toilet. It grew stronger. Made him think of another woman he had been in a bathroom with. It was six days ago. She no longer existed. And the thought that the woman now sitting on the toilet and emptying herself might no longer exist put a charge through his chest, as if a horse were galloping inside it. If she sees me, she'll never leave here, he thought. But if she doesn't see me, she'll live. She was the one who would decide it. Not him. Or it was a game of chance. Mercy, or the opposite of mercy. Because maybe it was all in God's hands, the God they believed in and prayed to in this house. The God who had sent him to them that night, and no other night.

The woman's name was Sara. He liked it. She farted down into the bowl, almost inaudible. He liked that too, that what was inside of her came out, that he was made a party to certain things she liked to keep to herself. Then she dried herself, got up, stood a moment with her small bum exposed to him, and then the nightdress dropped down to her ankles, and for a moment he had to struggle against the temptation to break the deal he had made, to tear down the curtain so that she'd see him, because then he would have to pull her into the shower cabinet with him and hold that warm body tightly.

He let her go.

The house would stand for another night. For another brief stretch of time Erleveien would remain a sheltered corner of the world. The fire tonight would be somewhere else.

He waited quarter of an hour before emerging. The child was asleep. He put the glass on the floor next to the bed.

– I'll be back, Rakel, he whispered. – I'll be back tomorrow.

He drove up along Sagdalen, towards the centre of Strømmen. The time was approaching quarter to three. When he got out of the car, an icy wind blew up at him from the river below. At Sæter's they had agreed on a security plan for Karsten Clausen. For the next few days, and longer if necessary, a team would keep watch over him. He himself had suggested a pre-emptive strike against the attackers, something that would compel respect. – That's what this is all about, he had said. – Pay a visit to the Chadar family, give them a message, talk to them in a language they understand.

Sæter liked the plan and spent a long time analysing it. It was rational, and if it was put into practice, it would produce a definite result; it would make it clear that there was a battle going on, that the wars of the future were already being fought. *We have started*, he said, over and over again in that reedy voice of his. In the end, it was all talk. *We have started, but are not yet ready to wage war. Not yet, but our time is coming, and when it does we shall be ready.*

As though the rest of the world was waiting. As though Old Man Sæter would ever be ready.

He pulled up his hood, rounded the corner by a bar called the Ram, walked on up the deserted street. The sweet shop was one of a little group of shops further up, next to a large old timber building that housed a store selling lamps. Posters in the window gave the prices of beer and soft drinks in fluorescent orange. He walked around the building; it was made of stone, so he had to get inside to make it happen.

He'd been there twice before. The first time was just over fourteen years ago. The man behind the counter was a Pakistani and looked to be in his forties. Khalid Chadar? he was on the point of asking. But it wasn't necessary. Even though he had never met Khalid Chadar, had never even seen a picture of him, he recognised him.

Can I help you? Khalid Chadar's gaze had flitted about. His hair was greying at the temples and he had bags under his eyes.

Elsa says hello, he could have replied, and then beaten the Paki shit out of the overweight body on the other side of the counter. Instead he just stared him straight in the eyes, then turned and walked out, without buying anything, without saying a word.

A month ago, just before the prince was due back, Elsa became distracted and worked up. Suddenly she had no time for him any more, and he went back to the sweet shop again. Khalid Chadar wasn't there; this time it was a boy of about twenty. A vain, spoiled Paki with a gold chain above his open-necked shirt and his hair full of gel. Someone who ran the world and talked down to him. I know you, Shahzad Chadar, he could have said. I know you and all of your scrounging family.

According to the company records up at Brønnøysund, Khalid Chadar owned a couple of other soft drink outlets and had an annual income of a few hundred thousand kroner. Afterwards, he told Elsa what he had found out.

They live as though they have made millions from a couple of sweet shops. Khalid Chadar drives round in a Merc and acts the big shot. Do we have to put up with that? Should people like that be allowed to come here and take everything over and force us to live by some fucking tribal laws?

But Elsa forbade him from going back there. Just wanted to let sleeping dogs lie. That was how she had managed, by focusing on the goodness and brightness in the world.

He found a window round the back, took off his jacket, wrapped it around the hammer and then struck at the side with the catches. One blow was enough. He was filled with a calmness. Erleveien is for me, he thought, but this one I'm doing for you, Elsa.

The cellar was the obvious choice, a kind of rest room. In a corner below a sink was a rubbish bin filled with trash. The wall was chipboard. He was going to treat himself to three separate ignition sites, because now he was doing a job for someone else, claiming what was still owed to Elsa, even though she would never know it.

He pulled one bottle out of his pocket, squirted liberally across both walls, placed the ignition devices. From the point at which they started to burn, he had between one and a half and two minutes. By that time, he'd be back in the car.

27

DAN-LEVI HAD NEITHER his father's cheerful openness nor
his talent as a speaker, and there had never been any question
of his taking over after Pastor Jakobsen. His father had accepted
it from the start and never criticised his son's choice of journalism as a career, however unspiritual it was. He had been
pastor at Bethany for several decades, but was in demand
across the whole country. These meetings in packed assembly
halls were among Dan-Levi's earliest memories. The whole
family went along on trips to Tønsberg, Molde, Mosjøen. His
mother noticed how anxious Dan-Levi became at the change
in his father's voice whenever he stood at the podium. She
used to reassure him by saying that his father had been raised
up into a greater world, into the presence of the Spirit. His
way there led via a joyous whispering that rose to a great
hallelujah, and then someone would stand and raise their arms
towards the ceiling, the tongue forming words in a foreign
language that everyone else in the hall seemed to understand.

This was what Dan-Levi was thinking of as he lay waiting
for the alarm to ring. It had grown suspiciously light outside
and still the phone on his bedside table hadn't made a sound.
He picked it up. The battery was flat. He leapt out of bed,
plugged in the charger. Message from Stranger; he had probably called several times already. Dan-Levi groaned. He was
on desk duty and obviously something must have happened
during the night. He was on the point of calling back,
changed his mind. It was Maundy Thursday, after all.

He treated himself to a shower as he prepared to face the wrath of his boss; it would hardly be any greater for being postponed for five minutes. Standing there under the warm stream, he again thought of the day when he might at last be allowed to transfer to the culture section. An end to desk duties, an end to racing off to cover accidents in the middle of the night. He would write about music, and amateur theatricals, interview authors and painters.

Still dripping wet, he sat on the toilet seat. The bathroom needed doing up too. There were patches of damp on the walls, and the door of the shower cabinet was missing. He had hung up a curtain, but the rod was always falling down. As soon as Sara felt better, he would make a start, he decided. Start with the room he was currently using as an office. Rakel could have that. Sara had already chosen a pink wallpaper with dogs on it. She was determined that they should have a puppy too, but right now she was too nauseous to discuss it any further.

As Dan-Levi emerged from the bathroom, he heard a noise from Rakel's room. Suddenly overcome with dread, he saw an image of the little girl dead in the bed. Thoughts like that could assail him at any time. He'd asked the doctor about it last time he was there. The chances of sudden and unexpected cot death were much reduced by the time a child reached eighteen months. But then there were all the others things that could happen. New possibilities that would arise as the child grew older.

In his head, Dan-Levi had a catalogue of every kind of accident Rakel might encounter. The common ones, like drowning, being knocked over by a car, meningitis, were hardly worth the trouble of listing; they were there all the time. It was the more unusual ones that he had to look out for. Choking on a playground ride, hanging from the strap of a cycle helmet, the thing that was meant to protect the head. And a few years back, he had read about two kids playing hide-and-seek who had climbed up into a disused freezer. The lid had closed over them, the vacuum pressure made it impossible for the little hands to push it open, and no one knew where they were.

Beneath the crushing weight of these thoughts – they could be images, sometimes whole scenes from a film – he would often drop to his knees and with hands together offer up a frail prayer. So far it had worked. But what about all the other children? What right did he have to pray that God hold a sheltering hand over his own daughter while millions of others suffered the most appalling fates every minute of the day?

He opened the door slightly. Rakel wasn't sleeping, she was sitting in bed chattering to herself. Dan-Levi lifted her up and held the little body close, drawing in the smell of freshly woken child. With his lips pressed into her hair, he said a little prayer of thanksgiving for every second of intense happiness that he was granted. He offered up thanks too for the worry that never let go of him, a trivial price to pay for everything he had been given.

He danced around the room with his daughter in his arms, and then raised the blind and let in the morning light. There was a half-empty glass of water on the floor. He hadn't heard her calling out. Again and again he had told Sara she was to wake him if Rakel needed anything in the night, so she wouldn't have to get up. But she'd got up anyway and given the little girl some water. The thought of Sara lying in their bed, the sight of her, the feeling of having her by his side, all that she said to him as they lay together, and the child that was on the way, the thought of all this made him close his eyes and offer up another prayer. His worries he could handle by himself, but this joy that consumed him so and at times threatened to make him burst into pieces was almost more than he could contain.

Rakel bent and reached for the glass.

– Thirsty.

It was one of the first words she had learnt. Of necessity, for she was always thirsty. His last job at night, his first job in the morning, and often in the middle of the night too, was to slake that thirst. It was a good sign, thought Dan-Levi. Because the search for God was also a thirst.

– Did Mummy bring you the water?

Rakel shook her head. – Water Man.

Dan-Levi laughed and held the little body close again. He had been toying with the idea of writing a story for her. It was going to be about a good fairy, maybe a guardian angel, who went round in the night visiting children who lay awake, a messenger from God. And he was going to call him the Water Man.

At seven thirty, he called Stranger.

– Fire, his boss announced. – In Strømmen. Once you've got yourself out of bed, you can get up there and relieve Gunders. He's had a rough bloody night of it.

Stranger was clearly too stressed to give him a ticking-off, and Dan-Levi took his time over his coffee, wrapped a sandwich in a serviette. As he pulled out of the residential area, he passed a silver-grey Toyota with two young men inside. He didn't recognise them. He made a note of that kind of thing. Even in a peaceful backwater like this, you never knew what could happen.

A grainy layer of smoke floated in the air around Strømmen centre, and the stench of burned plastic made Dan-Levi put aside his sandwich half eaten. The area around the site of the fire was cordoned off and the street closed. On the pavement, some distance away from what had once been the sweet shop, he saw Roar Horvath standing with a couple of other policemen he recognised. When Roar saw his friend, he gave a sign to the constable standing guard at the tape and the journalist was able to slip by.

– We meet rather too often at places that smell of burning, Roar greeted him. He was obviously trying to appear fairly nonchalant.

Dan-Levi had called him a couple of times after their evening in town together, concerned about how his friend was dealing with what had happened to Monica, but hadn't been able to get through.

– Any connection to the other fires? he asked now, notebook in hand.

– You'll need to give us more than five minutes to answer that.

– You must have some idea.

Roar shrugged. – We need to go through a whole list of possibilities. Electrical fault, carelessness, insurance scam. And then we'll get around to the sort of question you're asking.

– Who's the owner?

Roar pointed to the large timber building. – The whole shopping block has just been sold to Thon.

It was no surprise that the old property magnate had been busy even out here.

– The sweet shop was rented by Pakistanis.

– Name?

Roar pulled his own notebook out of his pocket. – Chadar. Lives in Lørenskog.

– So your first thought is probably insurance.

Roar gestured with the notebook. – You keep your prejudices to yourself, Dan-Levi. Tell me instead why I haven't heard any more from you about that cigarette device. He sounded a touch brusque.

– Tried to call you, Dan-Levi said in his own defence.

Roar wrinkled his forehead, and three deep furrows appeared above his eyebrows. They looked like birds in flight.

– As you can see for yourself, the other building here is made of wood, he growled. – It was built nearly a hundred years ago. A family lives up on the second floor, some youngsters on the first. If the wind had been from the north, you can just imagine what might have happened. So what the hell's the matter with you? Am I going to have to drag you in for an interview?

Dan-Levi was shaking. His friend was angry now, and with good reason.

– Give me a few hours, he said weakly. – I'll call you after lunch.

28

KARSTEN AWOKE SUDDENLY. Behind the curtains the day was grey. He turned over and picked up his mobile from the floor. It was past eleven. There was a message from Jasmeen. *Something's happened. Must talk to you.*

There were a few spiky drops in the air as he went out to fetch the newspapers, rain or perhaps hard snowflakes. The postbox was empty, and he remembered it was Maundy Thursday.

No one in sight on the road. Adrian had said that Shahzad and his gang would wait until he was somewhere there were no witnesses. He was to maintain caution, not take a step without having his phone ready. Be on the run inside his own home. He put his hand inside his vest, let it run over the cut that crossed his stomach. At some point he would have to sit down and take stock of the situation. Isolate exactly what it was that had changed everything. Find out how it had happened. Find a way to make sure it had as little effect on his future life as possible.

He took his cereal bowl out into the living room, sat in front of the computer, clicked on to *VG*'s web edition. Let his eyes scan the page until he came to a story about a fire. How many sweet shops were there in Strømmen? Abruptly he couldn't sit still any more, stood up, clicked on the link, recognised the old timber building in the picture.

He tried to establish a chain of thought. a) Jasmeen's family owned the sweet shop. b) Jasmeen had tried to get in touch with him. That was as far as he got. There was a piece missing. Lots of pieces. Maybe they didn't even exist. He pushed the bowl of muesli to one side, picked up his phone, called her. No answer. Her message had been sent from a hidden number. He pulled on his running gear, fumbled with the laces of his trainers. Just then the door-bell rang. He ran up to his room, peered down from behind the curtains. Dan-Levi was standing on the steps outside.

– Sorry I couldn't make chess, he said once he'd unlocked the door. – I should've sent you a message.

– You already told me. What happened to you?

– Banged into something. A door. Karsten ran a finger over his swollen lower lip. – Did you see about the fire at Strømmen? he went on, to change the subject.

– I've just been up there.

– Any news?

Dan-Levi wiped the drizzle off his glasses. – The police are pretty sure it was arson.

– Have they got any clues?

– Well they don't announce that kind of thing. But I'll be writing more about it, so don't miss it. He peered past him into the house. – Are you still on your own?

– Just till this afternoon. Why do you ask?

Dan-Levi put his glasses on again, swept back his long black hair. – You remember that morning last week when you called round to see me?

Karsten thought about it. – It was last Friday. Why wouldn't I?

– Remember I found something at the foot of the steps?

– You mean that figure?

– It wasn't a figure, or at least not a toy. I realised that afterwards.

It wasn't like Dan-Levi to be this serious when they spoke. He always seemed like someone who hadn't a care in the world.

– What was it then?

– Karsten, you mustn't tell anyone else this.

– Of course not.

– I think it might have been some kind of ignition mechanism

Suddenly Dan-Levi's gaze was quizzical. Karsten had to avert his eyes.

– And you're asking *me* about it? Why?

– Because I thought you might have dropped it.

– But it was just lying there, you were standing right next to me.

Dan-Levi was still staring at him. – And I believe it was coincidental, Karsten. The point is, a person who finds something like that, in this case me, automatically becomes a witness. And the police will want to talk to you too.

– The police?

– I want you to go and see them. Better that way than that you wait for them to contact you.

Karsten looked round. – I know the people who own that sweet shop. He lowered his voice. – It's the family of a girl in my class. Think that has anything to do with it?

Dan-Levi's eyes widened. He removed his glasses again, spent a long time wiping them.

– A friend of mine works at the police station, he said finally. – He's okay. Promise me you'll go and see him as soon as you can?

Karsten shrugged. – Don't see that I can help them much.

– You don't need to do anything apart from tell them what you know.

Dan-Levi dug his hand into his pocket, pulled out a piece of paper. Something was written on it: *Roar Horvath, Sergeant*, and a telephone number.

– Then we've got a deal, Karsten.

* * *

The Peugeot was standing in front of the red garage with its boot open. Before Karsten could ring the bell, the door opened. Elsa Wilkins emerged with her coat on, a suitcase in one hand.

– Hi, Karsten, she said. – You still look as if you've got troubles.

She put a hand on his arm. He looked down. – Bit stressed out. It'll be okay. Are you going away?

– Just for the Easter weekend. She smiled, and he was on the point of asking her to stay. As though nothing bad could happen as long as she was there.

– Where are you going?

– Åsgårdstrand, she answered, still with her hand on his arm. – I'm attending a seminar.

– Tarot?

– That too.

– You mentioned something last time I was here. That card with the burning tower. He said it mostly to detain her for a few more moments. – Some of what you said turned out to be true.

– I know, Karsten. You're right to come here. Adrian is good at taking care of people. She squeezed his arm. – Maybe I'll be able to help you too when I come back. She laughed. – I know how sceptical you are. And that's good.

She headed towards the car, turned.

– He's down in the basement. You've got the place to yourselves the whole weekend.

Adrian was sitting in front of the computer. – There you are, he said as Karsten knocked on the door and stuck his head round.

Karsten saw the piece about the fire on the screen.

– You know who owns that shop? he exclaimed. His voice

felt splintered round the edges. – Jasmeen sent me a text message. Maybe they think I had something to do with it.

Adrian indicated for him to sit down in the leather armchair, handed him a mug. – And you don't?

Karsten jumped up again, splashing scalding coffee across his hand and swearing. – Seriously?

Adrian looked at him, his brow furrowed. Then he broke into a smile.

– Had to ask. Now it's done. You can sit down again.

Karsten remained on his feet. – Does the fire have anything to do with Sæter and all that stuff?

Adrian folded his hands behind his head, looked up at the ceiling. – Well we agreed that they needed to be given a message, a line needed to be drawn. But sometimes things happen that aren't planned.

– So you know who did it?

Adrian shook his head slowly. – But there's no harm in taking a guess.

– Could you get them to hand themselves in?

– Listen, Karsten. That shop is insured for a lot more than it's worth. And they've already had a fire in another shop they owned. Maybe someone just got there ahead of them this time. Maybe they did it themselves.

Karsten couldn't sit still. In a few hours' time they'd be back from the cabin, his mother, father and Synne. Before that he had to get all of this tidied up.

– Once they realise you've got people backing you, they'll think twice before doing anything, Adrian reassured him. – That's the kind of language they understand.

– I'm going to the police, Karsten finally managed to blurt out. – They want to talk to me.

He tried to explain what Dan-Levi had said to him.

– What did it look like? Adrian interrupted.

Karsten described the ignition device as far as he could recall it.

– And it was lying on the steps of the house where this chess pal of yours lives?

– Or just next to them.

– Think about it. Adrian suddenly seemed irritated. – Was it *on* the steps, or just *next* to the steps?

– A metre in front of them, in the snow.

Adrian's eyes narrowed. – We've got to stay one step ahead, he said into the air, as though he was talking to himself. – Always surprise.

He leaned forward and patted Karsten on the thigh, then got up and crossed to the wardrobe, glanced at himself in the mirror.

– Elsa's going to be away for Easter.

– I just met her outside, Karsten nodded.

Adrian whirled round. – You didn't mention anything about this? And nothing about what happened at the weekend?

Karsten hadn't mentioned anything about secret meetings, or weapons training, or the sacrifice.

– Elsa is a good person, Adrian explained. – I don't want to bother her with things she doesn't need to know anything about.

He slid his hand below a pile of clothing on one of the shelves, pulled out a black leather pouch. – Vemund and Sweaty are keeping an eye on your house.

Karsten's jaw dropped. His upper lip still hurt, and his knuckles were sore.

– The guy who said he's going to kill me? You can't trust that clown. Or his moron buddy.

Adrian opened the pouch and took out the Luger. – My grandfather was at the Normandy landings. He was one of the first to set foot on Sword Beach.

He pulled out the magazine, inserted some bullets. – The

safety catch is on, but don't wave it about. Sit with it a couple of minutes, get used to the feel of it in your hand.

With a little smile, he handed the weapon to Karsten. – Less than a week after D-Day, my grandfather was sent inland with an advance troop, towards a town called Bayeux. They came to a barn. It was raining, and the captain ordered my grandfather to check to see if they could shelter there. Grandfather kicks open the door and there, lying behind the corpse of a horse completely covered in rats, is a German soldier. The German points his pistol at my grandfather. My grandfather is quicker. He kills him with two shots. That's how he came by this. Try to imagine what it's been used for.

He kept his eyes fixed on Karsten. – I'll walk back to your place with you. From now on you need to be very aware of who you're hanging out with. Know who they are, if they'll back you or stab you in the back. Neither Vemund nor Sweaty is what you would call a Nietzschean *Übermensch*, and they both hate you. Not without reason. And Vemund is a difficult bastard who's not afraid to take his revenge. But he does what I tell him to do. And I'm the one you can trust.

He emptied his coffee cup and pulled on his leather jacket, took the Luger from Karsten and put it in his inside pocket.

– You can spend the nights here until Elsa gets back. That gives us a few days to find a solution.

Karsten felt a bubbling in his chest. Something is going to happen, he thought again. He held on to the thought, went through it word for word. Something is going to happen.

As they were on their way out, a huge van turned into the drive and stopped next to the garage.

– Did you get hold of them? Adrian asked Kai as he clambered out.

– They'll be ready tomorrow evening.

– Not before?

Kai shrugged. In the biting wind he was wearing only a T-shirt.

Adrian turned towards Karsten. – We've had an idea about how to deal with this Paki gang of yours. We've got contacts in another gang. Vietnamese.

– The Lia gang? Karsten exclaimed.

– A cross-cultural co-operation, Adrian nodded.

– Excellent people, Kai added with a grin. In the afternoon light, his bleached hair looked yellow.

As they headed up the road, Karsten tried to find out if all this was serious.

– It doesn't solve your problem, Adrian answered. – But we'll make sure Chadar and his pals have something else to worry about this Easter.

Karsten tried to pull himself together. – Is that Kai trustworthy?

Adrian put a hand on his shoulder. – Kai is my cousin, he reassured him. – He knows what he's doing.

Synne was standing out on the steps as they headed up the drive.

– Oh shit, they're home already, Karsten groaned.

– Nothing'll happen to them, Adrian repeated.

– Hi, Adrian, Synne said happily. She was wearing a pink parka and black tights.

– Weren't you supposed to be back tonight? said Karsten.

– Mum had to prepare for a meeting. Can you help me with something? She looked at Adrian.

– Of course we can help you, Synne.

She blushed. – Dad promised to get my bike out, but he's so lazy. And now he's gone off to the petrol station to shop.

Adrian spread his hands. – Then we'll do it.

The bike was hanging from a hook at the back of the

garage, behind the Volvo. Karsten went to fetch the car keys. When he came back, Synne was standing there tapping something into her phone.

– Gave her my number, Adrian winked. – Never know when you might need it.

Karsten backed the car out, and Adrian followed with the bike.

– You need air in both your tyres. And the chain needs oiling.

He began pumping. Karsten held the bike. It was calming to be doing something together. Adrian ran the tip of the oil can over the dry chain. When he was done, he slid his finger around the frame with its half-torn transfers of Disney princesses.

– What are you doing today? Karsten wanted to know.

Synne sat on her bike. – Going to Tamara's. She's on her own at home.

– Just the two of you?

She nodded. – Mum and I were going to watch a film, but she can't after all. So I'm sleeping over at Tamara's instead.

Adrian patted her on the head. As usual, the thick brown hair was uncombed, with dense tangles at the back.

– You should be wearing a helmet, said Karsten.

She yawned. – No one at school uses a helmet.

Nothing must happen to her, he thought suddenly. He put his arm around her and pulled her towards him.

– Be careful then.

She reached up and gave him a hug. It had been a while since the last time, and he was taken aback, but he understood why when she then did the same with Adrian before pedalling away through the gate.

29

THE POLICEMAN WHO came down to fetch him had a naff moustache that ended in two twisted points. He had to be using wax on it, Karsten thought as he was ushered into a small, almost unfurnished office. A few folders and magazine holders on the shelf, a noticeboard with a duty list on it.

– I need to talk to . . . Karsten fumbled out the note Dan-Levi had given him. – Someone called Horvath.

– You need to talk to me, said the policeman, without making it clear whether he was or was not Horvath.

Karsten sat on the edge of the plastic chair. He didn't have much to tell. He was passing Dan-Levi's house one morning on his way to school, saw his chess-playing partner on the steps, went over for a chat. As he was about to leave, Dan-Levi picked something up from the ground.

– Describe what he found.

Karsten had hardly even looked at it that morning.

– A cigarette, some matches, a rubber band.

Mustachio shoved a pen and paper across the table towards him. – Draw it.

He did his best.

– And that was the first time you'd ever seen anything like that?

Even though it was easy to answer, Karsten disliked the question. The police guy took a bag from a drawer, placed cigarettes, rubber bands, paper clips and a few lengths of string on the table.

– Can you make one?

– You mean assemble all this lot?

– That is what I mean.

– Why should I do that?

The policeman looked at him for a few moments.

– Try, he said finally.

Karsten laid a couple of matches against a cigarette, fiddled with a rubber band. Made a sort of rough job of it.

– Is that what the thing looked like?

– More or less.

– No string, or thread?

– Don't think so.

The guy tweaked the ends of his moustache, first one side, then the other. Karsten felt a sudden urge to get up, leave the room, just get out of there. Or else tell the man everything that had happened. He did none of those things.

– Have you any idea who might be behind it? he stammered.

Mustachio gave a quick grin.

– We have our suspicions.

He leaned back in his chair, folded his arms behind his head. – So you play chess?

Karsten nodded. – Can I have a glass of water?

Mustachio got up, went out into the corridor. Half a minute later he was back with a plastic cup. The water was tepid and smelled metallic. Karsten forced half of it down. Then a thought struck him; he couldn't shake it off.

– Was that . . . water?

The policeman frowned. – What else would it be?

Karsten peered down into the cup, saw the tiny bubbles there, couldn't shake off the thought that something had been added to the clear liquid.

– I'm going to ask you about a few dates. I want you to try to remember what you were doing on those days.

Karsten squeezed the cup. The flimsy plastic cracked and what was left inside jetted in a thin stream on to his trousers. The policeman again studied him intently before turning towards the window. He took a few paper tissues and slung them across to him.

– The first date is Sunday March the thirty-first. To be specific, the night of April the first.

– Why are you asking me about that?

The policeman shrugged. – I've asked a hundred people the same thing and I'll be asking a hundred more. Or a thousand.

The answer didn't make Karsten feel any easier. A stinging pain spread through his stomach.

– Was at home, he managed to say.

– Sure?

The pain rose into his chest. There was something in that water, he thought again, something that was making his heartbeat heavy and uneven.

– I need some fresh air, he said.

– It can wait.

The policeman continued to question him about various dates, where he had been, if he knew where the Stornes stables were, and the Furutunet remand home. This last question was what tipped the scales. Karsten got to his feet. Dark shadows drifting in from the sides narrowed his vision.

– Sit down, said the policeman. – I've got a couple more questions and then we're done.

Karsten pulled the door open and staggered out into the corridor, ran towards the vestibule and out into the parking lot, where he stopped, bent over and gasped for breath.

His father was sitting in the living room watching TV when Karsten sneaked in through the front door. He wasn't sure whether his mother was back from the office. Something to do with a business dispute, or a quarrel over a will. Or was it political? After she joined the board of the local council, she always came home with two piles of documents, one from work, the other committee stuff.

– Is that you, Karsten?

Karsten looked in on his father.

– Everything all right?

He said yes. Everything was all right. Absolutely everything. He didn't scream; on the contrary, his voice was so calm it was almost inaudible.

– Spending the night at a pal's house.

– That's all right.

– Heard from Synne?

His father turned back to the TV screen.

– She's at that friend's, over at Vigernes.

– Tamara.

– Right. Good for her to get out a bit. By the way, there was a boy here asking for you.

– A boy?

– It was Synne who spoke to him.

Karsten closed the door. Ran up the stairs to his room. Called her. She didn't answer. Called Adrian, got no answer there either. He ran down again, shoved his feet into his shoes and raced out the door without tying the laces.

He pedalled as hard as he could over to Vigernes. Tamara lived in a semi-detached house just by the roundabout. He dropped the bike and ran up and down the road, looking out for the black BMW. Looking out for any car that might be waiting for him. Stood in the driveway. The rain had stopped. – Better calm down now, he instructed himself out loud. – Don't do anything stupid. Stand here until things are under control, that's the first thing.

He rang the bell. No response. They were playing loud

music inside, some heavy stuff. Not what Synne usually listened to. He charged in. The music was coming from a huge TV screen. There was a smell of freshly baked pizza. In the half-light he could make out three or four shapes. He found a switch and turned the light on.

– Karsten, Synne cried as she got up from a chair.

Tamara was on her feet too. She was dark and skinny, long legs and short skirt.

– Has something happened? Synne said, crossing the floor. Karsten looked round. There were only girls in the room. Thirteen-year-olds eating pizza and crisps. One of them grabbed a bottle from the table and hid it on the floor beside the sofa.

– No, nothing's happened. I was just passing.

– You want some? asked Tamara and turned down the TV. She held out a piece of pizza towards him.

He waved no with his hands, pulled Synne outside into the hallway. She looked up at him. Distantly he registered that she was wearing make-up, far too much mascara; she looked like a stranger.

– Dad said someone had been asking for me. What was his name?

– He didn't say. He was a Pakistani or something. Her mouth was full of chewing gum. She blew a bubble until it burst.

– You sure?

– He spoke a bit like *say hi to your brother all right kid*. She did the accent well and even added a little smile.

– What did he look like?

She described him. Suit and shirt, earring, thin strip of beard, the kind you could rub out with an eraser, according to her.

– Was he alone?

She shook her head, chewing and chewing. He felt like

pulling the gum out of her mouth and throwing it at the wall.

– There were some others sitting in a car out on the road.

– What kind of car?

– Black. Pretty cool.

– Did he frighten you?

– Not in the slightest. She blew another gum bubble that burst and stuck to her lips. – Cool guy actually.

He went right up close to her and grabbed her by the arm. – Now listen, Synne, listen properly.

– What's up with you?

– There are certain people out there you shouldn't talk to.

– Thought he was one of your pals.

– He's no pal of mine. So if he or any other Pakistani stops you, just keep on walking and pretend you didn't hear.

– Turned into a racist, have you?

He let go of her. – Just be careful, he said. – Be careful and look out for yourself. And one more thing. Not a word to Mum and Dad about me coming round here. I'll explain later.

She looked at him with large round eyes. Then she nodded. She liked secrets.

– Be sure to keep the doors locked, okay? If someone comes to the door, check who it is before you open it. And call me if someone you don't know wants to come in, understand? I'll be back in a couple of hours.

A sly look came into her eyes, as though at any moment she was about to burst out laughing.

– I can call Adrian, she said. – He rang me not long ago.

– He rang *you*?

– He was trying to get hold of you but you didn't pick up.

He thought about it. She was always lying about stuff

like that. He would never understand what went on in that head of hers.

He tried Adrian's number again. Still no answer. It was now seven thirty. He pedalled down Storgata. It was Maundy Thursday, not many people about. A car approached from behind, passed slowly by, a silver-grey Toyota. There were two people inside, could be Vemund and Sweaty. He braked sharply. The car drove on, then pulled in alongside the kerb and stopped. Karsten whirled the bike round, down a side street, then a right. Back on Storgata there was no sign of the Toyota.

At that moment he saw Priest emerging from Pizza House carrying five or six pizza cartons. Karsten turned, pretending not to have seen him.

– Is that *you* out at this hour? Priest came over towards him. – Tonje's been asking about you, he winked. – You two got something going on I don't know about?

A few minutes later Karsten was being ushered into the living room at the rectory.

– Look what I found! Priest shouted. – A real live genius.

Inga squealed with delight when she saw him. There were eight or ten others there, some from the school leavers' party committee, a couple of others from class. Some of them cheered and gave him the Mexican wave. No sign of Tonje.

– The lad's drifting around Lillestrøm all on his own. Has no one told him how dangerous it is?

– Good job we've got you, Priest.

Priest slung the pizza cartons on to the table. – And I'm not being the driver again until July. He grabbed a can of beer, took a swig, handed it to Karsten.

Karsten shook his head.

– A smart guy like him doesn't want to be swapping

germs with you, said Inga, picking up one that hadn't been opened. A little shower hit Karsten in the face as she released the ring pull and held the can up to his mouth.

– Where's Tonje? he asked after taking a swallow.

Inga shrugged. – Somewhere or other with Thomas.

That was how it was. It had always been Tonje and Thomas. A break every now and then. Before she started sending messages pretending there was something she wanted. And then it was back to her boyfriend.

Karsten took the beer can that was offered him again, drained it down. Now I'm going to puke, he thought. Instead he belched, and there was more cheering. Inga put an arm round him.

– I wanna be kissed by you, she sang hoarsely and pulled him into a few unsteady dance steps.

– Think you're going to lose your virginity tonight, Karsten, Priest grinned.

– Inga too, said someone on the sofa, followed by a short burst of laughter.

The music was turned up, some techno stuff. Karsten managed another couple of swigs of beer, and since Inga refused to let go of him, he put his arm around her. Suddenly he bent down and kissed her on the neck. She gave a start and looked at him, eyes wide in surprise.

– What's got into you?

He let go of her and turned away. Priest was standing at the table slicing up the pizzas with a pair of nail scissors.

– To operate on a pizza in a fair and just world requires surgical precision, he announced. – No one is to get one piece of corn more than anyone else.

Karsten forced the rest of the beer down, the bubbles from the bitter liquid rising to his head and fizzing there. Not the bubbles themselves, of course, he reasoned; the ethanol released certain transmitter substances, dopamine among them, in those parts of the brain that controlled the sensation of well-being. He felt lighter, as though he was full of helium, and if he floated any higher he would be able to observe everything from above. Call Synne every half-hour, he decided, telling himself that he was already seeing things more clearly. He had landed in something that resembled a labyrinth. If he could get a bird's eye view, it would be easier to find the way out.

– Got another beer? he asked Priest.

– Dear Brother Karsten. Have I ever stood by and watched a fellow human being suffer?

He went out into the kitchen, returned with a can.

– Let me know if you want something stronger. Or faster acting.

– You said Tonje was here.

– She's bound to turn up.

– You say you've got something stronger?

Priest grinned broadly. – That's my boy.

He put an arm around Karsten and led him out into the kitchen. He took a bottle from a cupboard next to the fridge.

– This is a special occasion. An experiment. What happens when the genius takes a drink? Does he become even more of a genius, or more like the rest of us? I'm certain my dad would be prepared to donate some of his cognac in the name of a scientific experiment.

It burnt in his mouth, but Karsten liked the sensation, a flash of light that travelled up from his palate to the back of his head. And when he swallowed, that burning sensation moved down into his stomach and drowned whatever it was that for more than a week now had been crawling around like an earwig.

– You know what, Karsten, you've always been a helluva good lad. I love you, and that's the truth of it. Priest embraced him. – Cheers, Brother Karsten.

They emptied their glasses. Karsten gasped for breath but did not protest when his was again filled to the brim.

– You and me, we'll bloody show them, Priest chortled, and kissed him on the cheek. – Together we are invincible.

Karsten took his phone out of his jacket pocket. – Have to call my sister.

Synne answered straight away. – No, no one's been here. No, I'm not afraid of Pakistanis. Relax. See you.

– I can't let anything happen to her, he said to Priest as he forced down more of the cognac. – The police are after me, he added once he had recovered.

Priest gave him a sidelong glance. Then he grinned. – Sure, brother, I'll take care of them if they show up.

– The police and a Pakistani gang, Karsten went on. – And Schrödinger and Heisenberg.

Priest frowned and stopped smiling. – That bad, eh?

Then Inga was there.

– Sorry about just then, she said. – You took me by surprise.

She gave him a hug. He squeezed her tight, pressing against her until her breasts flattened across his chest.

– I'm going to die, he shouted into her ear.

It looked like she was making an effort to look straight at him, her eyes swimming round in a great lake. Unless it was his own that refused to keep still.

– Hi, Karsten, said Tonje.

He broke free and turned. She was standing in the doorway.

– Tonje, he murmured, and took a few steps in her direction. And then it hit him. Not some vague nausea slowly spreading through his belly, but a fierce clawing that seized his stomach and twisted it tight. With no warning, it jetted out of him, splashing down across the carpet and the table. Although actually not that much ended up on the carpet and table. Something in the region of seventy per cent of it hit Tonje.

Afterwards, with a mixture of swearing and laughing and groans of exasperation, he lay on the floor with a cloth in his hand and tried to wipe up the remains of the contents of his own stomach. That's what I'm like inside, he thought or said out loud. Half-digested food and drinks he couldn't tolerate and would never be able to tolerate, masticated in hydrochloric acid.

Later, he's lying on a sofa, in a basement room. Someone is sitting there with him. – Tonje, he says out into the semi-darkness, but it isn't her. A phone rings. After a while he realises that it's his own, but he can't find it. Not until he pushes his whole hand into the hole in the lining of his jacket. By the time he retrieves it, the ringing has stopped. Synne, he babbles, and sits up in the room that is now in darkness. Supposed to be looking after her, and I can't even stand on my own two feet. Somehow or other he manages to reach the number of the caller.

– Kai.

– Kai! shouted Karsten, trying to remember who Kai was.

– Where are you?

He looked around the basement room.

– Lillestrøm, he slurred.

– Are you drunk?

Karsten had to concede that he was. Pissed, stoned, sloshed, as they used to say when his dad was a schoolboy. Rat legged, tight, tipsy and tanked.

– You having fun?

– Dunno.

Karsten thought he might start to laugh. Or just as easily the opposite. Sort of perfectly poised between the two. – I don't think it's fun. On a scale from one to ten, I'm minus nine. Are *you* having fun?

– Tell me where you are and stay there. I'll pick you up.

– The station, he managed to say before the call was terminated.

He opened the window, pulled himself up and out through a window well. Staggered through a garden that must belong to the rectory, over a fence, into another garden, finally ended up on a road. Tried to walk straight but it was impossible; all kinds of forces, centrifugal and centripetal and gravitational, pulled in different directions. The sum of these forces had to be controlled, and he was in no condition to do so. In his stockinged feet with his shirt hanging out he stumbled along the road beside the railway line, a dark stain covering one thigh of his trousers. – There's a walkway under the road here somewhere, he muttered. – I'm walking towards the walkway.

Kai looked him over as he climbed into the car.

– Not good.

He pulled out of the station, drove in the direction of Volla. The engine growled and sounded annoyed as well.

– We must find Synne, Karsten slurred.

Who is Synne?

He struggled to make himself understood. Certain consonants were impossible to articulate after each other. They responded as though they had opposing magnetic charges. Others were sticky and glued up against each other.

– We'll drive by, Kai interrupted. – But perhaps best not to let your little sister see you like this.

Karsten nodded and nodded. Kai was a four-square block of muscle, as well as being the most sensible man in the world.

– You're fucking all right, he tried to say, just as his stomach lurched again. He fumbled with a handle that might open the window before it was too late.

– Do not touch that!

Karsten forced the contents of his stomach back down again.

— It don't work, Kai barked.

Karsten raised his hands to show that he had no intention of touching anything else in the car.

— The winder mechanism is kaput. Been trying to get a new one for weeks. Kai said something or other about cables and wires. — And you probably think all you have to do is knock on the door of your local Chevy dealer and ask for a new one.

Karsten didn't know whether he was being asked a question, but he nodded to be on the safe side, and Kai carried on talking. That was fine by him; he could alternately grunt and nod without understanding a word of what this sudden outpouring was actually about. He gathered it had something to do with European winder mechanisms. That they stopped and slipped back down if you so much as breathed on them, so that kids wouldn't suffocate. Whereas in America the motors were as strong as horses and unstoppable, and looking after people's kids wasn't the responsibility of the car manufacturer.

Kai carried on in this vein all the while they cruised around the block where Tamara lived. There was still light on in all the windows. Karsten counted them and thought he'd worked out which was the right apartment. But even the simple addition involved in this process was tricky, as he sat there gripping on to the seat of the Chevy and trying not to puke.

— It all looks peaceful, said Kai.

— Got to talk to her.

Karsten tried to climb out, felt a blow on his arm.

— Remember what I said about messing around with that door?

— Sorry, Karsten muttered, again raising his hands to indicate his unconditional surrender.

Kai pulled in by the roadside. – Sit here and don't play with anything. He got out and walked over to the driveway.

Karsten couldn't keep his eyes open. Slumped down and landed on a ship's deck that rose and fell, and he had no business being at sea at all.

– Everything okay there, Kai announced as he slammed the door behind him. – I've called Vemund. He'll take care of it. Now we've got to get you up on your feet. We've got a couple of hours.

– What's happening?

Kai didn't answer. They crossed Storgata and carried on past the school. Shortly afterwards, they pulled into Adrian's courtyard, stopped next to the garage.

Karsten got out. Staggered towards Adrian's front door.

– Not there, Kai shouted behind him. – Adrian's not back yet.

Karsten looked around in confusion. When Kai unlocked the other front door, he followed him in.

– No need to take off your shoes. Kai grinned as he let him into the hall.

Karsten looked down. – Where are my shoes?

Kai shrugged. – Maybe you gave them to the Salvation Army. Or they've wandered off somewhere on their own. Can you manage to get up the stairs?

Karsten started on the bottom step, slumped against the wall. – A bit slippery, he tried to excuse himself.

Kai leaned down and lifted him, carried him upstairs. On the landing he opened the door to a bathroom, put Karsten down on the toilet seat.

– Take off your Sunday best. You need a shower.

– Can't hold it down any more, Karsten groaned, and slithered down on to the floor. Kai just had time to raise the lid before it came pouring out of him.

* * *

Later, he sat in the bathtub with the shower jet directed on to his face. Fragments of the events of earlier that evening broke through. Tonje's face as he walked towards her and his mouth suddenly gaped wide open. He rubbed the shower head against his forehead, tried to imagine the water forcing its way through the bones of the skull and flushing out everything inside, undoing the synapses that had been formed over the last few hours and days, from the moment when Jasmeen had appeared at his desk. Let everything he could recall since that day drain down through the plughole and disappear for ever. He saw in his mind's eye the gravestone penetrated by the cylinder. A fitting memorial for the time that was to be buried.

He climbed out of the tub. Kai had laid out a towel and some clothes for him, but he felt another evacuation on the way and didn't know where it would come from. There was no toilet paper left. He opened the cupboard below the sink. Four bottles of lighter fluid there. Had to take them out to find what he was looking for, just about reached the toilet in time before a warm shower burst from his gut. The right orifice at least, he consoled himself. Things are looking up.

– That helped, then, Kai remarked when Karsten came down to the kitchen wearing training pants that were several centimetres too short for his legs.

He put a cup of steaming fresh coffee down in front of him.

– I don't know how many of these you're going to need, but you better sober up quick. We're leaving in a few minutes.

– Leaving?

The consonants were no longer quite so sticky.

– You can't stay here. Kai poured himself a cup. – We think the Pakis know where you are.

– No one knows where I am, Karsten protested. He picked up his own trousers, felt in his pockets; his phone wasn't there.

– Shit, he muttered, and tried to recall where he had last seen it. – It's at Priest's place. I need to talk to Adrian.

– Leave it to me.

Karsten tried to get his head to work a little quicker.

– Do you live here? he asked.

– Yes.

– Adrian said you were his cousin?

No answer.

– And Elsa is your aunt?

Kai said at the table. – Do you know her?

– She told my fortune. Amazing that people believe in stuff like that.

– Now you shut your mouth, Kai interrupted. – No more crap from you.

Karsten cringed in his chair. – I didn't mean anything.

Kai leaned across the table, his gaze boring into him. – Here's something you better learn pretty damned quick, he growled, wagging his finger in Karsten's face. – You're not better than other people, not one tiny bit, even if you can solve maths problems. Got that?

– Of course, Karsten mumbled, staring down at the table.

– You make enemies wherever you go. Always provoking. If you don't wise up pretty soon, you will be in deep shit. Got that?

– Got it, Karsten said without looking up.

– I don't want to hear one more word of your shit. I don't want you talking about Elsa at all. Got that?

– Got that, Karsten echoed, not getting anything.

– You're not worth a toenail compared to her. So keep your mouth shut.

Kai stood up. For a moment Karsten thought he was

going to hit him. He raised an arm above his head to protect himself, but Kai disappeared out into the hallway and climbed the stairs. When he returned a few minutes later, he was much calmer.

– Has Adrian given you any idea of what we're going to do?

– Not any more than what you were talking about.

Kai leaned against the table. He was wearing a sleeveless vest and his bulging muscles shone as though smeared with oil. His forearm was covered in scars.

– The Gooks are going to do what we asked them to. They hate the Pakis. The Gooks are something else. You can trust them. They're not trying to take over the whole world. They're happy just to get on with their own business. But don't ever trespass on their territory, otherwise you're dead.

He straightened up. – Excellent people, he added.

Karsten was careful not to touch anything as he once again climbed into the Chevy.

– Where are we going?

– Sæter, said Kai.

– What d'you mean? I've got no business there.

Kai reversed out and turned into the road. – They're not there. You'll have the house to yourself. All you need to worry about is feeding the dogs. He laughed. Karsten didn't know whether or not that was a good sign.

They crossed the runway. As they passed the Statoil petrol station, a car swung out behind them.

Kai scowled. – There they are, I'm guessing.

– They?

– The BMW. Black.

Karsten leaned forward and looked in the mirror, could see nothing but the headlights of the car behind.

– That's a Paki Porsche, said Kai.

– Porsche?

– Or kebab cab or Punjab taxi, whatever you want to call it. Can smell people like that a kilometre away.

He speeded up at the roundabout. There was a rumbling under the bonnet as he put his foot down and changed gear. Karsten sat on his hands to keep them from shaking. By the flat stretch up at Hvam they were doing over a hundred. Round the corner Kai jammed on the brakes and wrenched the Chevy into the driveway of a business park, then on behind the closest building, coming to a complete halt a few centimetres from a fence. The contents of Karsten's stomach were still moving forward; somehow or other he got the door open, staggered out and bent double as the gush jetted out of him.

Several minutes passed before he was able to crawl back into the car.

– Pakis won't set foot inside an American car, Kai grinned as he handed him some tissue paper. – Fucking pigs. Full of prejudice. But when it really matters they always screw up.

He waited a few more minutes before reversing out in front of the building again, gliding off up the road in the opposite direction.

– Almost too easy to lose them, he chuckled as he took the turning towards Korset.

– Stop here, Karsten shouted when they reached Erleveien. Kai looked at him, didn't slow down.

– I'm not interested in feeding any dogs, Karsten protested. – I want to go home.

– The Pakis are waiting for you.

– Don't give a shit. Just let me out here.

Kai speeded up. – We're working like maniacs to help you deal with all this. Don't you understand that without us you're finished? Now just stop your bloody moaning. You're going to stay at Sæter's until tomorrow morning.

Talking to Kai was like playing Minesweeper. Part of the time you could work out where it was best to go, and then suddenly it all blew up anyway. Karsten chose to say nothing.

As they passed the church, Kai opened the glove compartment and took out a CD.

– Put that on.

Nirvana, Karsten noted as he slid it into the player. Kai clicked forward to the track he wanted to hear, turned up the volume. Behind the music Karsten noted a droning sound that he couldn't locate. Not until he turned and saw Kai sitting there, his thick lips moving as he sang along with Cobain.

– Kind of thing I listened to when I was your age, he shouted. – *I feel stupid and contagious.*

They turned on to the E6. Karsten slumped back into the seat. Still dizzy and nauseous, he made a tentative attempt to sum up the situation so far. First, he had puked all over Tonje. Second, Kai was taking him to spend the night completely alone at a deserted farmhouse in the depths of the forest. Third, they were planning something that involved getting the Vietnamese and the Pakistanis to fight each other. Fourth, this gang of Pakistanis was still keeping his home under observation. He could have kept on like that, reaching fifty or a hundred other points before he came to something positive.

– Adrian said you were his cousin, he said once more, as a way of approaching what he really wanted to say. He had to get Kai to lend him his phone so that he could ring Adrian, because this business about Sæter and the dogs was a misunderstanding.

Kai shrugged. – That's not correct.

Karsten sat up straight. – Why would he tell a lie about something like that? Is it such a big deal to be your cousin?

Kai grinned. Fortunately, because Karsten could hear that it sounded more sarcastic than he meant.

– Adrian is my brother.

– You're kidding.

– My half-brother, Kai corrected himself.

The information acted as a stimulus on Karsten's brain.
– Is Elsa . . .?

– Didn't I tell you not to talk about her?

– Yes, you did.

– Has anything happened to make you think that isn't the case any more?

– Not as far as I know.

At the turn-off to Kløfta, he pulled in and stopped at the petrol station.

– Sit here while I fill it up.

– I need a pee.

– Then you'll just have to wait until I get back.

He took hold of the petrol gun and began filling the tank. When he was finished, he headed off towards the shop.

Karsten found himself sitting there and cursing inside. Damned if he would stay at Sæter's place, even if it meant having to make his way home in the slippers Kai had lent him. There was a map in the driver's-side door. He leaned over and pulled it out. A road map of Europe; not much use for someone who wanted to navigate the Nannestad country lanes in the middle of the night. As he put it back, he noticed that the felt lining of the doorpost had come loose at the edge. He tried to press it back into place, but something was blocking it. He stuck two fingers inside, felt something that seemed to be made of plastic, caught hold of a corner of it and dragged it out.

A bag full of cigarettes. He'd never seen Kai smoking.

He took one out, a sort of figure consisting of a half-cigarette and three matchsticks bound together with an elastic band. It was as though his fingers recognised it before his brain did. There were five or six more of them in the bag, some with a long string-like tail.

He sat there, revolving the little cigarette figure between his fingers, knew that he had to put it back, couldn't do it. His thoughts prevented it, streaming in all directions, tearing up pictures, throwing them together, and suddenly he saw in his mind's eye one of the cards Elsa had laid out for him. *This might be dangerous, Karsten*, she said, and pointed to the picture of a burning tower with people tumbling down from the top of it. Part of him tried to classify the information. The policeman had asked him to assemble something that looked exactly like this. Suddenly he thought of Synne. What was she doing in the middle of this train of thought? She's sitting at the kitchen table. He pours muesli into her cereal bowl, the dry flakes filling it, he doesn't stop pouring, it runs over, flows across the tabletop, where the sunlight reflects so strongly he has to shield his eyes.

With a huge effort he pulled himself together, dropped the half-cigarette back into the plastic bag, forced himself to collect his thoughts. The reason the police wanted to talk to him was that these cigarettes had something to do with the fires. What was it Dan-Levi had said when he told him to go to the police? That these figures were some kind of ignition device.

He looked up as Kai hurried out of the shop. He wanted to squash the bag back behind the felt, but he wouldn't have time. Instead he rolled it up and pushed it underneath the seat. Three seconds later, Kai jumped back inside. He was carrying two hot dogs and handed one to Karsten.

– Bit of nourishment is what you need, he said.

Karsten managed to say something that sounded like

thank you. Considered throwing open the car door, running into the shop, screaming out something or other, holding on tight to the counter, or to the girl he could make out through the window. She didn't look much older than Synne.

The car started with an impatient growl. Kai drove with one hand, bolting down the hot dog with the other. On the motorway, he moved into the outside lane and pushed the car up to a hundred and forty.

– Not eating? he slurped.

– Still nauseous.

Kai laughed loudly. – That's what you get when you can't control yourself. People like you shouldn't drink alcohol. You burn your brain cells away and then you're not much use to us any more. All at once he seemed to be in high spirits.

Karsten squeezed the sausage he was holding between his fingers. It reeked of sweet fat and tomato ketchup.

– Will Adrian be coming? he managed to say.

– Adrian will be coming. Or not coming. He does what he feels like.

In the fields around the road patchy snow still lay like white scars across the darkness. Suddenly Kai turned the music down.

– Adrian grew up like a prince, he said, still munching. – That's what I call him. The prince. His father owns five or six factories and more properties than you've got fingers and toes. If ever anyone was born with a silver spoon in his mouth, it's Adrian. And now damned if he doesn't turn up and start taking over everything here as well.

He pressed the racing engine a little harder. If only a traffic cop would come after us, thought Karsten.

– Why does Adrian say he's your cousin? he asked, just for something to say.

Kai wiped around his mouth with the sausage paper, opened the window and threw it out.

– He doesn't like having anyone close to him, he growled. – And I was raised by our aunt, so that means he thinks we can call ourselves cousins.

He leaned back, put his foot down harder on the accelerator.

– Not too far from where you live, as it happens.

His voice sounded friendly again, but Karsten stayed on the alert.

– In Erleveien?

– Yes.

– Where?

– Never you mind.

Kai indicated and moved into the lane for the Gardermoen slip road. – The woman who called herself my mother took ill. And I ended up in a children's home. Not something I would recommend to others. But then Elsa came back.

The name made Karsten see that image of the burning tower again.

– That twat of a factory owner dropped her. And now don't you start fucking asking why.

Again Karsten tried to gather his thoughts. He fumbled with the door handle. Kai's hand came down so hard on his thigh he felt the pain shoot into his back.

– You just don't fucking get it with that window, do you?

Karsten shrank into his seat. – I forgot, he managed to say. – Need some fresh air.

Kai growled something or other, lowered the window on the driver's side halfway. Fortunately he turned the music up again, navigated back to the first song he'd played and started groaning away . . . *stupid and contagious*. Suddenly he howled something through the half-open window, and then he'd played it over and over again, and the fourth or fifth time Karsten was able to discern the words through the music.

– Fucking Furutunet!

Ignition devices, those things in the bag are ignition devices. The part of his brain where these thoughts accumulated was already full, but even more forced their way in. Furutunet was the name of the remand home that burned down; the guy at the police station had asked him where he was that night. A girl had died in the fire up there, and this creature sitting beside him and bellowing away at the top of his voice had four bottles of lighter fluid in a cupboard beneath his bathroom sink.

They turned into the driveway of Sæter's house. The headlights swept across the facade and the dogs began howling loudly. The old Mazda was still parked in front of the main house, but there were no lights on in any of the windows.

– Fucking mutts, Kai growled. – Sæter shouldn't keep dogs if he can't look after them himself.

Karsten stared through the windscreen. The window on the driver's side was still half open, and he sat there shivering in the thin borrowed shirt. His thumb touched a corner of the plastic bag sticking out from under the seat.

– Sæter asked Adrian to come up here and feed his dogs, but the prince always gets out of the shit jobs. So now it's your turn instead. Kai was angry again. – Hate dogs, he barked, and turned towards Karsten. – I'm locking you in. You'll stay here tonight and give the dogs their food. Someone'll come out and pick you up in the morning.

– Okay, Karsten muttered without moving his gaze from a point above the dark edge of the forest on the far side of the field.

Kai switched off the engine, opened the door; the light came on. He stepped out, stopped and bent forward. Karsten still didn't move. From the corner of his eye he saw Kai fiddling with the flap in the doorpost, stick his whole hand down inside it. Suddenly he got back in and slammed the door shut hard. For a few moments he sat there without saying a word. Karsten could feel his eyes burning through the semi-darkness. The sausage he'd been holding in his hand since the petrol station slipped from his fingers and on to his lap.

– Where are they?

He thought of asking for his punishment straight away; get it over with so that he could get out and away.

– What? he managed to say, and knew it was the wrong answer even before the bunched fist hit him in the temple so hard that his head was thrown against the window.

– Don't treat me like an idiot, Kai shouted. – Where have you hidden them?

The pain flared in every direction and met at a point somewhere in the middle of his head. He managed to wriggle a hand beneath the seat and pull the bag out. Kai turned on the light, examined it, looked as though he was counting them. As he pushed it back under the felt, Karsten opened the door and jumped out. He kicked off the slippers, raced towards the house in his stockinged feet, above the furious baying of the dogs heard the car door opening and Kai bellowing at him from behind.

He sped round the corner of the house, on through the garden and over towards the barn, pulled at the door handle he had tried the last time, found he still couldn't open it. He threw himself to the ground, on the point of surrendering, anything to lessen the anger of the figure storming towards him. Then he caught side of the place at the end of the wall where some of the planks hung loose. He squeezed in, tumbled down, remembered in the same instant that there was an animal in there. Several animals; he heard them over in a corner, crude grunting mixed with high-pitched squeals. He lay there counting. Four seconds later,

he heard footsteps in the slush outside. A low growling
sound as the door handle was shaken. Karsten lay frozen
to the ground. One of his legs began to shake, he held it
tight with his hands, forcing it to be still.

– Is that where you are?

Through the grunting of the pig and the squealing of
her young he heard Kai breathing heavily just behind the
loose planks. Yes, he could have shouted, here I am. Because
waiting for what was about to happen was worse than
anything. Then the sound of footsteps again, continuing
along the wall and disappearing.

He shouldn't have got up, should have carried on lying
there without moving a finger, but he felt something soft
against his throat, a damp snout grunting in his ear, and he
scrambled to his knees, feeling round in the dark. He found
a shelf, pulled himself up. A sliver of light entered through
the broken plank. He backed away, his foot hit something
– a bucket that tipped over and emptied its contents. The
pig began to run round him, her squealing shredding the
darkness into thin strips. Then Kai's voice was there again.

– Don't try to hide, you little bastard.

Karsten heard the rotten plank being pulled away with
a ripping sound. He ran into the darkness, banged into a
gate, hopped over it and staggered into a large space,
glimpsed a tractor and a plough. A ladder behind it. He
climbed up, pulling himself up from the top rung into an
open loft. There was the sound of a hard blow from the
room he had just been in, and suddenly the shrieking pig
fell silent and all that could be heard was the whimpering
of what sounded like newborn piglets. He crawled in towards
the back of the loft. Pale light fell from a small window
under the gable. There were some skis there, and tins of
paint. A spade. He squatted, not moving.

– You're going to have to come down. Kai was talking

to him from somewhere right next to the ladder. – I don't understand why you're so afraid. You haven't done anything wrong, have you?

The voice was friendly now, and for a moment Karsten felt like climbing down, shaking Kai's hand and apologising for having gone through his things like that.

– I'm coming up, said Kai. – And then we can have a little chat.

Karsten heard him step on to the ladder and begin to climb up, rung by rung. Suddenly he saw Synne, still sitting at the kitchen table and staring at him. She's afraid, and he wants to comfort her, because she doesn't trust anybody else.

Kai's head appeared above the edge of the floor, just about visible in the light from the opening. He seemed to be smiling, his eyes two black holes in his broad face. Karsten grabbed the spade by the wall, swung round and struck with all his might, screaming as the handle snapped. He heard the body tumbling down and hitting the floor with a dull thud, dragging the ladder with it.

He backed away towards the other end of the loft, couldn't bear to look down. He found a beam, clambered up and managed to get his legs round it. It sloped downwards, he slid briefly and a huge splinter penetrated his thigh. He let go, fell, landed on his feet and rolled forwards.

Getting up, he trampled in something wet and sticky. He kicked the overturned bucket away, found his way back into the room he had first entered. The hole in the wall was bigger now. In the grey vestiges of light that filtered through, the pig lay still, the piglets swarming round the body. Karsten stepped on to the soft body, pushed up against the loose planks and dragged himself out into the mud. The dogs began baying again. He ran across the yard. Keep running down the road, he thought, keep on running till I'm home. Then he saw that the passenger door of the Chevy was still open. He reached inside, the keys were there. He crawled across into the driver's seat, turned the ignition; the engine began to thrum. At that moment he saw a shadow from the corner of his eye. It grew larger as it pressed in through the half-open window.

– Leaving without me?

Karsten put his foot down. There were lights on the dashboard, but the engine wouldn't catch. Then Kai's hand was holding him by the neck in an iron grip.

– You're one of those types who likes to play alone, Kai whispered, his lips pressed to Karsten's ear. – You're the type who keeps to himself. You're afraid of everybody.

– I won't say anything, Karsten gasped.

– Say anything? About what?

Karsten opened and then closed his mouth, unable to speak.

– About what, Karsten?

Pyromaniac. The word sped through him, black, and the blackness swept over him from every direction, like a narrowing tunnel, and the voice in his ear was getting fainter and fainter. I'm going to die, he thought, fumbling at the buttons on the door, pulled one, didn't know which, heard the window glide up. It took him a moment to realise it had become a gravity-inverting guillotine. He heard tiny crackling sounds from the throat next to his ear, like the sound of small bubbles popping. They swelled to a howl of pain. Kai seized hold of the edge of the window, held it with one hand, grabbing for Karsten's hair with the other. Karsten threw himself forward, still pulling on the button for the window hoist.

– Keep away, he howled.

The face hanging from the side window looked swollen, eyes bulging like a boiled fish.

– I'll cut your head off. Understand?

He heard a distant sound from the bursting face, saw that Kai was forcing the window down with both hands and had opened it enough to pull his head free. Karsten fumbled for the key in the ignition, his right hand shaking so much he couldn't turn it and had to steady it with the other. The engine coughed. He stamped down with his foot, but there was no clutch there, and he turned the key again, felt the vibration up through his spine as the car roared and leapt forward a few metres, the engine almost choking. At the last moment he managed to pick up acceleration, and the car raced towards the steps to the main house. He yanked the gearstick into reverse, backed up and turned, was thrown against the steering wheel as he smashed into the Mazda that was parked behind him. He rammed the gearstick into drive. The open passenger door was banging loose as he pulled free of the other car. Something had landed in front of the bumper, there was a loud noise as he drove over it. For a moment he thought it was Kai's body he had smashed. Then he saw the short, broad figure coming towards him in the cone of light from the headlamps.

He put his foot down and accelerated straight towards it.

PART II

April 2011

1

DAN-LEVI MANAGED TO pop home for a brief visit. Sara didn't finish until three, and Pepsi had to be taken for a walk before that. Rakel had long schooldays, and the others were too small to take the dog out on their own.

The walk up to the end of Erleveien and back took him nine minutes. The whole time Pepsi was straining at the leash like a ferret, and if he tried to talk sharply to her, she would start biting at the leash. There was no shortage of information about how to train a dog, and there were obedience classes too, but they had long ago realised that they would never manage to squeeze anything like that into their weekly routine.

At a quarter past one he was in his car again. The paper was running a series on the new spirituality. He had interviewed a healer in Vormsund earlier that week, and the owner of a corner shop who had studied at Princess Märtha's Angel School. Now it was the turn of a woman who told people's fortunes by reading the cards. He had planned to do an hour's research for the interview beforehand but hadn't managed it, not that it worried him much. His greatest challenge would be to keep his scepticism at bay.

She lived in a house in Volla, not far from the swimming baths. Dan-Levi stood in the middle of the yard and studied the little semi-detached. It appeared to be from the 1950s but looked well maintained, painted white with red frames.

In the flat furthest away, the curtains were closed, but that wasn't where he was going.

The woman he had arranged to interview ran her own company, registered up at Brønnøysund, and she earned well in excess of four hundred thousand a year, after tax. She couldn't possibly make that much just from fortune-telling, he thought. But if that was the case, then maybe he should consider starting up in the branch himself. In his thoughts he added to himself that he was being ironic. Dan-Levi had grown up in a home where card games were sinful, and where the use of cards to tell fortunes was an even greater sin, since it represented an attempt to put oneself in God's place; in other words, become Satan. But his father had not been the kind of man who went about spreading the fear of eternal damnation. Right up until his final service at Bethany, five years ago, the word Pastor Jakobsen wanted to spread was one of joy.

Had he not checked beforehand, Dan-Levi would have thought that the woman who opened the door to him was well under fifty. She had dark brown hair and only a few lines around her eyes. As they shook hands, she looked directly at him. Secure, that was the first word that occurred to him. He didn't make a habit of judging women as members of their sex, but Elsa Wilkins had been and indeed still was a woman he would unhesitatingly have described as attractive. He allowed himself a good look at her as she led him into the living room, all what you might call part of the assignment. She was almost as tall as he was, and decidedly feminine in shape. Dan-Levi had always liked buxom women and didn't mind it at all when Sara began putting on weight each time she was pregnant. He thought it suited her, skinny thing that she was normally.

– So you call yourself a Parotist? he said once he had sat down on the sofa.

– Tarotist, Elsa Wilkins corrected him with a smile as she handed him a cup of herbal tea. – I also hold courses in other subjects.

– Courses?

– Self-development, meditation, getting in touch with yourself.

– I see, he said, picking up his notebook and writing down a couple of key words as he stemmed a tide of critical questions. His greatest strength as a journalist was probably his ability to get on well with the people he interviewed. People trusted him quickly and often told him more than they had intended. But he was careful about how he used this talent. No one should feel they had been exploited.

– And is that something you can earn a living from? He didn't reveal that he had checked her income beforehand in the tax office listings. – From tarot and meditation and that kind of thing?

– It's probably the same as with anything else, she said, gliding her fingers through her hair and tucking it behind her ear on one side. – If you're good at what you do and work hard, you can go as far as you want. It's probably the same in your job too.

Without him having to ask, she then began to talk about a centuries-old wisdom that had survived both the prohibitions of the Church and the arrogance of modern times. She talked about the collective unconscious and about archetypes, something Dan-Levi vaguely remembered reading about at university. She spoke about developing one's intuition, about finding different ways towards a knowledge of oneself. Hard to object to stuff like that. He chose to leave out the most critical questions he had intended to put to her, questions he had obliged both the healer and the angel school graduate to wrestle with. But nothing this woman said would have caused Pastor Jakobsen to raise his eyebrows.

Dan-Levi moved carefully over into the personal sphere.

– Wilkins, that's not a typical Norwegian name?

She was silent for a moment. – My ex-husband is English.

Dan-Levi waited, checking for any signs that she didn't want to talk about the past and the failed marriage.

– Have you lived in England?

– In Birmingham, and in Zimbabwe. It was half a lifetime ago.

Again she smiled, but he saw the trace of a shadow glide across the dark blue eyes.

– But you are from round here?

She sipped her drink, and he did the same. It tasted of peppermint and something sharper, he wasn't quite sure what.

– I grew up on a farm not too far from here. Stornes. We ran a stables.

– Stornes? he exclaimed. – That's where the fire was.

She nodded. – That was a long time after the place was sold. Once my parents were gone, there was no one in the family to take over.

– A tragic story, said Dan-Levi. – The fire, I mean. The kind of thing you don't forget, not even years later.

– It was eight years ago, she said. – Actually to the very day today. I remember it was on the first of April.

Dan-Levi made no comment on the coincidence. – Children? he asked as he turned a page in his notebook. – Please just say if you don't want to talk about that kind of thing. It is after all the Tarot I'm going to write about.

– It's quite all right. I have a boy. Elsa Wilkins interrupted herself with a smile. – Not a boy any more, actually. He's about your age.

Dan-Levi had a thought. — Maybe I . . .?

— I doubt it. He grew up partly in England and partly in Africa. He studied in Oslo one spring, many years ago, while he was living with me. But he didn't stay. He's always enjoyed looking for challenges.

— And he studied what?

— History and political science. Then he joined the army. He's been in both Iraq and Afghanistan.

Dan-Levi found this interesting. — Is he still out there?

She poured more tea. — He took over a firm his father started. They provide security for the people living in the south of Iraq. Adrian has never been afraid of anything. It keeps me awake at night sometimes.

She looked out of the window.

— I used to call him Lionheart when he was little. He was always wanting to protect me . . . I'd like to show you how I work. If you're interested.

Elsa Wilkins stood up, and Dan-Levi understood she didn't want to talk any more about this son of hers, this Lionheart.

— I wouldn't show this to just any journalist, she said as she went ahead of him up the stairs. — You seem a trust-worthy type of person.

The room upstairs smelled of incense and some kind of spice. Elsa Wilkins lit three candles on a table covered with a dark red cloth with black fringes that hung down towards the floor. She indicated for him to sit in one of the chairs; it was comfortable, covered in soft leather. She took a pack of cards from a drawer in the table. The cards were large and decorated on the back with yellow stars.

— The Tarot pack consists of fifty-six cards known as the Minor Arcana. That means the lesser secret. They are the basis of the normal pack of cards that I'm sure you use at home.

He made no response to this.

She spread the cards out in a fan across the table.

– The four suits are called wands, cups, swords and pentacles, and relate to differing material and spiritual sides of human life. The swords, for instance, are closely related to the world of thought, and the cups to feelings. You'll see why this is so in a moment. In addition to these fifty-six cards, there are twenty-two others known as the Major Arcana.

– The greater secret?

– Correct. These cards symbolise the most important themes in life, from growth and love to decline and death.

Dan-Levi resisted the temptation to ask how life's secrets and possibilities came to be hidden in a pack of cards. He had to admit he was curious. The room with its smells and its candlelight and the allegedly magic cards on the table made him think of circuses and wandering gypsies.

– Let's say you've come because you need advice regarding something that's troubling you in your daily life. Shall we pick a hypothetical problem, or talk about something real? You choose.

He thought for a moment. In his mind's eye he saw Pastor Jakobsen's friendly face. This is my job, he offered in his defence.

– Can't we just look at what the future holds? In a general sense.

– Then we choose the six-month special, she nodded, and laid the cards out in seven rows, three cards in each. – This first row relates to things that are on your mind at the moment.

There were a couple of wand cards there, and a jack holding a cup with a fish in it. Elsa Wilkins sat for a while studying the rows of cards, as though looking for a pattern. Dan-Levi glanced over towards the curtain. Through a gap he saw that it had started to rain. In a little while he'd head back to the newspaper and finish a couple of articles. Then he'd fetch Ruth and Rebekah from nursery school, then home and help with the dinner. After dinner, drive with Ruben to football. He was trainer and helped out at practice sessions whenever he could. Then back home again, help out with any homework, tidy up the kitchen, then off to the youth group he led at Bethany. Somewhere among all this, Pepsi had to be given her walk.

– You are a man who manages to get a great many things done, Elsa began, making an instant connection to what had been running through his mind. – You are an asset. People think of you as a good person. She paused. – Yet you are not completely happy with yourself.

Who is? thought Dan-Levi with a slight stab of irritation. Should a person be completely happy with himself? But Elsa Wilkins seemed to be asking rather than insisting. She looked straight at him, maybe debating whether to drop this about not being content. He noticed that he was tensing up and leaned back in his chair. The articles about alternative forms of faith and the new spirituality were not supposed to be a critical examination of New Age and other spiritual fast foods. At the editorial discussion they had agreed that he wouldn't write about charlatans and people being tricked out of their money but instead treat those he was interviewing as sympathetically as possible.

She pointed to the card with the eight wands.

– This might indicate new horizons. Are you planning a journey?

Now he was unable to hide his smile. If there was one thing he associated with fortune-telling, then this was it. Was there ever actually anyone anywhere who wasn't in some way or other planning a journey? For years he had dreamed of crossing the United States on a motorcycle, coast to coast across the endless plains, with the Rocky Mountains just visible on the horizon. He and his best friend Roar Horvath had planned to do it together, sharing the same attraction to all things American, the nature, the mindset, the music. And still, at times, Dan-Levi could start talking to Roar about this journey to end all journeys, although never without regretfully patting himself on the stomach, as though it was this that prevented it happening.

The final row consisted of cards that would reveal events to come in three to six months' time, according to Elsa Wilkins. She closed her eyes. All professionals have their tricks, Dan-Levi thought. Psychologists, lawyers and of course journalists. This was probably the tarotist's. Closing the eyes as though peering inwards in order to see what lay hidden within intuition.

The final card was called The Lovers, marked with a six in Roman numerals. Even though he was keeping a professional distance from the session, Dan-Levi was relieved, since this was obviously a love card.

– The Lovers, intoned Elsa Wilkins.

– The Lovers, said Dan-Levi, and repeating it like that, without any irony, alerted him to the fact that he was starting to take the ceremony more seriously than he ought to. He decided to talk to Sara about it once he got home.

– The Lovers, upside down.

– Upside down?

– The meaning of a card changes when it's upside down.

He felt himself frowning and again saw his father in his mind's eye.

– The card is upside down for you, but not for me, he tried to object.

Once more that melancholy smile, making him recall the fragments of her life story that she had revealed. A failed marriage, and a son who ran a security firm in Iraq.

– It's upside down for me, said Elsa Wilkins. – That's what counts.

– What does it mean?

Again she let her gaze glide across the rows of cards, as though searching for something.

– The Lovers upside down indicates problems in relationships, broken marriages and loveless sex. There might be jealousy, rejection, infidelity, or just a warning not to have a fling. It might also mean that faith is challenged by doubt.

Dan-Levi sat up straight in his chair. Infidelity had never been one of the themes of his life. He had known Sara since they were children. Their parents were friends. Sara was the sweetest girl in the circle around Bethany. She was a soloist in the church choir and played the organ. In secondary school she had left the congregation, at least partly, at the same time as she was the girlfriend of his best friend Roar Horvath, an atheist and son of a Hungarian refugee. But after a couple of years she returned to Bethany, and from that time onwards there was never any doubt about who she was going to share her life with. It had always been the two of them. Not in his wildest fantasies could Dan-Levi see himself with anyone else, and it had never occurred to him that this might be different for Sara.

Elsa Wilkins talked about the other cards too. Something about corn that had been sowed but had not yet ripened, and one of the cards indicated what could be either a genuine illness or just an exaggerated worry. But after she was finished, it was that business with the Lovers upside down that Dan-Levi sat brooding over.

Fifteen minutes later, he rounded things off by taking a series of photographs of her in the chilly April afternoon, noting that he'd captured the drops of misty rain that glinted in her dark hair. Even then the thought of that card cropped up. It stayed with him as he made his way back to his car, and on the drive back to his desk at the newspaper office, where his tasks included working out how to angle the story, what use to make of text boxes, and how the photos he had just taken would work in the piece.

2

I HAVE ALWAYS *felt a compulsion to lie.*

Synne Clausen looked up from the keyboard, sat a while gazing out of the window towards the stone wall on the other side of the grassy slope before lowering her eyes again and reading the single line there, the first she had written for months. She pulled out the earplugs so suddenly there was a stinging in one of her eardrums. From a room further down the corridor came the sound of a flute. She was relieved that Maja was obviously at home. She stood up, walked out of her bedsit into the kitchen, switched the kettle on, turned on the radio, tried a couple of stations, turned it off again, hoping that Maja would realise it was her out there and come out to see her. But the flute-playing continued, the lines of the melody interrupted and repeated, with small breaks each time, and Synne remained alone on the tiny veranda with her cup of coffee, wrapped in a quilted anorak and blankets. In about half an hour the sun would be setting behind the roof of the block next door. She tried not to think, just concentrate on the sounds drifting up through the endless hum of the city and disappearing again. A car accelerating up the hill in Sognsveien, a great tit in the pine tree, another answering some distance away, and from within the house, the dark notes of the flute.

It was almost a year now since the unbelievable had happened. She had sent a brown envelope out into the world. It contained words she had forced out of herself, then taken apart and reassembled, polished, roughed up, turned into miniatures, destroying most of them, keeping just a few. When she posted that envelope, she imagined it as a bottle with a letter pushed down inside it, tossed into the sea from a skerry or a boat. The unbelievable was that someone had found her message in a bottle. An editor at one of the big publishing companies had called her the following week. He assured her that her images were unlike anything else he had ever read. He insisted that after a few revisions they must be sent off to the printers and from there to the book-shops and the libraries, that they must be made accessible to a great number of people. Even more incomprehensible was the fact that several of the major newspapers had devoted valuable column space to her sliver of a book, and that a couple of them wrote that it was worth thinking about what she had to say.

Even before the book was published, she had started on something new. Worked night and day for a couple of months. For a whole autumn she was a genius. She was Virginia Woolf on the verge of madness, and everything she touched burnt her fingers. And then very suddenly it all stopped. She developed physical aversions, in the first instance towards the keyboard. Began writing by hand in notebooks, but the aversion spread until even holding a pen became painful and nauseating. She sat tensed and strained at her desk for hours on end. Around New Year, she realised she was ill. Pain moved around inside her whole body. It was painful to walk, painful to sit, painful to lie still. The doctor subjected her to all sorts of examinations but could find no cause. In the end he said it was fibromyalgia, a diagnosis he evidently regarded with contempt.

As the sun disappeared behind the rooftop, she suddenly stood up, took her coffee inside and slumped down in front of the keyboard again. She twisted the yellow earplugs into two pointed cones and wedged them into her ears, closed her eyes as the sounds from the outside world disappeared.

I never lie about big things and never about things where I might be found out. It's the tiny little things. I tell Erika I sent an email and made a couple of phone calls. I only called one person. I tell her I met someone I used to go to school with and we stopped for a chat on Karl Johan. But I walked straight past Tamara, sitting on the steps outside a shop in Dronningens gate. I nodded, and maybe she nodded back. If Erika decides to ask who it was, I can give her the name, or say I've forgotten it, and smile as though I find it a bit embarrassing. And if she asks what we talked about, I can laugh it off and say it was confidential, or invent the conversation. Naturally that will be enough to satisfy her. But if she really looked closely at it she would find all sorts of holes in the story of my life, little holes, but lots of them, spread all over the place.

Synne knew that she must not stop there. If she stopped, she wouldn't be able to start again. Not for weeks and months, maybe not ever. She mustn't begin reading what she had written, just let her fingers go, let it stream out through them.

I've got nothing to talk to Tamara about.

I turn and peer upwards along the dark scale.

Someone approaching me from up there.

Karsten, I say out loud, and a figure emerges from this word, face emaciated and eyes that don't recognise me, don't recognise anything at all.

You owe, says the voice that is no longer his.

You owe for everything you never had to pay.

I know, I murmur, I owe you more than I can ever repay.

You don't owe me, he says, that same mechanical voice that is no longer his.

You owe the grey, that's why you're sinking, you pay what you owe by sinking down, becoming part of the grey yourself.

Again she looked up from the keyboard and out of the window. A magpie landed in the fir tree. It was big and had something in its beak; could be a piece of bread it had found down on the playground. She carried on typing, writing about this piece of bread. About where it came from, about the mother who buttered it for her little girl that morning, as she was running from the house, to the nursery school, to drop her daughter off. She sat hunched over the keyboard, driving her fingers on. No idea where the sentences were going, didn't want to know, because then she would have to stop, give up, go back to bed again.

She had just put the machine in hibernation mode when Erika arrived. It was late afternoon. Erika had been giving a seminar at Blindern and she looked worn out.

– You people who can take time off whenever you like have no idea how lucky you are, she groaned as she stretched out on the bed.

The teasing wasn't malicious, but it irritated Synne.

– Do I work any less than you do?

Erika raised her hands in a gesture of apology. – Didn't mean to offend.

Synne went out to the kitchen and switched on the coffee machine. When she returned with two full cups, Erika was lying there, her eyelids flickering.

– I slept so badly last night after you left, she complained. – Come here.

Synne sat down on the edge of the bed, held out one of the cups to her.

– Just put it down.

She did so. Erika put a hand around her neck and drew her down towards her.

– Lie close to me. Just for a little while. I promise I won't fall asleep.

By the time Synne sat up again, the coffee was lukewarm. She added another spoonful of sugar, but it didn't help.

– I've written today.

Erika turned over on her side and looked at her. – Have you? But that's fantastic.

– No need to get carried away.

– Let me see.

Synne hesitated. It was new. The first tentative step. A wrong word from Erika, or even a look, could upend it. And then more days and nights with no hope of getting started again. And yet she woke the machine, put it in Erika's lap, opened the document in which Karsten had made his appearance. The other texts, especially the one about the little lies, she would never show to anyone, or at least not to Erika.

She turned away and leaned her forehead against the window. Tried not to think about Erika sitting there reading. Tried not to listen out for any changes in her breathing, or some other sort of sound emerging from her throat, or bodily movements that might express impatience or, even more intolerable to contemplate, enthusiasm. Erika was exact, and she was merciless. She had helped her with the poetry collection. Made it better. But what Synne wanted above all right now was a more naïve reader. Someone who didn't have that sharpness, someone who was easy to seduce.

Erika put the computer down on the floor. Synne waited, didn't dare turn round. Didn't Erika understand how she felt? Didn't she realise what was hanging in the balance through these waiting seconds? Whether the text was good or bad, or somewhere in between, which was probably what it was, surely Erika ought to know that a tiny word could be enough to transport her to heaven, or to the darkest pits. So then she must be tormenting her with silence deliberately.

Finally Erika got up. Synne stared out at the grey and

yellow slope between the blocks. The magpie of course was long gone. Not a sparrow in sight. Only that dirty lawn with the scattered patches of late winter snow that should have been rained away long ago.

Erika put her arms around her from behind. If she was doing this as a way of offering comfort, then it was the most unbearably clumsy attempt Synne had ever experienced. She pulled herself away.

– Don't cling to me. Say something. Is it that bloody difficult to speak?

Her eyes filled with tears. Not because this scrap of writing was so important. It had taken her five minutes to wring it out of herself, certainly no more than ten. She should have deleted it, but had let herself be tricked into showing it to Erika of all people, literary expert and assistant professor, writing her doctoral thesis on the subject of Beckett's anti-novels. Erika, most cynical, brutal and cruel of all the billions of readers in the world.

– You hate it, Synne announced. – You think it's the most banal little-girl twaddle that any hard disk has ever been compelled to save.

Erika burst out laughing, and Synne started laughing too. She cursed, but nothing could stop the laughter. It felt okay to laugh; that was the only thing her text really deserved.

– Don't ask me to pass judgement on that thing, said Erika, and it felt like another kick in the stomach.

– *That thing?* Is that how you refer to my work? As though it doesn't even deserve a proper name.

– Sorry, I didn't mean it like that.

– You hate it, Synne hissed. – You hate everything I write. You've never been able to endure having to read it.

Erika shook her head. – Synne, she sang, perhaps trying to sound cheerful.

– I'll tell you one thing I think, Synne interrupted. – You don't like the fact that I write at all. It makes you jealous.

Finally the smile disappeared, and she knew she must have touched a nerve. Not that she had been aiming. Throwing everything out, tossing it in all directions, sooner or later she had to hit something.

Erika wandered over and sat down on the bed again.

– I understand it was too early for you to be showing it to anyone, she said in a fairly controlled voice.

– No it was not, Synne fumed. – It was too early to show it to *you*.

Erika took a sip of her coffee, which must have been cold by now.

– Does that mean you don't want a response?

Suddenly Synne felt cold. She wrapped her woollen jacket around herself.

– I don't want a beating. That's all.

– Synne . . . Erika's voice had that maternal tone that had always been there in the early days. – Come and sit down, she said calmly and firmly, patting the blanket beside her a couple of times.

Synne did as she was told.

– If I really was going to say anything about good or bad, then I would praise rather than be negative.

– Because you feel sorry for me!

– There, there. Erika stroked her hair. – I understand why you're defending yourself, she said comfortingly. – It means there's something at stake here.

Synne rested her cheek on Erika's neck. – *Everything* is at stake.

– Well, fine, if you want to express it in such an operatic way. Let's not talk about turning points and ways forward and all that kind of thing. But it's obvious that what we were talking about last night has had some effect on you.

– Oh really.

– You've got so hung up on all this Knausgård stuff, trying to imitate his style – no, don't interrupt, I know what you're going to say – but the only thing really worth writing about in your write-your-life project is the one thing you spend your whole time avoiding.

– Oh really.

Erika continued to stroke her hair, and Synne didn't want her to stop.

– When you were talking about your brother last night . . .

– I'd been drinking.

– It's okay, I'm glad you told me about it.

– It's coming up for Easter. I always get like that at Easter.

– Stop apologising. What I said to you last night is exactly what you've done.

– Oh really.

– Find out where it hurts the most. When your brother appears in your writing, something happens. That's what I'm trying to tell you. Right then, I was so moved I could hardly breathe. Understand? That's where you have to go.

– Oh really, Synne mumbled and let her lips brush across Erika's neck. She couldn't remember the last time she had felt such joy.

Synne rang the bell. She'd started doing that one day, instead of going straight in and calling out hello. It was weeks now since she'd visited her father, maybe more than a month. There had been several postponements. Not that he would remind her of how long it had been, but she knew that it was a disappointment to him.

The front door opened. Her father stood there, glasses in hand. He had grown older these last few weeks, it struck her; his cheeks had started to sag. His hair was uncombed but didn't look dirty.

– Hi, Synne, he said, spreading his arms a little, a signal that she could give him a hug if she wanted to. She leaned over and pressed her cheek against his, held it there for a few seconds. He had shaved, and smelled of his usual aftershave. It was a relief to her, the smell recalling family holidays, on their way to the cabin, the trees flashing by.

She kicked off her boots. Was about to say something about why she hadn't come before, but didn't.

– Are you hungry? she asked instead.

In the end she made a plate of bread and butter for them both, as she had often done in the evenings, before she moved out. He didn't comment on it. Neither the fact that she was rummaging in a fridge that was no longer hers, nor that she sniffed the cheese to make sure it was okay, nor that she assumed the role of hostess and made him a guest in his own house.

Once they had eaten she said: – I'd like to see Karsten's room.

He peered at her over his glasses. His gaze sharpened, as though he had been pulled up out of his own train of thought.

– Karsten's? Why?

She had always told him what she did, and he had never expressed any displeasure at her doing something different from what he would have recommended. Studying literature was fair enough, even though he couldn't understand what use it would be. Publishing poems was fine too. He was visibly pleased when she handed him a copy of her first book, the one she had received herself from the publisher. He started leafing through it at once, hectically self-conscious. After that he had read each poem thoroughly several times, apologising for only having understood the occasional fragment. – They *are* only fragments, she had exclaimed.

But this vague idea of approaching Karsten through her writing was not something she could reveal to her father.

Not yet, and she realised she was already dreading the day when she would have to talk to him about it. If that day even came, because so far this was all just a few fragile strands of an idea that would perhaps never develop into anything more.

She went upstairs, stood a moment outside the room before opening the door. After that Easter eight years ago, she had avoided Karsten's room. The thought of going in there frightened her. She had started to imagine that she would find him in there. That he would be sitting at his desk with his back turned, as he always used to, before it happened. That he would turn, but that she would no longer recognise him. Fantasies like this tormented her. Two or three years went by before she dared to enter the room, realising that she had to, otherwise her fantasies would take control of her life completely. It was something she had understood herself, but she let the psychiatrist think it was his idea, let him continue to work on her for weeks after she had made up her mind to do it.

There was a smell of stale dust and something unidentifiably plasticky. Synne crossed to the window and opened it. Beyond the runway she could glimpse a bend in the river. That was what they had ended up believing, that down there was where he had gone on that Maundy Thursday.

The furniture was all still there, but most of his belongings had been removed long ago. Mother had insisted on it, when she still lived in the house. Synne sat at the desk, opened the top drawer, where a few things that had survived the clear-out remained. Not even after she had dared to enter the room again had she been able to touch any of them. Now she took out a calculator and a maths workbook. His name was on the inside, written in capitals and underlined once. Indicating a provisional answer, she recalled from her maths lessons. Two underlinings for the final answer.

Deeper inside the drawer she found a textbook. She flipped through it, saw Karsten's notations in the margins, crosses and doodles, a few observations. On one of the blank pages at the back her brother had drawn a hollow figure. Formulas were scribbled alongside it, and a calculation. On the figure, he had written his initials, his date of birth and a second date. Below it, RIP. She sat looking at the drawing, realised that it was supposed to be a gravestone. And the date of death noted there wasn't far off the day when he'd disappeared. Had he sat there and planned his own death, drawn his own gravestone, and then worked out the stone's volume and ratio? Maybe that was the way his thoughts worked. Calculations, analyses, formulae, and as an apropos, approaching death.

There was something else written there, lower down the page.

Schrödinger: 'I'll kill you.' Heisenberg helping him. Only A. can stop them.

These were names she associated with German science, possibly something to do with the war. Suddenly she took out her own notebook and copied down everything that was written below the drawing. A place to begin. In the tension between the analytic, where life was a given that could be revealed, and the unpredictable, threatening experience of living it.

At the back of the drawer she found a brown envelope with a pile of photographs inside. At the top, one of her brother. Looked to have been taken in front of the house. Just a few leaves left on the cherry tree. She studied the face, a pale ellipse, the narrow lower jaw he had inherited from his father. The eyes were light and looked happy. Had you already made up your mind by then, Karsten? A second picture showed the two of them together. She was holding on to his jacket; he had his arm around her, the same smile in that narrow face. The same as in the other pictures. Was that a mask he wore, and behind it, deep down in the eyes, had the death wish already taken over?

There was a school photograph there too, from secondary school. Karsten was standing in the back row, but was shorter and slighter than the biggest boys. Dark grey college sweater, collar-length hair. Not smiling here, seemed to be looking down and away. She let her eyes wander across the other faces, remembering some of them. Tonje, of course, with whom Karsten had been secretly in love since primary school. But not more secretly than that he had revealed it to his little sister one morning as he was making breakfast for her. She couldn't remember anyone from his class coming to the house. Only a Vietnamese boy he used to solve arithmetic problems with. She found him sitting on the front row, couldn't recall his name. Karsten didn't have many friends, maybe none; it ran in the family. Oh yes, there was one, several years older, a supply teacher who took over the class.

She found a programme at the bottom of the envelope. It was printed on stiff peach-coloured paper. The picture on the front was the one taken in the garden, with him standing beneath the cherry tree. Below that, in ornate black lettering: *Programme for Karsten's memorial service, 8 July 2003.*

They had waited a long time before holding it. Almost three months had passed since that Maundy Thursday. By then, what remained of their hope was gone. But not hers, not even when she realised that her parents had given up. At first she had imagined that one day he would quite simply be sitting here in his room, and open the door and come out to them. Without anyone having to explain where he had been or why he had been away. Then later she had imagined him showing up somewhere far away, maybe even in another country, that he had somehow ended up on board a ship, fallen ill, lost his memory, until a nurse at a hospital in England or Egypt or a Mediterranean island had managed to get him to talk and found out who he was. She had seen *The English Patient* and it would happen pretty much like that. Her brother had experienced something both wonderful and terrible, connected with love; he had been injured, but not as badly as the English patient. He would recover his memory, and one day he'd come walking up the road, stop in front of their gate and look up at the house. And she would see him through the living-room window and run outside, and she would be the first to throw her arms around him.

Many things from that time remained unclear, but she could remember the service. It was held in a church, which must have been her mother's doing; her father wouldn't set foot inside a church unless he had to. They had sung a psalm, something about thinking yourself weary unto death. And afterwards everybody talked about Karsten as though he no longer existed.

She opened the card from the memorial service. The words of the psalm were printed there, and she found the line that had stuck in her mind: *When I have thought myself weary unto death, say Oh Lord what thou hast thought.*

There was a piece of paper inside. She unfolded it. *Memorial address by the Reverend Olav Kiran.*

Hadn't she seen this before? She couldn't remember. But as she sat there reading at Karsten's desk, the images came back to her. The light in the church that summer's day. The pews full, though it was the middle of the summer holidays. Suddenly she remembered how she had been looking for *him*, Karsten's friend, Adrian Wilkins, but he wasn't there. She found out later that he had gone back to England to resume his studies.

Why must the best be taken from us? Why must those who

have so much left to do, who have so far left to travel, and
who have so much to offer to others, be taken from us? Where
can we turn in search of meaning when such a thing happens?

If the priest's answer was to God, then it didn't exactly
agree with what Karsten had believed. With the support of
his father, he had declined to be confirmed. And on the day
he turned eighteen, he left the state church. But the priest
hadn't even mentioned God in his address. He had probably
formed a picture of Karsten based on conversations with
his parents and classmates. The priest's own son was in his
class, she remembered now. And maybe some of what she
herself had said about her brother had found its way into
what the Reverend Kiran said that day in church.

He was unique. He could solve problems in maths and physics
that even the teachers struggled with. He was an outstanding
chess player. He took care of his friends and looked out for his
little sister.

And there it was. She remembered the priest being at
their home. He sat on the sofa by the window in the living
room, next to her mother. Synne couldn't place her father;
maybe he wasn't there. The priest had asked if she and
Karsten spent a lot of time together, and she hadn't known
what to answer. She was thirteen; he was almost six years
older. But he cared about her, she knew that much. In the
evening, when she was doing her homework, or reading or
playing a computer game, he might come into her room.
Stand behind her for a while, observing what she was doing,
and if she seemed to be stuck, give her a hint. Maybe pat
her on the head. She could hardly recall a single quarrel.
So yes, it was what she had said that had become, in the
priest's address, *He looked out for his little sister.*

After the service, she had stood outside with her parents,
she remembered now. A stream of people she didn't know
shaking her hand and saying that strange, stiff thing, *my*

condolences, as well as other, meaningless things, such as that she must get in touch if there was any way in which they could help.

She put the programme and the address back inside the envelope. If she was to get close to Karsten, it was the impression he had left inside her, the weight of his absence she would have to focus on. The greyness outside was denser now. She could no longer make out the river on the far side of the runway. She thought of what Erika had said about visiting your own pain, the only thing worth writing about. But she would never be able to write about the night Karsten disappeared.

His mobile phone lay in the drawer too. Back then, she didn't have a camera on her own phone. She remembered what a fuss she'd made; everybody else had one. She had envied Karsten his state-of-the art phone and was always asking to borrow it to take pictures with. And he good-naturedly let her. He didn't even keep his code a secret from her; he used her birthday.

She plugged in the charger. The display lit up. She tapped in the four numbers and unlocked the SIM card.

There weren't many pictures there; her brother wasn't exactly a keen photographer. She found several she had taken herself, including some of him. It was at Christmas, outside the cabin. He stood leaning on his ski poles and smiling that same smile. Afterwards she had taken one of them together. He had his arm around her, faces cheek to cheek, right up close to the lens. In another one he was standing by the kitchen table pouring muesli into a bowl. Then pictures from various locations. She stopped at the next-to-last picture. Karsten looked to be naked and was grinning at the camera, suddenly quite unlike all the other images. Must have taken it of himself. The last one was of a dark-haired girl. She was wearing what looked like

Pakistani costume and had almond-shaped dark eyes and the kind of full lips any girl would envy.

Synne got the class photo out again, found her sitting at the end of the first row. Again she studied the picture on the phone. To the right of the girl's head she saw the edge of a painting of a woodland scene, one that was still hanging on their wall down in the living room. The girl was holding out a hand and didn't seem to want to be photographed. The picture was taken the Friday before Palm Sunday, at nine thirty in the evening, the same time as the picture of Karsten naked. She remembered that she and her parents had gone to the cabin that weekend, leaving Karsten at home to study for his exams. She would never have imagined that a girlfriend came round to see him. He was shy with girls. Synne thought it had something to do with an operation, a hernia or something, but they never talked about it at home.

She opened the messages, clicked down to the ones from that Maundy Thursday, found some from Tonje, a number of short messages; it looked as though they had an arrangement. There was another name she recognised there too, a name that was to her at that time the most exciting in the whole world. Karsten had sent several messages to Adrian Wilkins that Maundy Thursday. He appeared to be trying to get in touch with him.

Suddenly Synne remembered something that had happened that evening. She was at Tamara's, was going to sleep over. Tamara was allowed to be home on her own, even though she was only thirteen. She had three girlfriends visiting and planned to ring some boys. They'd got hold of some alcopops. Synne had lied to her parents that Tamara's mother was at home. Later on that evening Karsten had turned up. Looking back on it now, it was obvious that something had been going on, something she hadn't understood. There was so much she hadn't understood. Karsten said he was worried about her. He was falling into a pit, and even then it was her he was looking out for.

She looked further down the list. In the days after Maundy Thursday there were a number of messages sent from her parents' phones. She couldn't bear to open them, knowing what they must say. But the final message on Maundy Thursday was from another number, received at ten forty-two. *Call me, it's urgent.* No indication who it was from. She took out her own phone, ran a directory enquiry. Thought that few people would hang on to the same number for eight years.

But the name of the person who had sent that last message appeared on her screen.

3

DAN-LEVI OPENED HIS iPhone playlist. 'Almost Cut My Hair' filled his ears as he started to clear the table. It was Friday. He realised how much he had been looking forward to an evening with no arrangements or programme. *It happened just the other day.* He scraped the taco remains into the rubbish. They threw away too much food. There was an economic argument to it, but mostly it was wrong. Rebekah was four and they were agreed that she shouldn't be made to eat everything up. Ruben was good at not taking any more than he knew he could manage. Rakel and Ruth, on the other hand, were hopeless. Ruth was only five, but Rakel was nine and got away with it too easily. Something happened to her eyes when Dan-Levi tried to be strict with her, as though the whole world around her were falling to pieces. Once he had allowed himself to get far too angry. It frightened him, but Sara laughed it off. In her own time she'd been the apple of her father's eye too.

Now she entered the kitchen carrying two half-full glasses of milk and emptied them into the sink. He always put anything left over back into the fridge. It never got drunk, but it was easier to throw them out a few days later, after they'd been standing there so long that drinking them would be a health risk.

– Satisfactory?

Sara ran a finger over the worktop, peered into the sink. Found the remains of an apple core.

– Not satisfactory.

He grabbed it from her and tossed it into the overfilled rubbish bin.

– Now?

– C minus, she offered after taking another look.

– Well that's a pass, more than a pass. So that means a reward.

He leaned against the worktop and closed his eyes. Heard her exaggerated sigh of exasperation. And then her lips were there, a light touch and then gone.

– That will not do, he protested. – Satisfactory is satisfactory.

He put his arms around her and lifted her up, sucked hold of one lip.

– You idiot, she murmured, pulling herself free as Ruth appeared in the doorway.

– Rakel, Mummy and Daddy are kissing, their daughter called into the living room.

– So what, came the response.

– Kiss more, Ruth demanded, holding on to her mother.

– All right then, said Dan-Levi, and placed his lips on Sara's nose with a blowing sound that made her jump. As she turned and tried to escape, he held her from behind and whispered in her ear: – I'll be back. When the children are asleep. Don't think you'll get away with this.

She turned towards him. – In that case, you'd better shave first, you caveman.

It was his turn to put the children to bed. That meant washing and then pyjamas, teeth to be brushed, around forty altogether in the two mouths. Ruben had made it clear long ago that he didn't want to be included in the bedtime cleaning ritual.

Every evening Dan-Levi made sure he had some time alone with Rakel before she went to sleep. She needed it, he and Sara were agreed on that, and once Ruth and Rebekah were wrapped up inside their duvets, and Ruben was busy in the bathroom, he quietly opened the door to her room.

– Rakel?

As he turned to go out again, he heard her answer.

– Are you here? he said in astonishment, and peered under the bed.

The wardrobe door opened and she peeked out.

He had to laugh. – What are you doing in there?

– Thinking.

He didn't ask why she had to sit inside a wardrobe to think. Rakel did that kind of thing. Her teacher said she had a rich inner world, but had no idea how true that was. It was Dan-Levi who most often had access to this world, of princes and princesses, wizards, trolls and demons. But what he noticed above all was something he recognised as the presence of the Lord, because Rakel had certain gifts that no one could completely understand. They had discovered this two years ago, one night when she came in to them and told them of a dream. She had seen her grandfather standing in the middle of the floor clad in a long white gown. According to Rakel, he laughed the whole time and spoke in a language she had never heard before. That same morning, Dan-Levi's mother called. His father had died in the night. Without any signs at all of being unwell, he had gone to bed that night, fallen asleep and never woken again.

They agreed not to talk about Rakel's gift, not until He had revealed it to others.

– I have a special place in there, she confided in him now.

– In the wardrobe? There isn't a door into another world in there, is there?

He had read the Narnia books to her and Ruben. Ruben had reluctantly allowed himself to be drawn into a universe that strained the laws of common sense, but Rakel had thrown herself into it, lapping it up.

She shook her head. – Just a secret room. Someone's written something on the wall there. Something nasty.

Dan-Levi was curious. They had lived in this house for over eleven years; he thought he knew every nook and cranny of it.

– If I show it you, you must promise never to tell anyone else.

He thought this over. – Okay, he finally decided. – This will be *our* secret.

She pulled out the desk drawer, handed him a torch. He opened the cupboard door wide. Besides Rakel's clothes, it was full of shoes, shirts and jackets, most of it his that had been hanging there for years, clothes he hadn't thrown out but that he never wore either. He lifted them aside and crept in. At the back was a board swivelled at an angle, and behind it a small opening in the wall. He stretched his arm inside and switched on the torch. The space was just large enough for a child to creep into.

– The perfect hiding place when you're playing hide-and-seek, he called out to her.

She groaned. – Then everyone would know about it. How secret is that?

– Not secret at all, he conceded as he backed out again. – It's good to have your own little place in the world, he added as he handed the torch back to her.

It struck him that this was hardly in line with what he and Sara had agreed to teach the children, but it felt good to say it.

With a glass of red wine in his hand, he flopped down on to the sofa. He came from a home in which alcohol had been forbidden, but after consulting the scriptures, he had come to the conclusion that a glass now and then wasn't against the will of the Master. He had tried for a while to persuade Sara to join him. Had she considered how Jesus would have reacted if she were a guest at the wedding in Cana and said no to the wine he offered her? She was never particularly impressed by these theological explications of his.

There was some crime series on NRK, just boring enough to switch off. He put his arm around Sara, his hand drifting down towards her neckline. There was a ring on the doorbell, Pepsi began barking loudly and Sara gave a start and jumped to her feet. She had a sister who was ill now and then. Last time she had turned up at their house, naked and frozen after walking miles through the middle of the night to ask for help in getting hold of fifteen litres of milk. That was several years ago, but Dan-Levi knew from Sara's reaction what the ring on the doorbell reminded her of.

– I'll go, she volunteered, already on her way out into the hall.

He heard her talking sharply to Pepsi. The dog calmed down; Sara was best at controlling her. Dan-Levi listened, couldn't make out the words, but from the tone of voice he realised it was someone she knew; his impression was that it was a man. And then, of all thoughts, this was what came to him: *the Lovers upside down*. He stood up, head shaking at his own whimsicality.

– Dan, it's for you, she called.

Something to do with work, he thought, exasperated and also a touch relieved. Sometimes people turned up on his doorstep with a tip, or even worse, tried to use him as a way of announcing something they wanted to have put in the paper.

– For you, she repeated, coming back inside and leaving the front door ajar. She did something with her mouth that was difficult to understand. – She insisted on waiting outside.

One of the bulbs in the outside lamp was gone. It had

happened weeks ago, but replacing it was way down on his list of things to do. At first, in the half-light, he had trouble recognising her.

– I'm sorry to bother you.

– Not at all, he said, certain that he would soon be able to place her.

– It's been quite a while, she said.

He nodded. – Time flies.

She was below average height, wearing a short black coat with a shawl around her head against the drizzle. He decided to move changing the light bulb further up his list of priorities.

– Do you have a couple of minutes?

He didn't answer. – Would you like to come inside? he said instead, just as he recognised who it was. Synne Clausen had grown up just a couple of hundred metres up the road, but since she'd moved out, he'd hardly seen her. The year before, when she'd published her first book of poems, the paper had done a portrait interview with her. Dan-Levi had borrowed the book from the journalist who had done the interview, and still not handed it back, he now recalled.

– Are you visiting your father?

She nodded. Relieved at having finally realised who she was, he stepped to one side and repeated his invitation.

– I know it's probably not convenient, she said, declining his offer. – But I must ask you something.

He had a feeling he knew what this was going to be about. – I'll just put a jacket on.

Pepsi stood whining above her empty drinking bowl.

– All right then, he decided as he pulled on his boots, – I guess you can come along too.

– Sorry for bothering you, Synne Clausen said again as they set off down the road.

– Don't worry about it at all. The dog needs her walk anyway.

Dan-Levi had to jerk Pepsi back as she jumped up at the young woman. He apologised for the dog's bad manners, and Synne laughed slightly. She had to be in her early twenties, he worked out. Her father was still working at the Institute for Energy Research, but the mother had moved away. She'd been active in local politics and he had interviewed her several times. That was before it happened.

– How are your parents keeping? he asked.

She thought it over.

– Mother lives in Stockholm. We don't see much of each other. Dad carries on as usual. Or that's the way it seems from the outside at least. No one's got over it.

– I can understand that, said Dan-Levi. Sometimes he woke up in the middle of the night, tormented by the thought of losing Sara or one of the children. Usually it was prompted by a dream, and it would leave him lying there, stricken and uncertain whether he would be able to go on if it really happened. Even with the help of the Lord.

– It's been eight years, she said.

– Is it really that long?

It brought it back to him, all the thoughts he had had back then. He ought to have known what Karsten was going through. He had pressured him to go to the police on the vague suspicion that the boy might know something about the fires. The thought that it might have been him who tipped Karsten over the edge bothered him for a long time afterwards.

– I found his mobile phone at home, said Synne. – Read some of the text messages.

Pepsi had caught the scent of something or other and dragged Dan-Levi over towards the ditch; he dragged her back with sharp tugs.

– Didn't he have his phone with him?

She shook her head. – Apparently he left it at a school friend's house. He was there earlier in the evening.

Maybe that was why Karsten hadn't answered when he rang.

– One of the messages on that Maundy Thursday was from you, Synne told him.

– That could be.

– But you never heard from him?

– No.

Dan-Levi was on the point of saying what he was thinking: I should have understood something was about to happen. Gone to his house. Tried to find him.

– Why did you want to talk to Karsten?

He pulled Pepsi away from a pile of dog shit she was sniffing; now and then she could quite unexpectedly take a bite at what other dogs had left. Should he tell Synne that thanks to him, Karsten had come to the attention of the police? Would it not be the same as lying if he avoided answering her question?

– Well I knew him from the chess club, he said vaguely. – We often played against each other. He was a real talent, even though he never put much effort into it.

He stopped to allow Pepsi to sniff away in the sodden grass. He knew the police had made a thorough job of their investigation. They had of course checked Karsten's phone, and they had interviewed a number of people, but without getting anywhere. They had also tried to find out whether Karsten had had anything to do with the fires, but had no luck there either.

– On the day he disappeared, he was asked to go to the police station to be interviewed.

Synne stopped. – Interviewed?

He explained. Wished he could leave out his own part

in it all, but having mentioned it, he had to let her know how guilty he felt.

– I'll never believe Karsten was capable of something like that, she said when he had finished. – Do you think so?

– I don't have any other answers but what the investigation turned up, he responded carefully. – Karsten was obviously in distress. Perhaps he blamed himself for something or other. That's all I know. If he'd been found, then perhaps we'd know more.

The dog tried to sniff under Synne's coat and she pushed it away.

– Well it might have been an accident.

He admitted she could be right and said nothing about the police's conclusion: that people very rarely disappeared without trace as the result of an accident. If they were walking in the mountains maybe, and fell down a crevasse in a glacier. But not round here. The third possibility had of course been included in the investigation, but no sign of anything criminal was ever found.

Suddenly she said: – I've had this strange feeling of guilt too, ever since it happened.

He turned towards her, relieved that she wasn't blaming him.

– Why should you feel guilty?

She looked to be thinking it over before answering.

– Something happened that evening. Something to do with me. Did you hear about it? I had an attack.

He knew nothing about that.

– I had them now and then when I was a child. They never found out what it was. For a time they thought it might be epilepsy. If so, I grew out of it. But that evening, the Maundy Thursday . . .

Suddenly Pepsi began tugging like a wild beast at the leash, obviously catching the scent of some other animal, probably a cat. Dan-Levi tied her to a lamp post, turned again to Synne.

– I don't remember much about it, she said. – I was found in a ditch down by Lillestrøm secondary school. My bike was lying next to me. Mum and Dad came to the hospital with me. I spent the night there. If that hadn't happened, they would have noticed that Karsten hadn't come home. Maybe he would have been found if they'd reported it straight away.

– I think that's unlikely.

– Maybe. But that was how I thought. Probably still do.

– Who found you?

She looked away. – Some bloke. My parents said he rang the bell. They were so shocked, they forgot to ask about anything, and then he was gone. Just told them where I'd been found, because my bike was still there.

Dan-Levi examined her more closely in the light of the street lamp. She didn't look like Karsten. Her face was rounder, and there was a different expression in the eyes. It made him think of her poems. Many of them were impenetrable to him, but here and there something did get through, something mysterious that opened up a world of unexpected connections. One of them began something like this: *If trees can't tell me who I am, then I talk to God in vain.* He didn't know if he liked it, but he had read it several times.

– What's made you think of all this now?

She shrugged. – It happens every year, whenever Easter's approaching.

He untied Pepsi from the lamp post. Only when they had started walking back did she add: – There's another reason too. Something I've started writing. That's why I had to talk to you.

4

LIGHT SLIPPED INTO the room through a gap beneath the curtains. He pulled the duvet over himself. Lay like that for a long time in the semi-darkness, tried to hold on to sleep, but it receded further and further from him. He opened his eyes and looked up at the ceiling. The joints between the planks didn't match, each one half a length too long. A couple of them looked as though they hadn't even been cut to size. Previously this had irritated him, but now his gaze followed them idly from the door to the window, rested there a moment and then back to the door. For about half an hour he lay like that, maybe longer, until he heard Elsa's car turning into the yard. She had left at nine; it must be past one by now. He sat up on the side of the bed. He'd give her ten minutes to get inside. He had worked out a reason to go in and see her. An offer to go shopping. She would ask how he intended to spend the day, and he would give his usual response, something about going down to the gym, about going online and looking for a job, or getting in touch with social security and finding a new doctor. He had no intention of doing any of this. He had no desire to be surrounded by people at all hours of the day. Had no need of money either.

If Elsa didn't want him to go shopping for her, then he could ask if her computer was still behaving itself after he had installed the new operating system. Even if he had already asked the same question every day for the past week.

He would keep the message from Adrian as a last resort. If he told her about that, then he would be sure to have her full attention, for however long.

He heard her footsteps passing below the window. He thought he'd locked the door, but she let herself in.

– Kai, are you home?

He jumped and pulled on his training pants, dragged his fingers through his hair, went out on to the landing. She was standing at the foot of the stairs, wearing her red coat. Newspapers in one hand, mail in the other.

– You delivering the mail? he couldn't help saying, and then added quickly: – Just on my way out. Anything you need?

She shook her head, and maybe that was a trace of a smile he saw on her face. He went down, stopped on the last step, where he was still taller than her.

– Were you asleep up there?

– No, he lied, knowing she could see through him. – Just looking at a few bills.

She said nothing.

– I'll transfer some money for this month's rent, he told her, not wanting her to think that last month's delay was because he didn't want to pay. In one of his last calls from Basra the previous autumn she had hinted she might be selling that part of the house. And when he came back, he wasn't sure he would still be allowed to go on living there. It was only a few days later that she told him he could stay for the time being, and he had offered to pay and asked her what she thought a fair rent would be. She shrugged, said it was up to him. He had checked the market to see what people were paying for similar rentals in other flats around Lillestrøm, and ended up paying five thousand into her account on the first of each month. She didn't say anything, not a single word about whether that was too much or not enough or just right.

– Want a cup of tea? he asked, and was surprised when she said yes. He slipped by her, out into the kitchen, put the kettle on, not certain that she might not change her mind.

– Heard from Adrian, he said as he fetched the cups.

– Have you? she exclaimed, the change in her voice at once apparent, as though he was standing there holding a present for her.

– He rang. It was close enough to the truth.

– Where is he?

– Basra.

– What did he say?

– Not a lot. Wondered if I was interested in going back to work for the firm.

That was some considerable way from the truth, but he wanted to see her reaction.

– Well don't you think that's a good idea?

Sure, he thought. Doing shit jobs for his little brother, taking care of everything that smelled of danger while Adrian himself sat on his arse behind a desk, raking it in.

– I'll think about it, he said evenly. – But if I say yes, it means I'll be away a long time.

She didn't look as if she minded that much.

– Can be pretty dangerous too.

She didn't say she would refuse to let him take that risk.

– You'll earn good money again, she said, as if that was all it was about. He grabbed the kettle and put it down in the middle of the table, dropped a box of her favourite brews next to it, slumped down into a chair opposite her. She chose camomile, he noted, and he did the same himself. He might have asked her to take off her coat, but that would seem stupid and might have the opposite of the intended effect and make her leave immediately.

– No mail for you today, she told him, placing the pile

of newspapers on the table, slipping the letters into her coat pocket.

– Great. It's only the taxman and a couple of others who know I'm back.

For that whole winter he had hardly seen anyone else but her. Before Christmas he had been down to Studio Q a few times, made a half-hearted effort to get back in shape again, but since New Year he had spent most of his time in the flat.

– Maybe you should do something about it, she said.

He glanced at her, a quick, sweeping look to see what she was talking about. Years ago, the last time she read the cards for him, she'd told him he would have no trouble attracting women. Maybe she was referring to something in that direction.

– Actually I read something in the paper. She opened *Romerikes Blad*. – There's something here that might interest you.

He listened for signs in what she was saying, mostly for the tone of voice. Quite often when she came in to him it was because she needed help, usually in making her way through the mysteries of the digital world in which she felt lost, or else a problem with the house, or the car. But now and then because there was something she wanted to share with him.

He leaned his body as far over as he could towards her, peering as she flipped the pages. It was the culture section she was looking for. How interested was he in amateur dramatics in Sørumsand? Or what some local peasant thought of the Hellbillies' new record? But she was pointing to the page opposite, turned the paper round and pushed it towards him. An interview, he noted, and studied the photo of the young woman. Then he read the headline. *Writing about a brother who disappeared*. He skimmed the three columns. Realised at once what it was about, knew it even before he came to the name of the missing brother. Disappeared eight years ago, never found. Kai didn't keep count of the years; it might have been seven, or nine, but apparently it was eight. But he could recall every detail of that evening. Most days passed by unremarkably, but that particular Maundy Thursday had left traces that cropped up constantly.

– Why are you showing me this? he asked without a hint of a tremor in his voice.

He met her gaze for a second, maybe two seconds, before looking back down at the newspaper with the photo and the interview. There were places into which she must never catch even the merest glimpse.

– You mentioned back then that you knew Karsten Clausen, she said.

– Did I? Her gaze was still on him; he couldn't ignore it. – I met him a couple of times maybe, with Adrian.

– Never without Adrian being there?

He shrugged. – It was eight years ago.

– You've always had a good memory.

What he should have done was give an exasperated shake of the head, maybe express some irritation and ask what she was trying to say.

– If I had anything to tell you, I would have done it a long time ago, he said, hearing himself how hollow it sounded.

But then she, who noticed every sign of unease, every slight alteration in his voice, patted his arm, folded the newspaper and stood up.

– I'm thinking how that family must have suffered, she sighed. – If there was perhaps something we could have done for them.

She looked so unhappy, and he wanted to comfort her.

But what he might have said would only make things worse, for her too. So much so that she would never get over it.

The moment she went into her own apartment he got dressed and headed down to Studio Q. He felt as though people were staring at him but blocked the stares out, did five kilometres on the treadmill, rowed even longer, pumped iron for an hour. By the time he returned, Elsa's windows were dark and the car wasn't there. He let himself into her apartment, took a look round the living room, then the kitchen. The newspaper was in the cupboard below the sink. He tore out the page with the interview and took it back to his own apartment. In an envelope in the top bureau drawer he had a number of newspaper cuttings plus some printouts from the internet. He quickly went through them. *Eighteen-year-old missing*, and *Still no sign of Karsten (18)*.

Abruptly he stuffed everything back into the envelope, stood there for a while with it in his hand, as though weighing it before putting it away. Then he undressed and walked naked into the bathroom. He turned on the shower and let the warm water plaster his hair to his head. They'd never found Karsten Clausen. No one knew shit about what he had found out before he disappeared. Not the police, not the family, not this little sister who had started going through his possessions. All the same, an idea had started to grow on him. He isolated it. Suddenly he uttered a low laugh, and somewhere in that laughter the sister's face appeared, the way it looked in the photo, and with it came an idea of the kind that demanded to be worked on.

He sat at his computer and logged into Facebook. Found her there. Her information and pictures were open to everyone. Showed that she wasn't exactly up to speed in regards to online security. Unless, that is, she actually wanted to be seen by as many people as possible. He took out the interview again. Even her eyes were round, as though there were something she was wondering about the whole time. On one of her Facebook pictures she was leading a horse.

On the yellow pages website he found three people called Synne Clausen. Only one of them lived in Oslo. If it was her, she lived in a student village. It took him fifteen seconds to trace her email address, and four minutes to prepare a Trojan. If she was naïve enough, that should be enough.

He stood up, stepped into the kitchen, opened a Red Bull. The page was still in his hand. There was something else about that article, something he'd seen but not actually noted earlier in the day. Now he knew what it was. The name of the journalist who had done the interview. The Pentecostal who lived in the house in Erleveien. There were connections out there, little pieces that fitted into a bigger picture. The journalist and his pregnant wife, and the child that was always thirsty in the night. In the eight years since that business with Karsten, he had stayed away from that street. He realised that he was standing there and saying this out loud to himself.

The sky had cleared outside, the heavens a bluey grey above the river. He opened the window, stood there sniffing the gentle wind.

– Hibernation time is over, he murmured.

5

THIS STORY WILL do everything in its power not to be written. I will circle round Karsten, my brother Karsten, who is gone. He is there when I write; not him, but the empty space that remained. Emptiness is a gateway to something else, and I can't manage to pass through it.

Synne pulled out her earplugs and closed the lid of her laptop. The sounds in the house were turned on. People out in the corridor talking to each other, the sighing of the water pipes, and Maja practising the flute in her room next to the kitchen. She sat listening for a few moments before she went online to check her mail. Loads of Facebook messages. All about the piece in *Romerikes Blad*. She had been furious when she saw it. When Dan-Levi called the day after she had been to see him and asked if he could write something about the book she was working on, she had been stupid enough to let herself be persuaded. He assured her it would be no more than a brief paragraph in a far-off corner of the culture section. She suspected the worst when he called her again that morning and apologised that the piece had turned out the way it did – there had been a misunderstanding with the editor, and the desk, which always went its own way, but above all it was he who had screwed up. She was only mildly annoyed and forgave him, if not wholeheartedly then at least half-heartedly. That was before she saw the piece on the net. And in the paper edition it covered a whole page, with a picture of herself and the most awful headline imaginable.

Her phone vibrated and she saw it was Erika.

– I slept badly last night, she complained, and wasn't sure that was actually correct. It was the kind of thing she said to Erika.

– Because of that piece in your local paper?

– I didn't see that until this morning. If I'd known what they were going to write, I would've stopped it.

– Is it that bad?

– Log in to *Romerikes Blad* and see for yourself, Synne groaned, and summarised what Dan-Levi had written. – I don't want anyone to have the slightest idea what I'm doing, and now I'm completely snowed under by so-called friends on Facebook.

– Maybe that's exactly what you do want without realising it, Erika suggested. – You want people to know about your book project.

Synne's anger flared up again. – Spare me the patronising pseudo-Freudian bullshit, she hissed. – Are you trying to shine floodlights on my subconscious?

She flew off the handle completely and ended up blaming Erika for the interview and the write-up and everything else that was wrong with the local paper. She laid it on so thick that in the end Erika burst out laughing, and then she couldn't go on being serious herself.

– I'll come over later, Erika decided. – Then we can talk more about this.

– I'm going out with someone, Synne told her.

– And who is someone?

– Sounds like a cross-examination.

– Cut it out. That foreign girl?

She was about to say that it was none of Erika's business but desisted.

– Her name is Maja, I've told you that several times.

Erika didn't respond for an unusually long time.

– All right, she said finally. – You're free to go out with whomever you want.

– Thank you very much.

– Look, you mustn't take it like that.

Obviously she had only now realised what she had said. Synne permitted herself a smile of satisfaction, closed the conversation and checked her mail again. More Facebook messages. She didn't open them, mostly to disprove Erika's irritating theory. There was also something from an unknown firm offering free help in making her computer run faster. Synne had heard about Trojan horses and the shit they left behind: worms and viruses that were impossible to get rid of. She did not open the attachment, glanced at her watch, went out into the corridor and knocked on Maja's door.

Maja poked her head out, wearing a towel, her hair wet.

– Just need to chuck a few things on.

– Do you do your flute practice in the nude? Synne exclaimed with an amused smile, and Maja blushed.

A few minutes later she came in and sat down at the little table in the corner of the kitchen.

– Have you been working out again? said Synne, attempting to sound exasperated.

– The last time was two days ago, Maja excused herself, these roles being a part of their relationship, with Synne acting even more of a couch potato than she really was, and Maja even more of a workout junkie. In fact it was part of a routine intended to help her control a serious case of diabetes.

– You know I'm not like you, Maja flattered her. – You're pretty. And famous and intelligent. You can get anyone you want.

Synne had to laugh, both at what Maja said and at the strange rhythms of her Norwegian speech.

– Neither fame nor intelligence is advantageous for a woman who's looking for a man.

– What does 'advantageous' mean? Maja wanted to know. She had been less than a year in Norway but was a quick learner. Synne didn't mind at all helping her out on some of these finer points. She poured coffee for them both. They had ten minutes before they had to go for the bus.

– What sort of man are you actually looking for?

She had discovered that she liked talking to Maja about men in this way. It didn't work with Erika. – Do you want a strong but silent Norwegian who takes his turn at doing the washing-up, or a passionate Greek who satisfies you sexually but sleeps with all your friends too? Or a Muslim who wants you to hide your face every time you step outside the door?

She offered up these caricatures with a little grin, but Maja appeared to take the questions quite seriously.

– First and foremost, he must have a stainless charabanc.

Synne stared at her uncomprehendingly for a few moments before she realised what she was trying to say. It took quite a while for her to compose herself sufficiently to explain why she was laughing. And then Maja laughed too. She disappeared to her room and returned with a notebook. In addition to Polish, French and German, she spoke fluent English, but they had agreed to stick to Norwegian for the sake of her education.

– So then it's *character*, she noted, and Synne agreed that it might be a good idea to ask a man for a character reference before a first date.

6

THE LIGHTS WENT out in Synne Clausen's room. Kai glanced
at his watch: twenty past five. Four minutes passed before
she emerged from the main doorway. She was not alone,
but with a small, dark-haired woman who didn't look
Norwegian. They headed for the gate into Sognsveien. He
followed them, so closely he could hear their laughter, Synne
Clausen's light, the other's deeper. Once he was certain they
were heading for the bus stop, he turned and ran through
a short cut that brought him out higher up on Sognsveien.
He sprinted round the corner, reached the next stop just as
the bus came crawling down the hill from Kringsjå.

He picked a vacant seat somewhere in the middle. Saw
them standing on the pavement as the bus approached. The
small, dark one boarded first, then Synne Clausen. Her gaze
passed over him; he half turned, peered out into the dusk.
They sat a few seats in front of him. Her hair was longer
than in the picture in the paper; it suited her, he noted,
made her face seem less round. In the interview she said
she'd found several of her brother's things. She'd obviously
started digging around. After eight years, the chances of
anything with a connection to him cropping up were
minimal, but he wasn't the kind of person who dealt in
odds. He intended to find out exactly what she was up to.
The thought had obsessed him ever since Elsa showed
him the interview. It was as though this was what she had
been trying to awaken in him without even realising it. It

thrilled him, lifted him up out of the soporific state he'd drifted in throughout the winter. He'd laid out bait on the net. Maybe she'd taken a sniff at it, maybe taken a bite, or maybe sensed the danger.

They were getting off at Majorstua. He waited until both of them were out before jumping to his feet and following them, remaining at the bus stop until they had crossed the street. He saw them disappear into the Colosseum cinema, followed, located them in a ticket queue. At one point Synne Clausen turned and looked around, her gaze holding his for a moment or two, perhaps recalling him from the bus. Suddenly he felt cheerful. Something inside him that had been dormant all winter had begun to stir. A frail, still frozen flame. Welcome back, Kai, he murmured to himself.

They had chosen the film in Theatre 4. Typical student film, not exactly a stampede for tickets. He glanced around. The place was only a quarter full. Synne and the dark girl had seats in the middle of the fifth row. He sat three rows behind them, slid down in his seat as far as he could, studied the outline of the two women in the light from the screen. After a while, Synne leaned her head towards her friend, but not to say anything, as far as he could see.

They had called the week after Easter. A sergeant who explained that they were going through the call lists on Karsten's phone. They'd found a call from Kai's phone on Maundy Thursday and now they wanted to know if he had any information that could be of assistance to them. Afterwards he kept waiting for something to happen. For them to call again, summon him for an interview, confront him with something or other that could be used against him, a pattern of circumstantial evidence, irrefutable proof. He lay awake at night, always ready to run. Until after a month he began to realise they had nothing on him. But a tiny insecurity continued to nag away at him. It was still there, like a seed, and something the sister had said in the interview had wakened it to life again.

On the way out to the car, he had an idea, called in at a hairdresser's in Bogstadveien. It had something to do with Synne Clausen. She'd seen him twice, and he didn't want to be recognised if it happened a third time. But it was more to do with the fact that he'd let everything go. Let his body swell up. In the mirror, when the barber asked him to bend his head, he could see the faintest signs of a double chin. So welcome back, he said to himself again.

There were lights on in Elsa's apartment. He didn't ring the bell but knocked on the door a couple of times before going in. In the hallway he called her name. For a moment he thought she might be up in the tarot room, in which case there could be no question of disturbing her. But her voice replied from the living room, and he pulled off his trainers and went in. She was sitting in a corner armchair with a book, a steaming cup on the table beside her. She raised her reading glasses, looked up at him.

– You've been to the hairdresser's, she exclaimed.

He listened out for any sign of whether or not she liked it.

– Had to do something, he told her.

– It's very fair.

– I used to have it like this, he reminded her. This was exactly what his hair had looked like that Easter eight years ago. – Have to get going again.

She nodded, as though that was exactly what she had been expecting him to say.

– Are you hungry? There's a pie in the fridge.

He'd popped in somewhere for a hamburger while he was out, but an offer from her could not be refused. As he sat in the kitchen munching away, she came in.

– Where did you go tonight?

– Went to the cinema.

She joined him at the table. Why did you come in and show me that interview? he should have asked her, but he didn't take the chance.

He was the one who had told her Karsten had gone missing that time. He remembered how distressed she had been. She had met Karsten a few times and obviously liked him. She'd been away on a course that Easter weekend, and when she came back, he went out into the yard, pretending he had something to do in the garage. That was when he'd told her. At first she wouldn't believe him. *What do you mean?* He could recall how sharp her voice became. *How long has he been missing?*

She insisted that he tell her everything he knew. Forced him to answer that he knew fuck all. She studied him, could see deep inside him, could see there was something he wasn't telling. Suddenly she'd said: *Whatever it is you've been up to, Kai, you've got to stop it.*

For once, he'd got angry with her. There were places even she didn't have access to. He turned and walked away, because she mustn't know about that anger. Afterwards she had never spoken like that to him again. But he could feel the same penetrating gaze on him every time Karsten's name came up. He couldn't bear it.

In the early part of the summer he had rejoined the army. There were wars in the world. He wanted to go to Afghanistan; tried the Telemark Battalion, but they wouldn't have him. They used his sick note against him, offered him office work instead, computer work. Adrian was in Iraq with the British forces. Elsa boasted about him the whole time, as though it was Adrian who was leading the battle to save civilisation. And when he took over one of his father's firms and began doing security work in Basra, that was clearly just as heroic in her eyes. In reality it was about making a helluva lot of money out of a lost war. Adrian was always one step ahead.

One day in April the previous year he had called and asked if Kai wanted to come out and try his luck there. Kai suspected that Elsa had put him up to it but said nothing. He worked for the firm for almost five months. Working round the clock for peanuts, doing all the dangerous jobs. And a single mistake was enough for him to get squeezed out. He hadn't slept for four days, was told to clear a foyer, fired shots. Adrian claimed he needed treatment.

When he came home early in the autumn, Elsa seemed glad at first to have him there. She invited him in to her place some evenings, made dinner, served wine. But what she really wanted was to talk about Adrian. Lionheart, she still called him that. She wanted to know why Kai wasn't working for him any more, as though his mission in life was to serve his little brother.

– Good to see that there's life in you yet, she said now, and her voice had that tone he was always listening for.

– Thought I'd better update your OS, he said quickly. – There's a new security package out. He'd helped her choose a computer, and made her a webpage for attracting new clients.

– Great, she said, smiling at him across the table.

Over an hour passed before he let himself into his own flat, and she hadn't mentioned Adrian once.

He had some monster roids in a bag in the fridge. Poor quality; he should have got something better. Considered calling one of his dealers, decided not to, injected five milli-litres, a little more than he should have, was in a hurry to build himself up again. In the cellar he stripped off, did push-ups and sit-ups, a half-hour workout on the punchball. When he came back up, he stood for a while in the dark living room and looked out of the window. *Whatever it is you've been up to, Kai, you've got to stop it.* Elsa had no idea what she was asking for. She couldn't know anything about the fires. She must never find out what he'd been doing that spring.

He went into his bedroom, opened a drawer. Found the interview with *Romerikes Blad, Writing about a brother who disappeared,* focused on the third paragraph from the end.

For the first time I've been going through his things. All the things he left behind, things that maybe only he understood the importance of. And his mobile phone with the last messages and photos. Things that bring him back to life again. I also want to talk to people who used to know him.

Kai rubbed his throat. The pain of that time when the car window was crushing his larynx came back to him, the moment when he thought he was going to choke to death. The longer he studied her picture, the more her gaze looked like Karsten's. Karsten looking terrified as he lifts up the bag he's been trying to hide under the car seat. The look that says he knows what the things inside it are used for.

He switched on his computer, checked the mail he had sent to Synne Clausen. She hadn't opened the attachment, was obviously too cautious to fall for something that simple. He would have to come up with something better. The idea came to him as he was going over what he had found out about her. He saw her with her friend on the bus, and the two of them a few rows in front of him at the cinema, their heads touching. He suddenly knew how to get access to what he needed. Synne Clausen would be unable to stop him, and the thought made him laugh out loud. He threw open the window and let the laughter stream out into the chilly April evening.

7

THE MAN WHO opened the door was the same age as Karsten would have been, but he looked a good deal older. The chin had almost disappeared, and the thin fringe did not hide the markedly receding hairline. From the way he looked in the school photo, Synne had tried to imagine what his face would look like now, eight years on, the way certain advanced software could. She hadn't been very successful, even though the man was not very unlike his father. Now and then she had seen pictures of the local priest in the newspaper.

Synne offered him her hand. His handshake was damp, but firm enough.

– Finn Olav. So you're Karsten's little sister.

His tone was very slightly paternal, something she was oversensitive to, according to Erika.

– I never met you back then, he added quickly. – But Tonje remembers you well.

Synne doubted if that could be true. – Is she home?

– She'll be back shortly. Hairdresser, you know. Or something like that. He smiled sarcastically, as though intending to convey a general comment on women and all the time they spent on that kind of thing. Synne let it pass, realising that it was her responsibility to make sure things went well, because after all, she was the one who had asked for the meeting.

– I saw the interview with you in *Romerikes Blad*, he said.

She took off her boots, gave an inward groan. – It seems as though everyone has.

He frowned. – Isn't that the idea? Isn't that why people give interviews? Without waiting for her answer, he turned his back. – It must be exciting, writing a novel about your own family, he observed as he led her into the living room. They lived in a flat that belonged to the hospital, where he worked.

– Not at all sure there'll be a novel in it, she informed him.

He put cups on the coffee table. – I see a sort of Knausgårdian dimension to it.

– Oh yeah, she answered, suddenly watchful. – So you find time to read novels?

She had found out that he worked as a doctor in the surgical department, and that he and Tonje had two young children. She recalled that his nickname was Priest and decided she would use that if he became part of what she wrote.

– Always been a very quick reader, he claimed. – Particularly if it's a subject that interests me. Read every volume of Knausgård's book. Every last word of it.

He was clearly interested in showing off, and listed a whole catalogue of books he'd read. Eventually Tonje arrived. *She* hadn't changed much since that old school photo.

– Hi, Synne, she said, and gave her a hug. – I had to drop my oldest off at a birthday party.

Synne understood at once why Karsten had been so taken with her. The high cheekbones and the slightly slanting eyes gave the face an exotic cast. She was small but looked fit and healthy, the kind of woman all Norwegian boys were attracted to, she thought.

– I'm glad you can spare the time for this. You've obviously got plenty to be getting on with.

Tonje brushed this aside. – But of course we can. If you only knew how often I've thought about Karsten over the years.

It was as though the air in the room became fresher after Tonje's entry, as though all the windows had been thrown wide open.

– You said on the phone you wanted to know more about the evening he went missing. She looked to be thinking back. – It was Maundy Thursday, at Finn Olav's house; we were joking about having a party in the rectory in the middle of Holy Week.

Finn Olav nodded. – Dad was never too fussy about things like that.

– How did Karsten seem that evening? Synne asked.

The two exchanged a look. It seemed as though each would prefer the other to say something.

– Well, said Finn Olav finally. – He drank way too much.

– School leaving party, Synne commented.

Tonje sat up. – Karsten never drank. Not ever.

– Never? queried Finn Olav. He sounded unconvinced.

– Not before that evening, Tonje said, brushing him aside. – He was very straight. A bit more mature than certain other people I could mention were at that time. He knew what he wanted to do with his life.

– Research, Finn Olav added.

– Just think what he could have achieved. Tonje looked upset. – He was really intelligent.

Synne fetched the school photo from her bag, which she'd left out in the hallway.

– I haven't seen that for years, Finn Olav exclaimed once he realised what it was. – Must be up in some loft somewhere or other.

Tonje took it from him and let her gaze wander over the three rows of eighteen- and nineteen-year-olds.

– Good picture of Karsten, she said, her voice quavering slightly.

Synne stood behind her. – Who is that? she asked, pointing

to the girl whose photograph she had seen on the mobile phone.

– Jasmeen, said Tonje. – What was her other name again? What's that politician called?

– Chadar, Finn Olav answered. He glanced up at Synne. – You know who her brother is?

– Chadar? Synne thought about it. – You don't mean Shahzad Chadar?

– Exactly, said Finn Olav. – He was two years ahead of us at secondary school. Didn't think he'd even manage to finish school at all. Just shows you how wrong you can be. I remember him as a bully who lived from stealing mobile phones and laptops.

– There's no need to keep your old prejudices alive, Tonje protested.

– Oh come on, everyone knew the guy was an associate of the Young Guns, or was it the Old Guns? Whenever he gets interviewed now, he never hides the fact that he used to be a petty thief and a gang member. He's managed to turn it into an advantage, an experience everyone ought to have.

– Jasmeen was completely different, Tonje interrupted. – A really sweet person, but we just never saw much of her. She never came to parties, not then and not at any later reunions either. She was clever, but for some reason or other she quit school just before the final exams.

– Muslims, Finn Olav interjected. – The girls are raised to abide by medieval standards of chastity. There are no restrictions on the boys at all.

– She and Karsten were an item. Synne offered this vague surmise as though it were an established fact. Finn Olav and Tonje looked at each other, and then Finn Olav smiled indulgently.

– I'm afraid you're mistaken there.

Tonje said: – I don't think Karsten and Jasmeen knew each other particularly well.

Synne shrugged her shoulders. – Maybe not.

– Has somebody said anything different?

Synne thought about it. – I found some pictures. It's obvious there was something going on between them.

– Pictures? Tonje sounded curious.

– All the things we don't know, Finn Olav said with a smirk.

Tonje gave him an annoyed look. Just then faint sounds were heard from upstairs.

– Your turn, she said firmly.

– To breastfeed?

She rolled her eyes. – You can give me a shout when you've changed his nappy.

Finn Olav stood up, still smirking, padded up the stairs.

– At least they're good for something, Tonje sighed.

– I heard that! he shouted down to them.

An upstairs door was opened. Synne heard him start to baby-talk.

– This business about Jasmeen. Tonje shook her head firmly. – I don't think Karsten had a girlfriend, not a proper one.

She sat up in her chair, crossed her legs.

– Actually, there was something that happened . . . Not being conceited or anything, but I think he liked me quite a lot.

– Yes, I think so too, Synne agreed.

– I was with this other guy, sort of on and off. But there was something special about Karsten. He was so completely himself. And always very serious and decisive about what he was going to do with his life. But I never thought about him in that way.

She drank some coffee.

– The week before Easter, we had a party at my place. A gang gatecrashed and beat up someone in our class, a Vietnamese boy. Nobody lifted a finger. Only Karsten. He ran outside and was going to stop them, and he wasn't exactly the fighting type. It must have taken a lot for him to do that.

She glanced over at the stairs up to the next floor.

– One day in the Easter holiday he came to my house. He seemed very changed. Seemed to radiate something or other . . . She started to fidget with the pearl pendant on her necklace. – And then he kissed me. On the front porch steps. And that last evening, Maundy Thursday, I was really wondering whether or not he'd come to the party.

She fell silent a moment. Synne realised she was rocking back and forth in her chair as she waited for Tonje to go on.

– When I arrived, he was already there. Not to make any bones about it, he was completely plastered. I was furious. Not at Karsten, but at Finn Olav, because it was him who got him drunk. And then lots of things happened. Karsten threw up and was in a terrible state. We managed to get him to lie down in the basement. And then he disappeared. His shoes were still out in the hallway. It would have made a great school leavers' party story, the kind we liked to talk about for years afterwards. Stumbles home in his stockinged feet. But it turned out very different.

Synne sensed that Tonje was on the point of crying.

– Because he never reached home.

From the floor above, her partner called down.

– Finn Olav doesn't like me talking about him.

She sat and looked again at the school photo.

– I should never have left him alone that night, she said suddenly. – I should have stayed there and looked after him.

She paused as Finn Olav came back downstairs.

– Your turn, he chirruped in an exaggeratedly cheerful voice.

Once Tonje had disappeared upstairs he said: – So our school leaving celebration fortnight didn't turn out quite the way we planned it. As though Karsten had ruined it for them, thought Synne, and almost as though he understood the way she was thinking, he added: – Naturally, *that* wasn't what was important. When someone kills themselves . . .

She put her cup down, jumped at the noise it made as it hit the table. – Do you know that? Do you know that was what happened?

He scratched his balding temples. – Know? Of course not. No one knows.

– Then why do you say it?

– A faint flush spread across his face. – It seems the most obvious thing.

– Hasn't it occurred to you that it might have been an accident?

He hesitated. – Not sure how important it is to discuss this really.

– It's important to me.

He looked as though he was thinking it over. – Karsten changed towards the end, he said after a while. – From being very shy and reserved. Something happened to him. And then there were those fires.

She took two deep breaths. – Do you really think Karsten was a pyromaniac?

Again he scratched himself through his thin hair. – Actually no, but there were rumours. And that evening when I brought him to the party . . .

Now it was his turn to start peering up towards the next floor. – Tonje doesn't like to hear this. Her idea of him is different.

– What happened to him at that party?

– When I picked him up, he was already pretty out of it. Said there were people after him.

– Who was after him?

– The police, according to him. And some gangs, Pakistanis and others. I've never been interested in psychiatry, but I did learn this much from my studies. He'd persuaded himself that all sorts of people were out to get him, and in his own eyes that made him important. It must have been some kind of substitute for all the things he didn't experience in real life. I mean, he never joined in anything. Today I would say that he was paranoid that evening.

Synne couldn't help herself. – So was that why you treated him with alcohol? she said, immediately regretting it as she saw how his face fell.

She stood at the bus stop looking up towards the hill. Blocks of flats below, villas on top. Carefully she began to make her way upwards. The pavement was covered in lumpy patches of ice with deep meltwater between them, and sometimes she was forced to walk out on the road. At the top, she looked at the map on her phone, checked she was on the right road, then carried on past the row of identical detached houses, each with a carport in between. The fifth house on the right was painted in a glowing turquoise that made it stand out from all the others in the neighbourhood. A dark Mercedes was parked outside. There was a small nameplate hanging on the postbox: *Chadar*.

There was no light in the window next to the front door. But something moved behind the cream-coloured curtains when she rang the bell, and she thought she caught a glimpse of a face. She rang a second time, holding the bell down a little longer. Another half-minute went by. It wasn't in her nature to find it easy to ring on strangers' doors, stick a foot in the doorway and ask questions until she got answers. Journalist was probably the last job she would ever have chosen.

As she was turning to walk away, she heard sounds in the hallway inside, then finally the click of a latch and the door glided open.

The woman who stood there was in her late fifties, maybe older. She was small and round, and her chin had been replaced by several layers of folds that looked to be held in place by her hijab. Her eyes slowly scrutinised Synne.

Synne said her name. – I would like to speak to Jasmeen Chadar.

The expression in the woman's eyes did not change. – There is no Jasmeen living here, she said in broken Norwegian.

In the hall behind her a younger woman appeared. The older one turned and spoke to her in what was probably Urdu or Punjabi. The younger one looked to be in her early thirties. She too wore a veil bound tightly around a full face.

– Where can I find her?

The younger woman began to say something, but the older one interrupted her in an angry voice. She turned to Synne once more.

– We don't know any Jasmeen.

Synne tried again. – I've come because there's something I want to ask her about.

– We know why you're here, the woman said curtly. – We can't help you. Without further answer, she closed the door.

As Synne reached the main road and was about to head back down towards the bus stop, she heard someone calling her. She turned and saw the young woman she had just met running in her direction with small steps.

– There's someone who wants to talk to you, she panted as she approached.

– Who wants to talk to me?

The woman stopped right in front of her. – Come. She took hold of Synne by the arm and set off walking.

The older woman was standing outside on the doorstep. She didn't look very friendly, but she said something or other that was probably a greeting, led Synne inside and up a flight of stairs, knocked on a door. No one answered, but she opened the door and ushered Synne into a bright room with the curtains pulled back and the windows opened towards the western sky. In a bed against the wall opposite sat a man propped up on pillows. He was very thin, his skin a yellowy brown, but his eyes were clear as they scrutinised Synne, standing in the middle of the floor with no idea at all of what to say.

– Sit down, he said in a frail voice, nodding in the direction of a chair.

The woman, who was probably his wife, was still standing at the door, but the man gestured with his hand, at which she withdrew, giving Synne a sidelong glance.

– So you are Karsten's sister, said the man.

Synne nodded. – And you must be Jasmeen's father.

He smiled with cracked lips and tried to reach a glass of water on his bedside table. She stood up and got it for him.

– Thank you, he murmured, and took a couple of small sips, swallowing with obvious difficulty.

He handed the glass back to her. She put it down and remained standing beside the bed, about to ask if there was anything else she could do for him.

– Sit down, he repeated with a smile that was barely visible. – If I had known you were coming, I would have arranged a proper welcome for you.

He looked towards the door. – My wife is probably more bitter than I am. Why do you want to meet Jasmeen?

She had rehearsed what she would say, told him she wanted to write about her brother.

He nodded at this information. – Words cannot bring anyone back. But they can be a comfort nonetheless.

– I think you understand me, she said, looking out of the window.

A little later, he was the one who broke the silence.

– I want to tell you a story. It is my story. Maybe it won't mean anything to you, or maybe it will.

She turned to look at him again.

– I came to Norway in nineteen seventy-four, he began, and as his story progressed, he seemed to come to life. His voice became stronger, and he reached out for the water glass himself and didn't need help. As he spoke, Synne sat listening and wondered why he wanted to tell her all this. And somewhere along the way she had the idea that she might need a story like this to give direction to what she was struggling to write herself. Maybe she had to distance herself that far from her material in order to be able to get close to it again.

Jasmeen's father paused and nodded towards the framed black-and-white photo on the bedside table. Synne took a closer look at it. Two young boys and a man standing in front of a house made of stone. All of them wearing tunics and baggy pants, sandals on their feet. The man was in his forties or fifties; his tunic was white, with embroidery on the collar, and on his head was a turban in a darker colour. He was looking down at the two boys with a very serious expression. One of them had a similar look in his eyes, while the other had his arms around a cow's neck, a broad grin on his face.

Jasmeen's father's reasons for wanting Synne to see this

photo, and to hear his story, remained unclear, but she had
a feeling that he was getting there. Khalid Chadar
had worked and lived on a farm in Nittedal. Something
had happened there, Synne wasn't quite clear what, but at
a certain point the people on the farm had turned against
him and he was literally thrown out. He was given no explanation and simply had to accept it. He described some of the
less salubrious places in which he had been obliged to live,
the hostels and the damp basements. At one point he was
holding down three jobs. Cleaning the toilets in schools and
cafés, delivering newspapers, and driving a taxi, having
earned enough to get his driving licence. The money he
didn't send back home he saved to pay for his return and
his marriage to the woman he would share his life with.

Back in Norway, he opened his own shop, worked there
day and night until it began to show a profit, and then started
another and worked twice as hard. After seventeen years in
this country, he was able to lead his Zainab up the short
driveway to a newly built house, the one they were now in.

This was what he had lived for, so that his children might
enjoy the sort of opportunities he never had. So that they
should be able to grow up in this unfathomably rich country,
put down roots and live here without being foreigners,
become Norwegian without abandoning the things that made
them good people: a belief in God, in justice, in purity, in
family.

Shahzad, the oldest, was now a highly respected lawyer
and politician. His youngest had also done well. But Jasmeen,
who had been the apple of his eye, who was even more
intelligent and strong willed than her big brother, had had
a difficult time of it. It was because she had developed a
weakness for Synne's brother, and because that brother had
exploited her weakness. And here he had reached the point
of what it was he wanted to say to her.

He drank more water. Slightly larger sips now.

– It destroyed so much for her. More than you could possibly understand. We were very angry with your brother. But at the same time I, who had spent so long in Norway, knew that this was what went on between the young people here, that this was how the Norwegians raised their sons and their daughters.

He looked directly into her eyes. – We decided to do nothing. And then your brother disappeared. We were truly sorry for your family. But because of what had happened with Jasmeen, we never expressed our sympathies.

He had to stop and catch his breath a couple of times.

– There was a collection in the class. They were going to buy a wreath for the memorial service. But we didn't contribute.

Again he looked directly at her.

– I shall meet Allah, and I know this is something we should have done. This is what I want you to take with you when you leave here. After all these years, I want there to be nothing left outstanding between our two families.

He half turned towards her and held out a bony hand.

8

JANUS KNEW THAT she would be coming. At least Synne liked to think that. And Åse, who ran the stables, firmly believed in that kind of thing. She reckoned Janus behaved differently in the hours preceding Synne's arrival, was restless in his box and pricked up his ears.

The animal Erika usually hired was called Sancto Spirito. He was a quiet gelding who stood alongside Janus, rubbed his head against his flank and had no difficulty in accepting that Janus was boss. According to Åse, Sancto Spirito was more concerned with the spiritual side of things.

In the same way, Erika accepted that Synne was boss when they were out on the horses. Before they met, she had never sat on a horse's back. It made up for some of the inequalities in other departments, and Synne could experience Erika's keenness to emphasise this as irritating: *I'm just a novice, you need to teach me everything.*

They let the horses trot up through the valley. The afternoon was fine and still, the sun flickering between the branches of the spruce. When Synne rode alone, the thoughts could come streaming out of her, away on ahead into the trees until they disappeared. But now Erika was right behind her, commenting on everything she saw, turning it all into language. Some days Synne didn't mind too much, but on this bright afternoon she would have preferred to ride alone.

Up on the forest track, Janus picked up speed in the slush. Somewhere behind her Synne heard Erika squealing with pleasure and had to laugh. Only when they reached the tarn above the moor at Tuftemyra did she slow down and wait. When Erika caught up with her, she jumped down, slipped off the bridles and replaced them with halters, then let the two animals wander on long tethers and graze in between the patchy snow.

Erika snuggled up against Synne on the blanket in front of a big rock by the edge of the water. – And when am I going to be allowed to read what you're writing?

Synne peered into the sun between the branches of the pines. It shone directly above the hill, uneasily, as though it wanted to come nearer but was afraid it would destroy her.

– I thought we were agreed you wouldn't go on about it.
– I'm not going on about it.

Erika seemed genuinely curious, and finally Synne relented and told her about the trip to Lørenskog.

– I'm noting down as exactly as I can what people who knew Karsten tell me. I can't just keep going over my own vague memories and feelings.

Erika couldn't resist. – Is it distance you're looking for? Finding a passage that's safe?

– I just don't want to drown in sentimentality.

Erika turned her head away and sat looking across to the opposite bank of the tarn.

– Don't you like the idea? Synne exclaimed.

It took a frustrating amount of time before Erika responded.

– I'm sure it will be quite interesting. It'll be like something any of the dozens of clever girls whose books will get published this autumn could have written.

The moment they dismounted, they had resumed their

familiar roles, with Erika as the mentor and Synne as the pupil.

– You're trying to protect yourself from what pains you.

– You don't understand, Synne snapped.

– Do you understand that yourself?

Synne got to her feet. Janus stretched his neck and looked at her. There was a divide down the centre of the bridge of his nose, with one side as pitch black as the rest of his body and the other a greyish white.

– Might just as well talk to *you*, Synne muttered, her mouth up against his muzzle.

The horse made a deep murmuring sound.

– At least you listen.

– Come and sit down again when you've finished sulking, Erika suggested, lighting a cigarette.

Synne gave up, slumped down beside her again, took the cigarette from her mouth and inhaled, drawing the cloud of hot fog as deep into her chest as she could bear.

– That's where you have to begin, Erika insisted. – With the evening your brother disappeared.

She was right. Frustratingly and obviously.

– Tell me what happened.

– What can I say that I haven't said before? Synne said. – It's turned into a jumble of threads, some things I remember, other things I've imagined, and all mixed up with what other people have told me.

She'd had to spend the night in the hospital. Her parents sat with her until the doctors had carried out their first examinations. Concluded that it was not serious. It wasn't until the following day that they discovered Karsten hadn't come home. Again and again the psychiatrist had returned to this. She was not to blame. It was all an unfortunate coincidence, something wholly beyond her control. But she had always thought there was something else. *There was something else*; the words ran through her every time she approached the subject. Like a child inside her standing up and shouting: *there was something else, there was something else, there was something else*. Not even words sometimes, just the rhythm, loud and harsh, and then it was like the screeching of gulls. Compulsive thoughts, the psychiatrist ended up calling it. There were ways of getting rid of such thoughts. She'd discovered some of her own. One required not thinking about that evening, and it worked after a fashion. Then a few days ago she had seen Tamara sitting on a step in Dronningens gate. And afterwards she had started writing about Karsten.

– Perhaps you shouldn't be concerned about the objective truth of what happened, Erika suggested.

Synne picked a blade of grass, held it fast between her teeth and jabbed her tongue hard against the pointed end. It had helped to stick to the version of events they had agreed upon all those years ago. She had been at Tamara's house. On the way home she had suffered an attack, the first in over a year. She had fallen off her cycle and hit her head. It happened right outside Karsten's school. Luckily someone came by, some bloke who found her by the side of the road. She was lifted up and placed in the back of a car. Did she remember this, or was it something she had been told? The man spoke to her. There was a strong smell inside the car. She was certain she remembered that. And something the man said: *I know Karsten*. He had driven her home and then disappeared. And by that time she was almost fully conscious again.

– There's something that occurs to me, said Erika, and Synne couldn't face asking her to please not talk about it any more. – That evening we drove to Lillestrøm and you showed me round. The place where you were found isn't on the way home from your friend's.

Of course the same thing had also occurred to Synne. But it took Erika to ask the question:

– If you cycled straight home, how come you were found outside the school?

9

Why do you write? Erika asks as a way of provoking. And when I don't answer, she thinks it's because she's found me out. I write because something is shattered, I could have told her, but I don't want to share that kind of thought with her. I write because something was crushed that evening when I had my last attack. Since then there have only been scattered fragments. I write to gather up those pieces, even if they no longer fit together.

She reached out and released the roller blind. Sat for a while staring out. The sun appeared and disappeared behind the clouds, now just visible behind a grey veil, and now as though completely extinguished. – Isn't this supposed to be about Karsten? she muttered to herself. – This is his story, not mine.

Through the closed window she could hear the rain trickling along the gutter, and behind her, from inside the house, Maja's flute. She stood up abruptly, strode out into the corridor, knocked on the door. The sound of the flute stopped.

– Does my practising disturb you? Maja exclaimed as she opened the door.

Synne shook her head. – No, I'm the one who's disturbing you.

– Doesn't matter. Want some coffee?

That was what Synne wanted. To drink coffee with her, think about something else.

– What have you written today? asked Maja as they sat out on the little veranda.

– I'd rather talk about you, said Synne.

– What about me? Maja had a funny look on her face.

– Okay, I've met someone, she confessed, and had to take a look round, even though there was no one else there.

– Really?

– Really really.

– Who is he?

Maja looked a little ashamed. – He's wonderful.

– Stainless charabanc?

They both laughed.

– He's very manly.

– That's good, said Synne without being quite sure she meant it. – Where did you meet him?

– On the metro. We got talking. He's very interested in music and Poland and everything.

It almost sounded as though she was about to burst into song. – And it turned out we were both getting off at the same station and he asked me to go for a coffee.

Synne liked stories like that. – Is he . . . I know it's not important, but do you think he's good looking?

– Very, Maja confirmed. – Not so tall, but very strong. She bent her arm and showed her own biceps, which wouldn't have scared a moth. – We're going out tonight, she went on. – To eat and *enjoy* ourselves.

Synne leaned over the table and gave her a hug. Talking to Maja was an antidote to the despair she was feeling about what she herself was trying to do and would never get right.

Back in her room, she stood in the doorway looking at the writing desk. The words she had written before the coffee break looked like tiny insects on the screen. If she approached any closer, they might take off and fly away.

Her phone rang.

– Synne? asked a woman's voice.

She confirmed it.

– You've been asking about Jasmeen.

She sat on the side of the bed, picked up a pen lying on the floor, with no clear idea of what she would do with it.

– There's something I want to ask her about, she began.

– You don't have to explain. The woman at the other end spoke with a very slight accent. – Do you still want to meet her?

Synne stood at the bus stop down on the ring road, glanced at her watch. Five past five. She had decided she would wait until ten past. Just then a dark green car indicated and pulled up at the kerb alongside her. The window slid down. Synne walked forward. In the grey afternoon light she recognised the woman from the house in Lørenskog, the young one with the chubby face who had come running after her. She wasn't wearing the hijab now; her hair was short and the collar of her jacket turned up.

– Come with me, she said.

Synne got in. The woman pulled out on to the ring road again.

– My name is Rashida. Jasmeen is my cousin.

– Where are we going?

The woman pulled into another lane. – To somewhere where it's safe to meet.

– Safe?

She drove on without answering. Not until they turned off in the direction of Vestre Aker did she say:

– I was stupid enough to tell Jasmeen about you coming to see us that day. I warned her, but she won't listen. If certain other people get to hear about this, things will happen that mustn't happen. It's been painful enough as it is.

Synne didn't know what to say. – Why does she want to see me?

– Why do you want to see her?

– I'm trying to find out about my brother.

Rashida shrugged her shoulders. – I can't tell you any more.

Sometimes in the summer Synne went out to Huk to bathe in the fjord. Now the grassy beach by the bay was deserted and grey. There was a car at the end of the parking lot. They pulled up a hundred metres away. Shortly afterwards, the lights in the other car were switched on and then off again.

– All clear, said Rashida.

Synne stepped out into the light rain and they walked together across the car park. The other car was a black Mercedes, possibly the one she had seen outside their house.

Rashida opened a rear door. – Get in.

There was a woman in the driver's seat, and in the back seat another wearing a black hijab. It occurred to Synne that she should have talked to someone before coming out here, Erika maybe; made sure someone knew where she was. She dismissed the thought and slipped into the back seat.

The woman in the hijab sat half turned away, She extended a gloved hand. – I am Jasmeen.

Synne tried to recall the large dark eyes from that school photograph taken more than eight years ago. – I'm glad you've agreed to meet me, she managed to say.

Jasmeen looked straight ahead. – Karsten talked about you a great deal. He loved his little sister very much.

Synne peered out through the raindrops running down

the windscreen, towards the bay and the greyness that hung over the fjord. – He did.

– I hear you're going to write about him. It's a good idea. Karsten deserves to be remembered.

That wasn't what her writing was about, but she didn't try to explain.

– I've come to realise that there is only one person in the world who is meant for you and no one else, Jasmeen continued in a quiet voice. – If you're lucky, you meet this one special person. Maybe that happens to only a very few people.

– Are you referring to Karsten? Synne asked, taken aback.

Rashida was sitting in the front. She exchanged a look with the woman in the driver's seat.

– Karsten felt the same way, said Jasmeen. – There's never been any doubt in my mind about that. We would have been a couple. Had we lived in another time, another place. He said he would become a Muslim for my sake.

Synne tried to take this in. In her thoughts she was already looking for the words she would later use to describe this meeting. For a moment she felt an enormous relief, as though the thing she had sat and struggled with over her keyboard had suddenly opened up in front of her eyes.

– You were at our house, she said. – Karsten took a picture of you in our living room.

The two women in front sat silent, obviously listening to every word that was being said. The one in the driver's seat had neither turned around nor said hello. In the dim interior she was wearing sunglasses, with a shawl loosely covering her hair.

– Do you know who Shahzad is? Jasmeen asked.

– Your brother? I never met him.

– He's afraid that I'll talk to you.

– Why is that?

Jasmeen shook her head. – He knows it'll bring it all up again. Her voice was suddenly filled with bitterness.

– You had to drop out of Karsten's class.

– I had to drop out of class, out of school, out of my whole life. They sent me to Pakistan.

She took out a pack of cigarettes. Synne accepted one when it was offered, even though she didn't feel like a smoke.

– I had brought shame on the family. According to Shahzad, I should count myself lucky to still be alive at all.

She lit Synne's cigarette with a gold lighter, then her own, handed the lighter across to the woman in the front seat, who also lit up.

– I don't count myself lucky.

The woman at the steering wheel said something in Urdu. Jasmeen ignored her.

– I was given away in an arranged marriage. But the price for me had dropped. My husband was from a lower caste. Thirty years older than I was. He despised me, and as recompense for marrying a woman without honour, he could do what he liked with me. My family let him. If he had killed me, they would not have lifted a finger. But he didn't do that. I was his ticket to Norway.

Again the woman in the driving seat said something. Jasmeen made a gesture of dismissal.

– I want you to know that I will never forget your brother. He is the best thing that ever happened in my life. The thought of the short time we had together is what keeps me going now.

Synne drew carefully on the cigarette, let the sharp cloud of smoke swell in her mouth.

– Can you understand that? The love I feel for Karsten is the only thing I have that is worth holding on to. The rest is hatred.

Another comment from the front, this time from Rashida. Synne fancied it must be a warning. Jasmeen's response was angry. It was raining more heavily now. The woman in the driver's seat gave the ignition a half-turn and set the windscreen wipers going for a few moments. The grey above the fjord in front of them appeared through the clouds of smoke inside the car and then was gone again.

– When I heard that you were going to write a book about Karsten, I wanted to get in touch with you. And you had the same idea.

Synne lowered the window halfway and blew smoke out into the rain. – I want to know what happened to him that time, she said, sounding more definite than she felt. – I want to know because it has some connection with me, with the way my life has turned out. It's the not knowing that nags away at me on and on. If he really didn't want to live any more, I want to try to understand why.

Jasmeen laid a hand on her arm. – Karsten didn't kill himself, she said.

Synne gave a start, turned towards her, but Jasmeen didn't look her in the eyes.

– Why should he? she continued. – He was a good person. The best. He was more intelligent than anyone else I've ever met. He went his own way. He was strong.

She fell silent. Synne couldn't sit there calmly and wait. – You talk as though you know what happened.

Jasmeen opened the door, threw her cigarette out, closed it again.

– They killed him.

Now both women in the front seats turned towards them. – This is not something you should be talking about, said Rashida in Norwegian.

Jasmeen stared at her. – I've kept my mouth shut long

enough. All my life I've kept my mouth shut. Haven't we promised each other that there should be an end to it?

– Jasmeen, I'm begging you.

Jasmeen shook her head. – I'm not afraid, she said. – I have nothing to lose.

Synne registered a feeling of numbness down one side of her face, as if it was about to go to sleep. It was many years since she'd felt such a thing.

– Killed him? she managed to say.

Jasmeen pushed a stray lock of hair into her hijab. – Whether my brother did it himself or got one of his monkeys to do it, I can't say. But he was behind it.

Synne was vaguely aware that she had started pulling at the skin on the side of her neck, as though there were an itch deep below.

– How do you know . . .?

– Shahzad was angry with me. So furious that he gave himself away. He wanted to kill me too, he said. I asked what he meant. And then he said that Karsten had been strangled and cut into pieces and thrown into the fjord.

Synne's grip on her own throat tightened. She sat there for some time, squeezing hard, scarcely breathing. And then suddenly a clear thought:

– Why haven't you told the police?

Now Jasmeen turned to her. She took hold of Synne's hands.

– I was afraid. Cowardly and afraid. But not any more. In the front seat, Rashida groaned.

– Today I would have gone to the police, Jasmeen whispered. – Now I will.

Synne could not stop staring into her face. The left side of it seemed to be shrunken in some way. The skin was thin and like a film of plastic across a confusion of scars that looked like tiny worms. The eye that was gazing at her seemed to be somewhere below the socket and was lacking eyelashes.

She realised she was sitting there with her mouth open, and shut it. Jasmeen lifted a hand and stroked her cheek with a gloved finger. She said something in her own language, low and indistinct, but Synne understood one word. Karsten.

10

Kai parked at the end of the square. They sat in the car for a while, looking out on the wet April night. It was almost one o'clock. After they had eaten, he had taken a long drive with this woman, to make time pass. She wasn't the talkative type, and that pleased him. He had asked about her background, how she had ended up in Norway. She told him she grew up in a little town in the west of Poland, in an area that had been German before the war, but clearly she didn't want to talk much about this, and that suited him too; it meant he didn't have to say much about his own background either. A few hints sufficed. That he was a soldier, what it was like in a war zone, all the things you had to learn to look out for, little things that could lead to your getting shot or blown to pieces. She was fascinated, no doubt about it.

He had spent the whole evening homing in on his goal. Asked about her life in Oslo, her music studies, where she practised, what it was like living in a student village, who she had got to know there, what it was about the girl who lived in the same corridor, the one she said she liked best of all the people she had met since coming to Norway.

They had been sitting there in the car for ten minutes. Time for him to make his move.

– Do you believe in anything, Kai?

He suppressed a smirk. Didn't know if it was because the question was so funny, or the way she said his name.

She split up the two vowels and separated them, Ka-i, as if she was making room for something in the middle. The first time he had approached her he had wondered whether to give himself another name, but contented himself with a change of surname.

– I believe in people, he said and looked across at her. – What's good in people, Maja. Regardless of gods and that sort of thing.

It sounded reasonable. He could see she liked hearing it, and realised that the time had come to lean over and give her a kiss. She had a pretty little face, large brown eyes beneath the black fringe. Her lips were thin but her teeth white and even. He couldn't stand bad teeth.

At first it seemed as though she was going to pull away, because she gave him a frightened look. But then she let it happen, parted her lips below his. Like a fish, he thought. And that was okay. He didn't mind fish. Didn't mind most things. Out of the corner of his eye he followed a couple who crossed the square and disappeared in the direction of one of the blocks.

Afterwards she sat leaning back in the seat, her eyes closed.

– I don't usually do that, she apologised. – Not the first time.

– I believe you, he assured her, and stroked her hair. She still hadn't opened her eyes; was probably hoping he would kiss her again.

– I'll come up with you, he said, and opened his door without waiting for an answer.

She came running up to him. – I don't know if that's a good idea.

– Don't have to stay long. He put an arm around her. – Just curious to see what your place is like.

She stood at the front door, feeling down inside her handbag.

– Lost my keys on Wednesday, she said. – It wasn't easy to get new ones.

– You're not the type to mislay things.

– I never do. I don't understand it.

The corridor was brightly lit. Four doors on each side. Shoes and boots outside several of them. Not a sound coming from any of the flats. It was quarter past one. He couldn't help wondering how a fire would spread here. Composite walls, the kind that didn't catch fire easily; there would be more gas than flames. Two smoke alarms on the ceiling and an alarm on the wall. According to what he had read on the net, they were connected directly to the fire station. A pair of wire-cutters would soon break that connection. Not unlikely that there were smoke alarms in the individual rooms, but almost certainly not with a direct connection. The kitchen was at the end of the corridor. A small oven, a fridge, a toaster, a microwave. If a fire were to break out here, the kitchen was the obvious place. A saucepan forgotten on a hot stove, a faulty fuse in the toaster, the electric kettle allowed to boil dry.

A toilet flushed. She put a finger over his lips. They stood without moving by the kitchen table. Obviously it was important to her to keep his visit secret, and that suited him perfectly. There was the sound of a door, footsteps in the corridor, and then silence again.

Her room was more or less as he had imagined. Tidy, with a poster of some trees on one wall. A music stand beside the desk. She switched off the ceiling light, switched on the bedside lamp. The room was about ten to twelve metres square.

– Nice place, he observed.

– You don't mean that, she protested in a low voice.

He put an arm around her.

– I'm tired, she excused herself, pulling away.

– I'll leave soon, he said quickly.

She looked at him, seemed suddenly sad.

– Can we just lie on the bed a bit? Not do anything much?

He nodded without reflecting on what *anything much* might mean.

She lay for a long time, holding him. He put his arms around her, stroked her back; that was what she seemed to want. Through the blouse he could feel two broad scars that angled down towards one of her hips. She twisted uncomfortably when he touched them. He didn't ask about them, just carried on stroking her, put a bit of feeling into it.

– Can we lie naked together? she said suddenly, and in his astonishment he laughed.

– Why not, he answered.

– Do you think I'm forward?

– Not at all.

She got up, took a little bag from a drawer in the dresser.

– I need the bathroom for a minute.

He nodded.

– Don't go anywhere, she added with mock severity.

– Promise I won't.

As soon as she closed the door, he checked her dresser. Sheet music and make-up in one drawer, panties, stockings and bras in another. At the back, four packets of ampoules. Insulin, he established. A syringe that looked like a pen next to them. He put everything back, opened the door and peered along the corridor. Synne Clausen lived two doors down on the other side. He had taken Maja's room key to a guy who had once worked on home security for the army. They had shared an office and the guy had taught Kai everything he knew about picking locks. He charged twelve hundred to make a bump key. The chances of it working were over seventy per cent, the guy reckoned; the rest was a matter of technique. If Kai wanted to feel even more certain, he could provide him with three, and that doubled the price.

He heard her flushing the toilet, closed the door, stood by the window as she came back into the room. Sorted out your blood sugar level? he could have asked her. Instead he put his arms around her, pulled her towards him.

– We won't do anything you don't want to, he said, and stroked her back again, avoiding the part with the scars.

– I want to, she said, and began unbuttoning the thin blouse.

After he was finished, she lay there whimpering and holding on tight to him. It took over half an hour before she fell asleep. As he prised himself loose, she grunted and turned but didn't wake up. He left his shoes there.

Outside Synne Clausen's door, he pulled out the bunch of keys and the file. All the bump keys fitted. He chose the second, put it in, hit it with the handle of the file and turned. Nothing happened. He had practised on a few locks at home, but it was five years since he'd been able to do this stuff blindfold. He tried another three times, the banging sounding like little explosions down the empty corridor. He realised a change of plan was called for, that he'd need another day or two. But as he slipped the keys into his pocket, it occurred to him that he would then have to see Maja again. He took them back out, tried the first one a second time, knocked on the head of the key. This time he could feel it in the fingertips holding the key. It turned, almost without resistance. The door didn't make a sound when he opened it and glided through into the darkness.

At first he couldn't hear her. But he could smell warm skin, and behind it the scent of something that must be from the inside of her body, redolent of sour milk. And right then she drew a breath, quick and strong, held it for a long time before releasing it in small jolts.

His eyes adapted to the dark. He saw the outline of the bed to his right, hair against the white bedclothes. She lay with her face to the wall. Her clothes were hanging on a chair beside the bed. He placed his hand on them, feeling his way forward, the rough touch of denim, cotton socks, a top. He put his hand down inside the tights, felt along the seams. Down one leg something scrunched up like a little ball. He pulled it up, opened it out; it turned into a thin, silky G-string between his fingers.

Abruptly he bent over her, his face almost touching the white neck. That sweet smell was coming from her skin; it too made him think of milk, not curdled, but lukewarm after being out all day. Suddenly a flash of another room with another bed he had bent across. It was eight years ago. That room no longer existed. Nor the girl either. He couldn't recall her name, or where she came from. If he'd wanted to he could have remembered, but the memory was clean and transparent; if he let it go, it would dissolve in the blackness of the night.

He turned towards the desk. Her laptop was there. Even in the dark he could make out that it was an iBook. He cursed softly, even though he was prepared for the fact that it might be a Mac. He didn't like Macs, and if he had to get into the hard disk, it would be a helluva difficult job. Then he noticed that the machine was in hibernation mode and he almost felt like waking the sleeping figure up and thanking her for all the bother she had saved him. He pulled out his memory stick and positioned himself so that the light from the screen wouldn't disturb her. It took him thirty seconds to install a key logger that would give him access to every touch of the keyboard and every image on her screen.

As he was finishing, Synne Clausen turned over on her back, muttered something or other. It sounded as if she was trying to comfort someone. For an instant her eyes were wide open and staring right at him. He didn't move, stood frozen in the darkness, but ready to act, get out of there, or put both hands across her face and start squeezing. But the eyes slid shut again, and a loud snore came from her nose.

On the way out, he stopped. Still that jolting breath of hers. He stepped back over to the bed, picked up the G-string he had dropped and stuffed it into his pocket. He heard steps out in the corridor, bare feet, stood there listening. Let thirty seconds pass before he slipped out.

Maja was standing in the kitchen doorway. She stared at him, open mouthed.

Don't scream, he thought, please don't scream. If you keep quiet now, everything will work out. His prayer was answered. She didn't make a sound, but suddenly she tore herself away and raced down the corridor back into her room. He was there the instant she started to close the door; wrenched it open and strode in. Still not a sound from her, but her eyes were quivering and she raised both hands towards his face. He turned her around, closed the door, held her firmly, one hand over her mouth, the other around the tiny body. She was wearing a bulky pullover, underneath which he could feel she was naked. The sight of Synne Clausen still dominated his mind. That body sleeping in the bed, the clothes on the chair, the panties he had stolen, everything came together in his mind now, mingling with the smell of this naked, terrified figure he was pressing up against his body, exciting him in a way he had not experienced when he lay with her.

– Don't be afraid, he whispered in her ear. – I'm going to let you go. I'll explain what happened.

He put her down on the bed, sat beside her, took his hand

away from her mouth. A few sounds came out, but not a scream, nothing that made it necessary to go any further with what had taken possession of him. Nothing had been decided yet. He could still go either way. It was a good place to be, with all his options open. It was like sitting in the secret room in Erleveien. He'd scratched her name on the wall, over and over again, because sooner or later it would make her come back. If he turned to the beam behind him, then it was the Fire Man's voice that would win. If he managed not to, it would be Elsa's.

Sitting there on the side of a bed in a room in this student village, he couldn't scratch Elsa's name into a wall, but it was the thought of her that protected the frail woman who lay trembling on the bed saying things in a language that must be Polish.

– Are you praying?

His voice was calm, and if he could continue to talk in that way, then nothing more was likely to happen.

She nodded.

– Why couldn't you have stayed in here? he asked.

She bit her lip. – You weren't here. But your shoes were here. And I had to go to the toilet. And you weren't there. I went looking for you in the kitchen.

She was speaking freely now, and he placed a hand over her mouth again, not hard, just enough to interrupt the flow of speech.

– You think I'm a thief, he said to her.

– What is a seef?

He laughed briefly. – Someone who steals.

She curled up as far away as she could in the bed. – Are you someone who steals?

He wondered whether this might be a way out. Leave, and let her think that was the explanation. Nothing had been stolen from Synne Clausen's room, only a pair of panties.

No one would take the trouble to go looking for him. And he could keep out of the way until it had all died down.

– I don't steal, he said.

– What were you doing?

– You mustn't ask me that.

Suddenly she sat up. – Have you done something to her?

Before he could reply, she repeated it, this time in a loud voice, and he had to lay himself over her and squash her down into the mattress.

– No more questions, he snapped. – Don't you understand, if I tell you what I did there, then not even Elsa can help you.

He pressed his hand so hard over her mouth that her eyes began to quiver again. She flexed her body like a snake and he had to push down with all his weight to keep her still.

– Her brother, he said suddenly, and he knew he shouldn't have said it, but the Fire Man behind him was laughing loudly, because things were going his way now. – She wants to discover what happened to her brother. But you understand nothing about it. You're someone who gets in the way, who's in places where she shouldn't be. You can't do anything about it, because you're a loser.

He grabbed a sock, forced it into her mouth.

– It's up to me now. He lay down beside her. – You want to know why, is that what you're saying? You should never have asked about it.

She made a noise in her throat and he placed a finger across her lips.

– Her brother's name was Karsten. I tried to help him. He found something in a car, something he should never have seen. He wasn't stupid. He saw the way things added up. He tricked me out of the car and then he made a break for it. Drove straight at me.

He could still see those lights coming towards him. He

leaps up on to the bonnet, convinced that Karsten will stop, but the kid is desperate and accelerates.

– I'm holding on for dear life to the windscreen wiper, yelling at him, but he keeps on going and drives straight into a fence. I get thrown off, I'm winded.

He lies there and sees the car stop outside the gate, drags himself to his knees. He hears the engine revving again, full throttle, into gear, and then tail lights disappearing down towards the forest track.

Maja whimpering in his ear. Impossible to know how much she had grasped of what he was saying. But she had heard enough, she had heard too much, and the road Elsa was trying to show him was closed long ago.

– Takes me hours to get to Lillestrøm. My phone's still in the car. I have to walk all the way to the petrol station. Try to thumb a ride, but no one stops, though that won't surprise you.

Everything that happened that night came back to him. Once he started to talk about it, it became impossible to hold it back; the story just surged on and on by itself.

– At the petrol station, I manage to ring for a taxi. The girl behind the counter is staring at my neck, there are marks there, from the car window. The kid tried to kill me. Little bastard.

He sits in the rear of the taxi and thinks about what he's going to do to Karsten when he gets hold of him.

– My car's by the side of the road when I get to Erleveien. The front windscreen is broken. No idea how that happened, but I know I pulled one of the wipers off when he tried to run me down.

The keys are still in it. He sticks his hand behind the felt. Nothing there. He searches the whole car; the bag with the ignition mechanisms isn't there. Karsten must have taken them with him.

– I run to his house and ring the doorbell. Not too clever maybe, but I was so furious I didn't have time to think about what was smart. And as it turned out, there was no one home.

All of this he told Maja while lying on her bed, and it was calming to lie there like that; he felt he could have spent the rest of the night there, holding her and talking quietly into her ear.

– So now you know why I was in Synne Clausen's room, he said without raising his voice. – She's going to write about what happened to her brother. Karsten met some people that night, and it's not possible that he wouldn't have talked about the ignition mechanisms. But for some reason or other the people he met didn't take it any further, at least they haven't so far. Maybe someone out there still has that plastic bag. Covered with my fingerprints. Other things too. A tiny flake of skin would be enough. That's why I need to get into her computer, see what she's poking her nose into.

He couldn't stop now, had to carry on with his story. About the secret room in the house in Erleveien, and the fires, about the night watch and the girl at Furutunet whose name he couldn't recall. About Monica with a *c* who died not by fire but by water. Afterwards he raised his head and looked down into Maja's face. It had frozen; she was lying there with her eyes open, a few tremors around her mouth the only sign that she was alive.

– And what makes me so sad now, he whispered, – is that you know all this too.

He grabbed the belt from the bathrobe that was hanging in the cupboard, held her hands behind her back and tied them together. She was staring at him again now, and he turned off the lamp. He took the insulin pen from the drawer in the dresser. Maybe she could hear what he was doing, because he had to roll on to her again to keep her still. With one hand he drove the syringe into her shoulder, and now he heard her screaming, though only a few muted cries penetrated through the sock.

– There there, he comforted her. – All I'm doing is giving you your medicine. There's nothing dangerous in that.

He pressed on the pen, waited, pressed again, kept on pressing until it was empty.

The time was a quarter to three. She hadn't moved for half an hour. He placed a finger on her throat, couldn't feel a pulse. He got dressed, wrapped the pen in a paper handkerchief and put it in his pocket. He was finished with her, but he couldn't leave her lying there, because like an idiot he'd come inside her while they were at it. Now he had to get rid of the body.

He draped her over his shoulder. As he was about to leave the room, he heard sounds from the corridor. Footsteps, a door opening. He laid her down again. Looked out the window. No blocks on that side; he could just about make out the roofs of a few detached houses. Again the sound of a door. Then silence. He waited three minutes, then opened the window wide. No lights in the rooms on this side of the block. He lifted the little body, held it down along the outside wall and let go. The sound when she landed two floors down was a hollow thud shot through with the noise of something shattering.

He closed the door behind him. Stepped down the corridor with his shoes in his hand. Not until he reached the staircase did he stop to put them on. It was blowing hard outside and rain had started to fall. He stationed himself at the corner, peered out along the rear wall of the block. Could see the bundle where she had landed. Still dark in all the windows. He made his way over. She lay like a rag doll in a position he had never seen before, her legs doing the splits, her head broken over on her back. He bent down quickly, dragged her along the block towards the shadows of the end wall.

He hurried over to the car, reversed along the driveway, lifted up the bundle, the arms and legs dangling as if about to fall off, and threw her into the boot. All in all it couldn't have taken more than five minutes. As he glided slowly up the drive again and across the car park, he was filled with a relief that seemed about to explode inside him. He turned on the radio, found a station playing music, something classical, an orchestra with a choir, sang along at the top of his voice to a melody he had never heard before, knowing as he did so what it was he would do with her.

Along Thereses gate he found the car he was looking for, a little delivery van that was obviously at least ten years old. He turned into a side street three blocks down, a cul-de-sac. Found a place to park at the end, in front of a skip. He had what he needed in the glove compartment, screwdrivers and steel wire. As calmly as he could, he walked back up Thereses gate, used the screwdriver to bend the door of the van, poked the steel wire inside and pulled up the lock button, removed the plate from under the steering wheel and hot-wired the engine.

After driving down and parking the van next to his own car, he tried to pick the lock on the boot. It jammed. He looked round. Lights in some of the windows in the block, no sign of anyone. It was three thirty. He opened the boot of his own car, lifted up the body and dropped it in the passenger seat of the delivery van, released the recliner catch on the seat and stretched her out. It looked as if she was lying there asleep. He grabbed the two bottles of lighter fluid, tossed them on to the floor in front and drove off.

He passed Ullevål stadium. The floppy body slid backwards and forwards on the seat next to him, the head dangling on to the chest. He pulled in and fastened her safety belt before driving on. Turned on the CD player. The owner of the van was a country music fan. He had always hated country music, but now it seemed like just the thing.

The rain fell more heavily up in Maridalen. He hadn't passed more than three cars since crossing the ring road. Up past the end of the lake he found a forest track, pulled in, drove on a hundred metres into the woods, stopped the van. At that moment he saw a flickering light in the distance ahead. It danced up and down between the trees, was still a moment, danced on. He tried to reconnect, fumbling with the wires, but the engine was dead. A dark rage invaded him. Who the hell goes out walking in the woods in the middle of the night? The light was no more than fifty metres away now. He could open the door and make a run for it, leaving her body there stuffed with his fucking genetics. They'd catch up with him sooner or later, circle him, get him in a corner.

He turned towards the body in the passenger seat, lifted the head up by the hair and moved over on top of it, pressing his cheek against her coldness. The skin had a different smell already, reminiscent of raw meat. Just then a torch beam was directed into the car. It glided over his back and his neck; he saw the shadow of his own head against the glass that divided the front and rear compartments. People wandering in the woods at night had the cheek to stop and peer in through the car windows; maybe they'd even open the door to ask what was going on. He turned up the collar of his jacket and pulled his trousers halfway down, twisting her long hair around his hands as he pressed his lips against hers. The taste reminded him of a solvent he had sniffed once; maybe it was Gunnhild's nail varnish remover. He turned the dangling head from side to side, his tongue disappearing between her teeth and into a mouth that was full of froth. The taste of rotting chemicals made him even angrier, and when the circle of light stopped directly outside the side window, he tensed the lower part of his body against what lay beneath him on the seat, ready to throw open the door and beat the owner of the torch across the head with his own flashlight. As he took hold of the door handle, the light glided on; he saw it dancing away down the track behind the van.

For a long time afterwards he sat there looking out into the darkness between the trees. The rain had eased off, a few drops snaking their way down the front windscreen. Slowly a tiredness descended on him. The same one he had felt all winter. A heaviness that had made him lie in bed, watching as the daylight came sneaking in beneath the curtains, and still be lying there when the light faded away again.

He wasn't going back to all that, shook himself free of it. With the sleeve of his jacket he wiped away the sticky goo that still coated his mouth and chin, opened the door, picked up the two bottles from the floor, started dousing the bundle in the passenger seat. Kept going until all he could smell was lighter fluid.

11

Jasmeen takes hold of my hands. 'I was cowardly. Today I would have gone to the police about it.'

Synne scrolled down. The meeting with Jasmeen Chadar had become seven pages of text. She had spent some time describing what the three women in the car were wearing, how they moved their hands as they spoke, the smell of perfume and cigarettes, details that had to be there if people were to believe what she was saying. If she herself were to believe it. She couldn't face reading through it, printed it out, took the pages out into the corridor, had to show someone what she had written.

She hadn't heard Maja's flute all day. Still she knocked. No answer. She saw the door wasn't locked, knocked again and then opened it. No one there. She had a look in the kitchen, then returned to Maja's room. She could be careless herself, and as recently as last night had forgotten to lock the door before going to bed. When she got up in the morning and found it ajar, she had felt a passing unease. But Maja was very particular about locking. And the sofa bed hadn't been made, the duvet lay in a bundle on the floor, all the drawers in the nightstand had been pulled out. That wasn't like her either. The flute was in its case on the desk, and the bag Maja always took to university with her was over by the wall. It had to be the first time she'd ever skipped classes in all the time they'd known each other. It might have something to do with her date the previous evening, and the thought made Synne pick up the duvet and straighten it out on the bed as she tried to persuade herself that these breaches of Maja's usual orderliness and routine were positive signs.

Back in her own room, she took out her phone. Erika was on her way to a meeting.

– I've met someone Karsten was seeing just before he disappeared.

– You're not going to carry on doing this interview stuff, are you? Erika interrupted, panting as though she was running up a staircase.

– She said Karsten was murdered. And that she knew who did it.

– Synne, what are you getting into here?

– Don't know.

– I'm worried about you.

– You should've thought about that before.

– Honestly, I mean it. You need a psychologist while you're working on material like this.

– I can use yours after you've finished with him. Seven years since you started going there, isn't it?

– Get with it. We're not talking about me. You said you had help back then, after your brother.

– I did not say I got help, Synne exclaimed, leaning against the sink, looking into her own eyes in the mirror. – I said I was seeing a psychiatrist for a while. He was hopeless and understood nothing. She took a deep breath. – But there was a contact of a sort. Now and then. In spite of everything.

– And you think you can hope for a bit more than that, Erika observed. – Maybe you could ring him again. Or was it a she?

Synne saw herself shaking her head in the mirror.

– The guy stopped practising as a psychiatrist. Know what he does now?

– Should I know?

– He writes crime novels.

Erika snorted, a mixture of laughter and contemptuous sneer.

– You must be joking. *Show me the money*. Instead of making himself useful.

Suddenly it sounded as if she had changed her attitude towards psychiatry. Synne ended the call and tried Dan-Levi instead.

– I've written something you've got to see, she told him when he picked up.

– Love to, he said, sounding surprised. – Are you going to mail it to me?

– I'm going to see my dad later. Can I call in?

In the background, barking and children's voices.

– Of course, I'm not working this afternoon.

What that meant she didn't try to find out. Suddenly the room seemed unbearably small. She pulled on her boots and grabbed her coat.

As she reached the foot of the staircase, the outer door opened. The man who let himself in looked at her with an arrogant expression and then turned to the noticeboard without offering any sort of greeting at all. She thought she'd seen him somewhere before, but he looked distinctly too old to be a student. She turned and glared at him. Am I invisible? she was on the point of saying, because people who ignored other people spread emptiness. The guy had peroxided hair and was short, and his outsize muscles made him look deformed. Stop letting other people get under your skin, she scolded herself. You only spoil things for yourself.

She didn't ring the bell this time.

Her father was sitting in the living room when she let

herself in. He looked up, his eyes big and grey behind his reading glasses, reflecting the sunless afternoon. But his face brightened when he saw that it was her standing there.

– Something happened? she asked, pointing at the TV screen, which showed ambulances navigating between ruins.

– Car bombs, he nodded. – Floods, droughts, radioactive leaks, environmental catastrophes and other unmistakable signs that the end of the world is nigh. Apart from that, not much.

She had to laugh. A touch of his old humour, being ironic about his own pessimism. He seemed to be in a better mood than last time she'd visited, and for a moment she thought of not saying why she had come.

She made cheese and tomato sandwiches for them, and fetched him a bottle of beer, a habit he'd developed recently. Before, he might have a glass now and then; now it looked as though it was every day. But there was no pile of empty bottles in the kitchen, so she didn't feel she had to worry about it. There was a meatball in the frying pan, and beside it on the kitchen counter the packet it came from. He shouldn't have to live like this, she thought, not on convenience food. He shouldn't have to sit here night after night watching TV, leafing through magazines. A couple of years ago, just after she moved out, she had suggested various activities to him, but he had insisted he was too old to start making friends and looking for a new woman, and too young to turn up at pensioners' events.

They sat at the living-room table with their cheese sandwiches, and he muted the volume on the TV. There was a nature programme on, something about insects that he had probably been looking forward to watching.

She said: – You saw the interview in *Romerikes Blad*.

He nodded, clearly expecting her to continue. It had always been that way; she was the one who had to bring things up.

– Actually it wasn't really an interview. Dan-Levi called and asked if he could mention this new project of mine.

– You're writing about Karsten.

– In a way.

– Why him and not somebody else?

– I don't know. Don't you like me doing it?

He shrugged his shoulders. – I think it's probably best to leave him in peace.

She put her sandwich down. – Sounds as if you think he's up there somewhere following what's going on.

– You know I don't believe that.

– Then you know that I'm not doing this for his sake.

He poured beer into his glass. – It's important to you.

The way he said it made her feel relieved. Maybe there wasn't understanding in his voice, but at least there was no censure.

– How do you think your mother will react? he asked.

– That's her business.

He chewed away, small bites.

– I want you to tell me about that evening, she said.

The wrinkles in his forehead lifted and furrowed.

– That evening?

Inconceivable that he might not know which evening she was referring to.

– Haven't we talked about it before? he continued after a while.

She could have spared him, but was determined to stick to her plan. – There are a lot of things I've been thinking about.

– Like what?

She glanced at the TV screen. The camera zoomed in towards the end of a large open plain, a savannah or a pampas. A few oxen were standing under some trees, and a swarm of green flies settled in a flesh wound on the back of one of them.

– I was at Tamara's house that evening. I cycled home, but the man who found me said I was lying in a wayside ditch just next to Lillestrøm secondary school. That isn't on the way home.

She was surprised at how odd it sounded when she said this to her father. He pushed his plate away.

– Obviously that's something we thought about.

– And? She was careful not to make her tone sharp.

– We never found a satisfactory explanation. Even you couldn't remember why you had taken that route.

– Tell me about the person who found me.

– What can I tell you? I don't know the first thing about him.

– What did he look like?

Her father appeared to think about it. – Average height, I think. Powerfully built, possibly. But of course it was very dark. And it was eight years ago.

– What about his voice?

– Normal, I think. No special dialect. But you must realise, we were profoundly shocked, your mother and I.

– Which one of you opened the door?

– I did. He closed his eyes for a few seconds. – I think he was holding you by the arm. You were sagging, confused, tired, the way you always were after an attack, with a lot of blood on your face and in your hair.

– Blood? She sat up straight in her chair. – You never told me that before. She could see how upset he was but didn't back off.

– Haven't I? Anyway, we were in complete shock. Your mother screamed and grabbed hold of you. And then the young man left. I'm sure we must have thanked him. Maybe we asked what his name was, that type of thing. I don't remember.

– So I had a head injury and no one has ever mentioned that to me before?

Her father glanced at her, suddenly seeming unsure. – Well you weren't injured.

– What do you mean? she exclaimed.

Another pause as he closed his eyes again, perhaps trying to remember, perhaps trying to reject the things that surfaced in his memory. His pale mouth hung open, and she decided that was enough for the time being. Already she was dreading leaving him with a head full of memories and images he had carefully packed away and archived in drawers that were never meant to be opened again.

– Was I hurt or not? she asked anyway.

He drained his beer glass and wiped around his mouth with a serviette, grinding the paper against his lips again and again. – I remember we asked the doctor at the hospital about it, he said finally. – They didn't find any injuries on you, not so much as a scratch.

– So why did I have blood all over my face?

– That is one of the questions we never found an answer to.

She sank back into her chair. On the screen, a little creature ran across the surface of some water, tiny feet that rippled but did not break the surface.

– You were exhausted, sleepy, worn out, all the symptoms of the sort of attack you used to have at that time. At first we thought you must have fallen off your bike and hit your head, but at the hospital they were a hundred per cent certain that's not what happened.

– What tests did they carry out there?

Her father removed his glasses, placed them on the table, rubbed his eyes.

– Did they check the blood?

– I'm sure they did whatever they thought was necessary. But you must realise that of course by that time we had something else on our minds.

She understood, suddenly thought of herself as self-centred, felt ashamed.

– Sorry, she said.

He shook his head; she wasn't sure what that meant.

– Is it okay if I take some of Karsten's stuff with me? she said as she got to her feet.

– Which things?

– Some books, his mobile phone, the programme from the memorial service. I'll put it all back.

He gave a little nod and turned his attention back to the TV, put his glasses on. A host of tiny dramas were being played out on the screen, minuscule animals that could adapt themselves to every change in the environment. But looking at him, she could see that for the rest of the evening he wouldn't be able to take in much of what was going on in the world of insects.

12

DAN-LEVI STOOD UP, adjusted the kitchen curtain, was about to sit down again but suddenly strode over to the fridge, took out a carton of juice and put it on the table, even though a recently opened one was already standing there.

– So she is implying that her brother may have killed Karsten, he said as calmly as he could.

Synne gathered up the printout she had just read to him.

– Doesn't imply it, says it straight out.

Dan-Levi still couldn't manage to sit down, stood instead behind the chair, tipped it backwards, released it. Over in her corner Pepsi gave a start, was on her feet and starting to growl. He grabbed the dog by the collar, dragged it out into the corridor and closed the door. Of all the thoughts that had been whirled up, it was those of the journalist that were uppermost. He could see the headlines and the lead paragraph. Eight-year-old disappearance becomes murder case, famous Norwegian-Pakistani politician accused. One of the most prominent advocates of integration appears to have been guilty of an honour killing in his youth. Please, Synne, he almost exclaimed, this is just too much.

– All right then, so what do we do? he said instead. And with that *we*, he realised how involved he already was. Last time she came to see him, he had encouraged her to share her troubles with him, and now he had to show that he meant it.

– I don't think Jasmeen will do anything on her own, she

said. – Maybe if it gets to court she'll give evidence against her brother, but she won't make the charge in the first place.

Dan-Levi felt an even stronger urge to get her to slow down.

– Court? Does she have any kind of evidence at all?

Synne nodded; a little too eagerly it seemed to him.

– Her brother wasn't home that evening.

Dan-Levi raised his hands in the air. – Synne, please, we're talking about Maundy Thursday eight years ago. If it's possible to prove she's right about that, so what? I wasn't home that evening either.

She leaned back in the chair.

– I know it's thin. That's why I've come to you. You're friends with someone in the police force. You can speak to him.

– Well yes, yes.

– Maybe the police can take another look at what they have. They don't need to make a big deal out of it, not until they have something more.

Dan-Levi sat down heavily in the chair. Of course, he could ring Roar Horvath. He had often got in touch with him about criminal cases; it had been to their mutual advantage.

– I'll have a word with my friend, he promised.

– Thank you very much. I'll carry on with my own enquiries.

– How do you mean?

Synne shrugged her shoulders. – I've tried to get in touch with Shahzad Chadar several times.

Dan-Levi sat up. – You mustn't even think about it.

– Why not?

He couldn't begin to answer her.

– As you know, I'm working on a new text, she said, and from the almost imperceptible edge to her voice it was clear she had not completely forgiven him for the interview. He chose to let it pass.

– But you can't use this business about Shahzad Chadar in a novel.

– I don't know if this will be a novel. It's heading in a different direction from what I expected. That's to say, I hadn't thought too much about it. I've started writing about other people who knew him. I think I'm homing in on something.

She stood up. – Promise me you'll call when you've spoken to your policeman friend.

He followed her out to the front door.

– There was something I meant to ask you, he said hesitantly as she pulled on her boots. – Which nursery school did Karsten go to?

She looked up at him, frowning.

– Nursery school? Same one as me, I think. Vollen.

– Are you certain?

– I can't remember ever talking about it. You're thinking about those fires, right?

He didn't want to lie.

– Are you trying to find out whether it was Karsten who did it?

Dan-Levi wasn't sure if that was the reason he'd asked.

After she'd gone, he got the mince out of the fridge, scraping it into a saucepan. Suddenly he put the packet down, fished out his mobile phone and punched in the number of Sara's sister, Solveig. She was a nursery school teacher and had worked in the school at Vollen in the nineties before moving into town. Dan-Levi had to admit that he slightly dreaded calling her. In every sense of the word Solveig was sharp. She had an eerily precise memory. And she was never afraid to say exactly what she thought. On three or four occasions she had experienced manic episodes. On each occasion Dan-Levi had been the first to notice, with Sara trying to deny it for as long as possible. He recognised the early signs. Solveig became a touch more abrupt, as though a filter had been removed, began reeling off comments about people, treading on quite a few sensitive toes. Gradually she became more hectic, started buying things neither she nor the family needed, hoarding food, milk especially. She could empty whole shelves in the shops, arrive home with the boot of the car bulging. Typically this would be just before the whole thing tipped over and her condition became obvious to everyone. The time he had helped to take her for admission to a closed ward against her will was one of his worst experiences.

– Lundwall, she said now as she took the call, even though she had to be able to see who was ringing. He listened out for signs in her voice but heard nothing untoward. In the course of a few days, though, she could change from being the well-dressed, energetic and efficient head of a nursery school into a person ridden by the blackest demons. Once when they'd visited her in hospital she'd lain on a restraining bed wearing only panties and a torn shirt.

Dan-Levi explained, without being unnecessarily precise, that he was working on a story. – I'm trying to find out something about that boy from our neighbourhood who disappeared.

– Karsten Clausen.

– Correct. Did he attend Vollen nursery school while you were working there?

– Yes he did. Why do you ask?

He would have preferred to let it go at that, but felt he had to tell her that it was in connection with the fire.

– And you think Karsten Clausen had something to do with that?

– Do you think he did? he wanted to know.

– The thought never crossed my mind. Tell me what it is about a six-year-old that might make you think he would turn out to be a pyromaniac in later life.

I'm sure it's possible, he thought, but said nothing.

After ending the call, he tore a page from a sketch pad one of the girls had left on the dining table along with some felt-tip pens. Not until he was sitting there with one of the pens in his hand did he realise what he was going to do. A sort of game he'd learned at a personal development course he had attended once in connection with work. The course leader called it *solar association*.

In the middle of the page he wrote: *Fires that spring, never solved, police believe they were started deliberately.* He drew several lines radiating from this sentence and wrote something at the end of each one of them. *Vollen nursery school: Karsten went there as a child. The sweet shop in Strømmen: owned by Khalid Chadar. Jasmeen Chadar says her brother killed Karsten. Stornes stables: Elsa Wilkins grew up there.* The Lovers upside down came to him immediately, as though this tarot card were inextricably connected to the thought of her. At the end of the line leading to Furutunet remand home he had nothing.

He glanced out at the bright evening, then picked up his phone again.

Roar Horvath sounded in good spirits when he answered. Pink Floyd was playing in the background and Dan-Levi guessed he was on his own at home.

– You sitting there knitting? Shouldn't you be out chasing thieves and robbers at this time of day?

He barked a few times to heighten the drama, and heard his friend grin at the other end. After his divorce a few years ago, Roar had got a transfer to the Oslo police and moved into an apartment block in Manglerud.

– Aren't you down at Bethany praying?

– Yes I am, and a voice came to me in a vision and told me to get in touch with you.

Roar laughed out loud at this.

– I've got a question about Karsten Clausen. Remember that case?

Roar had just graduated at the time and wandered about Lillestrøm in his uniform and a Kaiser Bill moustache that Dan-Levi had spent a long time trying to persuade him to get rid of.

– Are you implying that I'm suffering from dementia?

– Just testing to see if it's got any worse, Dan-Levi replied. He related the conversation he'd had with Synne.

– So Chadar's sister now hates him, Roar observed.

– I think there may be more to this, said Dan-Levi.

Roar began munching on something; Dan-Levi guessed it was a slice of cold pizza. He picked up the sheet of paper on which he had sketched the solar association diagram and gave an account of the connections between Karsten and the fires.

– I'm presuming you're not expecting us to drop everything and start investigating that disappearance again. Roar did not sound particularly impressed. – We're talking about something that happened eight years ago.

Dan-Levi remembered something else from that Easter, something affecting Roar. He had found his girlfriend dead in her bathtub and the verdict was that she had committed suicide. Roar would never talk about her and soon claimed that he had put it behind him, but Dan-Levi noticed that it continued to bother him. Later that spring Roar met someone else. They got married in the autumn and had a daughter the following year. His wife was a psychologist. The marriage lasted two and a half years.

– When new lines of investigation crop up in a case as

serious as this, don't you think the police should take another look at it? Dan-Levi persisted. – Shahzad Chadar had two good reasons for getting rid of Karsten. Besides this business with his sister, he might have thought Karsten was involved in the arson attack on the sweet shop. It's even possible he was right about that.

– Have you seen all these stories in the press about the percentage of crimes the police solve? Roar interrupted. – That rag of yours is always leading the charge about how useless we are. How likely do you think it is that we have the resources to reopen an eight-year-old case when we've already got piles and piles of pending cases no one has time to deal with?

– That's not something *you* should be asking *me* about.

Roar gave an exaggerated sigh. – I'll think about it, he said. – Can't promise anything.

– If not, then I guess I'll have to do it myself, said Dan-Levi, and realised that he had just had an idea. – I'm going to have a chat with him.

– With who?

– Shahzad Chadar. I'll interview him.

Roar groaned. – Are you going to ask him if he killed Karsten Clausen?

– Something like that. If he confesses, I'll bring him in for you. Case ready solved.

– Remember to take your handcuffs, Roar advised him. – How are things at home?

– Business as usual.

– Sara?

– Doing well.

– Say hello.

After he had disconnected, Dan-Levi sat for a while and wondered about that. Just recently Roar had started asking him to pass on his greetings to Sara whenever they spoke.

The Lovers upside down, he thought suddenly. And shook his head sadly at his own foolishness.

After he had fried the mince and put six litres of water on to boil, he made his way up to his office and woke the computer, returning to what he had been working on when Synne turned up. There was a draught from a gap under the ceiling, and he took the blanket that hung over the back of the chair and wrapped himself in it. It would take carpenters and electricians to upgrade that little loft space into a proper office. Where the money to pay for all that might come from he hadn't got around to thinking about.

What does the Lord want us to do? he typed, and then looked at his watch. He'd been sitting there for ten minutes already; the pan of water in the kitchen must have started boiling by now. He looked down at the question he had written. It had been with him for as long as he could remember. Pastor Jakobsen's answer had been simple. *You'll find that out if you listen to His voice. And if you don't hear it – yes, quite literally hear His voice inside you – then you must have got lost and you need to find your way back.* Dan-Levi had heard this voice on a number of occasions, but sitting there now with his fingers frozen on the keyboard and his allotted span ticking by, it was silent. Last night, before going to bed, he had put his hands together and felt the same silence. All he could hear inside himself were his own thoughts, and it frightened him. He had lain there listening to Sara's breathing, staring up into the darkness, and for the first time in ages he was unable to sleep.

The Lovers upside down he typed now, deleted it immediately and closed the document as the door slid open behind him. He knew who it was.

– Hi, Rakel, he said as he heard the sound of his daughter's bare feet against the rough floor planks. – Mind you don't get splinters, the floor hasn't been sealed yet, you know. He put his arm around her.

– What are you writing? she wanted to know.

– Just some thoughts.

– Are they about me?

He lifted her up on to his lap.

– Yes, he answered into her hair, – they're about you too.

– I had a horrible dream last night, she said.

– Oh no.

Since her grandfather's death, she had never talked about her dreams, as far as Dan-Levi could remember.

– You want to tell me about it?

– Don't know.

– Telling people your dreams isn't dangerous. I'll be able to take it.

She cuddled up to him. – It was about you.

– Oh?

– You'd been away travelling and then you came home. I saw you from the window.

– Well that's not so bad.

– I ran out of the house. And then I saw that something terrible had happened. They had destroyed you.

– Destroyed?

– On your face and everywhere. That was what was worst. That I didn't recognise you.

13

He followed Synne Clausen to Erleveien. As though she were a guide. He hadn't been there for eight years; it was the first time since the night Karsten disappeared. She went to her father's house. He carried on past and stopped at the copse. Drizzle in the air, not cold, not warm, still not yet those evenings when there was too much light.

For the past twenty-four hours he had not slept a wink. The sight of that delivery van burning met him every time he closed his eyes. Standing there amongst the spruce trees and watching the flames catch, waiting for the explosion, knowing there was a body in the front seat, that he was the one who had put it there. He was less than a hundred metres away when it went up. The voice of the Fire Man rose to a roar; he roared along with him. He stood there, roaring until he heard the sound of the sirens. Then he slipped away into the woods and was gone.

Synne Clausen re-emerged after an hour. And now there she was, walking down Erleveien less than a hundred metres in front of him. That morning, after he got back home, he had hacked into her machine and gone through every document she'd worked on over the last few weeks.

She stopped outside the journalist's house and rang the bell. No surprise that she should visit him. The guy had interviewed her and she mentioned him several times in what she was writing. That excited him even more; that thread connected to all the others and led him back to this house.

It was now six thirty and still not noticeably dusk. He passed the gateway, stopped, stood on the road outside. It wasn't the journalist's house. If a hundred families had lived there and tried to turn it into their home, it would change nothing. It was still the house where *he* had grown up. He let his gaze wander from window to window. Stood there as long as he could. Then over to the gate, read the names on the letter box. Six names there now. Two girls and a boy had arrived since the last time eight years ago. He wandered down an icy pathway between the fences. Tall white conifers that Gunnhild had planted for privacy lined the path. He stood there and waited. Two minutes later, Synne Clausen hurried past on the road a few yards away. He chuckled to himself. He took risks, but they were calculated risks. Not many hours ago she had encountered him on her way out of her block in the student village. She had looked directly at him and seemed curious. And still he had followed her to Lillestrøm. She hadn't recognised him, knew nothing about him, but he had access to what she was doing whenever he felt like it.

He peered out along Erleveien again as she reached the end of the road and disappeared in the direction of the bus shelter. He let her go, crossed diagonally towards the footpath and came out behind the petrol station. From there he ran into the middle of town. Called in at Studio Q and went through a double programme, and was still filled with that bright itching when he arrived back home. He broke off a couple of capsules, injected himself in the upper arm, got into the shower and turned the hot as high as he could stand. Then back to ice cold. For a minute he stood motionless, maybe longer.

But afterwards he had to go back to Erleveien. He walked

up and down the footpath next to the house. He still had the key he had taken that time at home in a drawer. Not unlikely that it would still fit. He imagined letting himself in, going from room to room, recognising the smells, from the damp cellar to the little loft space that Tord had planned to do something with. Ending up in the bedroom that used to be his. And the dark, mouldy odour of the secret cupboard at the back of the wardrobe. He imagined himself crawling into it. The only place where he could get any peace.

Under cover of the conifers he jumped over the fence and entered the lower part of the garden, stepped across to the corner of the house, glanced at the time, ten past nine. He continued up on to the veranda. The curtains were closed but he spotted a gap and peered in. The TV was on in the living room, the journalist sitting facing it. A bundle on the floor beside him looked like as though it might be a blanket, but then he heard a child's voice shout something and the bundle stretched and turned into a dog. The journalist stood up, still keeping an eye on the screen as he headed towards the door. The dog followed him. The child was in the room above, the room that had once been his. The window was slightly open. Shortly afterwards he heard the journalist's voice up there. Kai could imagine him entering the child's room, going over to the bed or wherever the child was, sitting down beside it. Maybe it was the girl he had fetched water for that time. Now the journalist was telling her something or other, comforting her. She had gone to bed and was afraid lying there alone, and Kai imagined that it was him who was sitting there on her bedside.

Before the journalist returned to the living room, Kai moved away from the window, down from the veranda. They had built a little shed by the garden fence. The door wasn't locked. There were a couple of bikes inside and a lawnmower.

He closed the door, walked back out through the garden. The grass was hard beneath his feet, with a few patches of snow still left underneath the cherry tree. Last time he had been here he had come to a decision about what was going to happen to this house. If that business with Karsten hadn't come up, the house wouldn't be standing there now. The decision he had taken that time had closed itself up, leaf by leaf. Now it was beginning to unfurl again.

Back home he sat down at the computer. Again looked through the files he had downloaded from Synne Clausen's machine. It was her life he sat there peering into. Assignments from the university, archived emails, pictures. But it was in this book she was writing about her brother that he could study how her mind worked.

When I write, he comes closer, Karsten, my brother who vanished, whom I had always thought would come back. I'm homing in on nothing. I'm writing to understand that Karsten is the emptiness. But this emptiness is a gate, one I have never dared to pass through.

Not even Kai had understood that Karsten was gone for good. Not until a long time afterwards. He waited and he waited, but no one called that night. Nor the day after. Nor the rest of that Easter. He stayed away from people, prepared to be arrested at any moment. Only after the memorial service later that summer did he finally relax. And not until the sister started messing around did the thought of what Karsten knew come back to him. Now she was going round talking to people who had known Karsten back then, and writing long accounts of what they had said to her. But so far not a word about ignition devices, and not a word about the fires.

She was clever. But he could see inside her head, into her brain. And she couldn't see him. He had hacked into her machine using an onion router. Not even the world's greatest computer expert would have been able to trace the hacking back to him, if anyone ever found out about it. He stood up and fetched the panties he had stolen from her room. Sniffed at them as he carried on reading. A new document was being opened. She was on her computer at this very moment. He could follow her thoughts the moment she had them. He fetched a mug of strong coffee. Back at the computer he saw that she was writing about Khalid Chadar. Instantly he was on his feet, shouting in pain as he knocked over the mug and the coffee spilled across his thighs.

Not until he had cleaned up and made himself another mug did he return to what she had written. Khalid Chadar lay in bed, seriously ill. Khalid Chadar spoke about God, whom he was soon to meet. Again Kai had to stand up and take a walk round the room. Pulled the curtains shut. By the time he sat down again, she had finished writing. He looked around inside her machine, came across a document she had created that afternoon. *Jasmeen Chadar* was the title she had given it. Jasmeen Chadar had been in the same class as Karsten. Adrian had worked as their supply teacher for a couple of weeks that spring. Kai hadn't liked Adrian getting involved in stuff like that, getting so close to people who were a part of his own life, but Adrian did as he pleased. He wanted to see what would happen if he brought a white Norwegian and a Pakistani girl of marriageable age together. It didn't end all that well for either of them.

Now Synne wrote that she had met Jasmeen Chadar at a car park on Bygdøy. Kai leaned in towards the screen in surprise.

Shahzad killed Karsten, he read. *Whether he did it himself or got one of his apes to do it, I don't know. But he was behind it.*

14

It was already rush hour by the time he reached Karihaugen, the traffic going slower and slower until it came to a complete halt at the Ulven junction. Dan-Levi had left early and used the time to run over the questions he had prepared. The editor had gone for his idea for a portrait interview with Shahzad Chadar. It was something he thought they should have done long ago. Even though Chadar had moved to Oslo years ago and was now a member of the city council, he would always be a Romerike lad, and *Romerikes Blad* his local newspaper, now and forever, whether he liked it or not.

Dan-Levi had planned to start with his years growing up as a Norwegian Pakistani in Lørenskog, or second-generation Pakistani he probably ought to say. He had drawn up an outline of Shahzad Chadar's life story. He would not be the first to point out how much it reflected Norway's changing history over the last few decades. He intended to ask him about the turbulent years of his youth, what it was like to be part of a gangland world, about growing up, condemning violence, becoming active in youth work, helping young lads on to the right track, studying law and coming top of his class in the final exams, starting in politics and finding himself on the way to the heart of the corridors of power. One political commentary Dan-Levi had come across in a newspaper mentioned Chadar as a likely candidate for the post of Minister of Justice after the next general election.

Chadar's party boasted that it had room for everyone who wanted to achieve something, and that it forgave the injustices and mistakes of the past. In the commentator's view it would be a smart move to invite a man like Chadar to join the government; it would make it difficult to criticise the party as anti-immigrant in a petty sense.

Shahzad Chadar was a busy man. The agreement was that Dan-Levi would meet him at his home, then accompany him to his office and conclude the interview there. By the time he parked outside the house in Nordstrand, it was quarter past eight. He strolled up through the large garden towards the vivid blue villa.

Shahzad Chadar opened the door himself. He was wearing a light suit and held out a hand with two large rings on the fingers. There was a warm sincerity about his smile and Dan-Levi reminded himself that his doubts about the Muslim faith and way of thinking must not be allowed to intrude on the job he had come to do. Again he thanked the busy politician-lawyer for giving up his time at such short notice.

He was led along what appeared to be a newly decorated corridor, through an arched doorway and into a large, bright room.

– This is my wife Iram, and my son Usman.

Dan-Levi didn't know whether he was supposed to offer his hand to a Muslim woman, but she was there before him. A slim figure in a turquoise costume with jeans underneath, a loose scarf covering only a little of the raven-dark hair. As always when he met an unusually beautiful woman, Dan-Levi felt a touch of melancholy.

The boy she was holding in her arms already had his father's eyes. Shahzad Chadar stroked his cheek and then made a sign to the mother. As she left with the boy, he gestured for Dan-Levi to take a seat on the sofa, the ring on his index finger a crescent moon of gold with a green gem. He himself sat in the high-backed armchair and crossed one leg over the other. He was clearly ready. A large red rug hung on the wall behind him, intricately patterned with gold thread.

– Beautiful rug, Dan-Levi remarked, without being quite sure what he really thought of it.

Shahzad turned towards it. – It's a text from a sura in the Koran called 'The Light'. I presume you read Arabic?

Dan-Levi had to admit that he hadn't got that far yet. Shahzad pointed to the top line. – *God is the light of the heavens and the earth.*

Iram came gliding in and served some kind of tea that smelled of camphor. Then she excused herself, saying she had to go somewhere, and disappeared out into the corridor. Dan-Levi had already found out that she worked as a doctor at the National Hospital.

– Now I am at your disposal for the next . . . Shahzad Chadar looked at his watch, – forty-three minutes.

As planned, Dan-Levi began with some questions about growing up in Lørenskog, the district in Norway with the highest proportion of people of Pakistani origin. Shahzad had never made any secret of where he came from, he said, and it had given him several advantages in his political life. He talked about gangs and fights, status and threats, in essence the struggle to survive as a young man. When Dan-Levi asked him about criminality, he said with a broad smile:

– I presume you mean things like shoplifting in the big shopping malls, fighting, driving without a licence, that type of thing? The answer is yes. I did all of those things. I have my parents to thank for the fact that I never got involved in anything more serious. My father had a great thought when he came to this country in the seventies. His family would be Norwegian, it would put down roots here, be accepted, make a positive contribution to growth and development.

– Has your father always lived in Lørenskog? Dan-Levi interrupted, looking to make the local angle even more pronounced.

– More or less. Quite by chance he met a family in Nittedal that owned a large farm. In his first year he lived there in a bedsit in exchange for helping out with the work. He knew everything about horses.

Dan-Levi grabbed at an idea that came flashing by.

– Which farm?

– It was called Stornes, I think.

Dan-Levi dropped his pen on the floor. – Then he must know the family who . . . Is he still in touch with them?

Shahzad Chadar shook his head firmly. His face darkened slightly.

– Certain things happened there that meant he had to break the contact. But surely this is not something you intend to write about?

– Not if you don't want me to.

– Then we have a deal.

Shahzad drank from his teacup and put it down on the table with careful movements.

– My father lived in a shed, not much more than a stable, and was poorly paid. When he raised the question with them, it became clear that they thought Pakistanis were something quite different from Norwegians, if I can put it like that.

– Do you know Elsa Wilkins? Dan-Levi offered.

– Who is she? Shahzad said, wrinkling his brow.

– She was the daughter on the farm at that time. I've just interviewed her. On a completely different matter.

Shahzad shrugged his shoulders, fell silent.

– You have a lot to thank your parents for, Dan-Levi said, resuming the thread.

– God and my family.

Dan-Levi recovered his pen from beneath the table. – Many people find a strength in their faith, he said evenly.

– For me it was a turning point in my life when I rediscovered God, said Shahzad. – The home I grew up in wasn't particularly religious. My father went to the mosque every Friday. He didn't touch alcohol and raised us to be believers, but he rarely prayed himself. My mother was more pious, but even she didn't talk about her faith much. I had to find it myself.

– How? Dan-Levi wondered.

– One summer when I was in Pakistan visiting relatives, I met a *pir*, a holy man who has achieved clarity through faith and self-denial. We're still in regular touch. It's thanks to him that I'm sitting here today and not in a prison cell in Ullersmo. Do you know anything about Sufism?

Dan-Levi knew that Shahzad Chadar had talked about this in an earlier interview, as he had Googled it. At first glance Sufism seemed to have quite a bit in common with what he believed in himself. Though there were New Agey sides to it, our joint soul, stuff like that.

– It is a branch of Islam, he offered.

– Not a branch, Shahzad corrected him. – Sufism can without difficulty be incorporated into other aspects of the faith. It is as strong within Sunni as Shia. You might say it's a direct channel to God.

Dan-Levi was immediately more curious than sceptical. Where he came from too, what mattered was to achieve direct contact with God, a state known to the congregation as being filled with the presence of the Spirit. Some of Dan-Levi's strongest memories were of sitting on one of the front rows and seeing his father, a calm man who rarely raised his voice at home, take his place at the pulpit. Then he was no longer his father; that was when he became Pastor Jakobsen. He could laugh and shout, condemn, plead for mercy. With the tears coursing down his cheeks, he could always make things happen in that crowded room: people fell to their knees or raised their arms above their heads and began to talk in tongues they had never learnt. For a long time Dan-Levi was afraid when he saw the change that came over his father, that normally friendly and taciturn man up on the podium suddenly alternating between loud laughter and weeping. Throughout his childhood this manifestation of the Spirit had frightened him, and he was still not at ease with it, the joy he could experience during the meetings always mingled with despair. He could never free himself from his childish fear that his father would remain where he was, in the presence of the Spirit, and never come down from the pulpit to be himself again.

– How can you tell that you have achieved contact with God? he wanted to know now.

Shahzad Chadar looked to be thinking this over for a few moments.

– Gratitude, he replied. – That is the most illuminating word I can find.

– Gratitude, Dan-Levi exclaimed.

Shahzad studied him. – In Arabic, the word *kufr* means both heathendom and ingratitude, because these two things are essentially the same.

Dan-Levi realised he was sitting there nodding.

– Sufism is the teaching of reconciliation, Shahzad continued. – Within it lies the possibility of our leaving this period of conflict behind us. It is the opportunity to come together, as Christian or Muslim. Or Jew.

He talked about this for a while, and Dan-Levi did not interrupt. He couldn't bring himself to ask a single question about sharia, and the Muslim plan for world domination and the expulsion of the unbelievers, the reverse crusade as they called it in his congregation.

* * *

Dan-Levi had another agenda too, and hidden agendas were a form of lying. His father, who was a very learned man, often spoke of a concept developed by the Jesuits called *reservatio mentalis*. By using an expression that was ambivalent and misleading, and in the privacy of one's own mind ascribing a distinct meaning to it, the Jesuit allowed himself to lie. According to Pastor Jakobsen, this was one important reason for the decline of the Church, and Dan-Levi had set his own limits on how far he could go during the interview. There was no question of employing the Jesuit tactic, and for the almost three quarters of an hour in which he was a guest in Shahzad Chadar's home, he had tried to avoid any thought of what Synne Clausen had said to him. Only once they were in his car afterwards, passing through the Opera tunnel on the way to the centre of town, did he decide to approach the subject anyway.

– You have a sister.

– I have two sisters and a brother, Shahzad answered. – I am the oldest.

– One of your sisters is named Jasmeen?

– Do you know her? Beneath the friendly tone there was a hint of scepticism.

– Not personally, but I know someone who has met her. Dan-Levi scratched the side of his neck. – I'd like to talk to Jasmeen too. It's good to have some other reference points in a portrait interview like this.

Shahzad Chadar's face tightened slightly. – My sister has gone back to Pakistan.

Shortly afterwards he added: – Who do you know who has met her?

Their conversation had reached a critical point. Dan-Levi considered backing off, but continued: – Her name is Synne Clausen. Her brother was in the same class at school as Jasmeen.

– Oh really.

– You probably know about him. He disappeared.

Shahzad Chadar didn't answer. Silence descended on the car, a change of seasons. Dan-Levi began to regret his persistence.

– Is it him you've come to talk about? said Shahzad once they were clear of the tunnel.

Dan-Levi made an effort to wriggle out of it. – I'm here to interview you.

– Was it this girl who asked you to come and see me? Synne Clausen?

His voice was cold now, and beneath the chill it seemed to Dan-Levi he could hear a real anger.

– No, he said. – I'm here for the newspaper.

Shahzad Chadar pointed to a bus bay at the end of Bygdøy Allé.

– Pull in there. This interview is over. He added: – There is no interview. Save yourself the trouble of writing it. It will never be printed.

He opened the door even before the car had come to a standstill, left it open as he walked away.

Dan-Levi was left there staring at the morning traffic heading in towards the centre. He felt like a Jesuit. Or more like Pepsi after the dog had received a telling-off and crept away into a corner. The shame made him nauseous, and suddenly he seemed to recall Elsa Wilkins saying that the Lovers upside down didn't just relate to the love between two people. It could also refer to faith and doubt. Through the still open car door, the stink of the morning rush hour filled the car. Sitting there, Dan-Levi knew that he was going to have to talk to her about just that.

15

MAJA WAS STILL not back. Synne had asked the others in the corridor. None of them had seen her that weekend, nor heard any sounds from her room. But they didn't know her very well and hadn't thought any more about it. Synne called the music school, finally got through to one of her teachers. Maja hadn't turned up for her practice sessions and hadn't called in with any explanation either. That was all he knew.

Then she called the police. Was put through to the duty group. The woman at the other end sounded about her own age.

– Might she have gone back to Poland? she suggested even before Synne had finished speaking.

– Without locking her door? Without telling anyone? Without packing? Without taking her flute, or her passport?

Again she was interrupted. – Give me her full name and national identity number and we'll look into it.

Synne went into Maja's room, looked up the details in the passport she had found in the desk drawer the previous day.

– And when did you say you last saw her?

She looked out the window, down at the lawn at the rear of the block.

– Thursday.

Then it hit her. Maja had been going to meet someone. Synne recalled how excited she had been on her friend's account. Suddenly she froze, exited the room and closed the door behind her.

Snowflakes drifting down. Halfway across the footbridge, I stop. Stand there looking down at the rows of cars streaming by beneath me, in both directions. Maja said something about the man she was going to meet, but I wasn't listening properly.

Carry on across the bridge. It's spring, and these light flakes are already gone by the time they reach the ground, but I reach out to catch them, and the warmth of my hands make them melt. Certain thoughts are like that too. Karsten's absence is a gateway. That's why I'm writing about those who knew him. I must write something about Adrian Wilkins. I was thirteen years old. Begin there. See with the eyes of the young girl I was then. Adrian Wilkins enters the room. Think it's the living room in our house. Adrian is Karsten's best friend. He's a few years older, maybe twenty-three or four. He stands in the middle of the floor. His eyes scare me, but I don't want him to look away. Because I become something else when he looks at me.

If I had not had an attack that evening, nothing would have happened to Karsten. But what Jasmeen Chadar says turns everything upside down. They were out to get Karsten. There's a reason he disappeared. I have never believed he took his own life. And now Maja is gone. Is it me who makes people disappear?

Synne deleted the last two lines. Without looking at the rest of what she had written, she stood up, picked up the towel and the make-up bag she hardly ever used. As she opened the door, she had the idea that she was alone, not just in the corridor, but in the whole block. She popped back inside, picked up the key and locked the door behind her.

In the bathroom, she pulled off her clothes, turned on the shower. *If you want to remember, you'll remember.* She had fallen off her bike. But why had she cycled down by Lillestrøm secondary and not taken the shortest route home? And where did the blood come from?

Afterwards she wiped the steam from the mirror, stood there looking at her face. Suddenly the door handle turned; someone was trying the door. She jumped, pulled on her dressing gown, stood there listening a while before starting to breathe again. As she took out her mascara, she changed her mind, pulled a face at her reflection in the mirror, which new layers of steam had almost obliterated, made a turban of her towel, packed her clothes into a bundle, let herself out. As she shuffled down the corridor in her slippers, she heard a noise from the kitchen, didn't turn round, stood there fumbling with her key. Just as she got the door unlocked, someone behind her shoved it wide open. She was pushed inside, was about to scream but a huge hand clamped over her mouth and her arms were trapped against her sides.

– Don't say anything!

Her head was forced up against the wall, she couldn't move. She felt everything freeze inside her.

– Not one sound. Do you hear?

Now it's going to happen, she thought. She tried to nod. The hold was released, the weight of the stranger's body moved and pulled away slightly.

– Sit down. The voice spoke Norwegian with a tiny displacement in the stresses.

– No, she whimpered, not daring to look at him. Registering that her bathrobe had slipped open, she fastened it around her waist.

– What do you want? she whispered, even though there could be little doubt.

He didn't answer, and at that same moment she knew something terrible had happened to Maja. She could scream now, she'd have time before he could stop her, but she didn't have the strength; her muscle fibre had stopped reacting. She could give up and fall into a pit, freeze solid and stay frozen until it was all over. I've been in that pit before, she whispered, so quietly she didn't even hear herself.

– I'm not going to touch you.

She didn't hear what he was saying; there was a ringing in both her ears and the room was spinning round and about to disappear. She slumped down into the chair.

– I am not here to cause you any harm.

Slowly she picked up these words, even more slowly gathered the meaning of them. But she couldn't believe them. They were said so that she would come up out of the pit again, up to the man who stood there waiting.

– I don't have anything, she tried to say.

– Relax, he said hoarsely. – I'm not going to steal anything.

She glanced up at him.

– Or touch you, he repeated.

He was dark, his hair almost black, and he was wearing dark clothes. She still didn't dare to look at his face. But he was sitting on the side of the table, arms dangling at his sides. And once again he said he was *not going to touch you*. As though he had not already done so.

– You're going around asking about Chadar.

She tried to understand whom he was talking about.

– Jasmeen, she mumbled, still confused.

The room around her slowed down. She was nauseous, but could feel herself breathing. Hold on to it. Take it in deeply. Hold it. Let it out. It was Erika's voice, telling her how to breathe.

– I met Jasmeen. Is that why you're here?

He didn't answer her question. Instead he said: – You're trying to find out what happened to your brother.

She didn't know if that was what she was doing, or if it

would help her to say yes, but she nodded. She could have said: Yes, I want to know what happened to Karsten, I want to know where he is, I want him to come back.

She started to cry.

The man's hands began to move, as though he wasn't sure what to do with them.

– I thought you were going to kill me, she mumbled. – My friend has gone missing.

– Sorry.

Dimly she realised that he meant it.

– Had to be sure you wouldn't scream. No one must know I'm here.

And then the rage came, like an avalanche.

– Fucking idiot, she yelled, leaping to her feet.

The guy stood up. He was a mountain of muscles.

– I know what happened to your brother, he said, and that made her sit back down in the chair again. But something was changed, and now she dared to look into his face. The description was recited inside her. Strong, wide face, scar on the forehead. Big mouth, small eyes close together, eyebrows meeting above the bridge of the nose. She was doing the reciting herself I've seen you now, she thought. You'd better get out of here without touching me. Or kill me. Though she no longer believed he would do that. She fastened the bathrobe tighter around herself.

– Does Shahzad Chadar have anything to do with this? she asked as firmly as she could.

The guy looked at her for a few moments.

– Shahzad knows everything, he said finally. – He picked your brother up that night.

– Picked him up?

– They were waiting outside your house. They took him off in a car.

She saw in a flash Karsten disappearing into a vehicle.

– How do you know that? she asked and got up again. – Were you there?

He shrugged. – Maybe I was, maybe not. That's not something you need to worry about.

She let that sink in.

– They drove off with him, over to the runway. Shahzad took him down to the river. No one has seen your brother since then.

– Why are you telling me this?

He took a step forward.

– We know you are writing a book about your brother. Someone wants you to know what happened. What you do with the information will be up to you.

She stood between him and the door. Wanted him to leave without saying anything else. Wanted him to stay until he had told her everything. She moved away into the corner by the desk.

– I can't just write something like that without proof.

He was standing with his hand on the doorknob. – If you dare to publish it, we'll give you more.

He left, closing the door carefully behind him.

Afterwards, she lay on the bed. Couldn't even lift her head up. Didn't have the strength to lock the door. She tried to organise all the things flooding through her. Had to abandon the attempt, closed her eyes, and there was that image of Karsten again, getting into the car. She's there too, very close, lying on the ground, or sitting on a step, trying to call out his name, but nothing comes out. She has seen this happen, or dreamed it. The car is dark, not very big; one of the rear lights doesn't work. Is this detail a sign that this really took place, or does it mean she is unable to prevent herself making things up?

It had grown dark outside. She got up from the bed, sat at her computer, typed without thinking, stopped for a moment, closed her eyes. She sees herself in another room. She's lying on the floor, peering down at her naked body. The door bursts open.

She stood up, opened the window; the cool spring air streamed in. She picked up her phone. Luckily Dan-Levi answered at once.

– Good to hear your voice, she burst out, and could hear how embarrassed he was.

Dan-Levi listened without interrupting. It took a while before she managed to say anything about the stranger who had been there. Once she started, it came pouring out. She told him about Maja, how she was sure something bad had happened to her, that for a while she thought something bad was going to happen to her too.

– Now the police'll have to do something, he said when she had finished.

– I must talk to him, she interrupted. – I need to get hold of Shahzad Chadar.

– You mustn't even consider it, Dan-Levi protested. – As it is, I feel very worried about you. If there is anything at all in this business about Chadar and Karsten then you must stay away from him, Synne.

– Must I?

– Don't do anything by yourself.

– I can't promise not to.

She ended the call, slumped down in front of the machine again.

Karsten on the way home. The garden dark, no one in the house. Somebody standing between the trees. Four shapes emerge from the darkness, form a circle around him. One grabs hold of him by the lapel. 'We've been looking for you, Karsten. Why are you hiding from us?'

It's Shahzad Chadar's voice. Karsten is afraid now, they're closing in on him. 'We're going for a little ride,' says Shahzad

Chadar. Karsten tries to break free, but they hold him, lift him up and drag him away. The car is parked at the end of the street, where no one can see it. They force him down into the back seat.

'What do you want?'

Nobody answers. They drive down along Fetveien, past the airport runway.

They turn off, carry on through the trees, stop. Karsten's hands are tied. Shahzad Chadar grabs hold of him, drags him out. Karsten tries to shout, but his mouth is taped shut. Shahzad Chadar pushes him ahead down towards the bridge. Down towards the river, towards the river.

She could feel a prickling in one of her temples. Had been feeling it all afternoon but ignored it. The prickling was like tiny flames that hadn't yet decided whether to turn into something bigger. She printed out the text she'd just written, folded the sheet into her back pocket, pulled on her boots, her blue coat.

She'd only been to Erika's place once before. It was last summer, at a party for students who had finished the semiotics course. There was drinking. Some eating, but mostly drinking, and when she woke up next morning in Erika and her husband's bed, Synne had trouble remembering exactly what had happened. He wasn't there, of course, nor their son. But now they were, or at least the son was; it was him who opened the door when Synne rang.

– Who are you? he asked, a four-year-old demanding instant answers to difficult questions.

– My name is Synne, and you must be Sturla. Is Mummy home?

Erika appeared behind him.

– Is that you?

The voice was layered in surprise and resistance and rejection, all packaged to sound like warmth.

– I must talk to you, Synne explained.

– Okay, said Erika, and the packaging was already quite neutral. *Does it have to be here?* was what her look conveyed.

– Aren't you coming in? Sturla asked, speaking for his mother.

Synne looked at Erika. The question clearly angered Erika, but she couldn't show it.

– Why didn't you ring instead? she whispered, struggling to remain poised.

– You don't answer the phone.

Erika looked as though she was thinking this over. She stood there flipping the door back and forth between her hands, apparently unable to decide whether to open it or slam it shut in the visitor's face. Behind her a door in the hallway opened. A tallish man with collar-length greying hair emerged. Synne recognised him from photos on Facebook. He was a saxophonist and had recorded CDs with his own quartet.

– Hi, he said, looking at her with a slightly milder version of the little boy's curiosity.

Erika appeared to have decided in favour of warmth.

– This is Synne, she told her partner. – Synne Clausen.

He approached and took her by the hand even before she had managed to offer it.

– Finally I get to meet you, Synne. It's about time. I'm Johan.

She muttered something about how she knew that.

– I hear you're working on a new book, he exclaimed with a show of real interest.

Synne glanced at Erika. – I wouldn't go so far as to call it a book. Not sure it'll get that far. Erika's helping me to get things going.

Johan nodded as though this were the most natural thing in the world.

– That poetry collection of yours is strong stuff, he said. –
I'm looking forward to seeing where you go from here.

He still seemed to be completely sincere, and as they sat
on the sofa in the large living room with its view of Tåsen,
he continued to talk about her poems. He even recalled
certain images she had used in them.

– Maybe I could do something with them, he said brightly.

– Music, you mean?

– Yep.

The thought of these fragile texts that hardly survived
being read being exposed to saxophone improvisations made
her laugh uncertainly.

– Johan always has at least four thousand ideas running
through his head at the same time, said Erika as she entered
the room carrying espresso cups and a coffee pot on a tray.

Later Erika took her up to her study. Synne looked out at
the bare apple trees. Tried to hold on to that strand of pain
in her temple and not let go of it. Perhaps that was the way
to keep it under control. It hadn't got any stronger, but she
was feeling more distant from things.

– He's nice, she offered, hearing her own voice out in the
room.

Erika made a sound between her teeth as though she was
releasing steam.

– What are you up to, Synne?

– So much is happening, I'm very confused. I had to talk
to someone.

– What do you mean by coming here? Don't you realise
this is my home? My family?

Synne pulled out the text she had written. – Read it,
please.

It took Erika less than half a minute.

– What is this?

Synne had told her about the meeting with Jasmeen; now she tried to tell her about the man who had forced his way into her room, and how Maja had gone missing. But she had to give up.

– This is what happened to Karsten, she said indistinctly. Erika glanced through it again. Suddenly she looked up.

– You can't just write something like this as though it really happened.

– Can't I?

– Christ, Synne. You're acting like a child. My son knows more about social relationships than you do.

– Do you want me to leave?

Erika breathed out heavily. – Maybe we need to take a break, she said, clearly trying to keep her voice down.

– Fine by me. Synne stood up.

– I didn't mean it like that. Erika held her back. – Call me tomorrow, we'll work something out.

Synne shook her head, opened the door and descended the stairs unsteadily. Johan popped his head out of the kitchen as she was putting on her coat.

– Finished already? he asked in surprise.

– We seem to be.

– Erika says you're writing about your brother. She showed me a newspaper interview on the net.

Erika joined them, face like an egg collector returning with an empty basket.

– I don't know what I'm writing about any more, said Synne. – I don't understand any of it.

She made her way slowly home. The drops of rain gathered in her hair. Above her right cheek that faint streak of pain had grown stronger again. Impossible not to recall what it reminded her of. Years ago she had experienced it several times. Not long before the attacks, it would appear as a warning, somewhere around the temple, a feeling as though a low, hot flame was burning close to her ear. And then suddenly she would be gone. It mustn't come back, she thought. Need to get hold of a doctor. As though any doctor in the world could prevent these attacks once they threatened to start.

For some reason or other she still had the number of the psychiatrist she used to go to in those days. She fished out her phone, called him. The number was no longer in use. – No one could help you back then, Synne, she muttered, – and no one can help you now.

Suddenly it was as though Karsten was talking to her. The voice came from some place where he was alone and where no other human could reach him. – I will write about you, she murmured down to the asphalt, where the street lights dripped orange patches on to the damp blackness. – I will write to you, Karsten.

She stopped and closed her eyes, dizzy, supported herself against the street lamp, pressed her forehead against it. As though in some flickering black-and-white film she could see him getting into a car. It's raining, he turns towards her. – Don't be angry, Karsten, she murmurs, – please, don't be angry with me.

16

After Synne had hung up, Dan-Levi called Roar. When his friend took the call, he could hear what sounded like a football match on the TV at the other end.

– You've got too much free time, he teased him.

– Don't you dare, you cheeky little journalist, Roar jabbed back. – I've had just about the worst day at work in the history of the world. Everything that could go wrong in Oslo Police District did go wrong, all at the same time.

– Maybe it's the full moon, Dan-Levi offered. – Actually, I've got more on that case we were talking about.

His friend groaned. Not once, or twice, but three times.

– Are you talking about a missing persons case and some arson attacks that were never solved?

– I've got something new for you, Dan-Levi interrupted. – Something pretty surprising. Maybe Synne Clausen needs police protection.

He repeated what she had told him and waited for Roar to be astounded.

– And the girl hasn't reported this? was all his friend had to say.

Dan-Levi lost patience. – The guy who forced his way into her room didn't harm her. But it's Shahzad Chadar who should be reported.

He stood up and looked out into the garden. Decided not to mention the embarrassing attempt at an interview.

– Dan-Levi, I'm sitting here trying to recover with a cold

beer and a Champions League game. Why don't you come over?

Before Dan-Levi could answer, Roar swore loudly, the game obviously commanding as much of his attention as the conversation.

– Actually, I did look into one thing for you, he went on, lowering the volume on the TV slightly. – If there's any question of bringing Chadar's sister in for an interview, it won't be that easy. It looks like she's moved back to Pakistan for good. So what does that leave you with?

He answered his own question. – If this mysterious intruder will agree to an interview, we might have a case. But if that happens, then it's up to Romerike to decide whether the investigation should be reopened.

– You talk like a civil servant, Dan-Levi complained.

– Maybe we should form a cold-case group with no other responsibilities but digging up old bodies? It sounded as though Roar was beginning to get really annoyed. – Give us fifty million a year and we might think about it.

Dan-Levi chose not to comment on the suggestion.

– I made a call to one of the lads in Lillestrøm, Roar added in a conciliatory tone. – Asked him to unearth a few documents from back then. A complaint was filed again Karsten Clausen for assaulting Jasmeen Chadar.

– Really?

– According to the complaint, Clausen seduced her and subjected her to sexually offensive acts.

– What did Karsten have to say to that? And the girl?

– We never got that far. The complaint was withdrawn after a couple of days. It was probably a consensual relationship, but consent isn't always the same thing when a girl from a Pakistani family is involved.

Dan-Levi could hear what sounded like several large swigs going down before Roar carried on.

– The whole thing was almost certainly connected to another complaint, one that Karsten's father made.

– About what?

– Someone vandalised his car. Broke into his garage and scratched it along both sides.

– So revenge then? And you didn't follow it up after Karsten went missing?

– Now don't go insulting the police force, Roar warned him. – That alone could lead to criminal proceedings. You know quite well that we interviewed Shahzad Chadar after Karsten disappeared. In fact we spoke to him twice. The guy had an alibi for the night in question. Although you might wonder about the value of it when the witnesses were all his gang buddies. All in all, a lot of work went into that case, Dan-Levi, and I shouldn't have to remind you of that. Roar was clearly on the defensive.

– I should think so too, Dan-Levi shot back. – Eighteen-year-old boy goes missing.

– All right, all right. Stop telling me off now. We had good grounds for believing that the boy probably took his own life. Several witnesses suggested that he was having some kind of mental trouble, including a certain Mr Jakobsen, who lived in the same area and was a member of the same chess club.

Dan-Levi tugged hard on his goatee.

– The fact is, Karsten Clausen made a run for it when I tried to interview him, Roar pointed out. – And there were no further fires of that kind after the lad disappeared. That was as far as we could take it. We spoke to everyone in his circle. Opinions about his mental state were contradictory. No one in his family had seen any signs of instability.

– I never said he was mentally unstable.

– Maybe not, but another witness went further than you. He more than implied that Karsten was suicidal.

– Who was that?

On the TV, the commentator began to bellow, and Roar swore.

– That was never offside, he growled.

Dan-Levi brought him back to the conversation.

– The guy had a foreign name . . . Wilkins, I think that was it.

– Adrian Wilkins?

– Correct. Do you know him?

Dan-Levi sat staring into the air for a few seconds. – I interviewed his mother a few weeks ago. What did he say about Karsten?

– Something about him being more and more depressed in the period just before Easter. Wilkins had made up his mind to talk to Karsten's parents and advise them to seek help, but the boy disappeared before he could get round to it.

Dan-Levi looked around for something to write on.

– I found out something else too, Roar went on. – There were investigations into Karsten Clausen that the lads in Lillestrøm don't have access to.

– What does that mean?

– Security Service.

Dan-Levi's jaw dropped. – Are you trying to tell me that the Norwegian Police Security Service were investigating Karsten?

– Your chess buddy's life was obviously not as quiet and peaceful as you thought, Roar concluded drily.

Pepsi needed a really good walk, and that was his job, but instead Dan-Levi closed the living-room door and left the dog to play with the girls upstairs. He could hear them throwing a ball and Pepsi barking, beside herself with joy. He should have gone up to them, told them again not to get her all jazzed up, that the dog shouldn't really be in their bedroom at all, but he leaned back into the sofa and tried to concentrate on what his friend had told him.

He suddenly felt very tired. He needed a break, and picking up the newspaper, he began reading an article about problems in the health sector. He felt his eyelids closing and smelled the newspaper as it landed on his face. The barking doesn't stop. He tries to get up from the sofa. It is dark, but neither Sara nor the kids are home. Pepsi comes bounding down the stairs and he raises a hand and plunges a knife into her chest. With the dog pinned to the knife he goes out to the kitchen, lays her on the work surface and starts to dissect her body, first in half, then in smaller sections. The coat is gone; only the head remains to show what it is he is dissecting. He feels cheerful as he stands there parcelling the pieces up into freezer bags and stuffing them down inside a rubbish sack. Out in the garden he buries them. Rakel stands at the door as he is about to sneak back inside. *Pepsi's gone*, she says, looking at him with sorrowful eyes, and in that instant he is overwhelmed by an infinite grief. *We'll go out and look for her*, he says, and jumps back down from the step. Ruth and Rebekah follow him into the back garden. Synne Clausen is already there. Everyone's calling Pepsi's name. Then Rakel notices that someone has been digging in the lawn. She kicks away the dirt Dan-Levi piled up there, sticks her hand down into the hole and starts to drag up the rubbish sack. *Don't do that*, he shouts, jumping up so that the newspaper falls to the floor.

Sara was standing next to the sofa.

– Lying here fast asleep in the middle of the day, she scolded, stroking his forehead. – You're sweating. Are you ill?

Not as far he knew he wasn't.

– What was Synne Clausen doing there? he asked, still confused.

Sara looked at him quizzically. He was about to tell her what he had done in his dream, but he couldn't bring himself to.

17

I am lying in a room. It must be a cellar, because there are no windows here. I am cold, and suddenly notice that I am naked. There is someone else in the room, a voice talking to me.

It is not a swan, Synne.

He says this. Or else I shout it. Or it is something I make up as I sit here typing away, as though the answers are to be found somewhere inside my head.

Don't be angry, Karsten, I whisper. Please, don't be angry with me.

The document had been created the previous evening, at 21.12. Kai read through it again but still couldn't understand what it was about. Of all the texts on Synne Clausen's hard disk, these were the type that irritated him most. All the same, he made a copy of it and put it in the folder where he kept things that might turn out to be useful. Synne Clausen called some of these texts 'dreams'; to others she had given different names, 'Sleep of a hundred years', 'The castle burning', 'Leda and the swan'. This last one turned out to be about Adrian.

Adrian Wilkins is Karsten's best friend. One day he calls at our house. I'm home alone, let him in. We sit talking for a long time in the living room before Karsten arrives. Adrian Wilkins asks how I'm doing. Not the way people usually ask, or the psychiatrist. He asks because the answer matters to him, so that's why I try to explain. Adrian Wilkins is an adult, but he still seems able to see things the way I do. Do they bully you? he wants to know. No, I answer, no one bullies me. It's just that there is something about me that's enough for them to keep a distance. I don't understand that, he says. Is it because you're cleverer than them at school? Maybe, I say. Or maybe it's the attacks, because I can even talk to Adrian about those. Don't you have any girlfriends? he asks. I hang out with Tamara sometimes, I answer. Tamara doesn't have anybody else either. We don't like each other all that much. But Mum and Dad want me to go round to her house. I'm not to sit up in my room because that way everyone can see I have no friends and it's embarrassing for them. Maybe they don't like the way I smell, I think, but I don't say that to Adrian.

Kai pushed her panties off the desk on to the floor, stood up, crossed to the window. Spring day outside. The sun hanging above the river. He felt a mixture of anger and relief. Inconceivable that Shahzad Chadar knew anything about the fires and the ignition devices. He wouldn't have kept his mouth shut for eight years. They must have killed Karsten before the kid had a chance to talk about it.

Another thought struck him as he read through Synne Clausen's most recent document. He picked up his mobile phone. A while since he'd called Adrian's number. For a time they had done things together. He'd worked for his little brother. It was unnatural. Couldn't last.

– You still alive?

The standard opening. Could mean anything. The continuation didn't make things any clearer, but the mere fact that Adrian had picked up was a sign that he was willing to let bygones be bygones.

– I'm just about to start a meeting, he said once they'd got the opening courtesies out of the way.

– Where are you?

– London. Try again later.

Kai heard the buzz of voices in the background. He didn't

need to call, didn't need Adrian's help or his money. He'd worked for him for almost six months. One mistake and he was out. *You fucked up* was how Adrian summarised it. And he was sent back home, like some kid who got legless on a school outing. How would Adrian have managed without the money his father gave him?

– It's about Synne Clausen.

Pause. Then Adrian was there again: – Are you talking about the sister?

– The very same.

– Wait a moment.

Adrian moved away into what sounded like a side room; the background noise was abruptly gone. Kai was surprised at how easy it had been to get his full attention. But Adrian had taken an interest in Karsten, had enjoyed the way the lad fell for Jasmeen Chadar. Had encouraged them, played along with them. He called it an experiment. Naïve boy grows up in Toytown, meets Pakistani girl who's been prepared for marriage to a relative in the Punjab. What happens if you bring them together and introduce a catalyst? As though a brainless idiot couldn't see what would happen. After the lad disappeared, Adrian soon lost interest in the experiment.

– What is this about the sister?

– You haven't heard that she's become a writer? Now she's writing some kind of documentary thing about her brother's disappearance.

– That was a hundred years ago.

– Precisely eight, Kai corrected him, prepared to be rejected, but Adrian was still there.

– When is the book being published?

– No idea. But if you can believe what she says in an interview, she's only just started. Thought I might try to find out a bit more about it.

Adrian said nothing, but Kai could feel that he was on the verge of breaking through the wall of hostility.

– There's more, he said, and waited.

– Let's hear it, Adrian grunted, and the tough-guy way he said it made Kai pull a face.

– Synne Clausen has a list of people she's contacting to ask about Karsten. She's been to see Shahzad Chadar's sister.

My sister, he was on the verge of adding, and flicked himself on the forehead with an irritated smirk.

– Jasmeen?

Kai didn't know what to make of the fact that Adrian still remembered her name.

– Jasmeen Chadar has told Synne that Shahzad killed Karsten.

There was a long silence after this. Kai knew that Adrian always fell silent when he was surprised, that he took refuge in the nearest shelter and assessed the situation before re-emerging and continuing his advance, or pulling back even further.

– Does she *know* that?

Suddenly Kai felt in high spirits. – She says she knows. You were in no doubt about it either back then. That it was Shahzad and his gang who got rid of Karsten.

They hadn't spoken much about this. Just recognised that they had failed to protect the lad, that they had lost a battle but that the war was only just beginning. But perhaps this defeat was the reason Adrian had gone back to England.

– You seem very well informed about who's been talking to whom.

– You're right there, Kai confirmed. He was enjoying this conversation more and more. – You don't seem to have noticed that Shahzad Chadar has been busy making himself a career as a politician.

– From small-time crook to politician? That's not exactly a long journey.

– He's backed the right horse, the party that's most opposed to immigration.

Adrian blew out his breath. – In Norway all politicians think the same. They assign each other roles and then try to make it look as though they're quarrelling. And Shahzad Chadar is a total creep.

– If he gets had up for murder, he's finished, said Kai. – Once and for all.

– Why do I need to know all this? Adrian interrupted irritably.

– Because I'm thinking I might just crush that Muslim bastard.

That was the way he had to talk to get Adrian on his side. – Iraq is a lost cause. Things are even worse in Afghanistan. Resistance here at home is what matters now.

Kai could hear that Adrian had opened the door back into the room he'd started out in. A confusion of background voices welled up again. But he was obviously still listening; he hadn't ended the call.

– Elsa's on Synne Clausen's list of people to talk to.

Adrian coughed at the other end. – What does she want to talk to Elsa about?

– I'm sure you'll realise if you think about it. Karsten spent a lot of time round here before he disappeared.

– Elsa has enough on her plate. We can't let people start worrying her.

He was right about that. Elsa reached out in all directions. That winter eight years ago, Kai had got closer to her than ever before. He was at her place every day, because Adrian had decided to live with his father in Birmingham. She'd opened up to him, started to talk about things she had been through, and Kai had helped her in any way he could. It was the best time he'd ever had. And then the prince had decided to come back to her. And again Kai found himself banished to a far-off land. Not a land even, just a dank, cold place.

– Interested in copies of what Synne Clausen is writing? he joked. – She's writing about you too.

– Fucking hell, no, Adrian swore. – Leave me out of your snooping.

Kai smirked, surprised by his outburst. – I'll get in touch if something comes up.

– I'm going to Basra, Adrian told him.

– I'll keep you posted, Kai replied, and made sure he was the one who ended the call.

Chadar lived in 47B, the central of three detached houses with carports dividing them. The house was painted in a loud turquoise colour that made him smile indulgently. There was a light in the hallway, the only one, and no car outside. Kai carried on past, on to the next group of houses, found a path between the gardens, passed 47B on the far side. The living room faced this way. He noticed that the curtains were closed and there were plants on the window-sill. He stood for half a minute before withdrawing into some bushes and then heading up towards the copse.

The April day was bright and sharp and the biting wind colder than it had been in the morning. He pulled his collar up, took out his phone and punched in a number. From his position between the trees he could not be seen from the house.

– Who is this?

The female voice was old, the accent broken. He guessed it must be the wife.

– I'm calling from Interflora, he said. – Is Khalid Chadar at home?

– No.

– Will he be long?

The woman said something in a foreign language and then another person came on the line.

– What's this about?

A younger voice this, no accent. He went through what he had planned to say.

– We can take the flowers here, the woman said.

He dismissed the suggestion, saying that the greeting had to be delivered in person. He could hear how stupid it sounded, but she fell for it.

– Then you'll have to send it to Lørenskog Nursing Home, she informed him.

He asked which department, was told, again declined the offer to take the flowers out to him. – A floral greeting, he murmured to himself, and was still laughing as he got into the car.

When they let him into the ward, he had a bouquet of flowers with him, bought at a nearby Esso station. The corridor smelled of piss. He was shown through a room in which four or five skinny old men sat staring at a blank TV screen. Kai felt himself getting irritated.

– Are you family? asked the chubby girl in the pale blue nurse's uniform.

He nodded and tried to look sad. – Close family. Has there been any change?

– He spends most of the time sleeping. Doesn't eat much. He's on liquids.

She opened a door at the end of the corridor. – Visitor for you, Khalid, she chirped. – Your nephew.

Kai had no idea where she got that from but had no need to correct the assertion, because the figure that was half sitting and half lying in bed didn't move his eyelids at all; they looked to be stuck to the sunken eyeballs. The chest moved jerkily two or three times and then was quite still for some time before the jerky movements were repeated.

– He is awake, the chubby girl informed him. – He hears everything you say to him. He's just *so* thrilled when he has a visit. If only every family looked after their own as well as yours does.

Kai gave her a suitably modest smile. She took the flowers he handed to her, filled a metal jug and put them in it, set it down on the bedside table.

– I'll let you have a little time on your own, she said warmly, and let herself out.

Kai remained standing by the bed, looking down at the almost translucent figure. A needle in the back of his hand was attached to a tube, clear liquid dripping from a bag up on the metal stand. He had met Khalid Chadar once before, in the sweet shop in Strømmen. Kai was fourteen and had played truant after the lunch break and ridden up there on his bike. Didn't buy anything, just stood there and looked Khalid Chadar in the eye. *Can I help you?* the man had asked. Kai had left without a word. And now, after all these years, he answered:

– Yes, you can help me.

Because now he knew what he should have said back then. He dragged a plastic chair over to the bedside, sat down.

– The first time I heard of Khalid Chadar was when Tord Hammer told me about you. Tord Hammer called himself my father. He knew who you were. For some reason or other he couldn't stand you.

It seemed to Kai that the glued eyelids moved, and he took that as a sign that the man lying there was awake and hearing every word he said. He felt an itching inside himself. The kind of itching that might lead anywhere.

– Tord Hammer couldn't stand me either. Not so

surprising really. He couldn't have kids of his own, his sperm was rotten, so he had to look after a boy who wasn't his. I wasn't supposed to know, Gunnhild wanted to shield me as long as possible, but Tord Hammer thought that was just rubbish. And he was right about that. Why shouldn't kids be told where they come from?

There were a few photos on the bedside table. Kai picked one up, a black-and-white picture. It looked to be from the village back in Pakistan. An elderly man with a turban, two children standing in front of him, one with his arm around the neck of a cow.

– Tord was pretty mad at me the day he told me. It was the time I set fire to a field just down from our house. It almost spread to the next-door garden, and if that'd happened the whole house could have burned to the ground. But Tord and a few others managed to put it out just in time. He came up to my room afterwards. I'd been sent up there to think about what I'd done. I thought and I thought and I wasn't in the least bit ashamed. And that's what I told Tord Hammer when he came up to hear the conclusion I'd come to.

Kai shook his head and placed the picture back on the table.

– There's an art in being ashamed. It wasn't for me. Something stronger was called for. Tord Hammer understood he had to get right down to it. *You don't even know who your mother is*, he told me, because it seemed to him now was the time for the truth to come out. And it was right, what he said. I'd already realised it wasn't Gunnhild. *Your mother is married to a rich man in England*, Tord Hammer explained, and suddenly his voice was softer. *The trouble was, this man didn't know she already had issue. When he found out, he probably wasn't all that pleased, but he didn't lose his rag completely till he learned who the father of this bastard was.*

A bloody Mohammedan, having it away with the woman who was now his wife. I had to think about what he was saying for a while. I wasn't familiar with the words *issue* or *bastard*. But it wasn't too hard to work out. And before Tord Hammer left my room that afternoon, he informed me that he had always thought of me as *the Paki kid*, and it was the sort of useful information that made a lot of things fall into place.

Kai pulled his chair closer to the bed. The creature lying there was breathing differently now, quicker and more evenly. There was a slight rattling sound from the throat, and a rivulet of spittle that had gathered at the corners of the mouth trickled down over the chin.

– But this is not what I came here to talk about, said Kai, and leaned down towards Khalid Chadar's ear. A smell of decay came from the body; it was hard to tell whether from the mouth or the hair, or whether the skin itself was releasing the stench. Kai held his nose.

– You stink, he announced. – But Shahzad smells even worse. I understand why you Muslims wash yourselves all day. Shame it doesn't help. The stink is embedded. And soon everyone's going to know what I know about Shahzad. Yes, that's who I'm talking about, Shahzad Chadar, your son. A little Paki criminal who thought he was clever because he stopped stealing mobile phones and began to play at being grown up and acting responsible. Who acts the friendly, enlightened man, the man who thinks it's wrong to beat his wife up, who preaches tolerance and free speech. But he's still a little Mohammedan shit. And soon everybody is going to know who he really is.

He leaned right over into the stinking ear.

– A killer. Someone who supposedly kills to protect the family honour. As though there is any honour in your family. Well now he can go to hell. Every fucking journalist in this country is going to be after him. They'll camp outside his house, follow his wife to work, his kids to nursery school. Nobody in that whole fucking family of yours is going to get a moment's peace until the newspapers and the TV have had their fill and people can't be bothered to pay attention any more. Not just that bottom-feeder Shahzad but the whole of the fucking Chadar family might as well move back to that hole in the Punjab you crawled out of. No one here will miss you.

Suddenly the thin eyelids moved, and Khalid Chadar's eyes opened, looked at him, or past him, and at that moment the thought of Elsa came to Kai. That she would get the revenge she had never asked for. If she could see him now, he thought, she would be happy that he was able to do something for her, that he didn't back away, that he protected her.

18

SYNNE SAT ON the side of the bed. Slowly the dream images were sucked into the afternoon light. She didn't try to hold on to them.

When she stood up, that line of tension was still there in her head, like a warning.

Four messages on her phone. Janus had a cold, nothing serious, but Åse obviously thought she ought to come and take care of him. Two of the others were from Erika. Synne deleted them, regretted it, should have read them first. Erika had rung too, three times according to the call list. Synne was about to ring back but didn't. For a few days she would make herself inaccessible, maybe a whole week, maybe for ever. The thought of how that would hurt Erika gave her an intense and pleasurable glow.

She was still tired and could have slept on, but after a Coke and a visit to the toilet, she sat down at the machine.

Don't be angry, Karsten, I whisper. Please, don't be angry with me.

She had typed this after staggering in through the door the previous evening, with the pain twisting from her ear and into her head. She had been outside herself. It was as though someone else had written it. Someone who knew more about her than she did about herself.

Janus was worse than Åse had said. He shook himself as she entered the stable, greeting her with that little movement of the neck. She pressed her face against the warm muzzle, stroked his mane.

– I missed you too, she said into his ear, and stood there without moving. Janus stood motionless too. – I've had so much on my mind, she confided to him. – I don't know what's happening. Don't understand any of it.

Afterwards she took both Janus and Sancto Spirito over to the riding hall. Walked them round the large room. Janus was stepping a little oddly, and she got the hoof pick and lifted one of his hooves, gave the inside of the shoe a clean. The door swung open. Synne half turned, saw a male figure silhouetted against the afternoon light. He was black haired, fairly tall.

– Hello? she said.

He pulled the door to behind him, walked towards her. She recognised him now, had seen pictures of him in the newspapers and online. What are you doing here? she wanted to ask, but couldn't get a word out. He came nearer. Her fingers tightened around the scraper. She tried to carry on with the cleaning job, but Janus was too restless. She dropped his hoof and stroked him, couldn't tell if it was the tremor passing from her skin into the big animal body or the other way round.

– You've been trying to get in touch with me, said Shahzad Chadar.

If he didn't know what she looked like, then she had a chance. If she just carried on stroking Janus without saying a word. The jabbing pain that had been absent since she woke up now returned and began to throb between her ear and her forehead.

– So I need to find out what it is you want of me.

She dropped the hoof scraper, didn't hear it fall against the soft surface.

– You could have called, she managed to say.

He was standing less than a metre away from her. Janus began stamping with one hoof. She whispered something in his ear, sounds that only he understood.

— I could have called, but now I'm here.

For a moment she thought of climbing on to Janus's back, because once she was up there no one could harm her, not even Shahzad Chadar. She looked at him. He was a head taller than she was. Dark jacket. Smell of aftershave. The smell was out of place here. That was the thought she held on to, that he was bringing a disturbing smell into this world.

— What's your horse's name?

She wanted to ask him to get lost, just take his smell with him and get out of there, but she was afraid to, afraid that something might happen to her.

— Janus, she said, and saying the name of the horse helped.

— That one there is Sancto Spirito.

— Nice names, he said, and grabbed Sancto Spirito's halter. — I've done a lot of riding too.

The horse allowed itself to be stroked, dipped its muzzle and rubbed against his hand. She could see he wasn't lying; he was used to being around horses. Janus noticed it too and the trembling eased off.

— You're interested in stories, Shahzad Chadar said. — Now I'm going to tell you one. About my family.

She breathed out. But she still wanted to tell him to leave, as soon as she could manage it.

He began to speak in a low voice. She couldn't grasp everything he said, but she didn't dare to stop him. Janus grew restless again. She was still standing with her face towards the horse's tail, but she could feel Shahzad Chadar looking at her. As if he wanted something in return for what he was telling her.

Abruptly she made up her mind. — I've met Jasmeen.

Of course he knew that.

– Then obviously you must know what she told me.

As soon as she had said this, she dared to turn round to face him.

Shahzad Chadar looked down into her eyes. – Jasmeen hates me. He never took his eyes off her. – She ruined her own life. I did what I could to help. Was she grateful?

He raised his voice, the superficial calm cracked. Synne could hear something else beneath it, a massive anger. Janus stepped away, treading on the hoof scraper on the soft ground. Synne held on to him.

– My brother was killed, she said quietly, talking as much to Janus as to Shahzad Chadar. – I knew it all the time. Someone killed him. It was you.

She shouldn't have said that, not here in the riding hall, alone with him. But she had started; now there was no turning back. – I've told the police about you, she lied. – If anything happens to me . . .

He lowered his hands. – Nothing's going to happen to you. Not here.

– Are you threatening me?

– I'm trying to make you understand what you're doing. He looked to be thinking something over before continuing. – Jasmeen does everything she can to harm me. I have lost a sister.

– I have lost a brother.

For an instant she saw something in his eyes. A sort of regret, perhaps.

– Karsten was just a kid, he said, his voice once again smooth and even. – A child who was given a toy. Just like you, he had no idea what he was dealing with. I tried to talk to him. He wouldn't listen. Afterwards I realised that other people had put him up to it, told him what to do.

– Put him up to what?

He shook his head. – His friends were a bad bunch. They persuaded him to trick my sister. I tried to protect her. She was naïve, thought Karsten was serious.

– Wasn't he?

– They got him to set fire to my father's shop.

– Oh come on, she protested. – Karsten had nothing to do with that.

Shahzad shrugged his shoulders. – You're gullible. It's fine by me. But it could be dangerous for you.

She froze. It had started low down in her spine; now the cold had reached every part of her.

– Someone came to the place where I live, she said. – A man who knows you. He told me you met Karsten that evening, that you took him away in a car.

Shahzad stared at her for a long time. It looked as if he was struggling to control himself, and she thought she could see the anger that floated round inside him, a flow of magma forcing its way upwards.

– I have enemies, he said finally. – A lot of people who don't want me to succeed. Some of them are Norwegian, with racist reasons. Others are Pakistanis who think I owe them something. The world I used to live in is probably not all that much like yours. You think I could have survived there if I just wagged my tail at everyone I met?

She didn't know how she felt about that. – You made him get into your car. I saw you.

He came a step closer, stared down into her face.

– You were not there, he said in a low voice. He touched her on the shoulder. – This is what everyone who wants to stop me has been waiting for. You understand that. The chance to push me back down into the dirt again. You could be the useful idiot they're looking for. Is that what you want?

She couldn't give an answer to that. Again she pressed

close against the warm body of the horse. *I'm lying in a room. It must be a cellar because there are no windows there. I'm cold, and I realise I'm naked. Then the door is thrown open. Karsten stands there, calling to me, but I can't hear the words, because everything is like a film with the sound turned off.*

– Then tell me what happened that night, she mumbled. – Without lying about anything.

19

DAN-LEVI PICKED UP the remote. He had been sitting there zapping after the news, enjoying the anaesthetic release of watching a bit of a reality show, then changing to a nature programme, until in the end he had to force himself to turn it off.

He took paper and felt-tip pens and sat at the kitchen table, created a new solar association diagram, with the facts spread out at the end of the rays.

Khalid Chadar worked at Stornes farm. Stornes burned down. Karsten knows something about this. Karsten had a relationship with Jasmeen Chadar. Shahzad Chadar threatened him. Jasmeen (and others) claim that Shahzad killed Karsten. Another ray led to Elsa Wilkins. *A son in Iraq. His name is Adrian and he knew Karsten, was with him a lot the spring Karsten disappeared.*

He took another shot at it, this time with Stornes farm in the centre. Suddenly something occurred to him, and he made a note at the tip of one ray: *Sara's father bought our house from someone who was related to the Stornes family.* He sat there pondering this. Wasn't sure if it was correct, even less sure why it had now become part of his solar association diagram.

He rang Sara. She answered within two seconds.

– Has something happened? she burst out.

Dan-Levi couldn't bring himself to say that he had just called to hear her voice, that he was looking forward to her coming home, the sort of things they said in the early years. Not that it was all no longer true, because he could suddenly experience that same sensation of missing her, even if she was only out shopping. Right now she was in the changing room of the gym at Kjellervolla School.

– Everything's fine, he reassured her. – Just something I wanted to ask you.

She breathed a heavy sigh of relief. – Don't scare me like that, Dan.

– All I'm doing is ringing you.

– I'll be home in twenty minutes. It must be something really important if it can't wait. Are the little ones in bed?

They were. Ruben was sleeping over at a school friend's, and Dan-Levi had had a long conversation with Rakel just before the news.

– Didn't you once tell me that your father bought this house from someone who was related to the people at Stornes?

She gave a demonstrative groan. – And that couldn't wait?

– Is that right?

– I think so. Solveig's the one who knows about things like that. Why do you ask?

He couldn't lie, but didn't want to reveal what it was he was working on.

– I'll tell you later, he promised, and hoped she would forget all about it.

Of course he could have rung Solveig immediately instead of bothering Sara. But he didn't like to call his sister-in-law unless he really had to. He knew that the dramatic changes in her personality were a result of her illness, and that should have engaged his feelings of sympathy. But even when she was well, there was something about her that made him feel uncertain. He ought to have tried to find out why this was. Working on yourself is a job for life, he reminded himself as he called her number.

She sounded surprised, probably because it was the second time he had rung in the course of the last few days. With no attempt to explain, he put to her the same question he had asked Sara.

– Gunnhild Hammer, Solveig replied. – She was the oldest daughter at Stornes.

– Hammer, Dan-Levi echoed thoughtfully. – Do you know her?

– No, but I remember her from the time Mum and Dad bought the house.

– Tell me about her.

– Tell you what?

– Did she have a family? What work did she do? How long had they lived there?

– Have you started up as a private eye?

– Yes, he said with a slightly forced laugh.

– Well, she was married to a man by the name of Hammer. An army officer, if I'm not mistaken. They had a son, about your age. He was adopted, I believe. It's not the kind of thing you ask people about.

– Where do they live now?

Solveig gave a low grunt, a habit of hers when she was thinking.

– Gunnhild Hammer had an illness, something that made the muscles waste away. That was the reason they sold up. She became increasingly disabled, couldn't manage the staircase.

– Is she still alive?

– How would I know? Actually, Dad met them, it must have been a year or two after they bought the house, and by that time she was in a wheelchair. She wasn't much older than me. It makes you think.

Dan-Levi didn't allow a pause into which thoughts on the subject of Sara's fate might enter.

– What about the son?

An impatient sound from the other end, and he began getting ready to close the conversation.

– Apparently he was in some kind of institution, she said. – They couldn't manage him any more.

Afterwards he sat studying his solar diagram, and then added: *Gunnhild Hammer, muscular disease. Husband military, son in an institution.*

He removed his glasses and cleaned them as he climbed the stairs. Something or other flitted away from his thoughts. He couldn't keep hold of it. It had something to do with what he had just written on the diagram.

The little ones were asleep, but Rakel's light was still on. The cupboard door was open; he poked his head in.

– Time to return to our own world.

She crept out, torch in hand. – The man who lived in there has written things on the wall, she said.

– Man? You sure it wasn't a girl?

She nodded definitely. – He's written a girl's name in there. Carved it into the beam.

– Maybe it was her own name.

Rakel climbed into bed. – I've seen him.

– You don't say, said Dan-Levi, and sat on her bedside. – Where was that?

She looked up at him. – Here, I think. Not completely sure.

Dan-Levi was about to turn her light off. – And what did he look like?

– He had completely fair hair. Nearly like the angels in the pictures. She closed her eyes. – But he's had very bad thoughts, you can tell from what he's written.

Dan-Levi dropped the subject, didn't think it was a good idea to talk about bad thoughts just before going to sleep.

After he'd sung evening prayers to her and tucked the duvet in around her, she said: – I had a weird dream last night.

He stopped in the doorway, sat down beside her again.

– Lots of what I dream I forget straight away. But I can't forget this one.

– It's not a secret, is it?

She shook her head. – But it was awful. I dreamed about you.

He was curious. – Again? Tell me.

She hesitated. – You took Pepsi out, you were going for a walk with her. And then you disappeared.

They had agreed never to ask her about her dreams but just let her describe them if she wanted to. Sara said that people thought her big sister could see the future in her dreams when she was a child. The thought that Rakel might have inherited something of the same unstable interior world that had spoiled so much of Solveig's life was intolerable, and whenever it came up, Dan-Levi rejected it.

– I dreamed that you killed Pepsi.

He started. – What are you saying?

She stared at the wall, as though she was the one who had done something wrong. – I'm sorry. I shouldn't have said it.

He took hold of both her arms. – Tell me exactly what happened in your dream.

– Don't remember.

– Try.

He realised he was too tense and let go of her. She hid her face in the duvet.

– I heard Pepsi whining and ran down into the kitchen and you had stabbed her with a knife.

He made a half-hearted attempt to give her a reassuring pat on the head, but she pulled away.

*   *   *

Elsa Wilkins squinted in the sharp light from the lamp above the door.

– Is that you? she exclaimed, clearly placing Dan-Levi immediately.

– I was in the neighbourhood, he explained. – Remembered there was something I wanted to ask you.

The visit was on impulse and he had not worked out any excuse for bursting in on her like this.

She held the door open for him. He stepped inside the small hallway. – I'm sure you must be busy.

– That doesn't matter, she assured him. – The interview was really good. But that's probably not why you're here?

Even though she was offering him the chance to do so, he didn't want to lie.

– No, that isn't why. He kicked off his shoes. – Last time I was here, you talked about your son.

She went ahead of him into the living room. – Did I?

– You mentioned him in passing. That he ran a firm that was working out in Iraq. What I didn't realise then was that he was a friend of someone I also know. A boy who disappeared.

Only when she was seated in a chair opposite him did she say: – You're referring to Karsten Clausen.

Dan-Levi nodded. – Karsten lived near me. We were members of the same chess club.

– A terrible story.

He thought that was a pretty good summation of it.

– It was so awful for his family, she went on. – And the worst thing must be never knowing what actually happened. She shook her head.

– Karsten saw a lot of your son that spring, said Dan-Levi.

She pulled her hair back behind her ear on one side. – Adrian liked him a lot. Looked after him, as I'm sure you noticed. Karsten was a sensitive boy. Adrian's very big hearted. Tea or coffee?

He declined, assured her he wouldn't take more than five minutes of her time.

– So you're here because of Karsten.

A relief not to have to deal in evasions. – I'm trying to find out what happened to him, he confirmed.

She looked at him as if she had realised this much earlier. – Do you think there's anything else Adrian can help you with? He contacted the police as soon as he knew Karsten had gone missing. Told them everything he knew. He went to see the parents too, spent a long time talking to them. They appreciated it.

She leaned back in her chair. She was wearing a dark dress and was nicely made up. Even when she wasn't expecting guests she looked good.

– I'm sure you know Karsten was in trouble, she said. – He'd started a relationship with a Pakistani girl. Her family threatened him.

– Might that be the reason he disappeared? Dan-Levi asked without saying anything about what Synne had told him.

Elsa seemed to think about it. – Maybe not directly, even though Adrian didn't rule it out. Mostly he believed it all got too much for Karsten, all these threats. They followed him around. He was assaulted.

– I didn't know that.

– As far as I remember, it was the week before he disappeared. He came here afterwards, desperate and afraid. They cut his stomach with a knife. Adrian went with him to the police, I think.

– Are you sure it was reported?

– Well it must have been. Adrian said he'd sorted it out. She sighed. – It's never easy to know when to let old ghosts die and when to open up and let the light in.

Dan-Levi wasn't sure how to respond to that.

– I'll call Adrian, she said decisively. – Ask him to get in touch with you. He'll do all he can to help clear up what happened back then.

– Is he in Iraq?

– Right at the moment he's in London.

– So he's back here now and then?

Elsa looked out of the window, and Dan-Levi realised he was being intrusive.

– I miss him, she said finally. – But he couldn't stay here. It was too provincial for him. He has to live somewhere where there's a place for people of above-average talents.

Dan-Levi glanced at his watch. It had been well over five minutes.

– I discovered by the way that my parents-in-law bought their house from someone who must have been related to you. It's in Erleveien.

Elsa Wilkins sat upright in her chair.

– My wife and I have taken over the house. Was it your sister who lived there?

– That's right, she said, and smoothed out the tablecloth.

– Gunnhild and Tord Hammer, said Dan-Levi. – They have a son, too.

Elsa gave a slight nod.

– Your nephew, then. Maybe I know him. I think he was in some sort of institution. When your sister fell ill.

– Excuse me a moment, said Elsa, and stood up. She turned and went out into the hall. Moments later she was standing in the doorway. – Sorry, I have to make a phone call.

He stepped past her and out towards the front door. – I'm the one who should apologise. Turning up at your door with no warning.

She gestured with her arm. As he was putting on his

shoes, he added: – I've been thinking about those cards you showed me. That thing about the Lovers. You mentioned it could also relate to love in a wider sense. Like faith.

She gave him a long look.

– I can see that there is doubt in you, she said. – That's what the card wanted to tell you. That it will grow.

20

The light at the far end of the corridor was gone. Synne stood in semi-darkness outside the bathroom. Strong smells came from the kitchen. Saffron or turmeric, she couldn't tell the difference, garlic and cooked meat. And from the floor above, the sound of bhangra music. A burst of laughter. Passing Maja's room, she saw that it was locked. Certain that her friend had reappeared, she knocked, waited. No answer. The previous evening she had again contacted the police, was asked the same questions, could tell them nothing new. Tried to accept what they suggested, that Maja had returned home because of an emergency, that she would probably get in touch soon, they usually did. Who are *they?* she asked, but by then the conversation was over.

She let herself into her own room, locked the door behind her. Bent over the machine, tried to read what she had just written as though seeing it for the first time.

You don't deny you met Karsten that evening?

Shahzad Chadar takes a step closer. Again Janus starts to tremble, and I think that this horse, my *horse, is wiser than any thought, it can fathom the depth in what is said, the truth of it, more reliably than any lie detector.*

As you say. I met him.

You were waiting for him. You were going to get him.

That's right. We were going to get him. Make him understand what he'd done.

You were going to kill him.

*Shahzad Chadar puts his hand on Janus's muzzle, strokes
him.*

*We were in your garden. He came up the drive. We surrounded
him. He tried to yell but my cousin stopped him. When he let
go of him, Karsten said: 'I know who started the fire.'*

'Started what fire?'

'Your shop, and lots of other places.'

*We weren't going to let him bluff his way out of it, but I
told him to tell us what he knew. Then he turned, dashed away
and threw himself over the hedge. We were after him, but of
course he knew the area well and we didn't find him. My cousin
and another guy headed up the road and caught sight of him.
They caught up with him as he was trying to start a van, a
huge van. One of them smashed the front windscreen with a
club. When I got there, they were sitting on top of Karsten. We
put him into my car.*

*I remember that, I say. Karsten was bundled into a car. You
bundled me in there too. In the back seat next to him.*

Now Shahzad Chadar stares at me.

You don't mean that, Synne.

*The moment he says my name, I know he's right. He didn't
bundle me into any car.*

You weren't there.

*You're lying, I say, or perhaps I shout it out, because I want
him to be lying, I want it to be the way I think it is, that I was
on my way home, that I saw what Shahzad and his gang did,
that they dragged me into the car and threw me out by the
school.*

*Shahzad Chadar offers to drive me home from the stables.
I'm still not certain he's telling me the truth, but would I
have gone with him if I really believed he was the one who
killed Karsten? He talks as he drives, giving me the circumstances of the case. Maybe this is what he sounds like when
he's pleading a case in court. I let him get on with it. He*

*talks about his father, who came to Norway in the seventies,
how honesty and hard work got him where he was, the same
story I heard Khalid Chadar himself tell, how he sacrificed
himself so that his children would have the opportunities he
never did. Then Shahzad talks about himself, what he's become,
and about his own son.*

*I've taken a big step, he says. And this is true of many others
besides myself. Do you understand what it will mean if I am
successful?*

*I do understand. But there is another story in there too, enclosed
within the one he has just told me, lying there like a serpent's
egg.*

You still haven't told me what happened to Karsten.

*A long silence ensues. It lasts until he passes the turn-off to
Oslo and carries on in the direction of Fetveien.*

I'm going to town, I protest.

*He doesn't answer, drives on for a while, pulls into a bus bay
and stops.*

Come with me. I want to show you something.

*He gets out. Would I have gone with him if I still believed
he was a murderer?*

*I follow him in the low evening light, across a muddy field,
towards a stand of trees. I can hear the sound of birdsong through
the noise of the traffic from the road behind us. It's late April,
a few days until Easter; it will be even later this year than it
was eight years ago.*

Here.

*Shahzad Chadar stops and points. The river is brown and
dull, it twists its way through the trees like a slow, half-frozen
snake.*

*I brought Karsten here. I was alone, the others stayed in the
car. I was the one who had to do it, for our honour to be upheld.*

Honour?

That's the way we used to think. Not even think, it was more a way of speaking. We didn't understand ourselves what it would lead to.

I look down into the water streaming by at our feet.

Karsten was terrified, I say.

Shahzad nods.

He was afraid. His hands were tied behind his back. He thought he was about to die. He was still raving on about those fires, that he knew who was responsible. He wanted to show me something he had in his pocket. He called it an ignition device. I said I wasn't interested. Then he started to talk about you.

I turn towards him.

About me?

He said that if he died, there would be no one to take care of you. He said you were ill, that you had no friends. I was certain he was bluffing. But it worked. He stood there sobbing and certain he was going to die, and then started talking about his little sister.

You killed him, I say again, and hear the way it almost sounds like a prayer. Admit it.

Shahzad Chadar looks back in the direction of the road, where his car stands with the engine still going and the headlights peering blindly out into the spring night.

When I think back over my life, he begins, and then falls silent for some moments. When I think back to the moment when everything changed, I realise it was that evening. If I'd cut his throat and let him vanish into the river, my life would have been ruined.

You killed him.

I pulled out the knife, cut the tape that held his wrists together. Told him to lie there until I'd gone. I knew something decisive had happened. I wanted a day before the others realised I hadn't done what I said I would do. I used that time to make up my mind to take another road.

But he was dead, I shout.

Shahzad Chadar turns towards me.

Perhaps Karsten jumped into the river. Or fell. Perhaps he met someone who did him harm. I did not kill your brother.

21

SHE HAD CREATED a new document the previous evening. Kai opened it. She was writing about Shahzad Chadar. He had followed her to the stables.

'I know who started the fire.'

'Started what fire?'

'Your shop, and lots of other places.'

Kai jumped to his feet and ran into the kitchen, refilled his coffee cup, put the cup down, went out into the yard, over to the gate, ran up the street and then ran back. By the time he returned to his room, he was calm enough to read through it again. Karsten had the ignition devices with him. That was why they hadn't been in the car. It sounded as if he was trying to tell Shahzad what he knew about the fires, but Shahzad wouldn't listen to him.

Kai drank his coffee in two deep gulps, had to get up and pace about again. It took a while before he was able to concentrate on what else Synne Clausen had written.

Shahzad Chadar threatened her. Still she went with him to the place where Karsten disappeared. *Perhaps Karsten jumped into the river. Or fell. Perhaps he met someone who did him harm. I did not kill your brother.*

Kai scowled at the screen, annoyed that Synne Clausen had been taken in by that slimy toad. But it made no difference what she believed or didn't believe. From now on, he would be the one who made things happen.

Synne was working now; he put what she was writing

up on his screen and read it. Word by word it appeared before his eyes. He was deep inside her thoughts; he could see them in the moment of their being born.

This is what I remember from the evening of Karsten's disappearance: I wake up in a car, lying in the back seat. Outside it is dark. Street lamps approach and pass across my face. There is a smell of vomit and sweat. Perhaps I'm the one who has vomited. Perhaps it's the seat that smells. When I come to fully, it is always the smells that hit me hardest. Unbearable, but these are what draw me back into this world. My senses wake first, and they wake up my thought. Is this all there is to me? I've always felt a compulsion to lie. That is why I write. I can create a world in which there is no difference between what I lie about, what I remember, what is happening around me right now, and what I think is going to happen. When I write, no one can insist that I distinguish one from the other.

Kai hit the table with his fist. She was sitting there with what looked very much like a confession from Shahzad Chadar, and then she started making things up, mixing up her fantasies with things that actually happened. For a moment he saw her sitting there typing, the sentences tumbling out of her fingers. No earthly use could be made of the things she wrote.

I'm lying in the back seat. The man driving is wearing a cap. I can just see his eyes in the mirror. Or perhaps I can't see them. An animal dangles below the mirror, a spider made of fabric or plastic or something. When the car drives over a bump, the spider dances.

We stop, the doors open. The driver leans over to me, the smell is unbearable. He tugs at my arm. I want to scream but I daren't.

Where am I? I might possibly ask.

Home, he answers, but I don't believe him.

He drags me to my feet, lifts me. He's where the smell comes from. His pullover is drenched in sweat, that's where the vomit smell is coming from, as if someone has puked rotten apples all over him. I feel nauseous, can't move, flopping in his arms.

I know Kasten.

He has a lisp, I remember that now. Without saying anything else, he carries me up the driveway, and I see that he is telling the truth. I am home, but I can't bring myself to think the thought yet, that I'm not going to die after all.

What else can I remember? Dad's frightened face when he opened the door. That I heard the sound of sobbing and didn't realise that it came from me. Dad taking me in his arms and talking to the stranger. The stink of apples, rotten apples mingled with vomit, and the weariness that overcame me and swamped everything, sleep for the rest of my life, never wake up again.

Kai sat staring at the screen. Of all the things whirling around in what she was writing, it was the spider dangling and dancing below the mirror that arrested his attention.

He got to his feet. Heard himself swear. He was agitated. Not angry. Not yet, but something was growing inside him, and he knew it would turn into anger.

He shouldn't ring Adrian now. Should wait until he was calmer. Go down to the gym for a while. He should only talk to Adrian when he was in control. But he couldn't wait.

– What's new?

Whenever he heard Adrian's voice, something happened to him. As if he was being held down. Just through the tone of his voice Adrian could put him way down beneath him. Kai imagined him sitting there in his office in the middle of Birmingham, leaning back in his armchair. Prince Adrian, who had turned into a king now; Adrian the Lionheart.

– I'm inside Synne Clausen's computer, he answered quietly.

Two or three seconds passed before Adrian's reaction came.

– Shit, you're kidding, right?

– I'm sitting here reading her thoughts just as soon as they come to her.

Another pause.

– You make so much trouble for yourself, Adrian said patronisingly. – Is that the idea?

It was the tone of voice rather than what he said that caused Kai to explode.

– Now you just shut up. He took a few deep breaths. Discovered a pocket of silence, a place in which he could portion his anger in a way that left him calm enough to speak. – Just shut up, he repeated so calmly that it brought a cold smile to his face.

Adrian was about to say something, but let it drop.

– Shahzad Chadar followed Synne. He confronted her in the stables.

He waited, feeling his way towards another pocket in which he would be able to continue.

– Did he threaten her?

– I told you to shut up and listen. His anger had thickened to something almost solid, something he could shape and put to any purpose he wanted. – He told her what happened that night. What he wants her to think happened.

– What else did you expect?

Kai fished the Zippo lighter from his pocket, lit it, closed the cap, lit it again.

– Maybe what he says is true. He was going to kill Karsten. He let him go.

– Well it's obvious the girl is sitting there and making things up, Adrian objected. – Isn't it a novel she's writing?

– There's more, Kai interrupted. – It looks as though she's remembered things that happened to her that evening.

– And this is not just stuff from her imagination?

– She describes someone driving her home. He smelled

bad. Stank of vomit, and his pullover was soaked in sweat. He lisped, said *Kasten* instead of Karsten. And then suddenly she mentions something else. In his car there's a fluffy toy hanging from the mirror. A spider.

– Shit.

– Don't try to tell me she made that up. There's someone out there who knows something and he's keeping quiet about it. And I'm going to make it my business to squeeze it out of him.

Adrian didn't answer straight away. Kai studied the flame from his lighter and enjoyed the silence, enjoyed hearing Adrian struggle to take all this on board. No way was he still lounging back in his armchair; now he was up and walking about, Kai could hear it in his breathing.

– Maybe it's not such a good idea to go digging up all that old stuff right now. If you chase the rats out into the light, a lot of other things might show up there too.

– That we knew Sæter? That we did a bit of target practice? Who the hell cares about that after eight years?

– For God's sake keep Elsa out of this, Adrian warned him.

– For *God's* sake, Kai mimicked, though he agreed with him about that. Elsa had enough troubles already. He grunted irritably. – I'll do it my way, he announced. – The guy we called Sweaty was named Morten. What was his surname?

– I don't go around keeping stuff like that in my head.

Adrian never forgot a name. Kai didn't know anyone with a better memory for names than him.

– You know I'll find out. Think hard.

Adrian was silent for a few moments.

– There's something you need to think about, he said finally. – You were involved in some stuff back then.

– Was I? Kai hissed.

– Easy now, I'm trying to help you. Sweaty found out

you were up to something or other. He was going to use it against you. I made sure that never happened. You understand?

Kai grunted. – Am I supposed to be grateful for that?

– I don't give a shit what you get mixed up in, Adrian snapped. – I'm thinking about Elsa. So I'm asking you to stay away from Sweaty and the rest of that gang. He did what I told him back then. There's no guarantee he will now.

– We'll just have to find out, said Kai, and closed the lighter.

The time was five past ten. He had the whole day ahead of him. With a sound that was somewhere between a laugh and a growl, he turned to the computer and navigated to the phone book.

22

SYNNE PICKED UP her phone and stood up, clicked down
to Erika's name on the recently used list and then stood
looking at the display. She forced herself not to ring, forced
herself to put the phone down again, stood over by the
window and looked out at the fir trees, the needles vibrating
almost invisibly. It was the wind showing itself. It always
had to show itself through something; by itself it was
invisible.

This was no longer a literary project she was working
on; it wasn't something she had control over. She was in
thrall to what lay behind the text, what drove it on, the
thing that manifested itself through the words. Memories.
Everything she wanted to remember. Did she want to
remember? Why couldn't she recall more of what had
happened to her that night? She was supposed to be circling
in on the emptiness left behind by Karsten, centring on it.
Instead she had ended up talking to people who had known
him, and left herself out of it completely. There was a shadow
there; it followed her as she wrote, stopped when she stopped,
carried on when she did, always a pace or two behind, and
if she turned around, she saw nothing.

The shadow is me, she thought. It's myself, that evening.
Where were you, Synne? she tried to ask.
I was at Tamara's.
You left there.
I left. I got on my bike.

Why were you going home? Wasn't the idea to stay the night?

Don't know.

You don't want to know.

I don't want to know.

Again she sat down in front of the machine.

I want to know. This is not about Karsten. This is about Synne. Karsten disappeared. Synne didn't disappear. Synne was taken home by a stranger, never seen again. Or have I seen him again? Has he been following me the whole time? Synne's face and hair were covered in blood. They washed it away at the hospital. Found no wound. It wasn't her blood. Could anyone understand what that meant? Do you, Synne Clausen, understand what it means?

Afterwards she read it aloud to herself. Like an accusation, it seemed to her.

I accuse you, Synne Clausen, of not wanting to know.

I want to know.

If you want to know, why are you avoiding the only thing that can tell you what happened that night?

Distantly she heard the sound of someone hammering on the door. She jumped, took out her earplugs.

– Who is it?

A man's voice replied from the corridor, something about the police. Reluctantly she unlocked the door. The man standing there was wearing a short black jacket and a cap with a police badge.

– Synne Clausen?

She managed to nod.

– Come to the kitchen, please.

She looked up and down the corridor. The door to Maja's room was wide open. As she passed, she saw a figure in a white suit doing something inside.

A man was seated at the kitchen table taking notes. He

stood up as she came in. He was thin and rather stooping, not much taller than she was, wearing a grey suit and a white open-necked shirt. He looked to be about her father's age.

– Viken, he said, offering his hand, squeezing hers but not too hard. – Detective inspector, Oslo district police. If you can just spare us a few minutes.

– Maja, Synne managed to say.

The policeman looked at her. – You knew her?

Synne slumped down into a chair. – Have you . . .?

– We have opened an investigation. So far we don't know much. You were the one who reported her missing?

Synne tried to say how worried she had been; that was the reason she had contacted them several times.

– Can you repeat for me what you told the duty group?

She pulled herself together. Told him about the door not being locked, why she thought something must be wrong.

– Have you found her? she almost whispered.

– It's too early to say whether it's her.

Synne was scraping the back of her hand with her nail, back and forth, without noticing it. They've found someone, but they don't know if it's her. She couldn't bear to think what that meant.

The policeman continued to question her. She answered as well as she could. How long had she known Maja, did Maja have many friends in Norway, how about her relationship to the others in the corridor, did she have any kind of drug problem. He made a note of what she said about diabetes, and then Synne had to repeat what they had said to each other in their last conversation.

– So she was going out with someone?

– Someone she had just met.

– Who?

Synne thought about it.

– A man. I don't know anything about him.

– Do you have a name?

She shook her head. – I don't think she said his name. Nor where they were going.

The policeman had introduced himself as a detective inspector. She wanted him to say his name again, but hadn't the energy to ask. He leaned back and ran his fingers across his balding head, moved a few of the long, thin wisps. Studied her in what seemed a friendly way.

– Anything else you want to add?

She looked quizzically at him. – Such as what?

Now he smiled. – That is what you're supposed to be telling me. Anything else at all that occurs to you. There's no need to think it's important.

She closed her eyes, let her thoughts flow.

– Karsten, she said finally.

– Who is that?

– My brother.

When she looked at him, he was busy taking notes.

– He disappeared too.

The inspector put his pen down and leaned over towards her. She picked up a faint waft of aftershave; it reminded her of the kind her father used.

– It was a long time ago, she added hurriedly. – Eight years. In a few days' time.

– And what makes you think there might be a connection?

She couldn't give any answer to that. Only that people around her disappeared. That she had a feeling it was something to do with her. That maybe she should stay away from people. She was talking incoherently and noticed that the inspector's interest had faded. Again she pulled herself together, talked about Shahzad Chadar and the man who had forced his way into her room. This final detail made the policeman follow what she was saying with the same look of concentration as earlier.

– So he broke into your room?

She thought about it. – The door wasn't locked.

– But he didn't harm you?

She breathed heavily. – He frightened me.

– I can understand that, the inspector nodded. – But you didn't report this?

– Should I have?

– I'll make a note of it, he said. – If we find there's a connection to your friend, then we'll follow it up.

– And if not?

– Then you'll have to decide for yourself whether to report it.

23

SWEATY CAME WADDLING out from a back room at the Statoil petrol station. Eight years ago he was overweight; now he was fat. A couple of shirt buttons had given up the struggle and a tuft of belly hair stuck out from between them.

Kai turned and examined the selection of engine oils. It wasn't very impressive. When the only customer had paid up and gone, he ambled over to the counter and said hello. A lot of *Christs*, and *how greats* and *what a fucking surprise* and all that kind of stuff. Soon enough, there wasn't much left to say.

– Pretty busy right now, Sweaty coughed, gesturing around the empty shop. – But you can always ring me, he said generously, making an imaginary receiver out of his thumb and little finger and holding it next to his cheek. – We can go out and get rat legged.

Kai shook his head. – I can't ring you, he answered tonelessly. – I'm here because I have a question for you. Very simple question. It's about the night Karsten Clausen disappeared.

Sweaty's eyes were as big as saucers.

– Kasten, he lisped. – That nerd from Lillestrøm?

– The nerd from Lillestrøm, Kai confirmed.

– The one who disappeared?

– The one who disappeared. It turns out that his sister

was found in a roadside ditch that same evening. She was driven home.

– Oh yeah? Sweaty's gaze flitted around the interior of the shop.

– And for some reason or other, it was you who drove her.

It looked as though Sweaty's grin cost him a day's work by the time it came. – Now you're pissing me about. Never met his sister. Didn't even know he had one.

– That's not my question, Kai said, leaning across the counter. Sweaty's smell hadn't changed at all, it struck him, a stench that put him in mind of rancid butter, with an added dash of deodorant thrown in in an attempt to drown it out. – I want to know why you did that. That's the question I need you to answer.

– You've got no business here, Sweaty protested, trying to swell himself up, a barrel of fat wobbling under his Statoil shirt.

– That's certainly something we can discuss, Kai conceded. – But sooner or later you are going to answer my question. It might as well be now.

– That's bullshit, and you know it.

Kai raised both hands. – You got it, he said with a wink. – Just bullshit. He gave Sweaty a pat on the jaw. – Didn't mean to be rude. Now I'll let you get on with your work in peace.

He drove further south, crossed the border into Sweden, turned off towards Strömstad. Walked up and down the quayside, went into a café, treated himself to a pizza, but he had no appetite and instead knocked back two cups of black coffee. Over and over, as he sat there, he shook his head. Could have grinned. Could have laughed out loud. But contented himself with this shaking of the head. He drank a Coke, ordered more coffee. He had all the time in the world but couldn't sit still, had to get out and pace up and down the streets again. Sweaty lived on a boat. He'd checked his income tax details on the net; his given address was Bryggvägen, Vallabostrand. No number. Kai had taken a look down there. Logically enough, Bryggvägen ended down at the quayside, where a number of boats had already been prepared for the summer. But only one of them looked like a house-boat. There was an envelope with Sweaty's name on it in a sack of rubbish on the deck.

After another three coffees, he got back into his car. Took the coast road up. It was a bright spring evening. He stopped at a headland. Jumped out and had a pee in some bushes while watching the nervous flight of the gulls above the fjord. Carried on northwards, keeping to minor roads, played a few old Nirvana tracks. Every so often he had a conversation out loud with Sweaty. As though he couldn't wait for the exchange, and had to rehearse it, over and over again. Sweaty's like a balloon, he thought. If he bursts, his body's going to shrivel down to a scrap of damp rubber.

At ten thirty he parked close to Bryggvägen. It had grown dark. He clambered up a rise that gave a view over the quay, located the boat he had boarded earlier in the day. A faint light showed in the little cabin. He watched it for a while. Thought he saw Sweaty. Sweaty didn't see him. He felt like a great bird circling in the sky. The darkness calmed him, but he remained unable to keep still.

At three minutes to eleven he crossed the road a little higher up, turned back in the direction of the quay. He slipped over the rail, the boat so big it didn't move.

The door to the cabin wasn't locked. He yanked it open. Sweaty was stretched out on the bunk with a duvet over him. He gave a start and tried to sit up, but Kai was on him, twisted his arm behind his back, drove his fist into him, once into each kidney.

– Shit, Sweaty coughed as the huge body snapped first backwards, then forwards. Kai tipped it down on to the floor.

– Fat pig, he hissed. – I asked you a question. You know who I am, right? You know you shouldn't talk to me like that.

Panic oozed from every pore of Sweaty's body, the stench of butyric acid growing even stronger.

– I don't know any of that stuff about his sister, he lisped.

Kai bent down, grabbed hold of Sweaty's shirt, dragged him up then dropped him again so that his head bounced against the floor.

– Stop squealing, pig. Or I'll have to kill you.

– Shit, said Sweaty again. This time it sounded more like a sob.

– We're talking about Synne Clausen, got it? Why did you drive her home that night? If you tell me why, I'll leave you alone.

– What the hell are you talking about?

Kai took a bottle of lighter fluid from his back pocket, removed the cork and emptied half of the contents across Sweaty's shirt.

– No!

He took out the Zippo lighter. – You're going to get one more chance, he barked as he lit it. – Tell me what you were doing that evening.

– I don't know what happened. Sweaty stared at him through the flickering light.

Kai put his foot on Sweaty's stomach, squeezed a couple of litres of air out of him.

– I was passing, Sweaty sobbed. – There was a girl lying in the ditch. I didn't know who she was.

Kai laughed. – So pure chance, then.

– She was ill. She'd had an attack. Blood all over her face.

Kai pressed down again. – What did you do with Karsten? he hissed.

Sweaty lay there as though paralysed, and then tried to wriggle away.

– It wasn't me who picked up Kasten.

Kai let him get his breath back. – But you picked up his sister?

– Was told to, Sweaty managed to say. – Nothing to do with me. Don't know anything else. She'd fallen off her bike, passed out.

– Who told you to do that? Kai circled the open flame above the saturated shirt.

– Randeng, Sweaty moaned.

– Who's Randeng?

– Vemund Randeng. When I arrived, he was standing there taking pictures of the girl with his mobile phone.

Kai struggled to stay calm. Vemund Randeng was Sweaty's best friend, he recalled. That weekend at Sæter's place, the two of them had done everything they could to provoke Karsten. Kai had spoken to Adrian about it, thought it was best to keep them apart, but Adrian wanted to see how it would turn out. Adrian had a thing about studying other people, as though life was a series of experiments, and he was the one conducting them.

Again Kai bent low over Sweaty. – Was Karsten there?

– Jesus Christ, no! His eyes looked as though they were about to roll out of his head. – Just Vemund and the girl. Then Vemund left. He was the one who dealt with Kasten.

Kai studied his face. – Where does he live?

– I don't know any fucking more.

– Vemund is your only pal, and you're telling me you don't know where the guy lives?

– Not seen him for ages, he snuffled. – Not for years.

Kai took the bottle out again, began sprinkling it around the room, grabbed a couple of blankets that were piled in a straw basket, soaked them in the lighter fluid too.

– Before Karsten disappeared, he told you something. Something to do with me.

Sweaty stared at him.

– Maybe he showed you something as well, something he was carrying with him in a plastic bag.

– I never fucking saw him again after we were at Sæter's, Sweaty lisped.

Kai was uncertain. The guy was terrified and stood to lose everything but still insisted he was telling the truth.

– I don't like it when people tell lies, he said calmly. – This world would be a better place if only people wouldn't lie all the time. Have another think.

– I swear, Sweaty groaned. Froth was bubbling from the corners of his mouth.

– Please, do try to help me, Kai said. – This thing here could all go so completely fucking wrong.

Just then Sweaty lunged upwards and grabbed hold of Kai's trouser leg. Kai felt a sharp pain in his leg. He kicked out as hard as he could and caught Sweaty full in the head.

– You do not bite me, he growled, and dropped the lighter. It landed on the pile of blankets, and he leapt backwards, out of the cabin.

He heard the coming of the flame, like the barking of a playful dog as it caught hold of the clothing of the person lying inside. For an instant he thought perhaps he should look for a fire extinguisher and stop it. He jumped over the rail and on to the quay. A wave of sound burst through the air behind him and struck him like the kick of a horse. He got to his feet, ran off.

Further down the quay, he turned and took a quick look over his shoulder. The flame rose high above the cabin, a flickering eye in the light evening.

24

I WAS THIRTEEN and couldn't talk to Mum or Dad about what had happened. Couldn't talk to anyone about it. A week after the memorial service, I rang Elsa Wilkins. She invited me to visit her. I never went. I was probably afraid she'd ask me how I was bearing up.

Only yesterday, almost eight years later, did I again ring Elsa Wilkins. Began by explaining who I am, but that wasn't necessary, because she hadn't forgotten me. She knows I've published a book of poems, and she's read in Romerikes Blad *that I'm going to write about Karsten, and it was like getting in touch with a friend I haven't seen for a long time.*

Synne crossed out what she had written and put the notebook back in her bag as the train pulled into Lillestrøm station. She'd met Elsa Wilkins once before, outside the church after the memorial service, and it would be silly to call that a friendship. When writing, she got carried away by whims, by the need to exaggerate and distort things. The little lies crept in everywhere. In the article in the local paper it said that she wanted to try to approach what had happened to Karsten. If she wanted to do something like that, she would need to use words in another way, constantly measuring them against the reality they were supposed to be describing. Maybe she wasn't capable of it.

Before she could change her mind, she called Erika.

– Synne, are you trying to kill me?

She sounded genuinely concerned. Went on about how

many times she had tried to phone. Had called round at the student village on several occasions. Synne enjoyed hearing all this.

– Where are you now?

– I'm going to meet a woman named Elsa. She stepped down on to the platform.

– Who is Elsa?

– She reads the cards.

– Reads them?

– The Tarot.

Hard to interpret the meaning of the noise Erika made.

– I'm sorry, she said after a while.

Synne decided the war was over. – Forgotten about it already, she replied. – Forgotten everything that was said. Forgotten that I came to your house and got thrown out. Had no business being there anyway.

– I'd like to read what you showed me again.

– I've already deleted it.

– Don't talk nonsense. I've just apologised.

– I'm serious. I'm not going to be writing this story.

Synne crossed the street without looking and jumped when an approaching car gave a blast on its horn.

– Someone else will have to do it, she said once she had reached the safety of the pavement on the far side. – Someone who won't be drawn into that void . . . It just hurts too much.

– You mean you want somebody else to take over? Erika asked.

– Perhaps.

– What about asking that psychiatrist you used to go to? Maybe you could turn it into a crime novel. Erika gave a forced laugh. Synne pulled a face. – Sorry, I'll stop being flippant. I know how much this means to you.

– Do you?

Erika didn't answer. It sounded as if she was thinking.
— Maybe *I* could try, she said after a while.

When Synne had woken up, the string of pain along the
side of her head had almost gone and she had unwisely
drunk two cups of coffee before taking her shower. Now it
was back again.

— Are you saying *you* want to write this book?

— We'd need to work together closely on it, Erika added
quickly. — It would be good for us. I know you. You'd be
in safe hands.

— I'll need to think about it, Synne said curtly, knowing
it would never happen.

As she headed down Grensegata, she recalled something
from Elsa Wilkins' website: *The purpose of life is to make
the world right, restore it to its original state of order and
harmony. Every good deed helps in this.* Synne would have
liked to continue that thought, follow it somewhere, but it
didn't lead anywhere.

A car swung out from a driveway in front of her further
down the road. As it approached, it suddenly stopped a few
metres away from her. A dark blue Audi, she noticed. The
driver was looking straight ahead, and for a moment she
thought it was her he was looking at. Then it moved off
again and passed her. She caught a glimpse of the driver's
face in profile, still staring straight ahead. He reminded her
of someone. But it couldn't be him.

She found the house she was looking for, a white semi
with red frames, and was almost certain that that was where
the car had come from. Still confused, she rang the bell.

After the memorial service, Elsa Wilkins had been in the
line of people queuing up to offer words of comfort. She
had introduced herself as Adrian's mother. She was pretty
and had kind eyes. She held Synne's hand for a long time

and said she should get in touch if ever there was anything she could do for her. It was then that Synne had enquired where Adrian was. A stupid thing to ask, but Elsa didn't seem to mind. She told her he had gone back to England to carry on his studies there. The roses she had brought were from them both.

Now she opened the door and gave Synne a hug. She had hardly changed at all.

– I'm on the phone to a client at the moment, she explained, and showed Synne into the living room before going upstairs and closing the door.

I can just about hear her voice. Somewhere out there someone needs advice, needs to get their life on another track. Deep inside I want to believe it's possible, that there are people who can see threads that are invisible to others.

She had to wait a few minutes before Elsa Wilkins came down.

– Sorry to keep you waiting.

– I saw a car driving along just as I got here, said Synne, even though she had decided not to mention it. – For a moment I thought it might be Adrian.

Elsa raised her eyebrows and seemed to be blushing. – Funny you should say that.

She disappeared into the kitchen, came back with a teapot and cups.

– I had such a vivid dream about Adrian last night, she said as she laid the things out. – You know, one of those dreams you can't shake off after you wake up, that stay with you all day.

Synne nodded.

– Adrian's been in Iraq for months. He came back to England a few days ago and I'm so relieved. It gets worse every time he goes out there. You know how mums worry. And now you come here and tell me you've just seen him.

She poured a dark brown brew into the cups.

– Try this. It's what we call a three-year medicinal tea. It'll do you good.

Synne sipped the bitter drink.

– I just wish you were right, Elsa went on. – I miss him so much I can hardly bear it.

– I understand. I miss him too. Synne shook her head. – I mean . . .

Elsa looked surprised.

– I'm not quite myself at the moment, said Synne, trying to explain her confusion. – All this with Karsten, it affects me so much. And it starts up so many things.

Elsa seemed to accept the explanation.

– And then there's this friend of mine . . . she lived in the same corridor as me. Now she's gone missing. The police have interviewed me. On the train here I was reading the paper and they think she may have been that person burnt to death in a car a few days ago.

– You mean up in Maridalen?

– I don't know any more details. But it feels as though all this happened because I started getting close to Karsten again.

Synne rubbed her forehead with both hands, studied the wave pattern on the tablecloth. Next to a vase of tulips was a recently started embroidery. There were pins sticking out of it, and the point of a pair of scissors protruding from below it.

– People round me go missing.

Elsa nodded. As though the idea was not as unlikely as Synne wanted it to be.

– And then there's this Pakistani family. The father's name is Khalid Chadar. You know him.

Elsa's eyes opened wide. – So this book you're struggling with, she said, – that's what brought you into contact with them. I think all of this is connected to what you're writing.

Synne looked at her in surprise, even though she was the one who had voiced the thought.

– How is Khalid?

– He's very ill, Synne replied. – But he told me you had meant a lot in his life.

– Khalid's always used words that are too big for him. Elsa gestured with her hand as though swishing something away. – Tell me more about how you work.

Synne leaned back in the chair. – I go to see people who had some connection with Karsten, she said. – And then other stories crop up and they all weave together.

– But you write about things that really happened, not things you've made up?

Synne searched for an answer.

– Something broke, she offered. – Not just once, but many times. I used to have these attacks, and when I woke up afterwards, there was always something missing. And that night when Karsten disappeared, everything got smashed and the pieces flew all over the place. I struggled to put the world back together again. Writing became the glue. I think that was how I felt.

– You're talking as if you no longer feel that way.

Synne shrugged. – When I write, I can create all the pieces that are missing, shape them in my imagination so that they fit. It's led me deeper and deeper into a false world.

Elsa seemed to think about this. – You've come here looking for help, she said finally.

Synne didn't know if that was true, but couldn't bring herself to deny it.

– Everything that upsets you goes back to that evening when Karsten disappeared, Elsa continued. – If you can manage to recall what happened, you can put it behind you and move on.

– I've tried to remember. Nothing helps.

Elsa put her cup down on the table and stood up. – Maybe the cards can. Let's go up.

25

Kai turned up the gravel driveway. He hadn't been there since that evening eight years ago. Tufts of grass sprouted from the wheel ruts and the barn was on the verge of collapse, but the main house at least looked to have been painted in the intervening years. The dog pen was still to one side of the house, and when he opened the car door, he was met by a wall of howling and yapping. Four or five dogs were standing up against the fence, trying to outbark each other.

He crossed the lawn. How Vemund had come to take over from Sæter he had no idea. Since the spring of Karsten's disappearance he had had no more contact with Sæter. And the following winter the old man hung up for the last time.

There was no doorbell, so he rapped on the window. More baying, coming from inside this time. After knocking again, he tried the door; it slid open and a black dog appeared. He backed out again, heard a woman's voice inside, talking to the animal. Moments later, the door opened slightly. The woman standing there had a child in her arms. She was pale and looked tired. Kai had the feeling he'd seen her somewhere before.

– Have you come to look at the puppies? she yelled. – We're not taking callers until the weekend.

Kai had to smile. If there was one thing he hadn't come for, it was to look at the puppies.

– Is your husband at home?

She shook her head. The child did the same. It looked

like a girl, the spitting image of her mother, with huge eyes. A dummy filled her mouth.

– What do you want to see him about?

He bunched his fist, could have smashed her face. Instead he forced a smile.

– I'm an old friend of Vemund's. Was just passing and thought I'd drop in and see how he's doing. He hadn't called, had everything to gain by arriving unannounced. – I can wait for him. Is he at work?

She nodded. Suddenly she asked: – Is your name Kai?

He was startled, controlled himself. – Are you psychic?

She smiled. The dog in the corridor, which had been emitting a low growling since the conversation began, now started howling again. She put down the child, grabbed the animal by the loose skin around its neck and dragged it away to a door, pushed it into the room and shut the door.

– Maybe I am psychic, she said as she made her way back across the floor. – Got a good memory anyway.

Slowly it began to dawn on him where he knew her from, but he couldn't remember her name.

– I'm Vera, she said, and then he had her. The grand-daughter of Sæter's sister. She was living with her grandmother back then and hung around at several of the gatherings they had.

– Hi, Vera, he said and held out his hand.

She invited him into the kitchen. It was occupied by the beast he had encountered out in the corridor, and a litter of small black creatures about the size of fully grown rats. He had never liked dogs and pushed the bitch out of the way when she started to welcome him by licking him with her drooling tongue. The animal didn't take the hint but Vera did, and with a surprising show of force she persuaded the bitch to lie down with the pups, which at once swarmed around their mother's nipples.

– Do you breed dogs? Kai said, struggling to keep his composure. He had checked Vemund's tax return on the internet. Eight years ago, the guy had worked at an asphalt plant. They'd been there on training exercises, in the quarry and the surrounding woods. Kai seemed to remember that Vemund had talked about getting back into electronics, but the lad really didn't seem to have any kind of future as a rocket scientist. It wasn't easy to understand how he'd come by an income of about eight hundred thousand kroner a year and three million in the bank. Somewhere on the net he came across his name with the word *consultant* next to it.

Vera strapped the kid into a chair and gave her a baby bottle, which was immediately thrown to the floor.

– Fourth litter we've raised here, she told him. – Selling them next week. Probably keep one of the bitches.

She put coffee and biscuits on the table.

– So you and Vemund teamed up, Kai said, rubbing the palms of his hands up and down his thighs.

– You could put it like that. Vera nodded towards the kid and the dogs, as though that was the explanation.

He looked at her. She still had freckles all over her chubby face.

– See anything of Adrian? she asked suddenly. – Wasn't he your cousin?

For the third time she picked up the baby bottle, cleaned off the teat with her hand and shoved it back into the baby's gaping mouth.

– Why do you ask?

She shrugged.

– Spoke to him as recently as this morning, said Kai, just to keep the conversation going. – He's got something or other going in Iraq.

– I knew that, she answered. – Security work.

He hid how surprised he was. Tried to worm out of her how she knew. She stood up.

– I'll call Vemund. He should've been here by now.

He could hear her talking on the phone out in the corridor. Thought he heard his own name mentioned.

– He's out in the woods, she informed him when she came back. – But he's going to pop in. I'll get some grub ready.

She bent into the fridge and emerged with a casserole dish covered in cling film.

– You're very welcome to eat with us.

Ten minutes later, a van pulled up outside, a Transporter, Kai could see. Moments later, Vemund appeared in the kitchen doorway. He hadn't changed much either, still that same look of a sulky teenager, the eyes as red rimmed as ever, like a guy who didn't sleep well at night. Gone was the wispy hair, all shaved off.

Kai repeated what he had said to Vera. Not a word about what Sweaty had told him. Not a word about how Vemund had been beaten up by Karsten in the room directly above where they were now sitting. Not a word about Vemund swearing he would kill Karsten the first chance he got. As they ate, Vemund kept glancing over at him, clearly not particularly convinced by Kai's explanation for his visit, a story he probably found even thinner than the lapskaus stew they were eating.

After chewing the last piece of bacon and cleaning the bottom of his dish with a crust of bread, Vemund pushed it away and got to his feet.

– Ring before you come next time, he suggested, and Kai almost burst out laughing at the manifest lack of sincerity in the invitation. – Have to get back. Got a fence down. People wander around in these woods and completely ignore the fact that it's private land.

Kai acted as though he could take a hint and went out with him. They walked across the lawn.

– I take it you realise it's not just chance that brings me here.

– Oh really.

– Adrian says hello, by the way.

He didn't know why he said that; it was probably because Vera had mentioned him.

– Are you trying to tell me Adrian sent you?

– He said I should call in, he lied.

Vemund looked to be thinking. – Can't talk here, he said after a few moments.

– Why not?

Vemund nodded in the direction of the house behind them. Kai turned and saw Vera's face at the kitchen window. At the same moment he sensed a movement behind him. He raised his hand but that was as far as he got before he felt something being pressed into his back, and then a shower of needles sucked into his body and exploded inside his head.

26

THE WINDOW IN the upstairs room was wide open. Elsa closed it.

– It's important to air the room between every story I work on in here, she said.

Synne stood in the doorway. Afternoon light entered between the dark red curtains, and the smell of something sweet and burnt mingled with the smells of the spring day outside. *Maybe I should have done that. Not let all the stories get mixed up with each other but organised them, aired my inner rooms, got rid of old thoughts.*

Elsa lit a candle. – You're doing an important job, Synne. Daring to confront the burden you've been carrying along with you.

That sweet, spicy smell got stronger once the wick caught fire. Elsa spread six or seven cards out on the table in the shape of a cross. The cards were larger than normal playing cards. Dark blue on the reverse, with golden stars in different sizes. She turned over the first one. A cup, held up towards the sky by a hand. Columns of water emanating from it.

– Joy. Joy and love.

Several more cards were turned over. Synne felt something between confusion and calm. Each image gave rise to a little story that could be related to the other cards. Everything could be woven together into a comprehensible whole. *Writing is the same thing, trying to gather up the pieces of something that was once broken. Not being paralysed by doubt about what things are, what they want of me. If trees can't tell me who I am . . .*

Elsa turned the final card.

– The past.

At first Synne thought it was an image of the sun, but it had *The Moon* written on it.

– The Moon turned upside down is a bad card, Elsa informed her. – It means loss. In relation to your past, it's easy to connect it to Karsten, who disappeared and never came back.

A stern and closed face was depicted inside the yellow globe in the sky.

– The worst thing is that you never knew what happened to him. It lies there and is part of the past, and always will be.

– Will I never find out what happened?

Synne heard that she had asked the question in all seriousness. Elsa closed her eyes. Sat like that for a while, apparently in deep concentration, and yet relaxed.

– The most important thing right now is the asking. Not some answer or other we can work our way towards. You have to ask the question, and then enter it. What do you find in there? What is grief? What is guilt?

– Ought I to feel guilt? Synne asked in surprise, and knew that this lay at the heart of all her thoughts about Karsten.

– You alone know that, Synne.

– But I don't know what happened that evening. I don't know where Karsten was, I don't know where he went, whom he was with. The only thing I see in my imagination is that he was completely alone.

Again Elsa studied the cross of cards laid out on the deep red tablecloth.

– I believe he was too.

It is April, just before Easter. There are no leaves on the trees in the garden. The sun is somewhere above the river but not visible. Elsa sits watching me, waiting. She is so calm, it feels as though she contains everything. If she believes what I'm saying, then it's possible for me to believe it too.

– This same card appeared when I did a reading for Karsten, she said.

She pointed to the one in the centre of the cross. A burning tower, people falling from the top of it.

– It indicates a profound desire for change. But also something that might be dangerous for you. Tell me the first thing that comes into your head when you see this picture.

Without thinking, Synne said: – Just recently I've been remembering more.

– What have you remembered?

– Something about a room. I'm lying on a floor. A basement.

– Is it cold there?

– Not in the room, I don't think. I'm cold inside. And then Karsten comes.

– Where does he come?

– Through a door, someone opens it. And then he's standing in the middle of the floor, shouting.

– To you?

– I don't know . . . There's someone else there.

– Female? Male?

– The voice is deep. It's a man. He's saying something to Karsten.

Elsa shut her eyes tight as though trying to see the scene for herself. – Now we're approaching the limits of what you're able to remember, she said in a low voice.

Synne held her breath. – I must have been there, she whispered. – I must have been there when Karsten died.

The sinew in her temple began to throb.

– I can't, she mumbled, and noticed that she was shivering.

– Open your eyes, Synne.

She did as Elsa told her.

– Are you there?

– I saw him, Synne mumbled. – Suddenly it was very vivid.

Elsa laid a hand on her arm. – Now you're back here again. Feel where your breath is. Feel what you can smell. And hear, and see.

– Is that thing with the basement something I remember?

Elsa wrinkled her forehead. – It might have really happened. Or the basement might have a symbolic meaning. Whichever it is, those pictures are true for you.

– Will I remember any more?

– You're the only one who can answer that, Synne.

– But you can help me?

– If you wish. There is another method.

– Using the cards?

Elsa shook her head without taking her eyes off her. – Something more direct. We can find a way round whatever it is that is guarding your memory.

Synne pressed her hands against the sides of her head. Between each throb of pain, it felt both heavy and empty.

– Do you mean hypnosis?

– Something like that. It might be worth trying. You'll have to decide. But we won't go any further today. You're exhausted.

Afterwards, they sat downstairs in the living room again. Synne had told Elsa about her headache and had been given more of the three-year tea, and still the lightning flashed up through her temple.

– Drink more, it helps, said Elsa, and stroked her hair.

– Pain in the head increases the closer you get to the thing you've been carrying around with you all these years.

It sounded logical.

– I've often thought about Karsten too, Elsa continued. – So much happened to him so quickly that Easter. More than he could handle. Both Adrian and Kai warned him against being with that Pakistani girl.

Synne struggled to follow what she was saying. – Who is Kai?

Elsa blinked several times. – He was raised by Gunnhild. She lifted her teacup, put it down again. – My sister, she added. – She was ill and unable to take care of him any more. Since I came back, he's been living with me.

She stood up, and Synne had to do the same.

– Adrian's always trying to help other people, said Elsa. – But Karsten was in love. Or perhaps mostly very confused. When I read the cards for him, they told me a lot more than I was willing to say out loud. Since then, I've often thought I should have stayed home that Easter weekend.

– Would it have changed anything?

Elsa looked out of the window. – I don't know, Synne. There are forces that are way beyond our control. But something inside us tries to choose which of them we allow ourselves to be used by.

Synne hadn't the energy to feel if it was possible to see the world in such a way.

– Jasmeen Chadar says her brother killed Karsten, she said. – I met him. He told me he took Karsten to the river, that he was furious with him, but that he let him go.

Elsa nodded. – I think he's telling the truth.

27

WHAT HAVE YOU done with my head? Kai shouted. It was as though it was rolling about on the ground next to his body. He tried to turn; his arms wouldn't move, nor his legs. He had to vomit. His mouth was taped shut but it came anyway, a violent lurching that filled his mouth and spouted out through his nostrils. He twisted round, his face downwards. *Don't breathe,* he ordered himself. *If you breathe in now, you're finished.*

The car he was lying in came to a halt with the engine still running. He concentrated on getting enough air into his lungs. Remains of the stomach acid burned in his nose. Exhaust fumes mixed with the smell of dogs.

The boot was wrenched open abruptly.

– We're going to release your legs. If you keep still, we won't have to give you another dose.

It felt as if his eyebrows came off as the tape over his eyes was ripped away. Kai peered up at Vemund, who was holding the stun gun in one hand.

– Nice fucking mess you've made here.

The figure who appeared beside him looked big. He had long grey hair that was partially contained beneath a black cap.

Two pairs of hands took hold of Kai, lifted him out and leaned him up against the car. He made noises for them to remove the tape that was still covering his mouth.

– Shut up, Vemund hissed. – Or do you want me to break the teeth you have left?

Kai tried to nod that he understood, they were the ones in charge. He had to think tactically now; if he panicked, he wouldn't stand a chance. They wouldn't take him out there, not right next to the two cars. He still had some time, maybe a few minutes.

They were in a forest. The well-built guy pushed him through the trees, Vemund following. A few minutes later, they came to a lighting mast. Kai recognised it. Beyond the orange light he saw the outlines of the factory complex, the asphalt plant where Vemund used to work, the place where they'd had the combat exercise that Easter.

They clambered down a slope and emerged on to a works road. The quarry was a few hundred metres away. Kai could see a digger and something that looked like a drilling rig. They set off in the opposite direction.

After a few metres, he stopped and doubled over, pretending to be heaving again.

– Cunt wants to puke, said the big man, and Kai recognised the voice. He hadn't seen Noah since that Easter at Sæter's. He was big and unpredictable, but in poor physical shape. – Should we let him drown?

– No way am I going to drag that lump of meat around, answered Vemund, and took hold of Kai by the shoulder. – Fuck you.

He ripped the tape away from his mouth. Kai coughed and spluttered, doubled over again as though he was about to fall. Noah held him.

– You can walk yourself.

Kai staggered a couple of steps forward and then sank to his knees.

Vemund took a run at him and kicked him in the side. – You're not *that* bad. Get up.

The pain helped him to think more clearly. He no longer felt the nausea. Focused his mind on a single thought, held on to it as he groaned wordlessly and struggled back to his feet. Let his head hang, was careful to stumble even though he now had his balance and his strength back.

Noah was on one side of him, a pistol in his hand; it looked like a Colt. – If the cuckoo goes down one more time, I'm going to shoot.

– We're not going to shoot him, Vemund interrupted. – If he's got lead in him, the metal detector goes off and the stone crusher stops.

– Ah shit.

Noah walked on for a few more metres, turned again. – What about his teeth?

– We'll check them, knock them out if they've got fillings.

Noah shook his head. – You think of everything.

– Just don't want this bag of shit getting off too lightly, Vemund murmured. – He's going to suffer ten times more than Sweaty did by the time I'm finished with him.

They continued along the track, piles of fine-ground gravel covering the slope on the lower side. There was a shed a couple of hundred metres further on, with a platform behind it. Kai recognised it. Eight years ago, when Vemund showed them round the place, this was where the biggest stones were crushed. Kai had stood on the edge of the platform and looked down into the dark chasm. He remembered Vemund explaining how chipping and coarse gravel were made, how the most finely ground stone was then used in the production of asphalt.

He could hear hoarse breathing in his ear, like a great wind slowly picking up. It was his own breathing, and when Noah stepped out on to the platform, he slumped forward again, pretended he had collapsed. As he felt Vemund grab his arm, he spun round and rammed his head into his stomach. The skinny body snapped like a dry twig. Kai swung his arms, hit him above the temple with such force that he felt the pain all the way up to his shoulders.

Noah came at him from behind. Kai managed to turn, but the giant wrapped his arms around him, growling like a dog. Kai dug his teeth into his ear, tearing it from side to side. With a howl, he ripped it off. The hold broke; Noah staggered backwards, put his hands to his head, a thin shower of blood jetting through his fingers. Kai leapt forward and drove his foot into Noah's crotch. The giant collapsed like a folding deckchair, and Kai hammered his wrists down on to his exposed neck. Noah fell to the ground, flattened, but immediately started trying to get back to his feet.

Kai managed to grab up a stone. It was medium sized, with rough edges, and he was only just able to hold it in his taped hands. With Noah on his feet again and step-ping towards him, he raised his arms above his head and hurled the stone at the giant's face. Again Noah collapsed backwards, lay on his side. Kai kicked out at the side of his jaw, and connected so hard that suddenly the point of Noah's chin was bulging out of his cheek on the other side. He landed a few more kicks before grabbing Noah's jacket and tipping the huge body over the side of the platform. It rolled down the chute, and there was a thud as it hit the base of the crusher, followed by an avalanche of stones.

Vemund was still lying where he had fallen. Kai limped over to him, pressed his foot against his neck, spat out a few lumps that were probably gristle and blood. – Now I'm going to kill you, he said, so calmly that it almost made him laugh out loud. And for a moment he could feel how easy it would be to lift his foot and tread down on that defence-less larynx. He forced himself to wait.

– Get out your knife.

– Ain't got one, Vemund groaned.

Kai pressed down with his foot. There was a whistling sound from beneath him, and Vemund fumbled a flick knife out of his pocket. Kai kicked it out of his hand, picked it up, held the handle between his knees, sprung the blade and starting filing through the tape, all the time keeping his eyes on Vemund.

– Just got a few questions for you, he wheezed.

With his hands free, he picked up the stun gun and pressed it against Vemund's throat. Fired once there, once in the ribcage, another one in the back. Bent over and looked at the face, the storm of little twitches that came and went.

– A few questions I want you to answer. Why the hell do you have to make it so difficult?

Kai found the car keys in Vemund's jacket pocket. He shoved him into the passenger seat; Vemund lay there like a bundle of clothing.

There was a towel in the back seat. It stank of dog, but it was all he had. He got into the driver's seat, switched on the interior lighting, looked at himself in the mirror. Blood dribbled from a cut on his cheek, but otherwise most of the blood wasn't from him.

Once he'd wiped off everything that hadn't coagulated, he turned towards the slumped shape.

– Now the two of us are going to have a chat, he said.
– It's going to go like this. I ask questions, and you answer them.

He could see in Vemund's eyes that he understood.

– We can get this over with in just a few minutes, he went on, noticing how mild his own voice sounded. – But if I have to use this . . . he prodded the pistol into Vemund's stomach, – then it's going to take us quite a bit longer. Your choice. I'm in no hurry.

Still no answer.

– Maybe we'd better go back to your place and have a word with Vera and the little one, would you like that?

– No, Vemund murmured.

– Okay, we'll try and get it sorted out here then. Keep the wife and kid and dogs out of it.

He started the engine, left it running.

– We're going to talk about the evening Karsten Clausen disappeared, he said, prodding Vemund again with the barrel of the gun. – You still with us?

Vemund groaned. With a little goodwill, it might have sounded like a *yes*.

– The first question is, what did Karsten say to you that evening?

– I never spoke to him.

Kai suddenly jabbed the barrel of the stun gun into Vemund's neck.

– This is going to hurt. I really don't think this is what you want. I know you were the one who bumped off Karsten Clausen. I know you got Sweaty to fetch his sister and drive her home.

As he was speaking, he remembered something Sweaty had said.

– I also know you took photographs of what happened that night. And I intend to get a look at them. My question is, what did Karsten say to you while he was still in a condition to speak?

Vemund tried to lift his head; it flopped down on to his chest again.

– He didn't say nothing. He was dead when I got there.

28

PEPSI WAS THERE before the first piece of fish had reached the bottom of the food dish. The dog wasn't interested in dried food any more, would only eat the same as they ate. The vet had told them she had an allergy and shouldn't eat fish, but Dan-Levi liked to sneak her some of the leftovers. He could never get used to the idea of throwing away good food.

Afterwards he parked Ruth and Rebekah in front of the TV. Another emergency solution, because Sara was at a parents' meeting and Ruben had asked for help with a written assignment. And then there was Rakel. He ought to have sat down beside her and listened to what she had to say. What had happened at school, or on the way to school. Or what hadn't happened. Why she hadn't been with her classmates for the whole of that week.

The phone rang. He was on the point of turning off the sound, but when he looked at the display, he felt he had to take it.

– Am I disturbing you? asked Synne.

Dan-Levi put the plate of fish on the cooker and shut the door to the TV room, where Ruth and Rebekah were arguing about which channel to watch.

– Quite all right, he said, trying to keep the stress out of his voice. – How's the writing going?

He knew that was the worst thing you could ask a writer,

and added: – This won't be an interview, I promise you. He gave an embarrassed little laugh.

– It's difficult, she said. – Difficult in a way I hadn't expected. I don't think I'm going to carry on with it.

In the living room, the girls were involved in a full-scale quarrel.

– Excuse me just a moment. Dan-Levi opened the door wide and spent the next thirty seconds arbitrating. He was only partially successful; neither one was satisfied with the solution. He shut out the protests and returned to the conversation.

– I'll call later, Synne offered, but he said that wasn't necessary.

– You're surely not considering abandoning the whole idea? She didn't answer that.

– Shahzad Chadar was going to kill Karsten, she said after a pause. – But he didn't do it.

Dan-Levi took off his glasses, and while Synne told him about Shahzad's visit to the stables, he peered out through the dining-room window at the vague contours of the trees in the garden. Sometimes it was almost a relief not to see things in sharp outline.

– He might have taken you to the river to make a lie seem more credible, he objected once she had finished.

It sounded as if the same thought had occurred to her.

– Do you believe in coincidences, Dan-Levi?

He hesitated. – It's a useful word on occasion.

– I've been to see a woman who reads the cards. She's the mother of Adrian, who knew Karsten.

He sat down on the stairs. – You mean Elsa Wilkins.

– Do you know her?

He told her about the interview. That she had read the cards for him too. But not a word about the Lovers upside down.

– Adrian was one of Karsten's best friends, Synne went on. – One of the few he had. Adrian and his cousin helped Karsten when his life was threatened.

A thought was circling round in Dan-Levi's head. It took a few seconds for it to land somewhere he could get hold of it.

– So you're saying Karsten knew this cousin. Do you know anything about him?

– His name is Kai. At least I think he's Adrian's cousin. Elsa said he grew up at her sister's.

– Gunnhild?

At that moment, an ominous sound came from the kitchen and Dan-Levi ended the conversation. Even before opening the door, he knew what had happened and was preparing himself to see the floor covered in pieces of fish and broken plate, with a very happy dog snuffling about sorting one from the other.

Rakel helped him to tidy up. Every accident could be turned into something good, he liked to think. The good on this occasion was that it gave him a little more time with her.

– Here's the rest, said Rakel as she offered him a handful of smashed fragments. – Maybe it can be glued together.

– Probably not, he announced.

– You mustn't be angry with Pepsi, she said.

He patted her on the head. – Pepsi is an animal. Animals aren't responsible for their actions in the same way you and I are.

Rakel looked him straight in the eye. He had often thought she had the eyes of an old woman.

– I had the same dream again last night.

He shivered. – Not that one about Pepsi?

She shook her head, and he noticed he breathed easier.

– The other one I told you about. That you've been away a very long time. I dreamed that I crept into the secret room. Then I heard you outside the house and I ran out, but they had ruined you so badly that I didn't recognise you.

For a few moments Dan-Levi stood there staring straight ahead. Then he put the pieces of the broken dish into a milk carton and squashed it down into the rubbish basket. When he stood up again, he saw that his daughter had tears in her eyes. He hugged her tightly.

– Show me this secret room of ours, he said.

– You've already seen it.

– I want to see it again.

He followed her upstairs. She took the torch out of her desk drawer, crawled in underneath the clothes and removed the plank.

– Didn't you say there was something written on the wall in there? Bad thoughts?

She handed him the torch. He put his arm into the opening, then squeezed his head and upper body through. There was a smell of damp, but when he shone the torch, he didn't see any signs of it. All he saw were a few dark patches on one of the beams. He wriggled so close that he had to take off his glasses. The patches were scorch marks, framing words that had been cut into the wood. *Fire Man come tak them hom with you.* He discovered more on another beam. He had to use his fingertips to read them. *Elsa*, it said. Those four letters repeated over and over again in a descending column.

He crawled out again, ended up squatting on his haunches and peering between the clothes in the cupboard. Rakel was sitting on the side of the bed and didn't say a word. He could hear Sara downstairs in the hall. She shouted something, probably very annoyed that the two little ones still weren't in bed. Directly afterwards, her footsteps on the stairs. He could tell from them how irritated she was and pre-empted her.

– I have to go to the office, he said. – Yes, it's important. No, it can't wait until tomorrow.

29

KAI PULLED UP next to the garage. He saw Elsa's car in there. Another car parked outside, a dark blue Audi. Rental, he noted when he took a closer look at it. He stayed out in the yard for a minute or two. There was a change of weather in the air, warm spring winds sweeping from the marsh down by the river. In the darkness above him, clouds raced by like a herd of animals without a leader.

She didn't answer when he rang. He went into the back garden. The light was on in her workroom. He could see shadows moving within up there.

He let himself in. In the hallway, he looked in the mirror. There was still blood coming from the cut in his cheek, and above one eye was a bulge the size of a golf ball. The front of his shirt was soaked with the blood of another man.

– Hallo, he called up the stairs.

No response, but he had to go up. He stopped outside the room, heard subdued voices inside. He told himself he shouldn't go in. Not even if she was alone should he go in there. And now there was someone with her. He knew who it was and pushed open the door.

The room was lit by small candles on the table. She was sitting in one chair, her legs tucked underneath, Adrian in the other. She gave no sign of surprise at all at what Kai looked like as he stood there.

– Is that you? she said, and her voice sank down towards

the ground, down beneath the ground, to the place where he lived.

He wasn't invited in, could have backed out again, run down the stairs. He stood there on the threshold.

Adrian pointed to the third chair. – Sit down, he said.

The voice was commanding, a prince to an underling. Kai didn't move.

– Sit down, Elsa repeated, and then he couldn't resist, slipped down on to the outer edge of the chair, ready to leap up, overturn the table, grab hold of the candlestick and spread flames around the room, through the whole house.

– I hear you've been talking to Vemund, said Adrian.

– Yes, that's exactly what I've done, he answered in a voice much too loud. He tried to keep it quieter, couldn't. – Now I know everything I need to know about you, little brother.

Adrian gave Elsa a look, one eyebrow raised.

– You *think* you know, she corrected him.

Kai felt a shuddering inside his chest; it spread up into his throat.

– He killed Karsten, he shouted, pointing at Adrian. – Adrian killed Karsten Clausen. He got him in his car and he beat him to death.

Elsa stood up and gave him a slap. It happened so quickly he didn't have time to lift his arm. And so slowly that he saw it coming, had always seen it coming.

– I will not allow you to talk like that, she hissed, and sat down again.

The candlestick was standing right next to his hand. He could set her clothes alight. Stay there with her until everything was burned up. Because they belonged together; without her he was nothing.

– You don't decide what I can say.

His voice had become alien, as though the words were being said through him.

– Listen to me, he howled. He stood in front of her, but he didn't touch her, and Adrian sat there quite calmly. – Listen to me, he howled again, but he saw no fear in her face. – Now I'm going to tell you what happened that night.

She didn't respond.

– Synne Clausen was here. Adrian had called her. The girl was thirteen years old. Do you understand? Your son, Adrian, the one who's going to save the world, had a thirteen-year-old girl *visiting here*.

Still no response.

– Karsten arrived. Somehow or other he knew his sister was in the house.

– Her bike, Elsa interrupted. – He saw her bike outside.

Kai slumped back down into his chair. – You knew?

– Adrian has told me everything.

He stared at her. – Has he told you she was lying half naked in the back of the car? Vemund had to help her on with her jacket and pullover.

Elsa waved her hand dismissively. – She came here of her own free will, took her clothes off without Adrian knowing anything about it. She was in love and she misunderstood what was just meant as friendliness.

– You weren't there, Kai raged. – You don't know anything. He killed Karsten to hide the fact that he was having it away with his little sister. If Karsten had gone to the police, there would have been precious little left of your prince. He gave Vemund a job in his firm and paid the guy a bloody king's ransom to keep his mouth shut.

Elsa shook her head. – You've never understood anything. You've never managed to make anything at all of your life.

Kai pulled a memory stick out of his pocket. – Here are photographs of everything that happened that night. Vemund took them so that Adrian wouldn't trick him.

He offered it to her; she didn't take it.

– Adrian says he has no blame in what happened to Karsten. I believe him.

She laid her hand over Adrian's, but Kai had kept his ace to the last. Now he flung it into her face.

– Has he told you that he told Vemund to get rid of me? That he paid someone to have his own brother killed?

She lifted her arms in exasperation. – You're exaggerating. As usual.

– Look at these pictures, he shouted, holding the memory stick in front of her. – It's the worst thing I've ever seen. Do you know what Adrian did to Karsten?

– You were the one who was after Karsten, she interrupted. – He found out what you were up to. It's the most primitive and disgusting thing I've ever heard. We've kept it to ourselves all these years. The only thing you can do for me now is to leave Adrian in peace.

She leaned across the table towards him.

– If you don't, we'll tell the police what we know about you.

He reached for the candlestick, but his hand had withered.

– *He* has a life, she said calmly. – If you destroy that, I never want to have anything to do with you again.

She stared at him until he had to look away. The sweet scent of the incense seeped from the walls and into him. This was the room in which she told people what they should do with their lives. He'd sat here many times himself and seen his own fate laid out across the table. His task was to follow Adrian, help Adrian, protect Adrian when he needed it, make himself invisible when there was no longer any use for him.

– You knew, he mumbled. – You know they were going to kill me.

– Now go, she said.

He glanced up. Adrian sat half turned away and looking out of the window.

– Go, she said again. – You will never, ever say a word about this to anyone.

Finally he managed to get to his feet, out on to the landing.

– And those pictures you've got there, you're to destroy them, every single one.

As he reached the foot of the stairs, he heard the door being shut.

He sat in his room. Couldn't even face closing the curtains. In the dark sky above, the clouds had been piled into a mass and pushed down over the river. He sat for an hour, maybe longer. He heard a car engine starting down in the yard. Without looking, he knew that it was Adrian leaving. Maybe off to London, or Birmingham, or Basra. Or maybe it was just a quick trip out. Maybe he had returned to stay. Live in the house with Elsa, be her son, be the prince she'd waited for, the one she lived for. He opened a drawer, removed a packet of cigarettes, some elastic bands and lengths of string. His thoughts journeyed on into the darkness as he began putting the pieces together.

After he had made five of them, he turned to his computer, woke it, clicked on the path to Synne Clausen's machine. There he opened a new document. *How Karsten died*, he called it.

He began to type with two fingers.

It took Dan-Levi nearly three quarters of an hour to get hold of a key to the archives. By the time he unlocked the bomb shelter in the basement of the newspaper's office, it was quarter past ten.

It would be inaccurate to say that the paper had invested a lot of money in making things efficient down there. To get to the card indexes, he had to move aside a computer from a previous century, a punctured tyre and a sack of topsoil. After searching for a while, he found four cards on Furutunet and started looking in the cuttings folders, created in an era when online newspapers were the stuff of science fiction. He started when he saw one of the headlines: *Two near-fires in one week*. The article was from the autumn of 1991. The fire brigade had been called out, but in neither case did a serious incident develop. Nothing was said about the causes of the fires. At the foot of the page was a brief interview with the head of the remand home.

Up in the editorial office, he grabbed a cup of coffee. The news editor and a couple of online journalists were bent over a desk at the far end of the room. None of them looked up. Once he was online, he navigated to the phone book, glanced at the clock, decided to risk making a call.

The person who answered sounded like an old woman. Dan-Levi introduced himself, said he was writing a piece about unsolved cases of arson in Romerike. Which was not too far from the truth.

– I can't tell you anything about former residents of Furutunet, the woman answered in response to his question. – I am sure you'll understand that.

It was what Dan-Levi had expected. He stressed that he fully respected her duty of confidentiality.

– I'd just like you to think about whether there might have been a connection between the fire eight years ago and those two incidents back in nineteen ninety-one when fires nearly broke out.

Silence at the other end. Then she said:

– We had our suspicions. These things do happen in my line of work.

– Were these attempted arson attacks reported?

– We wrote a formal note of concern.

– To whom?

– The county children's services.

– Were the police brought in?

– I'm sure we considered it, but I don't know what happened in the end.

After hanging up, Dan-Levi spread out the sheet of paper with his solar association diagram on it, pencilled in a new ray and added the thought that had been circling around in his head the whole evening: *Gunnhild Hammer's son Kai, adopted. Sent to an institution when his adoptive mother became ill.*

He sat there studying the diagram. Suddenly he picked up his mobile phone and called Elsa Wilkins' number. She didn't answer. He Googled her website, called the number given there.

– Elsa's tarot service.

He apologised for using that number to contact her and for calling so late, apologised for calling at all.

– Then you don't want me to read the cards for you again?

– I'll get back to you on that. Right now, I have another question I'd like to ask you.

– I'd prefer it if you called me on my private number. When I'm not working. You know what it costs to use this?

He apologised again, even though he was the one who would be paying for the call.

– You sound uneasy, she observed.

– A bit stressed out, that's all, I'm still at the office. And I came across something I have to ask you about. I asked you last time we spoke as well. But you were interrupted.

Silence at the other end. He still hadn't said anything that was not actually true.

– I found out that your sister and her husband once lived in the house we now live in, so that means her adopted son Kai must also have lived there.

– What does this have to do with me? Elsa interrupted.

Dan-Levi felt a drop of sweat trickling down his back.
— I'm not quite sure, but it would help me if you could answer one question in particular.

— All right.

— Kai Hammer spent some time in a remand home. I was wondering if he was there at the same time as someone else I know.

Now he *was* lying. His ear was burning. He switched the receiver to the other side. Maybe this was how the Jesuits felt, at least in the beginning.

— Dan-Levi, I really don't know where you're going with this.

He realised he was heading full speed into a dead-end street and asked straight out: — Was he at Furutunet up in Nannestad?

She sighed. — I really can't remember. I wasn't even living in this country at the time.

Kai turned off straight after the roundabout and headed up the side road towards the low buildings grouped at the top of the hill. He left the car in the almost empty parking lot. For almost ten minutes he waited around the corner from the entrance to the nursing home. At last someone came out. The automatic door remained open and buzzing after them, and just before it closed, he slipped out of the shadows and glided through.

The smell in the corridor was even more overpowering than the previous time he had been here, urine and faeces and disinfectant. Two decrepit old men sat in front of a TV in the day room, maybe the same two as last time, and the screen was still black. No one else in sight. Kai slipped down the corridor, away from the ward office.

The window in Khalid Chadar's room was slightly open, and somewhere in among the stench coming from the bed was a waft of fresh evening air. For an instant Kai felt relief that he would never end up like this, floating around in his own bodily fluids.

He heard Khalid Chadar breathing and turned on the bedside lamp. The thin body jerked, the eyes opened immediately. In the dull light, the membranes were amber yellow. Khalid lay there looking up at him. Waiting perhaps to be turned, or for something to drink. On the bedside table, next to the photograph of the two boys and the man in the turban, was a glass. Kai picked it up and held it against the old man's lips, tipped it, tipped too much. A gurgling sound came from Khalid Chadar's throat, and beneath the yellow membrane his eyes widened.

Kai put the glass down. – You don't know who I am?

Khalid blinked, but his face didn't change at all.

– You're my father, did you know that?

No reaction.

– My father, Kai repeated.

Khalid Chadar's cracked lips moved slightly. Water trickled from the corners of his mouth.

– You probably know what Mr Wilkins in Birmingham did when he found out who the bastard's father was. He kicked Elsa out.

He looked over towards the balcony. A bird carved from wood was fastened to the railing; he felt he wanted to pull it off and toss it away into the darkness.

– All of that happened because you hung around her, followed her everywhere, forced yourself on her. In the stable, among the horses . . .

He stood there a while longer, looking down at the old man. Then he opened Khalid Chadar's mouth and poured more water into it. Emptied the whole jug down his throat, pulled the duvet over the gurgling, staring face and slipped away.

* * *

A thin sliver of moon was visible above the river as he walked down Erleveien. Only one thing left now, he thought, and when had he last felt this calm, this relaxed? The garage door was wide open and the journalist's car wasn't there. He knew how he was going to do it. It had thought itself out inside him.

– Now you'd best tell me what it is you're up to, Dan-Levi, exclaimed Solveig at the other end of the phone, her voice sounding beyond exasperation.

While he told her what he had discovered about the fires, he played with the associative diagram that lay spread on the desk in front of him.

When he had finished she said: – Well that sounds completely crazy.

He knew that. – You don't have to believe me, Solveig, he said in his own defence. – I'm only asking you to do me a favour. You must know someone who worked in Vollen nursery school before you. I want to know if Kai Hammer went there. This must have been in the early eighties.

– Have you talked to the police? she asked.

He mentioned his conversation with Roar Horvath. – I need to find out about Vollen before I call him again. Can you help me?

– I'll make a couple of phone calls. This is important, Dan-Levi.

He knew it, but it wasn't until she said it that he realised the extent of what he was involved in. He turned the piece of paper over and made a new diagram. In the centre he wrote *Kai Hammer.*

Kai used one of the bottles of lighter fluid on the garden shed. He took his time, allowed it to soak into the dry woodwork, put down three ignition devices. He glanced at his watch. Twenty to eleven. He crouched in the corner, unscrewed the top again, inhaled the smell. Purity through fire, he thought. Elsa's words. She didn't know what they would lead to. He was the one to show her.

Almost fifteen minutes passed. He heard the sound of the front door opening, and then the voice of the woman of the house. He knew her name, but stopped himself from thinking it. She said something to the dog, clearly trying to get it to calm down. It must have picked up the scent of the lighter fluid, and for a moment he feared its nose would lead it out to the shed where he was waiting. He thought he could hear it by the corner of the house, snuffling and straining, but the woman jerked it back, and shortly afterwards he saw her silhouette out on the road.

He lit all three devices, glided away round the house. He had a key, didn't know if it would still fit after eight years, but the woman hadn't locked the door. He let himself in without making a sound, made his way up the stairs that were so familiar to him. Nameplates hung on several of the doors now, but he avoided relating to any names. A girl was living in his room. He could smell it even though she hadn't yet started using deodorant and perfume, and he realised at once that it was the girl he had met that time, the little one who was so thirsty and who thought the stranger had come to give her a drink.

How lightly children breathe, he thought as he stood beside the bed. You can only hear a tiny bit of it, where it ends and lets go. He stood there listening to it, because all sounds and smells had a final meaning now, and they were pointing to one thing only.

He prised the cupboard door open. Mostly children's clothes in there, felt like frocks and blouses, and small shoes arranged on the floor. He removed the plank covering the hidden room, switched on his torch and in the cone of light saw again what he had once scratched there. There was something else there too, written in pen and in another hand; maybe that thirsty girl who was asleep right behind him. *I shall not burn.*

Three minutes had passed since the woman left the house. He had very little time left. He pulled out the other bottle, sprayed the surfaces in the secret room, the clothes in the cupboard. Some dripped on to his hands, some on to his face. He had to laugh. The cleansing fluid burnt his eyes; he rubbed it into his cheeks, into his hair.

– Are you an angel too?

He jumped. Stuck his head out, looked up at the girl standing there in a white nightdress.

– What is that smell in here?

He took out his lighter. – Go away. Get out of here. Get out of the house.

– I can't go anywhere. It's dark.

– Yes, he said, – it's dark.

It was fifteen minutes before Solveig rang back. She sounded out of breath.

– Kai Hammer did go to the nursery school.

– He did? Dan-Levi added *Vollen* to his solar diagram.

– He was a strange child, Solveig continued. – They were worried about him. But there wasn't really much they could do. His adoptive parents didn't want anyone else getting involved. Quite an unusual story. Kai was actually the son of Gunnhild Hammer's younger sister.

Dan-Levi was on his feet. – He's Elsa's son?

– Do you know her?

He was too agitated to answer.

– She had a child as a teenager, said Solveig. – The father was apparently a Pakistani who lived on the farm for a while. It was all hushed up.

Dan-Levi bent over his diagram. With an unsteady hand he added another ray. *Khalid Chadar, sweet shop.*

– Are you still there?

He confirmed that he was as he walked around the office and came back to his desk again.

– Solveig, I'm going to have to hang up now.

– There's something else.

He was suddenly unsure whether he wanted to hear anything else.

– I know someone who knows someone who knows someone, Solveig began. – It ended with me calling her. She worked at Furutunet in the early nineties.

He knew what was coming.

– One summer, fires broke out on a number of occasions. They were pretty sure which of the kids was capable of something like that, but they could never prove it. He was removed from the home shortly afterwards. His biological mother, Gunnhild's sister, was back in the country and said she would have him.

After he'd hung up, Dan-Levi sat there studying the diagram, reading the last thing he had added to it. A thought took possession of him. If it was not Karsten who had dropped the ignition device back then, it must have been someone else. *Kai Hammer grew up in our house,* he wrote, then folded the sheet of paper and put it in his pocket. The time was now five past eleven. He called Roar's number, got no reply. Doubted whether his friend had gone to bed that early. Sent a text. *I know who started the fires. And who killed Karsten?*

He was on the way out to his car when the phone rang. He grabbed it, but it wasn't Roar.

– This is your neighbour.

Which neighbour? he was on the point of asking.

– Listen, I'm on the road outside. Sara's going crazy . . . an ambulance is on its way.

– Ambulance? he shouted.

– A fire engine too, just coming round the bend.

Dan-Levi could hear the distant sound of sirens, and a few moments later heard them on the phone.

– I didn't see you here, that's why I'm calling. Your house is on fire.

He didn't notice that he was tugging at the car door handle. It was locked. He fiddled with his keys, jumped in, started the engine, backed into a lamp post, still with the phone held to his ear.

– The kids, he managed to say. – Sara.

– Not quite sure what's going on, said the neighbour. – I think it's best you get over here.

He raced down Fetveien. There was a queue at the traffic lights, and he sat there revving the engine with the clutch in. Finally he let go, laid over on to the other side of the road and sped across on red. He'd tossed the phone down. The neighbour was still talking away on it.

He'd been on emergency call-outs before, in the days when his job was writing about accidents. He'd covered several fires. Now the photos he'd taken came flickering back to him. He was unable to keep them out, and he howled at the car in front that had braked and was now standing still in the middle of the road.

Erleveien was cordoned off. A policewoman in a high-visibility jacket waved for him to go back.

– I live there, he shouted through the window.

– I understand, she said, – but you can't come past, your car will block the way for the rescue services.

For a moment he considered just putting his foot hard down and driving through the tape, but at the last moment he wrenched the gearstick into reverse and backed up on to the pavement.

– This road is closed, the policewoman said again, but

he ran past her and kept running. There was a smell of open fire and burnt pitch. He saw the house. Smoke leaking from it, but not much. Then a thin flame leaping up the rear of the house, a yellow gash across the dark grey sky.

Two huge fire engines were positioned across the road, forming a new barrier. There was a group of people in the garden on the other side.

– Dan!

Sara came running up, clung to him, her whole body shaking, unable to speak.

– The children?

One of the neighbours came across.

– The children? he repeated.

– Ruben's at a friend's house, said the neighbour.

– The girls?

– The two youngest are at our house.

Suddenly Dan-Levi shouted out: – Rakel?

He looked down into Sara's eyes. She shook her head.

– We've told the firefighters there's one missing, the neighbour said.

– Missing? Dan-Levi screamed. – Have they been inside and looked for her?

He turned towards the house. Black smoke was rolling out of the living-room windows.

– They'll probably go in as soon as possible.

It took three seconds for the meaning of the words to sink in. Then the thought hit.

– I know where she is, he shouted to Sara.

She stared at him as though what he said had not got through to her. Dan-Levi broke away, ran across the road.

A loud voice behind him: – Hey, you, get the hell away from there.

The hell away, Dan-Levi repeated, get the hell away. The

words echoed round his head as he bounded up the steps. The front door was ajar; he swung it wide open.

There was hardly any smoke in the entry. He took a deep breath, opened the door to the hallway. A wall of blackness met him; he felt as if his eyes were boiling. He shut them tight, pulled off his jacket, pressed it against his face, threw himself to the ground and began crawling into the blackness.

Maybe two metres over to the staircase. Something was happening to his hair; it felt like it was melting. He forced himself not to breathe, hauled himself up on to the first step. There were fourteen to the top. He counted them. At four, he had to stop. Tried to call out to her, but it wasn't possible to open his mouth. A foaming sound in his ears, something running inside them, and then the pain. Rakel, he thought, and brought her face into his mind. That frightened little face as she lay in the dark, the tiny ears, the little voice. He made it to the topmost step, could no longer think. Right, he kept telling himself, second door. He wriggled his way in, and the wall of smoke seemed to be even denser, the floor so hot he couldn't touch it.

With all the strength he still had left, he kicked himself forward off the wall, reached the corner of the cupboard. Something had wedged itself beneath the door, a shoe. He pulled and pulled at it. It was stuck to a leg and didn't move. Now he had to open his mouth to the blackness. Rakel, he breathed as his whole chest filled with acrid froth.

30

SYNNE WOKE FROM her reverie, realised she was still standing by the window, looking up at the sky above the roof of the block opposite. She registered the sounds from the adjoining rooms, heard her neighbour's TV. The late evening news was beginning. It was just after eleven; she had been standing there miles away for over half an hour.

She slumped down in front of the machine again, sat there resting her forehead in her hands watching the screen saver go through its cycle, the wave patterns that dissolved, re-formed, dissolved again. She had tried four or five times to write about the evening Karsten disappeared. If she tried again, she would have to start writing about herself in the third person.

She was at Tamara's house, supposed to be sleeping over but changed her mind. Suddenly she had to leave.

Who did you call, Synne?

You know who it was.

Synne pulls on her jacket. It's pale blue. Her boots have laces with two buckles at the top.

It's windy out. The kind of spring wind she loves to feel in her face, in her hair, the kind she lies and listens to in the evening when she's falling asleep, a wind that sings in a low voice and wraps itself around her.

Where are you going, Synne?

You know where I'm going.

Something missing here. She rides away, but can't see

herself doing so. Remembers the wind, the drizzle in the air just moistening her face, a patch of snow in a wayside ditch. Can't get any further than that.

Karsten comes through the door.

What's she doing here? he shouts. What is Synne doing here?

He's not shouting at her but at the man bending over her.

Synne is lying on the floor. Why has she taken her clothes off?

You know why she has.

She sat there looking through what she had written. Felt far away. The pain in her head had increased as the day went by; she couldn't seem to shake it. It stung at a point on the outside of her ear and moved backwards in waves. She should go to bed. Take some paracetamol.

She closed the document she had been working on, put it in the Karsten folder. Next to it was another document. *How Karsten died.* A title like that would never have occurred to her. She leaned forward, touched the screen with her index finger as though to see if it was something that could be wiped away. Her phone rang; she fumbled it out of her pocket. It was her father. She couldn't talk to him now but had to take it.

– Synne, he said, and in just the short sound of her name she could hear that something was terribly wrong. Even though he kept his voice low, it sounded as if he was shouting. – There's a fire.

– At your house? she shouted back.

– No, no. I can see it from the living-room window. Loads of people out there, fire engines. The whole house is in flames.

For an instant, before the pain resumed its free flow, her head cleared.

– I'm coming, she said, and realised that was what he wanted. That he was afraid and that he had no one else but her.

– Take a taxi, he said indistinctly. – I'll pay.

As they swung on to Fetveien, she heard the sirens.

– Apparently there's a fire over in Kjeller, the taxi driver said.

– Really? she muttered, crushing a torn paper handkerchief between her fingers.

Cars were queuing at Vestenga.

– Drop me off here, she said.

Smoke flowed across the sky like a black river, darker than darkness. She headed nervously up the hill. The entrance to Erleveien was closed off by a police car. People were swarming round it.

– You can't come in here. A uniformed woman blocked her way.

– My father lives up there. He's alone.

– You'll have to take another route.

She stepped up to the copse, took the path down between the gardens on the far side, and suddenly found herself looking directly down on to the burning roof. Sparks were shooting up into the green-grey night, as though someone with enormous lungs was lying inside the house, breathing. Only now did it finally dawn on her which house it was: it was where Dan-Levi and Sara and their four children lived. She stopped at the end of a fence. People were standing in their gardens, staring. Some in small groups, some alone.

– Did everyone get out? she asked someone, a woman in a tracksuit.

She shook her head. – They think there's someone in there.

A man in a leather jacket turned suddenly and looked at her. – Do you know them?

She couldn't answer, staggered back along the fence, back along the path between the houses. Couldn't stand to see any more, couldn't stand to leave. The pain streaming through her head grew worse; it was draining away all her strength.

Mustn't disappear now, she thought.

– Are you okay?

She had sat down in the wet grass and a man was bending over her. In the dark she couldn't see him properly, got the impression it might have been the person who'd spoken to her a couple of minutes earlier.

– I know you, she said indistinctly, but that wasn't what she meant to say; it was Dan-Levi she knew, and for some reason or other this man needed to know that.

– Maybe so, he said. He took her hand and helped her up. She held on to the sleeve of his leather jacket, afraid to let go.

– You aren't well.

Pain flashed into the grey darkness like the beams from a lighthouse. She raised her face and tried to look into his eyes. – I'm Synne. Karsten's sister.

Part of her realised how crazy this must sound. But he nodded. – I'll help you. You need a doctor.

She was still holding on tight to the sleeve of his jacket. Now he put his arm around her, steadied her as they walked down the hill. I have to get home, she said, but neither of them could hear it.

He took her to the Statoil petrol station, opened the door of a dark blue car. This is the same car, she thought, but she had nowhere to catch the thought, nowhere to put it, and it disappeared again. He helped her into the front seat, got in behind the wheel, didn't start the engine, didn't ask where she was going. She laid her head back and closed her eyes.

– I know the people who own that house, she said after a while. She pressed her hands against the pounding in her head, as though it would break apart if she didn't hold it together. – I know you too, I know your voice.

She thought he nodded, had to see him, reached out a hand and switched on the interior light.

She had imagined so many pictures, but he was unlike any of those she remembered. The hair thinner. The facial features sharper, the nose more crooked. She noticed all of this in the first glance. It was the eyes she recognised; they were unchanged, dark, almost black. But they were not smiling at her as she had always imagined they would be.

– Synne, he said, and she suddenly had the idea that she was asleep, she had to wake up, get out of there.

Suddenly she realised he was holding her hand.

– Adrian, she managed to say, and with that their names were once more bound together. Synne, Adrian.

– You came back, she heard herself say.

He flashed a quick smile at her, and that caused new images to float up, and a rain of thoughts that flew in all directions.

– Something I had to sort out. I'm not staying long.

– How long?

– I'm leaving tonight. Would have left already except I saw there was a fire.

– Where are you going?

– Gothenburg. And then flying on from there. He squeezed her hand. – I hear you published a book.

– Just some poems, she stammered.

He smiled again, broader this time. – That's how I remember you. You never believed that what you said or thought was of any importance.

– I was thirteen. Why did you want to meet me?

A wrinkle appeared in his brow.

– I was thirteen, she repeated, and at that moment she realised that she was about to tell him everything she remembered, and everything she still hadn't yet managed to remember.

– I was at Tamara's. I called, you asked me to come round to your place.

He looked out through the windscreen, up at the Statoil sign shining above them. Close by, a siren started up, an ambulance; it flashed by, but the sound didn't fade, it carried on inside her head.

– You were a special girl, he said. – Different from all the others. You still are.

He leaned over to her, stroked her cheek. The smell of him was everywhere, the smell of leather, of his skin. I'm thirteen years old, she thought suddenly. Even if this kills me, it's what I want.

But then something else appeared. She tried to keep it away.

– Karsten came, she said, and couldn't take it back.

He loosened his hold on her hand; she wouldn't let go of him.

– Will you do something for me? she heard him say, and when she didn't answer, he said it again, said her name too. – Will you do something for me, Synne?

She could feel his breath on her face, his mouth coming closer. Maybe he said her name several times, maybe it was the echo in her thoughts: Synne, Synne.

– That was the worst night of my life, he said. – Will you help me to forget it?

Was he asking for help? – It was you, she murmured. – You were in the room when Karsten came in. It was you he was shouting at.

She could see it now, a film flickering and juddering, but now with a soundtrack.

– He was furious, he attacked you. You grabbed him and pushed him to the floor.

His mouth was very close now, the lips brushing against her ear.

– Yes, I pushed him to the floor.

She saw him raise his fist. – Did you hit him?

He put his arm around her, pulled her close to him.

– I hit him, he said in a low voice. – I kept on hitting him until he was dead.

– I was there. I saw it.

– You were lying right next to him. And no one else in the world knows. Just you and me, Synne.

He said it as though it was a pact, something that would bind them together.

– I was thirteen years old, she said, and felt his grip tighten around her neck. – Now I'm disappearing, she whispered, and heard the words repeated in the tiny voice of the girl on the floor.

31

DAN-LEVI IS ON his way home. The thick grey clouds have sunk to ground level and are all around him. But there are pockets within them with light from some unseen source.

– Right-hand side, says a man's voice. – Start over on the right-hand side.

He turns in that direction, but the smoke is thicker there, and he doesn't know if he can trust the voice.

– Give more, it says, and Dan-Levi is glad when he hears these words, because this whole thing is all about giving more. That's the way it has always been.

– How much?

The woman's voice comes from a different place, further above him and to the left. It is as though the pockets of light form wherever he hears it, and he raises his head to see.

– Ten milligrams, says the man's voice, and that makes Dan-Levi laugh, because it is such an easy answer. He laughs and laughs at the thought that there are such easy answers to questions he has always struggled with. His laughter comes from below, opposite where the woman's voice is. He decides to make his way over in that direction. The smoke is now even denser, but he can still just make out a way through the pockets of light, and if he follows that then he will reach the house.

– Pastor Jakobsen, says the man's voice. – This is the way you spoke of, isn't it?

– Yes it is, but it's blocked further ahead. To his surprise, Dan-Levi hears that it is his father who answers. – It's that road-building they never get around to finishing. He mustn't go there yet.

– But that's exactly what I have to do, Dan-Levi protests. – I have to get home, they're expecting me.

It feels as though he has been away from them for a long time. He has no idea how long. Months, years maybe. He looks down, realises that he is barefoot. He can't remember where he took off his shoes.

– You can't go here, Dan-Levi.

– As long as the fog is this thick, I can't see any other way.

– Then you must turn back. The road isn't ready yet.

This looks to be the case. The asphalt hasn't set; it's soft and full of bubbles that he treads underfoot.

– My feet, he groans. – They're burning to pieces. But he feels nothing. – That's serious, isn't it? If I can't feel the boiling asphalt?

– How is he reacting?

The man's voice is back; now it's hidden in the thickest layer of cloud to the right.

– No reaction, says the woman's voice, and that surprises him, because he's moving all the time, and for a moment he wonders if she's talking about someone else, but then who could that be?

– The pressure? Even that gruff male voice becomes friendly when it talks to the female voice.

– We can't keep it up.

– That's all right, says Dan-Levi reassuringly. What she can't do doesn't need to be done. And as long as he can hear her voice, he'll be able to find his own way through the dense smog.

– Then they should be allowed to see him.

He's reached a hill. He notices how much harder it is to keep going, but he's also glad because it means there isn't far to go.

– Dan!

It is Sara calling out his name, and only now does he realise that the woman's voice up on his left has been Sara's the whole time. He can't understand why she sounds so worried, because he's on his way home, and it's actually clearing up now, it's as though those pockets of light are about to shatter the grey smog from within.

He could have told her where he's been all this time, why he had to leave, about the Lovers upside down, but none of that is important any more.

– Is everyone there? he asks.

She doesn't answer, but he can hear them. Ruben talking about a game of football. Ruth humming quietly, and Rebekah asking Sara something.

– Rakel? says Dan-Levi, but Sara doesn't answer.

– Why can't you tell me?

Finally she responds. He feels her leaning in towards him, senses her shadow in the flickering light.

– She's at home, Dan. She's the one who's coming to meet you.

– No!

He wants to stop, but can't. His feet burn when he isn't moving them; they are black with tar, and where his toes should be is only a row of gaping wounds.

– I don't want to go there, he shouts, but carries on up. Just then the clouds part, and the house on Erleveien comes into view.

32

SYNNE OPENED HER eyes, recognised the horse racing over the grassy moors on the mountain plains, mane flying. Lay there looking at it. She remembered the day she had been given that poster, how happy she had been when she unrolled it. It was her father who had bought it for her, and he'd helped her hang it up on the wall opposite the bed, so she could look at the horse until she fell asleep, and look at it when she woke up.

She heard sounds from below and swung down on to the floor, realised she was standing there in panties and a T-shirt, her jeans hanging over the back of a chair.

Her father was sitting at the kitchen table, sunlight from the window behind him so sharp it made her squint.

– Now that is what I would call a really good night's sleep, he said.

– What time is it?

– Ten past ten. You've hardly made a sound for the past day and a half.

– Someone was here.

He nodded. – I called a doctor.

She could vaguely remember it.

– You're to call and make an appointment with your own doctor. He gave me a list of the tests they should take.

– I didn't have a fit, did I? Not anything like I had back then?

Her father scratched his unshaven chin. – You seemed

far away when I got down to the petrol station. I'm not sure you knew where you were.

– But I didn't have any seizures? she asked, and had to struggle not to drift back into that greyness she'd been floating about inside for the last forty-eight hours.

– Not as far as I could see.

She sat down opposite him at the table, *Aftenposten* open beside him and a steaming mug. He peered at her over the rims of his spectacles. Tell him now, she thought. If I wait to tell him how Karsten died, I'll never manage it. She rehearsed how she would say it. *I know what happened to Karsten. Who killed him.*

– Dreadful tragedy, he said.

She took a drink of the orange juice he had poured for her. Not until a few moments later did it dawn on her that it couldn't be Karsten her father was referring to. And then she remembered it.

– The fire . . .

He turned the newspaper towards her and pushed it across the table.

– *Died in fire*, she read in a weak voice.

– Maybe we should talk about it later.

She pulled her hair back, so hard that it burnt at the roots. – Who is dead, Dad?

Romerikes Blad was lying on the table too. He pushed it in front of her. Then he took off his glasses and began to clean them.

There was a black border around the whole of the front page. *One of our own died in the fire.*

– Dan-Levi, she murmured, and the siren from the ambulance she had heard as she sat in the car at the petrol station sounded in her ears, as though the echo had been there all the time.

– Didn't he manage to get out? she sobbed, and in her

mind's eye she saw the burning house, the shower of sparks breathed up through the roof and scattering across the dark sky.

– He wasn't home when the fire started.

– What do you mean?

– By the time he got back, the fire was out of control. No one knew where Rakel was. He ran inside to look for her.

– Rakel too? cried Synne.

Her father put his spectacles back in their case, wedged it down into his pocket. – She wasn't in there, he said, his voice expressionless. – She'd run outside but no one saw her, must have used the veranda door. And then she probably just ran off in panic. They found her not far from the footpath. She was sitting by the river talking to herself.

Synne collapsed, laid her head on the table, heard her father stand up. Felt his hand stroke her back a couple of times.

– I've ordered flowers from us, he said, – but there's nowhere to send them.

She almost flared up and started shouting at him, how could he think about flowers when something like that had happened? And then it passed, and her head felt heavy again. The newspaper crackled as she rubbed her forehead against it.

– Why aren't you at work?

He was still standing behind her. – I've taken a couple of days off. Had to make sure you were all right. I might go out for a walk in a while.

– You can go, she snuffled into the table. – I'll be all right now.

She sat on the sofa looking out at the evening light. There was a cup of tea on the table. She'd taken a few sips; now it was cold. Call Erika, she thought again. In the few seconds it took to pick up the phone her father had left on the table before going out, she changed her mind, suddenly couldn't bear the thought of talking to her. She looked through the list. Instead called the number Dan-Levi had given her.

– Horvath.

It sounded like a threat; she felt like hanging up again, forced herself to say who she was. Remembered that Dan-Levi had said this policeman was a good friend of his.

– I'm so sorry about what happened, she said. – About Dan-Levi.

– Is that why you called? he said abruptly, and she felt suddenly weighted down with guilt. As though not just Karsten's death but Dan-Levi's too was her fault.

– There's something else, she stammered.

It had to be said, and once it was said it would unleash an avalanche of events over which she had no control. In its wildness it could easily blow her away too.

– This is a pretty unusual day for me, said Horvath. – You're going to have to tell me why you're calling or else report it at the police station.

– I know who killed him, she said quietly.

– Are you talking about Dan-Levi?

– I'm talking about my brother. Karsten Clausen.

She was led down a corridor painted red. Other corridors were painted in other colours; it made her think of the toy houses in a theme park they'd visited one summer. It had been cold, she didn't want to swim, but her mother had kept on at her. Karsten went down to the chutes with her; he helped her up the ladder and disappeared down, vanished round a bend. She couldn't remember what had happened, if she'd closed her eyes and gone down behind him, or just stood there, or turned round and climbed down again. Only that she woke up in a bed, with everybody standing round her and looking sad.

She couldn't climb back down from this red corridor. The man named Horvath was walking ahead of her. His greeting had been brisk, not a word in the lift on the way up. She felt she was bothering him, stealing his time, intruding on his grief for his dead friend.

The door to his office was ajar. She looked at the name-plate; his first name was Roar, she remembered that was what Dan-Levi had called him. She would prefer to do the same. *Horvath* still sounded like a threat.

There was a man standing there when they came in. He was short, skinny and slightly stooped. She recognised him from the kitchen at the student village. He held out his hand. – How are you? My name is Viken, in case you'd forgotten. I'll be conducting this interview.

Interview, she thought, as though it had only now dawned on her why she was here.

The inspector pointed her to a chair by the table. Horvath sat down at a computer. Clicked and clicked with the mouse. Sat there staring into the screen, his face closed, waiting. Waiting for her.

The man named Viken smiled, and his upper teeth became visible. They looked artificially white. – I'd like you to begin by repeating what you said earlier today on the telephone to Horvath. Then there'll be some questions.

She dragged it all up again, began uncertainly with her father's phone call, going over there, meeting someone in the crowd outside the burning house, someone she recognised, getting closer to what he said to her as they sat in his car.

– I should probably tell you what happened eight years ago . . . She broke off with a pleading look into the inspector's bony face, as though she thought she couldn't manage the trip back there without his help. Again he smiled. She couldn't tell if it was friendly, but it didn't seem like the opposite of friendly either.

It was a long story, beginning with the time she first met Adrian Wilkins, and the evening at Tamara's when she'd rung him. Horvath kept typing away, never moving his eyes from the screen. The detective inspector appeared to be listening, but one leg was bobbing up and down, and she had the feeling she ought to frame what had happened as a story, one that built to a climax, so that they would understand that something of crucial importance was about to happen before they grew impatient and lost interest. She thought she made a reasonable job of it, at least managed to tie the threads that connected the two evenings, that Maundy Thursday eight years ago, and the one two days earlier, when she sat in that dark blue Audi at the Statoil station and realised who her brother's killer was.

Afterwards she felt naked and ashamed. She needed a blanket to wrap round her, outside the jacket and the thick pullover.

Viken cleared his throat thoroughly. – So on both evenings, the evening of your brother's disappearance and the one two days ago, you suffered some kind of attack. Has that been diagnosed?

She shook her head.

– And we can't rule out the possibility that other factors might have been involved. I'm thinking of various types of stimulants, hallucinogenics.

– I don't use anything like that. And I hardly drink at all.

– Medications?

– Paracetamol for my headaches. But I haven't had any of those for years. Not until just very recently.

– But back then you did use something?

She had done. They made her try several different tablets to control the epilepsy. She refused to swallow them, but resistance was useless. Viken lingered on this subject. Medications, her physical condition, what she could remember, what she couldn't remember, why it had taken almost two days for her to get in touch with them, how unreal she had felt in the car, whether her hearing had been affected, her sight, her general awareness before the attack. He stopped a couple of times and stressed that he wasn't dwelling on all this because he didn't believe her, and she tried to hang on to this, because if he didn't believe her then she knew she could never again face telling the story of what had happened.

Suddenly Horvath interrupted. – A few days again, you contacted Dan-Levi and said you knew who had killed your brother. You gave a different name on that occasion than the one you're giving now.

She would have preferred to carry on talking to Viken, and looked over at him. He nodded slightly, indicating that he too was interested in hearing what she had to say about this. So she told once more the story of how Jasmeen Chadar had contacted her, and about Shahzad coming to the stables.

– And you were convinced that this particular person you mention was the one who murdered your brother, Viken said.

Synne thought his tone of voice had changed.

– Not convinced. Thought it was likely, though. Right up until he took me down to the river.

She noticed the way the detective inspector's lips moved, had the impression he was sitting there and tasting what she was telling them.

– I gather that you're in the process of writing a novel.

She started breathing quicker, felt as though she needed

more air. – Not exactly a novel. I don't know. I wanted to write something about Karsten.

– Will you be including this episode in the car?

She slumped a little.

– Will you be writing that this person you mention by name confessed to the killing of your brother?

– I don't think so. I don't know. Can't decide things like that beforehand.

– I understand, said Viken. – Something to do with inspiration, I suppose.

She had always loathed that word.

– As you may have read in the newspapers, two people were found dead in that house, he went on.

She didn't know that.

– One of those was Dan-Levi Jakobsen. The other is a so far unidentified person. We believe that this person may have had something to do with the outbreak of the fire. I'd like to ask you a few questions about that. It also concerns your brother.

She glanced over at him, looked away again immediately.

– Karsten came in for questioning just before his disappearance. It seems that he knew something about a series of arson attacks in Romerike that spring. Do you know of anyone in his circle at that time who later became involved in criminal activity?

She shook her head, wished he would stop asking her about things like that, that he would lean forward and tell her he believed her. But at the same time, if she was mistaken, she would feel relieved. If she had made up that encounter with Adrian Wilkins in his car, maybe everything else she thought she could remember was also just her imagination. Was it possible not to believe that she had ridden her bike over to Adrian's to meet him that evening? Not to believe that she was partially to blame for the fact that Karsten was killed? If *they* didn't believe her, maybe she wouldn't have to believe it herself.

At last the questioning was over. The typing ebbed away. Detective Inspector Viken stood up.

– What happens now? Synne managed to say.

He flattened a few wisps of hair on his head, laying them sideways across his glistening scalp.

– We'll hand a copy of your statement to the legal department at Romerike police station. Then it will be a matter for them whether there is enough to go on here.

Horvath turned round suddenly. – Naturally you're aware that it is a very serious matter to accuse someone of murder.

– Yes, she mumbled.

– If it turns out that any of what you've told us is incorrect, it will reflect very badly on you.

She looked at him questioningly; he stared back at her, and she turned to Viken again.

– Horvath has just lost his closest friend, he said.

– I understand, she replied in a low voice. – I knew him too.

– No one is accusing you of giving false witness here, the inspector continued. – But there is a degree of probable cause required before we start searching for a man who's somewhere or other out there, or bring him in for questioning.

She noted that phrase *somewhere or other out there*.

– I know how to find out where he is, she said weakly.

Viken glanced over at Horvath. A slight flutter passed across his lips, as though he was suppressing a smile.

– That's very kind of you, but I think we can manage that ourselves should it become necessary.

A sliver of sunlight lit the roof of the neighbouring block as she let herself back into her room. She turned on the machine and opened her window to the sounds of the city. The cars along Sognsveien, the distant hum of a building site, three seagulls circling above the lawn and squawking. She listened out for what wasn't there: the dark tones of a flute from a room further down the corridor.

Dusk was starting to fall as she sat at her desk. The thought was not quite yet a commitment, but she knew she would be doing it. The notes she had made over the past few weeks, the passages in which she had tried to get close to those she had met, Tonje and Priest, Khalid Chadar, Jasmeen, Shahzad. And the fragments of what she thought she could remember from that time but which were mixed in with her own fantasies. All of it would be deleted.

Among the host of things that appeared on her screen, there was one document in particular that attracted her attention. *How Karsten died.* She had noticed it just before her father rang and told her about the fire. She remembered thinking she would never use a title like that for a document. She selected it, dragged it to the recycle bin. As her fingertip rested on the delete button, she changed her mind. She dragged it out again, opened it.

I am going to write what happened from when Karsten ran off in my car outside Sæter's house in Nannestad until when he was killed. And what we did with the body.

Synne stood up, the chair fell over behind her. – I didn't write this, she whimpered. – I can't have written this. She leaned forward gingerly, touched the mouse as though afraid it might bite her. She scrolled down through the text; it was a couple of pages long. – I didn't write this, she muttered again, hearing that her voice was more certain this time.

After two weeks I realised Karsten hadn't been to the cops. He was gone. They thought he'd killed himself. They searched for him for a while. Then they gave up. But he didn't kill himself. First he went home. Shahzad and some other Pakis were waiting outside for him. Shahzad told Karsten's sister this. Shahzad tells the sister that he let Karsten go. I don't trust Shahzad. I thought that prick had killed Karsten. But he hadn't. Karsten got away. I know that now. And then he went to Adrian's.

When I get home that evening, Elsa's door is wide open. That's weird because Elsa's away for the weekend and Adrian said he was going to Oslo. I go in. There's no one there but the light is on in the living room. And in the basement. And in the bathroom upstairs the tap is turned on full. I go back outside. No car there. I see a bicycle. A girl's bike. It's hidden behind the garage. But I don't think any more about that. Maybe someone stole it and hid it there. But now I think about it. Because Karsten came here that evening he ran off from me. Adrian had the house to himself that weekend. Adrian had a visitor. A female visitor. She was thirteen years old. She hid her bike behind the garage. Karsten came here and he found it.

Eight years on, the sister starts writing about that evening. She remembers lying naked on the floor in a basement. Then Karsten comes charging in and finds them there and asks what the hell Adrian is up to. A few minutes later Adrian calls Vemund Randeng. I need you here. Where are you? In the car over near Nebbursvollen. Come alone, don't talk to anyone. Vemund stops at the entrance to the street. Walks the last few metres. Adrian's sitting on the bonnet of the car. What's up? Vemund asks. Adrian is completely calm, speaks without raising his voice. Vemund remembers it after all these years. How Adrian sits on the bonnet of the borrowed Peugeot. Talking that calmly. Seems almost like he's bored. I've got Karsten here. He's dead. I need you to help me get rid of him.

Holy shit! says Vemund, who isn't calm at all. Adrian tells him Karsten was going to tell people what we were doing out at Sæter's place. He was on his way to the police but Adrian got him into the car. He killed Karsten there with a hammer. And Vemund is stupid enough to believe that's the reason. He peers inside. Karsten in the front seat. Blood everywhere, on the dashboard, on the front windscreen. The hammer in the front seat. The kid sister lying in the back completely out of it.

Vemund hates Karsten. Said lots of times how he was going to kill him. Vemund is all mouth. He could never have done it. But that mouth stayed closed. Every fucking year since then he's had half a million from Adrian and never said a word about what happened that evening. Not even to that moronic pal of his, Sweaty.

Sweaty picks up Karsten's kid sister. He 'finds' the girl in a wayside ditch nearby. Adrian got Vemund to dump her there. But Sweaty doesn't know anything about this. He doesn't ask. Sweaty's the type of guy who keeps his mouth shut when someone tells him to keep his mouth shut. Vemund's a little brighter. When he's asked to help get rid of what's left of Karsten, he asks questions, but once he starts getting paid, he stops asking.

Later that night they went out to the asphalt plant. Adrian was the one who worked out what to do with the body. Adrian was the one who dumped it down the stone crusher. When the machines were started up again after the Easter break, the body was pulverised along with the stone mass and became part of the asphalt-making process. I got all this out of Vemund earlier this evening. After Easter they had a road-making job up in Eidsvoll. Karsten became part of it. The pictures Vemund took are in your inbox. Some of them are of you.

Synne fumbled with the mouse and finally managed to navigate to her inbox. A folder of pictures had arrived. – I can't take this, she moaned, but tried to open it all the same. She got an onscreen message: the machine didn't have the right program.

She hadn't eaten for several days, but there was something in her stomach and it was on its way up. She swallowed it back down. The bike, she thought. Karsten arrived and saw my bike. And then he ran in and down into the basement. She forced herself to read through the whole document once again. How she was lying in the back seat when Karsten was beaten to death with a hammer, how she was dumped in a ditch and Karsten was driven away to an asphalt plant.

She was standing up when her stomach convulsed again. She managed to get to the bathroom, stick her head down the toilet bowl and empty herself.

The time was seven thirty. The policeman, Dan-Levi's friend, didn't answer when she rang. She tried the reception, told them who she was trying to get in touch with. His name was Horvath, Roar Horvath. The call was transferred.

– He isn't in today, said a woman at the other end.

– That's not so. I was interviewed in his office a few hours ago.

– Well he's gone home for the day now.

– Then you've got to put me through to someone else, a detective inspector. Vik something or other. He was the one who interviewed me.

– Viken?

– I must talk to him.

– You can't just ring anybody you want here.

– My brother was murdered, Synne shouted. – I've found something out.

The woman at the other end breathed a few times.

– I'll make a note of your number, she said finally.

Viken called ten minutes later.

– Hi, Synne. I got your message.

She was relieved to hear him use her first name. She thought she liked the sound of his voice.

– I found something on my computer.

– Oh yeah?

– It's a description of what happened when Karsten was killed.

– Did someone send you an email?

– A document's been put on to my hard disk. I just found it. Somebody else must have written it while I was gone.

She tried to explain. Could hear how crazy it might sound to his ears.

– Are there any signs of a break-in in your room?

She glanced at the door, at the window, shook her head.

– I don't know how it happened, she groaned. – You have to see it. Someone has described in detail how Adrian Wilkins killed Karsten. Other people are mentioned there too, by name. I don't know who they are. One of them took me home. They call him Sweaty. It fits, it all fits. You must believe me. Plus I've been sent a lot of photos that I can't access. My machine's too old. It was a present from my dad for my eighteenth birthday, it's a Mac. I've had these kinds of problems before, not being able to open attachments—

– Now listen, Synne, the inspector interrupted. – We know this has been difficult for you. Do you have someone you can talk to?

– You must believe me, she urged again, but with less conviction this time.

– It isn't my job to believe things, he said. – We leave that sort of thing to the priests. You're saying that there is a document on your machine. I don't doubt that's true. The question is, how did it get there?

– You don't believe me, she whimpered. – You think I wrote it myself.

Viken made a coughing noise at the other end. – If you send me an email with the files you found on your computer, we'll have a look at it.

– Have a look?

– If we decide that further action is necessary we'll get

in touch with you, and in that case you can bring your machine with you. If someone's been messing about with it, we'll find out. And if there are pictures in an attachment you can't open, we'll sort that out too. But things like that are very time consuming, and we can't involve our computer people without good reason.

After Viken had ended the call, she remained sitting on her bed, staring straight ahead.

– He doesn't believe me, she murmured. – They're never going to believe me.

She sat for a long time looking out into the gathering dusk. Then abruptly she stood up and woke her machine, printed out the document she had found, put it in her jacket pocket and went out.

She climbed the steps and rang the bell. While she waited, she looked around. She'd left her bike round the side of the garage that time. Was that something Adrian had told her to do, or had it been her own idea? The bike mustn't be visible from the road, no one was to know she was there to see him.

Now a car was parked there. It looked like the one Adrian had taken her to at the petrol station a few days earlier. She seemed to remember him saying it was a rental he was just returning.

The door was opened. Elsa's eyes were red rimmed, as though she'd been crying. Without thinking, Synne leaned her head against the dark red velour pullover, not knowing whether she was offering comfort or asking for it. Elsa pulled her into the entry and wrapped her arms around her.

– Are you feeling better now?

Synne couldn't give any answer to that.

– I heard you had some kind of attack. When there was the fire up in Erleveien.

Synne pulled away. – Did he tell you that?

Elsa looked into her eyes. – We have a lot to talk about, Synne.

She went ahead into the living room.

– How is the writing coming along?

Synne was offered the same as last time, what Elsa called her three-year tea.

– I'm not going to be writing any more, she said.

Elsa looked at her without saying anything.

– I don't just mean this story, but writing any more at all.

– You're saying you don't want to be a writer after all? You who always thought it was the only thing you could really do?

Still Synne didn't know if she could say a single word of what she had come to say. – All this business of writing about life has been an excuse for not living, she said instead.

– So Karsten's story isn't going to be written after all? The story of what happened to him?

– Not by me.

– But by someone else?

Synne shrugged. – What did Adrian tell you? she managed to ask at last.

Elsa took a sip from her cup, looked at her for a long time before answering.

– I am the only person who really knows him. She turned, looked out the window. – Adrian is too stubborn to feel regret. Too strong. Too clear headed. He's got everything it takes to be a leader. I've always known that. From the day he was born I knew it. Even before that. I've done what I could to smooth his path, but the power of life finds its own course. It forces a way of its own, in whatever direction it chooses.

Synne couldn't work out where she was going with this, but didn't interrupt.

– When I got up this morning, I knew that this was going to be a fateful day. I sat here like this and looked out of the window. The clouds flew off at a furious pace. There was something both lovely and unpleasant about that sky. I often see in the clouds what the day has in store for me. Not only did they fly away, they looked to be flying away from me in whichever direction I looked.

Synne lifted her cup to her lips. The tea smelled even more acrid than last time, like the bark of a tree, and it tasted even worse.

– I skipped breakfast and walked out in the bright spring morning, Elsa went on. – The kind of morning in which there's a meaning behind everything you experience. Something you have to deal with, something you must break with. There is a time for everything, Synne, and a day like this shows you what it is time for. Everyone I met was telling me that, even though they had no idea themselves what was happening. A flock of children from a nursery school, little bodies warmly wrapped up and with rucksacks on their backs. Two women of my own age shepherding them along. That reminded me of Adrian too. The Adrian I went for walks with, looked after, cared for, cooked for. His first pair of shoes is still in a box up in the loft. Sometimes I take them out, run my finger over the cracked leather, smell them.

What did he tell you about that evening? Synne wanted to ask again, but still she couldn't bring herself to interrupt.

– I went up to the tarot room. Laid the cards for myself. Was going to lay Adrian's too, but started with mine, because his life and mine are connected in a way no outsider could ever understand. The five of wands came up. The card of inner turmoil. Risk of irrational behaviour. The five of swords. A difficult card. But also one that points towards the solution to an old problem. What you don't want to see,

Elsa, I said to myself. What you see all the time without seeing. Open your eyes to what you know. But the sword is double edged. It can cut the hand that holds it.

She leaned back in her chair. Synne summoned all the strength she had.

– Adrian told me what he did to Karsten.

Elsa closed her eyes. – One day you'll be a mother yourself, Synne. Maybe you'll have a son. Then you'll know that no matter what happens, you will support him. If something's about to go wrong, if something threatens him, you will do anything at all. You have no idea what you are capable of, because there is nothing stronger than these forces.

It dawned on Synne exactly what it was she was saying.

– You knew, she burst out. – You knew he killed Karsten.

– Did I know? Just like you, I hid all thoughts of that evening away.

– But I was thirteen years old, Synne protested.

Silence descended on them.

– Long before the first time Karsten came here, I knew that he would appear in Adrian's life, Elsa said at length. – I saw it every time I laid Adrian's cards. What threatened was approaching closer and closer. After Karsten disappeared, the cards changed too. But now it's back again.

– Do you know why I've come here? Synne asked.

Elsa sighed heavily. – You want me to talk to him, persuade him to hand himself in.

It was more clearly expressed than Synne herself had dared to think.

– But I can't do that, I'm sure you understand.

Synne pressed a hand against her stomach. Suddenly the nausea was there again. And beneath it the exhaustion that threatened to take over completely and wipe out all the thoughts she had brought there with her. She felt she had to get up from the chair and go out into the spring light before it was too late. Instead she said: – I want you to read this.

She laid the printout on the table. *How Karsten died*, she thought, didn't dare say it out loud.

Elsa leaned forward and picked up the sheets of paper. Synne watched her as she read, saw a different expression appear in her eyes, more anger than sorrow now.

– This was sent to you by someone who hates Adrian, she said once she had put it down again.

– You know who wrote this? Synne exclaimed.

Elsa picked up the teapot, went out to the kitchen, came back and refilled her cup. – You've met Khalid Chadar, she said.

Synne had had enough of the bitter drink but couldn't bring herself to say no.

– He lived at Stornes for a year, Elsa went on. – Then he was thrown out.

She began telling a different version of the story Synne had heard from Khalid. It was like the reverse of the same tapestry, all the loose threads hanging there making the motif unrecognisable. Synne sipped at her three-year tea and heard about the horses, the stables, about a man named Tord Hammer who was engaged to Elsa's sister. But mostly about the handsome chieftain's son from a country far away in the east.

She had forced down another couple of sips by the time Elsa was finished.

– There I was, sixteen years old and pregnant. Nobody had ever brought such shame to the family before.

– Surely Adrian isn't . . .?

Elsa laughed briefly. – You can rest assured he is not. Adrian has an older half-brother. His name is Kai.

Synne was surprised. – Isn't he Adrian's cousin?

Elsa shook her head and topped up her teacup. – Kai would

do anything at all to hurt his brother. I had to keep him away from Adrian at all times. I looked after him, gave him something to live for. But I couldn't save his soul. It was eaten up by hatred. You can see that for yourself. She pointed to the sheets of paper still lying on the table. – Slowly eaten up.

She got up, stood there looking out of the window.

– I know how difficult this has been, Synne. To lose a brother. Let me tell you something.

She opened the curtains wide. In the sharp evening light a rim of grey was visible at the roots of her hair.

– Let me tell you about the greatest day of my life. The day Adrian was born. The instant he came out, all my pains disappeared. His little voice, not weak, not screeching. It had an undertone, a depth that sang out through the dark room. The sky outside was crystal clear. A star twinkled high above the hill. It started to grow, and in the darkness was the sound of voices, at first an indistinct chanting, but then suddenly I was able to understand them. *This is your son, Elsa. To whom you have given birth. His name shall be Adrian. And he shall change the world. Your task is to do everything in your power to help him.*

She turned. There was an intense glow in her eyes.

– I've got something that a great many people are looking for. A reason to be here. I gave birth to Adrian. It is not I who gave him life, but I who was chosen to be the instrument of his coming. Adrian has powers that only a very few are able to comprehend. Even those who admire him have only the vaguest idea of who he really is.

Synne froze. – Adrian might have gifts, she said in a low voice. – But surely you can't mean that gives him the right to—

Elsa cut her off with a wave of the hand. – Different rules apply for Adrian than for other people. That's what you don't see. Not yet.

Synne felt something descending over her head, a tiredness that came not from inside but from somewhere in the room. She couldn't hold back any more.

– Don't you realise that Adrian is dangerous? She tried to pick up the pages from the table. – Do you still not understand what he did?

Elsa shook her head. – You really believe that something scribbled by a sick man is proof of anything at all?

– But Adrian said the same thing in the car, that it was him who—

– Adrian is the type who protects others, Elsa interrupted. – Even those who don't deserve it. She turned away. – A failed abortion, she murmured. – The harder I tried to get rid of it, the harder it held on.

Synne blinked in confusion. – There are pictures of what he did to Karsten. They're on my computer.

– Have you seen them?

– Can't manage to open them, not yet.

Elsa crossed the floor slowly, stood directly opposite her.

– Last time you were here, we agreed that I would help you try to get deeper into the things you can't remember.

Synne had been there too long. She should never have come. She tried to stand up, but it felt as though her body was that of some great animal that lay sweating in the shadows.

– Come with me. Elsa walked round the table, helped her to her feet. – I told you there was a more direct method of remembering. Now you're ready to try it.

She led Synne across the floor, opened a door. – Recognise where you are?

The stairs were much too steep.

– Not down there, Synne snuffled.

– This is important. I want to know what you remember too.

She clung tight to the banister, Elsa holding on to her other arm.

– I'm so tired. Was it the tea?

The ceiling was low, the room dark. A TV in one corner, a table next to a sofa, something lying on it: the embroidery she had seen in the living room last time she was there, and in a basket a set of needles and a pair of scissors.

She slumped down on to the sofa. – I don't think I'm up to this now.

– Yes, you can do it. Elsa pulled a chair over to the sofa. – Breathe deeply and calmly. Feel how your breath fills you up completely, feel yourself letting it go.

Synne felt unable to resist.

– It doesn't matter if you're tired. Follow my finger with your eyes. She began to move a finger from side to side in front of Synne's face. – Just keep watching. Let everything else go. Feel how heavy your hands are becoming.

It felt as though the topmost joints of her fingers were filled with lead. The weight spread into her hands, and from there up her arms.

– Raise your right hand.

Synne tried; it flopped down on to the armrest again. – What did you give me?

– Don't let any thoughts disturb you, just keep looking at my finger. You are awake, you are not falling asleep, you are here, you are safe as long as you stay with me.

– I am not falling asleep, Synne murmured.

– We're going back to that evening. Nod three times if you want to follow me there.

Synne felt herself nodding.

– You came here.

– I came here.

– You hide your bike behind the garage so that no one will see it.

– I hide my bike. Ring the bell. Adrian opens, gives me a hug.

– What do you feel inside at this moment?

– How many people in the whole world do I know who say they're happy to see me? But Adrian was a prince.

Elsa nodded. – Adrian *is* a prince.

– He brings me down here into the basement. It's warm here, there's a big mirror on the wall. He goes upstairs, comes back down with a Coke and two glasses.

– Adrian cares about others. He'll always help people who are suffering.

– *Go over there and stand in front of the mirror, Synne*, he says. *Look at yourself. Can you see how pretty you are?* Yeah, right. *You'd have to be blind not to see it*, he says. He sits down on the sofa, right here. *A girl as pretty as you shouldn't be wearing so many clothes.*

– That is not what he says, Elsa interrupts. – Concentrate now, follow my finger, don't fall asleep.

– *You are lovely, Synne,* says Adrian. I'm not, I'm fat and ugly. *I've never seen anyone like you.* It's warm in here. *Isn't it? It's much too warm to have all these clothes on.* Just the pullover. I can't take my blouse off.

Synne blinked, noticed that the weight had reached her eyelids. – I stand by the mirror, take off my clothes. He sits on the sofa, watching me. And then he begins to take his clothes off too.

– Now you're lying, Synne. You're making this up about the clothes. Anything you can't remember you make up.

– He gets up and comes over towards me, and my whole body starts to tremble. Karsten!

– Why are you shouting that?

– The door is slung open, suddenly Karsten's there. I fall over. Lie on the floor, trying to reach a hand out towards him. He's furious. He goes up to Adrian. Adrian holds him back, gets him on the ground. Adrian said he hit him. He didn't. He didn't hit him. Someone shouts to him, and he lets Karsten go.

Elsa stopped her. – This did not happen, Synne. Repeat after me: *This did not happen.*

Synne's eyes flickered as she tried to concentrate on the outlines of the face in the semi-darkness of the room. – This did not happen.

– Repeat after me: *I am not naked.*

– I am not naked.

– Repeat after me. *Another man comes in. His name is Kai.*

– His name is Kai, Synne says.

– What happens next?

– Someone's sitting near the sofa, talking to me.

– Kai is there, said Elsa. – Repeat what I say.

– I don't know any Kai. There isn't anyone here called Kai.

Elsa leaned over her, whispered into her ear. – Who is there?

– Someone asking me to stay calm. Someone who gives me a pill and a glass of water, tells me to swallow it. Synne opened her eyes. – *You are there*, you've come home.

Elsa stared at her. – So now suddenly you remember that. She stands up straight. – Yes, I came back home. I was too ill to finish the rest of the course. Do you think that was sheer chance?

Synne tried to lift a hand; it didn't move.

– Someone shouts, she murmured. – It's Karsten. *Calm down now,* says Adrian. He puts his shirt back on. *I'll drive you home,* he says. *And we'll take your sister too. She needs help.*

– Adrian wanted to help you, Elsa whispered. – Do you understand?

– *I'm not going home*, Karsten shouts. *I'm going to the*

police station. Fine, says Adrian, *then I'll drive you there first.*

Synne didn't dare to meet Elsa's gaze; she had to look away.

– You take the car keys from him. *I'll drive Karsten,* you say to Adrian. *I can talk to him in the car. It helps to talk things through.*

Sleep was enveloping her now, but Synne forced herself to stay awake.

– You got into the car, she went on. – Karsten hugged me, helped me into the seat, said he wouldn't leave me. *You* are the person driving the car. Adrian isn't there.

Elsa's face was now so close that Synne could no longer see it.

– There's no helping someone like you, she said loudly. – You're making things up even now.

– I'm lying in the back seat. It's cold. Karsten is in the front. *Not this way,* he says. *Don't you understand anything, we're going to the police.* He is still very angry. *One of your sons is a pyromaniac. He tried to kill me after I found out.* He's holding something in his hand, a plastic bag, he tosses it into your lap. *But Adrian is even worse,* he shouts, *he's a fucking paedo.*

All of a sudden Elsa started screaming in her ear, her voice penetrating through layer upon layer of fuzziness.

– Yes, I hit him, over and over again, and I've never regretted it for one moment. He was going to destroy my son. Karsten was an instrument, do you understand? His role was to destroy. Adrian protects people. I called him from the car and he was there within a few minutes and took care of everything. Everyone who comes near Adrian has been attracted to him. Including you, of course. You were head over heels in love with him. You called him. You came over here. And you haven't the faintest idea why.

Synne shook her head.

– Because *your* part was to be the temptress. You couldn't do anything about it. You have no idea of the forces that move you along.

– I was thirteen years old, Synne whispered.

– I was thirteen years old, Elsa mimicked. – As if that mattered. You knew exactly what you wanted and how you hoped to get it. And then these attacks, so you didn't have to take responsibility afterwards.

Synne sank even further down into the sofa. – I'm not like that.

– That is exactly what you are like. Slutty, and seductive. You're still doing everything you can to try to get Adrian to want you. With every word, Elsa tapped her index finger on the tabletop. – He laughed at you, tried to keep you at arm's length, but you wouldn't give up. You came here of your own free will, isn't that so?

– I was thirteen years old.

– You can say what you like, no one will believe you.

The words sank deep inside her. No one would believe her. And in that case she would never be able to believe herself.

– The pictures, she groaned. – I have the pictures.

She shouldn't have said it, but she couldn't stop herself either.

– The police want to see them. The inspector's name is Viken, I remember that now.

Elsa grabbed her by the hair and pulled her up.

– That is not going to happen. There is nothing in the world that can stop Adrian becoming what he is meant to be. There's no way a person like you could ever understand that.

She picked something up from the table.

– You think it was just chance there was a hammer in the car? Nothing happens by chance. Every grain of sand on every beach has been put there for a purpose.

She grabbed Synne by the throat, raised her hand. Synne could see she was holding the scissors, but she couldn't move. She heard footsteps on the stairs – maybe they were her own – then a door opening. She could leave. It was dark outside but she was no longer afraid.

Adrian was standing there.

– Not again, he said, his voice filling the room and making all other voices disappear. – Don't you touch her.

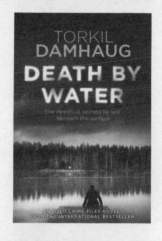
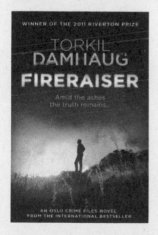

THRILLINGLY GOOD BOOKS
FROM CRIMINALLY
GOOD WRITERS

CRIME FILES BRINGS YOU THE LATEST RELEASES FROM
TOP CRIME AND THRILLER AUTHORS.

SIGN UP ONLINE FOR OUR MONTHLY NEWSLETTER AND BE THE FIRST
TO KNOW ABOUT OUR COMPETITIONS, NEW BOOKS AND MORE.

VISIT OUR WEBSITE: WWW.CRIMEFILES.CO.UK
LIKE US ON FACEBOOK: FACEBOOK.COM/CRIMEFILES
FOLLOW US ON TWITTER: @CRIMEFILESBOOKS